Praise for *He Who*

"Even better than the first . . . re
the feedback loop wherein queer-coded characters are reviled, which drives them to unbearable viciousness, which in turn fills them with self-loathing. Parker-Chan's characters struggle to break this cycle, and the nuance with which they're portrayed makes us root for them. In the end, Parker-Chan seems to suggest, power belongs not to the most ruthless but to those who are most successful at self-forgiveness."

—*The Washington Post*

"The most finely crafted fantasy novel of the year . . . Sentence by sentence, Parker-Chan's prose is unrivaled in modern fantasy. It's so consistent in its richness, so precise in its sequencing that even the grimmest of moments become enthralling and vital. . . . The fearless Parker-Chan pulls no punches, repeatedly pushing characters to their limits and beyond."

—*BookPage* (starred review)

"Intricately plotted and devastatingly brutal historical fantasy . . . Parker-Chan admirably continues the nuanced and compassionate examination of gender, sex, and desire that began in book one while simultaneously dialing up the intensity. . . . Parker-Chan successfully steers the complex political machinations to a satisfying conclusion."

—*Publishers Weekly*

"A powerful historical fantasy filled with complex people and high stakes . . . Paying equal attention to fierce battle scenes and deep conversations and filled with desperate decisions and brutal actions, this book is immersive and intimate."

—*Library Journal* (starred review)

"A heart-racing, emotional story that is also heartrending and shocking . . . The conclusion of the Radiant Emperor duology makes use of every last word and stamps this series onto the map as a new must-read of the fantasy canon."

—*Booklist* (starred review)

"Gender, power, queerness, sex, and empire are explored in complex and sometimes shocking ways. This duology will leave you breathless." —NPR, "Books We Love" feature

"Just as exciting, epic, and stunningly written as the first. It will leave you on the edge of your seat until the final page."

—*Ms.*

"An incredibly compelling novel, vividly written, with fascinating thematic arguments about gender and power—there are entire essays to be composed on that aspect of this novel alone—and with a startlingly fresh approach to combining the fantastical with the historical . . . I suspect I'll still be thinking about this duology in a decade's time. In either case, *He Who Drowned the World* is a worthy successor to *She Who Became the Sun*: a vivid and entertaining novel whose characters, for all their flaws, are never less than wholly fascinating." —*Locus*

"A dark, often brutal, and occasionally gory follow-up to (excellent) historical fantasy *She Who Became the Sun*. Shelley Parker-Chan sends their Radiant Emperor duology off in style."

—*Paste*

BOOKS BY SHELLEY PARKER-CHAN

THE RADIANT EMPEROR DUOLOGY

She Who Became the Sun

He Who Drowned the World

HE WHO DROWNED THE WORLD

SHELLEY PARKER-CHAN

TOR PUBLISHING GROUP

New York

This is a work of fiction. All of the characters, organizations, and events portrayed in this novel are either products of the author's imagination or are used fictitiously.

HE WHO DROWNED THE WORLD

Map by Jennifer Hanover

A Tor Book
Published by Tom Doherty Associates / Tor Publishing Group
120 Broadway
New York, NY 10271

www.torpublishinggroup.com

The Library of Congress has cataloged the hardcover edition as follows:

Names: Parker-Chan, Shelley, author.
Title: He who drowned the world : a novel / Shelley Parker-Chan.
Description: First. | New York : Tor Publishing Group, 2023.
Identifiers: LCCN 2023942506 (print) |
ISBN 9781250621825 (hardcover) | ISBN 9781250621832 (ebook)
LC record available at https://lccn.loc.gov/2023942506

ISBN 978-1-250-62184-9 (trade paperback)

Our books may be purchased in bulk for promotional, educational, or business use. Please contact your local bookseller or the Macmillan Corporate and Premium Sales Department at 1-800-221-7945, extension 5442, or by email at MacmillanSpecialMarkets@macmillan.com.

First Tor Paperback Edition: 2024

Printed in the United States of America

0 9 8 7 6 5 4 3 2 1

A hero is one who wants to be himself.

JOSÉ ORTEGA Y GASSET

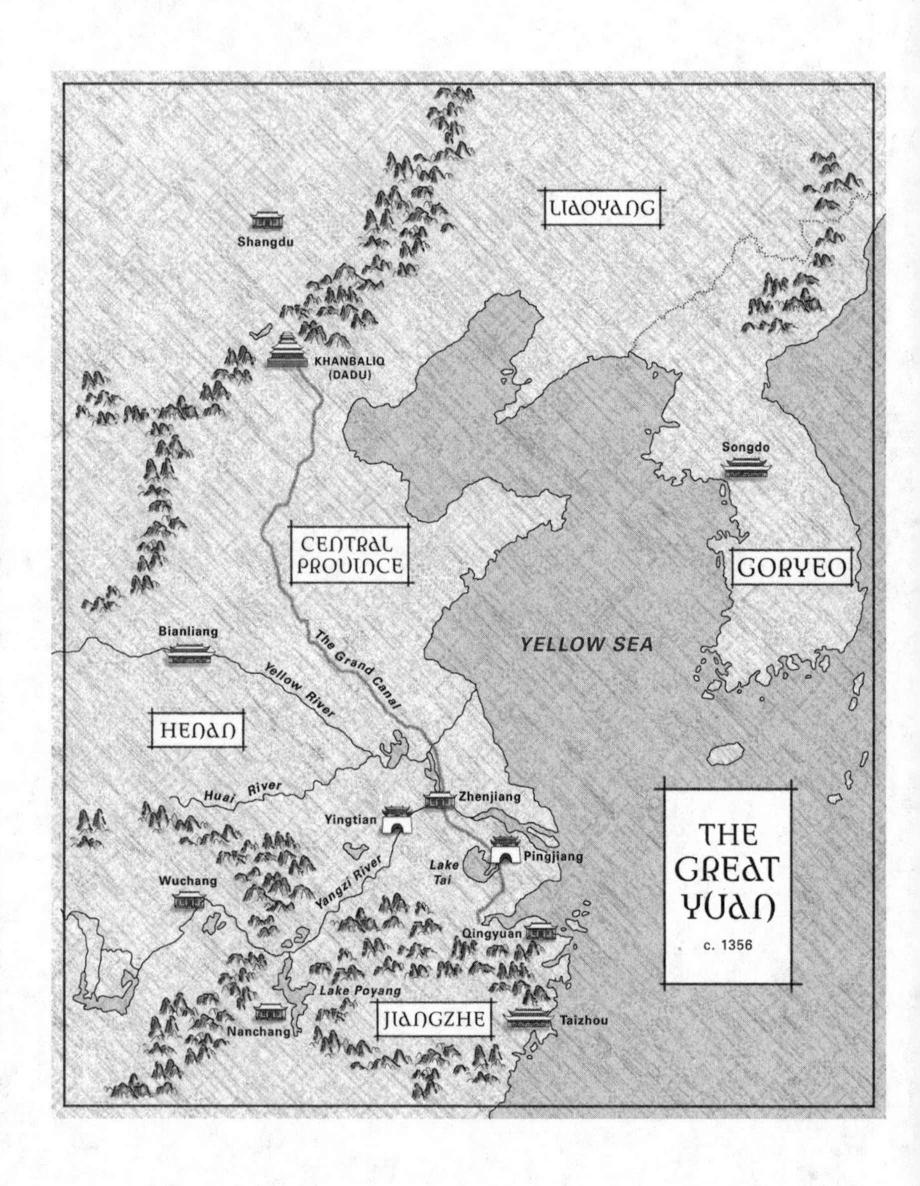

LIAOYANG
Shangdu
KHANBALIQ
(DADU)
Songdo
CENTRAL
PROVINCE
GORYEO
Bianliang
The Grand Canal
YELLOW SEA
Yellow River
HENAN
Huai River
Zhenjiang
Yingtian
Pingjiang
Lake
Tai
Yangzi River
Wuchang
THE
GREAT
YUAN
c. 1356
Qingyuan
Lake Poyang
JIANGZHE
Taizhou
Nanchang

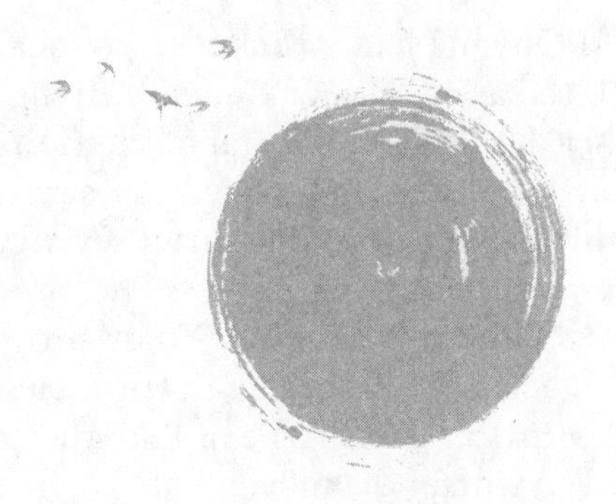

CHINA, 1356

In the twenty-third year of the reign of Toghon-Temur, the fifteenth Great Khan of the Mongol Empire of the Great Yuan, the Mongols suffered such defeats against the empire's internal enemies that control of the southern part of the empire was lost.

Merely one year past, the southern rebel movement known as the Red Turbans had been on the verge of extinction by the Yuan's redoubtable defenders: the Mongol lord Esen-Temur, of Henan, and his eunuch general Ouyang. However, under the new leadership of a young former monk, Zhu Chongba, the Red Turbans not only survived, but caused such losses to their opponents that the Yuan was forced to withdraw.

While Esen-Temur and General Ouyang regrouped, and sought the support of the powerful, Yuan-loyalist Zhang family—salt merchants who controlled the eastern seaboard—Zhu Chongba climbed the ranks of the Red Turbans. There he found allies—his sworn brother, Xu Da, and his wife, Ma Xiuying—as well as enemies, including amongst the movement's leaders. Bolstered by their success against the Yuan, and despite internal divisions, the renewed Red Turbans seized city after city in the south, culminating in their capture of former imperial capital Bianliang on the border of north and south.

Esen-Temur and General Ouyang, working in concert with the Zhang family, aimed to retake Bianliang for the Yuan. However, unbeknownst to Esen-Temur, his trusted lifelong companion General Ouyang had struck a secret deal with the Zhang family. With the assistance of General Zhang and Esen-Temur's own brother, Lord Wang Baoxiang, the traitor eunuch slew Esen-Temur at Bianliang and seized his army with the stated aim of marching to the capital to enact revenge upon his father's killer: the Great Khan.

General Ouyang's betrayal of the Yuan provided Zhu Chongba with the opportunity to betray in turn. He ruthlessly deposed the Prime Minister and Prince of Radiance of the Red Turbans, and gained control of the movement.

Zhu Chongba made his new capital in Yingtian, on the Yangzi River. He took a name of imperial ambition, Zhu Yuanzhang; styled himself the Radiant King; and proclaimed his possession of the Mandate of Heaven.

The Zhang family renounced their loyalty to the Great Yuan and claimed the resource-rich eastern seaboard as their independent kingdom, with walled Pingjiang as their capital.

The last surviving former Red Turban leader, the urbane but brutal Chen Youliang, fled the slaughter of Bianliang and established himself at Wuchang, upriver from Zhu Yuanzhang.

Unnoticed by many, Lord Wang Baoxiang of Henan took his dead brother's title, the Prince of Henan, and laid claim to the single largest estate in the Great Yuan.

Such was the state of the world in the eighty-fifth year of the rule of the khans descended from Khubilai Khan, the first Great Khan and founding emperor of the eternal Mongol Empire of the Great Yuan.

PART ONE

BORDER OF THE KINGDOMS OF ZHU YUANZHANG AND THE ZHANG FAMILY EIGHTH MONTH, 1356

"Surely it requires no extended consideration," the woman's voice said from behind the stirring gauze curtain of the carriage. "Why not give me your answer now, Zhu Yuanzhang, and save us both the time?"

Even here, far from the sea, the plain beneath the carriage's hilltop vantage point blazed white with salt as though the wealth of the woman's kingdom overflowed without restraint. The hot tiger tail of the southern summer had vanished the shallow lake that usually lay here on the border between the two territories. Above their armies, quickening flags dashed colored reflections onto the expanse. Yellow, for the rebel army of the Radiant King. Green for the Zhang merchant family, the former loyalists of the Empire of the Great Yuan, who had finally broken with their Mongol rulers that spring and proclaimed their rule over the salt and shipping lanes of the eastern seaboard.

Zhu Yuanzhang, her golden king's armor and gilded wooden hand matching the color of the grass under her horse's hooves, saw the generals of the opposing armies walking towards each other with deliberate courtesy. Their small noonday shadows sliced over the shattering crust beneath their boots.

To the casual eye there was little between the two generals to set them apart. Two winged helmets in the Nanren style, two sets of lamellar armor with the dark leather taking in the sun and the metal lion's-head bosses on their shoulders sending it flashing back like mirror signals. But to Zhu, whose general was her brother in all but blood, their distant shapes were as easily distinguished as two faces. That was Xu Da's unmonkishly tall frame, his joyful stride that of a young man eager to taste the world. The other, General Zhang, of lesser height and build, but carrying himself with the reserved confidence of a man with the life experience of Zhu and her general put together. Zhu knew just how quickly General Zhang had moved after his family's separation from the Yuan. In the space of a few months he had taken all the remaining cities along the southern reaches of the Grand Canal and moved the Zhang family's capital to walled Pingjiang on the eastern shore of Lake Tai. Now all that separated the Zhangs in the east from Zhu's own kingdom in the west was a stretch of flatlands in the curve of the mighty Yangzi River as it wound its way to the sea.

"Surrender to me," said the woman behind the curtain. Her voice had a throaty quality, low and flirtatious. It was a voice for a closed room, velveted with suggestion: that though they were strangers who had only just met, perhaps they were moments from becoming as known to each other as two bodies could be. It was one of those tactics that worked only as long as the calculation underneath it remained unseen. Zhu, who not only saw it but also considered herself generally immune to the urges of physical desire, was interested to feel a mild tug in response. As someone lacking in femininity herself, it had never occurred to her that it could be weaponized. The novelty of having it wielded against herself amused and impressed her in almost equal measure.

On the plain the two generals inclined their heads in respect; conveyed and received the formal message of surrender; and withdrew. Their tracks lay bruised blue behind them.

Zhu finally turned to her interlocutor. "Greetings to the esteemed Madam Zhang."

"I see you refuse my title," the woman said archly.

"Why shouldn't I, when you refuse mine?" Zhu returned. The snap of words sent a current of vitality through her. It was the delight of power mixed with play, as thrilling to her as the tang of brine in her nose and the hot wild wind that snapped her banners and sent the grass rushing and leaping down the hillsides. In a tone of matching archness, she added, "Perhaps my surrender is better given to he who holds the true title. Your husband, the king. I would rather be received face-to-face by my equal than by his honorable wife speaking from behind a curtain of propriety."

The woman gave a manicured laugh. "Don't worry. Your surrender will be given correctly. My husband's reputation may precede him, but a weak man, well managed, is a woman's greatest strength." A shadow rippled against the gauze, as if the woman had leaned close. Her lowered voice issued an invitation for Zhu to lean down from her horse, to let her ear drift so close to those murmuring lips that she might have felt each syllable on her skin had it not been for the thin barrier between them. "I don't think you're a weak man, Zhu Yuanzhang. But your position is weak. What hope can you have against my larger army; against my general who was even hailed as an equal by the Yuan's feared General Ouyang?

"Give me your surrender. Bring your forces under my command. Instead of waiting for the Yuan to send their Grand Councilor and that central army of theirs to put us down, we'll march on Dadu together. We'll take their capital, and the throne. And when my husband is emperor, he'll grant you the title of your choosing. Duke, prince? It will be yours."

Zhu said dryly, "When the histories are written, such a title will surely commend me to their authors as a great man."

The men she and Madam Zhang had each brought here were only for show. This was a meeting, not a battle. But Zhu was under no illusions about her situation. Her army, an infantry-dominated force built from the former Red Turban rebellion and additional peasant recruits, was barely half the size of the Zhangs' well-equipped professional army. And with the exception of her capital, Yingtian, none of the dozen cities she held in the south could match even the poorest of the Zhang family's canal-linked economic centers. It was clear what the outcome of a battle would be. Had their positions been reversed, Zhu would have counted herself the victor and demanded surrender, just as her opponent was doing now.

Madam Zhang murmured, "Is that what you want? To be great?" Her tone was as smooth as the trailing caress of fingertips along skin. "Then accept me, and let me make it happen."

Greatness. Zhu had wanted it her entire life. With a certainty as crisp as shadow cast across salt, she knew it would always be everything she wanted. She straightened in the saddle and gazed eastwards over the sweep of the Zhang family's realm. The wind rushing against her from that distant tawny horizon seemed to bring it close; it turned that abstract line into something palpable, something fiercely visceral. *Reachable.* The thought filled Zhu with sharp joy. Stationary and yet soaring on her hilltop, she had the curious sensation of seeing her entire path to her future stretching before her. From her eagle's vantage she could see no true obstacles on that path—only small bumps that would barely check her as she ran headlong towards her goal.

With a surge of delight, she said to the faceless woman behind the curtain, "I don't want to be great."

She savored the pause as Madam Zhang's mind churned, wondering what she had misunderstood about Zhu's character—where she had gone wrong with her seduction.

The stump of Zhu's arm ached inside the too-tight cuff of her wooden hand. But that discomfort, and the daily repercussions of being a one-handed man in a two-handed world, was merely the cost of her desire, and Zhu was strong enough to bear it. She was strong enough to bear anything, or to do anything, for the sake of what she wanted.

"Then—" Madam Zhang began.

"I don't want to be great," Zhu repeated. Her desire was the radiance of the sun, an immensity that filled every part of her without exception. Who else understood what it was to feel something of this magnitude; to want something with the entirety of their self, as she did? "I want to be the greatest."

Sparkling crystalline eddies scrubbed across the bare surface of the plain. Life-sustaining salt that, in such concentration, became life-denying.

"I see," Madam Zhang said after a moment. Her flirtatiousness had taken on a sheen of disdain, and Zhu had the mental image of the door to a private room slamming in her face. "I forgot how young you are. Young people are always too ambitious. They haven't yet learned the limits of what's possible."

Lacquered fingernails tapped the inner frame of the carriage, signaling the driver. As the carriage moved off, Madam Zhang said, "We'll meet again. But before we do, let this elder tell you something. Cast your eye upon my general down below. What respect does he lack from the world around him, for his manner, his appearance, his accomplishments? The natural place of a man like that is above others. You would do well to consider your natural place, Zhu Yuanzhang. If the world can barely stand to let its eye fall upon a man as lacking as you, do you think it would accept you on the throne? Only a fool would risk everything for the impossible."

Zhu watched the carriage wheel away down the hill. If Madam Zhang had known the true extent of Zhu's physical lacks—which, as far as matters of masculine anatomy went, included more than broad shoulders or a right hand—no doubt she'd have considered even Zhu's present accomplishments to have been impossible. But if you were determined to want the impossible, there was a better way to get it. Zhu thought with amused defiance: *Change the world, and make it possible.*

YINGTIAN

A king and queen strolling through their palace grounds proceeded without impediment, since everyone in their way stepped aside and bowed, but the sheer profusion of construction workers in every direction made Zhu think of herself as a boat cutting through a weed-clogged pond. As they passed yet another building shrouded in bamboo scaffolding, she said admiringly, "I wasn't even away that long. You've been busy."

Her wife, Ma Xiuying, delivered a look of deep indignation. "Of course I've been busy. When you said you wanted a new palace to reflect your status, did you think it would build itself?"

It wasn't even just the palace that was under construction. When Zhu had returned to the city, she'd seen the rising foundations of Yingtian's new walls, and ridden down sunbaked avenues lined with seedling trees that wouldn't give shade for decades yet. The sunshine sawdust smell and the breeze flowing unchecked through the construction sites; the uncluttered sky that seemed bigger and bluer than anywhere else Zhu had lived: the possibility contained in all that newness thrilled her to her bones.

Ma added, "Whereas it sounds like *you* rode all the way to the border just to posture." The enormous volume of her embroidered silk dress barely slowed her stride. Since she was of Semu nomad stock and her feet were as big as a peasant's, she moved several times faster than the aristocratic Nanren women who could be seen tottering about Yingtian under parasols.

Zhu hustled to keep up. "Better to posture than to take them on. Which is something Madam Zhang knew as well as I did. She wanted me to surrender."

"Which would make sense for both of you. So of course you refused."

But as long as there existed something greater in the world than what Zhu had, she knew she would desire it. She could have as readily given up that desire as she could have stopped breathing. "It makes sense according to that particular situation. So what I need to do is change the situation."

"Oh, is *that* all. Perhaps you can double your army just by wishing it."

Zhu twinkled at her. "Maybe I can! But I'm going to need your help."

Ma stopped and shot her a look. "My help."

"Why does that seem so surprising? You're a very capable woman." Zhu indicated the hammering, shouting chaos on all sides. She switched to one of the languages she'd learned in the monastery (but never practiced) and said very badly, "You can speak Uyghur, can't you?"

Ma went blank in surprise. Then she laughed and replied in the same language, "Better than you, apparently."

Uyghur wasn't a world away from Mongolian, which put Zhu in mind of the eunuch general Ouyang and his flat, alien accent when he spoke Han'er. She had always found that accent rather ugly. But she could have listened to Ma's Uyghur all day: there was something purely delightful about finding a new facet of someone she already knew so well.

"It's been so many years. I thought I might have forgotten." Ma switched back to Han'er. She had a nostalgic look. "When I was growing up in Dadu, when my father was a general of the Yuan's central army, we spoke our own Kipchak language at home. But we'd use Mongolian with the Mongols, and Uyghur with other Semu people. Once you know one of those three, the others come easily. But Han'er is completely different. I barely knew a word when my father brought us to Anfeng and gave me to the Guos."

Her father, who had betrayed the Yuan and joined the Red Turban rebellion in Anfeng, only to be betrayed in turn by his rebel compatriots and left to die on General Ouyang's sword. Zhu felt a pang at the thought of the life Ma had lived before they met. Everything she had suffered. She found she couldn't muster up much regret for the deaths of Ma's father, or the two Guos: Old Guo and his son Little Guo, Ma's unfortunate fiancé. "None of them saw your talents."

She realized she'd been too callous when a flash of pain crossed Ma's face. She knew Ma still grieved them. Not for who they'd been to her, or how they had treated her, but simply as human beings. Even after a full year of marriage, Zhu still found Ma's compassion mysterious. When they were together she sometimes thought she might understand—might even feel it, as if it were being transmitted by the vibration of Ma's tender heart against her own—but as soon as they were apart, it faded like a dream.

She changed the subject. She'd spent the greater part of her life trying to escape her past, and unpleasantly sticky feelings such as grief and nostalgia still filled her with the vague urge to run. "Can you find me a dozen or so other Semu people who speak Uyghur?" she said. "Women too, if you can find them. And while you're at it: a couple of camels."

To her satisfaction, the request jolted Ma out of her grief. She gave Zhu an incredulous glare.

"Who doesn't need the occasional camel? I'm sure you have some sort of ancestral facility with them," Zhu said cheerfully. "I'll also need as many rolls of silk as you can get."

"Maybe you have an ancestral facility with the turtle who

laid you as an egg!" Ma exclaimed. "Fine: Semu people, camels, silk. The sun and moon and all the magpies flying over the River of Heaven. When are you leaving?"

"As soon as possible. It's a long march. I'll need to ask Xu Da to start mobilizing the forces immediately. But you've got one thing wrong." A group of palace maids fluttered past, saw the Radiant King and his consort approaching, and flung themselves into reverences. Zhu flicked her fingers benevolently to bid them rise. "It's: Are *we* leaving soon."

Ma frowned in confusion.

"Am I as much a fool as the Guos, to overlook the talented woman in my own house?" Zhu felt a frisson of excitement at her own audacity. "We'll do it together."

The image of a beautiful, jade-cold face rose in her mind, and set all her senses tingling in that eerie recognition of someone else who was neither one thing nor the other. Her stump sang in remembered pain.

"Zhu Yuanzhang," Ma said, low, mindful of passersby who might hear her addressing the Radiant King so informally. "What are you planning?"

Zhu smiled at her. "I need an army on top of the one I already have. So we're going to Bianliang to get one."

After a long pause, Ma said, "The eunuch general—"

"Don't worry—"

"Don't *worry*!"

"—I'm not going to walk into the tiger's cave. Believe it or not, I've learned some lessons from the past." Zhu laughed. "This is a battle-free mission. But we have to move fast. Imagine you're him: you've just spent a lifetime biding your time and pretending loyalty to the ones who murdered your family. But now they're dead, and you're finally in a position to get your revenge on the person who's responsible for everything you suffered: the Great Khan. You'd be desperate to get moving, wouldn't you?

"The only reason General Ouyang hasn't left Bianliang already is because the Great Khan summers in Shangdu and doesn't return to Dadu until mid-autumn. But the very instant he hears the Great Khan is back, he'll be on the march. So we have to get to Bianliang before that happens."

Ma said with deep suspicion, "No fighting. Are you going to make him an offer like Madam Zhang made to you?"

"Not exactly. But it'll be fun, I promise."

Before Ma could reply, there was a roar and a dust cloud rose into the sky where an old building had been an instant ago.

"Buddha preserve us, it looks worse than before," Ma cried, as bricks rained down on a plaza that had already sprouted the skeletons of several new constructions. "Are you sure we couldn't have just kept everything?"

The air was full of brick dust and yellow dust and the familiar dark pickle smell of fire-powder. For an instant Zhu saw a vision of future Yingtian through that dusty curtain: a gleaming metropolis of such brash, tasteless, shocking newness that it stood as radical dismissal of everything that had come before.

Her stamp upon the world, made new.

She felt wild with speed: as if she was running as fast as she could towards that tawny horizon. "Have faith, Yingzi. It's going to be magnificent."

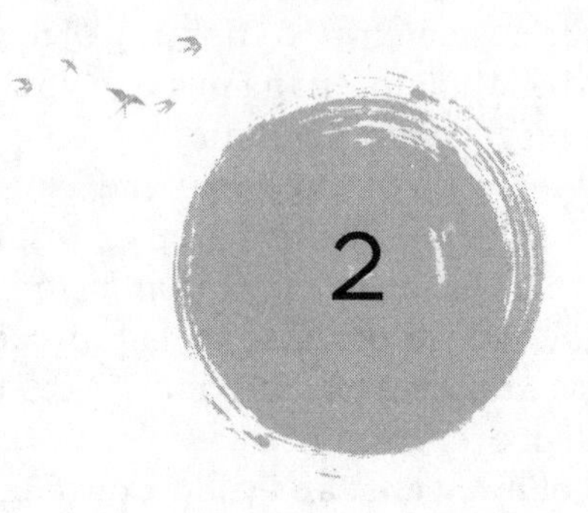

2

BIANLIANG

Esen had been buried on the long foreshore of the Yellow River. The wild grasses, scattered with the last of the summer flowers, had reclaimed what centuries ago had been farmed landscape. It was as close as Ouyang had been able to find to Esen's ancestral steppe with its endless grass sea. A jagged blue range rose in the distance: not mountains, but the broken shell of Bianliang's long-ruined outer wall. As Ouyang knelt on the marshy ground beside the freshly swept tomb, he felt himself slowly sinking. Eventually, everything around him would disappear the same way: Bianliang's walls, Esen's tomb, this entire wild landscape. And he—he would be gone sooner than all of it.

His pain rose. Since Esen's death there was never a moment without pain. Under every breath he felt an unbearable throb of grief rending the qi that knitted his spirit to his flesh and bones and organs, so it felt like the very fabric of himself was being wrenched apart. But the worst pain came upon him in waves, like this. To be caught was to be swept into a raging firestorm—to be trapped in an agony so intense it shelled away the outside world and left him as nothing but a burning mind curling upon itself in an endless, futile attempt to escape.

He knelt there, shuddering, burning. For a moment all he could think about was how much he wanted the yellow waters to rise around him, to quench his pain and bear his body away to the sea. But it was impossible. Even obliterated by pain, he knew there was only one way out. He would endure, though he didn't know how he could, simply because he had to. When summer was over and the Great Khan returned to the capital from the Summer Palace, Ouyang would march to Dadu and have his revenge upon the one who had written his and Esen's fates into the pattern of the world and stolen from them their choices in how they lived and died. And with the murder of the Great Khan, that one final act of Ouyang's life, every awful thing he had done—everything he had suffered—would be made worth it.

He stood. As his shadow fell across the grass, a shiver passed through it and sent the nesting larks flitting away. Farther away, cattails swayed in a half-glimpsed glimmer of bright water. The sun was hot enough to bring out their oniony smell, but he could feel the season turning. Summer was nearly over. It was almost time.

The sun had angled by the time he came within sight of Bianliang's intact inner wall. He realized, distantly and without concern, that he'd been away for most of the day.

"General Ouyang!"

A rider who had been waiting for him swung in beside Ouyang's black mare as he rode through the portal. Ouyang glanced over, irritated by the intrusion. Of the six original Nanren commanders who had been his co-conspirators in his treachery against the Mongols, only three remained, with Commander Geng being the least memorable of the three. Even his face, as square as the character for "nation," seemed less a stamp of individual character than the pronouncement of the commanders' cause: to return the Great Yuan to native rule. Like the other commanders, Geng had changed his hair from Mongol braids to a proud Nanren-style topknot. Ouyang wondered if they looked askance at his refusal to undo his own braids. Not that he cared if they did. Unlike for them, his Nanren identity was beyond recovery. It felt like something that had been cut out of him, along with everything else that made a man.

Geng's pleading expression increased Ouyang's irritation. "General, the matter of Commander Lin—" To match their newly Nanren-led army, he spoke Han'er rather than Mongolian. "With respect, I strongly urge you to meet with him to resolve the situation."

The urgency was baffling. Ouyang wasn't even sure which of his commanders Lin was, let alone why he should merit personal attention. "Why are you bothering me with this? Let Senior Commander Shao handle it."

Ouyang recalled the fate of two of those six co-conspirators. He had no love for Shao, but he could appreciate how his second-in-command's methods of dealing with problem people tended to remove the problem permanently.

He barely heard Geng's protests as they reached their headquarters in the former Yuan governor's residence, and dismounted. As Ouyang strode through the splintering wooden gateway, a stray dog raised its head and growled softly.

He knew what the dog was responding to, just as he knew why birds fled his shadow and flames dipped as he passed.

His ghosts.

He couldn't see them, like those with the Mandate of Heaven seemingly could, but they were there. They were always there. Ever since Esen's death, they filled his dreams: those dead members of the Ouyang clan in tattered white rags, staring at him with their empty black eyes, waiting for him to release them.

In a blaze of agony he thought: *Soon.*

The goatskin leather parted easily under Ouyang's knife as he cut a strap to size to replace the worn cheekpiece of a bridle. A small table, placed next to him on the bed, held a beeswax candle and his tools. Fixing tack was a groom's job, but as their departure approached he found himself seizing upon menial tasks in the hope it would make the time pass faster.

He held his knife into the candle flame. It was easiest to make runnels for the strap's stitching by scoring the leather with the back edge of a heated blade. He was staring into the sinking flame when, in some sudden horrible alchemy, the smells of candle and heated metal and leather combined into memory—not even a specific memory, he thought in anguish, but the *feeling* of Esen. And the instant he felt, the pain came.

It was unfathomable. A desperate instinct came upon him, nothing more than a reflex provoked by his mindless howl for the pain to stop, and before he knew what he was doing he had wrestled up his narrow left sleeve and laid the flat of the heated blade against his own skin.

That hurt. He stared down at it in dumb agony. It hurt so much it burned the grief out of his head until the only thing inside him was a clear-edged white scream.

Even before Ouyang had been a soldier, accustomed to every kind of bodily grievance, a heated knife had turned him into what he was. He knew this pain. He knew that—unlike the other pain—it was a pain he could survive. He snatched the blade off his wrist with a gasp. Underneath, parallel to the bracelet made of Esen's jade and gold hair beads, his skin bore a furious stripe. Inside his head the white scream went on and on. He let himself disappear into it. Instead of a burning mind he was a burning body, and inside that body he was wiped clean of everything he was and everything he felt.

He didn't know how long he floated. It seemed a long time.

"General."

Ouyang jerked around. Shao was in the doorway. How long had he been there? The bridle lay forgotten in Ouyang's lap. He yanked his sleeve down over burn and bracelet, feeling an obscure shame. The burn was still singing.

Shao came in. Apparently he considered that however many times he'd said "General" to Ouyang's back, that constituted invitation enough. Geng and Commander Chu, the other original co-conspirator, followed. Ouyang stood up. Without his armor, raw with pain, it felt less like a meeting than a confrontation. He was suddenly conscious of the knife in his hand.

"General Ouyang," Shao said without saluting. His eyes drifted to the knife. His mouth, a mirthless lopsided line of ironic acknowledgment, put Ouyang in mind of a sword slash. But Shao always looked like that. It didn't mean he had seen what Ouyang had been doing. "Didn't you receive my message?"

With a start, Ouyang recalled brushing aside a young soldier some time earlier. When had that been? Morning, perhaps. It was already afternoon. "You're here now," he said shortly. "What is it?"

"Commander Lin and his engineering company didn't report from their barracks this morning." Shao's mouth always hung open very slightly when he stopped speaking, like a fish about to bite.

Was it Geng who had said something the other day about Commander Lin? Perhaps it had been Chu. "So?"

"So, Commander Lin, who asked to meet you three days ago to discuss his dissatisfactions, but failed to receive a hearing, has now deserted."

Ouyang met Shao's gaze with dislike. He had zero interest in personnel issues, and felt sticky and furious with the desire to be left alone. "Aren't there still three more companies of engineers? I don't see the problem."

Geng and Chu shifted uneasily, but it took more than a sharp tone to quell Shao. "Waiting is hard on the best of armies. *Your* army is an army of conscripts who were just involved in murdering their commanders in cold blood. They've lost all prospect of being paid. And now they've all seen a hundred men leave. Trust me, loyalty isn't going to keep the rest of them here." The flatness of his reply masked whatever contempt he felt about the obvious: that a eunuch like Ouyang was barely capable of winning the respect of whole men, let alone so much as loyalty. "If you want them to stay, you have to make it worth their while."

"The cause of Nanren freedom from the Mongols should be enough," Ouyang said tightly.

Shao's mouth slanted further downwards. He wasn't one for causes.

"Dedicated as they are, don't forget they're just ordinary men with families to support," Chu put in. Ouyang found Chu unspeakably annoying. Something about his soft round marmot face, his excessive gentleness, the way he walked too lightly on his toes—it all filled Ouyang with the urge for violence.

"Remember the floods last year?" Geng added. "Nearly every farmer in Henan lost a year's income. It wasn't so bad for those of us on the Prince of Henan's estate, since Lord Wang forgave our debts. But elsewhere people suffered. If you can pay those men something to send back to their families, gold or silk or salt, they'll stay."

Ouyang had a distant memory of Wang Baoxiang borrowing his soldiers to dig ditches. He supposed Lord Wang was the

Prince of Henan now. With Esen and Ouyang out of his life, no doubt he was counting his gold and nurturing his peasants into ever-greater productivity. The idea that Lord Wang might be happy because of everything that had happened made him taste bile. "It's a moot point. We don't have gold. Or silk, or salt."

"We can get it," Shao said brusquely. "Several of Zhu Yuanzhang's cities are within reach. When he moved his capital from Anfeng to Yingtian, he left himself weak on the periphery. We can take those cities easily enough, and get what we need."

"And delay our march to Dadu? *No.*" The thought of waiting—waiting *longer*—choked Ouyang with fury. "Enough! Put together a small force of light cavalry. Hunt down those deserters, and flay every last one of them, and hang their skinned corpses from the walls. Do the men need an incentive not to desert? Perhaps that will be sweet enough for them."

He turned his back on them and sat down. The candle flame flickered, low on its wick, as he placed his knife into the flame. When it had heated and he took up the leather strap again, they had gone.

"Why are there broken roof tiles everywhere?" Ouyang snarled as he came into the hall that served as their command center. For some reason the compound's front courtyards were strewn with what looked like the aftermath of an earthquake.

Shao, Geng, and Chu looked up from a huddled discussion. Shao said with false pleasantness, "To answer the General's question: the men have been expressing their gratitude for the new decorations you've had strung up around town. I suppose tiles are easier to throw than rocks."

The hot wind brought a wavering sour odor into the building, carrion and sewage and smoke, but Ouyang had a strong stomach. He stared hard at Shao. "And yet: there haven't been any more desertions. So they got the message."

Shao said sardonically, "Indeed." He flipped a message tube to Ouyang. "This just came in from the northern observers. You'll be pleased."

Ouyang's heart leapt so strongly that he nearly dropped

the tube as he pulled out the letter. He could barely focus long enough to let the Mongolian script tell him what he knew it would. "The Great Khan has returned from the Summer Palace. He's back in Dadu." The intensity of his feelings pushed his voice into that loathed high register, but he found he no longer cared. Somehow he had become that soiled madman roaming the streets heedless of everyone's disgust. "This is it. We can finally leave this shithole of a city. Senior Commander Shao! Make the arrangements for departure."

He left them to it, feeling a strange lightness. Being in motion didn't lessen the effort needed to endure the pain, but now he could finally believe that the effort was finite. He only needed to hold on for a short while longer. And then he would have his relief.

He didn't realize Shao had followed until he heard from behind, "General."

He was in a long empty stretch of corridor. He turned in surprise and saw Shao regarding him with hate. Ouyang was taken aback. He'd always disliked Shao, to the point where all their interactions seemed in bad faith, but Shao had always pretended to accept Ouyang as his superior. The bald return of dislike was new and disturbing.

Shao said coldly, "Listen to me. I know you don't give a fuck about surviving Dadu, but you need to make it less obvious. How do you think the men are going to react if they realize you're on a suicide mission? If morale gets any worse, we're not even going to *make* it to Dadu, let alone get near the Great Khan. You want to see how bad it is? Walk out the front gate of this compound right now and see how they respond. I tell you what: they're not going to cheer."

"I don't need them to cheer for me," Ouyang said with instant fury. "I need them to *obey* me. I've made them obey before. I'll make them do it again." But instead of looking away in deference, this time Shao stared back. The defiance filled Ouyang with the sudden desire to hurt. He had the urge to force Shao's obedience the way he wrung it from his conscripts with the whip. "Shao Ge, sometimes I wonder. You don't have the Mandate yet, do you? It seems to be taking its time coming. Do you think I should take it as a sign I need someone else as my partner for this endeavor?"

He and Shao had never spoken explicitly about what Shao would get out of their partnership. But, Ouyang thought disgustedly, it was hardly a secret.

Shao's lips whitened. "You can't bluff me. I know how much you need to get to Dadu. Don't think you can do it without me and this army."

He glared down his nose at Ouyang. Without the leveling influence of being on horseback, their height difference was marked. Shao's icy expression reminded Ouyang of that rainy day over a game of weiqi, the last time he'd seen his commanders Yan and Bai alive. When they'd had doubts about the plan, Ouyang would have simply let them go, but Shao had had his own ideas. Even then he hadn't been Ouyang's man, but purely his own.

The only thing that superseded their animosity was what they both knew: that they needed each other.

"Right now, I'm in charge," Ouyang said. "Obey me and we won't have a problem. Get this army ready to leave, even if it means you need to beat one half of them to death in front of the other half." He didn't bother to stop the contempt from leaking into his voice. "And when we get to Dadu, I'll make sure you get your throne."

3

KHANBALIQ (DADU)

"So you're the new Prince of Henan. We have to say, your brother suited us better."

Wang Baoxiang rose, delicately, from his prostration, and saw familiar disgust animate the Great Khan's torpid features. It felt like an accomplishment. Everything about the Great Khan resisted the idea of disturbance, as though he were a squatting boulder that worked itself further into the hillside with every passing year. The Son of Heaven's heavy cheeks drew the eye down to long-lobed ears, which dragged the eye lower again to the drooping arcs of his braids. Behind his head, golden dragons yawned and writhed across the engraved woodwork of the throne.

The court had returned to Khanbaliq to find the capital in the grip of an unseasonably hot autumn. Even the soaring rafters of the Hall of Great Brilliance couldn't make the situation bearable. There was acrid desert on Baoxiang's tongue. The taste of the north. Out of perversity he had worn his favorite gown for his first audience before the court, a flamboyant lettuce-green provocation his father had hated beyond belief. Now its winter-weight embrace made his head spin. But fainting in front of the Great Khan would do little to advance his purpose. He slipped his fan from his sleeve and fanned himself instead. The Great Khan's silver-paneled walls fluttered back at him. The dimpled metal made too many reflections, as if it were showing pale figures lingering in the shadowed corners of the hall.

The Great Khan's eyes tracked Baoxiang's limp-wristed fanning. His expression soured further. It was the expression Baoxiang had seen on other people's faces his whole life, as if his very person offended dignity. As if the mere fact of his obstinate, unrepentant effeminacy made their own honor impossible.

His anger surged. Lately, since—*events*—he had the idea of his anger as a permanent dark sea inside him, sloshing and unstable. All it took was a single disturbance for that potential to gather into a tsunami of rage and hate. It was hard to imagine how he hadn't always been like this. He loved how completely the black feeling grabbed him. How obliterating and consuming it felt, and how it would never not feel that way because, unlike other emotions, it was infinite and inexhaustible. He imagined himself soaking up the Great Khan's scorn with his teeth bared in invitation. *Go ahead. Revile me.*

The Great Khan wasn't the only one scorning him. Three other unfriendly faces looked down at him from chairs a step down from the Dragon Throne. He recognized the Grand Councilor, commander of the Great Yuan's central army; and the Great Khan's favorite consort, Lady Ki. He was barely worth their notice. But the third person! He had *her* attention. Her hate struck Baoxiang open-handed. The Empress wore the towering red column hat of female Mongol nobility, and from inside its shadow her doll face promised vengeance. There was nothing poetic about that vengeance. It was the kind of ugly hatred that demanded its subject ripped limb from limb, his guts on the floor.

He knew he deserved it, but he barely remembered the cause. Oh, he knew what he'd *done:* destroyed the Empress's younger brother Altan, and left her entire family with the stigma of treason. But all he had was a distant impression of having enjoyed himself. It was what had come afterwards that was seared into his memory. Being disowned. Framed for his father's murder. Thrown, unknowing and unwilling—initially, at least—onto the path that led to his brother's death.

His brother. That was more than a disturbance. The explosion of black anger swallowed him whole. Esen, the perfect warrior prince. The epitome of Mongol culture in mind and body and spirit, who until the moment of his death had never experienced a moment of scorn or rejection or anything other than the world's love. Who had loved the world in return, even his own killer, except for the person whose wickedness he believed without doubt.

Baoxiang might not have been guilty of patricide. But by the time he'd reached the end of that path, he'd been as wicked and dishonorable as Esen had always thought him. He'd proved himself entirely worthy of hate.

He gestured, and his servant came forwards with the golden eagle on his fist. He felt drunk with anger. He was almost sure it didn't show. "Great Khan, this unworthy servant would be honored for you to accept this most lacking gift! Worthless though it must appear to you, it was my brother Esen-Temur's most treasured possession. My brother loved our Great Yuan beyond measure, and gave his life in service of it, so I dare hope the memory of his loyalty may please His Majesty."

The Empress said with sudden venom, "A dead man's castoffs for the Great Khan?" The tip of her column hat attacked like an enraged ostrich. Despite her rank, she was an ordinary-looking young Mongol woman: round-faced and pink-cheeked, lipstick painted fashionably inside her lip-line so her mouth looked even more pinched than it was. Everyone knew she had been made Empress because of her father the Military Governor of Shanxi's contributions to the capital's shrinking coffers—just as they all knew how the Great Khan showed her no favor, and kept on preferring Lady Ki. "The Prince of Henan's estate was once rich enough to fund armies. And now you can't even afford a proper gift for our Great Khan?" Her viper eyes dissected Baoxiang's shabby manservant. "Don't tell me you managed to lose your family's wealth along with its honor."

There was a subtle change in the room: someone's attention summoned by their enemy's mistake. A moment later Lady Ki leaned forwards and smiled warmly at Baoxiang. It was an astonishing transformation—haughty distaste into pure graciousness—and Baoxiang was under no illusions that it had anything to do with *him.* "The Prince of Henan has made a most noble gift," the Great Khan's favorite said. Her Goryeo-accented Mongolian was charming. As the mother of an adult prince she was well past youth, but her refinement gave Baoxiang the idea that if he looked away she might slip into her unobserved true shape: a luminescent stone; a white crane. Under her smile, the dagger of her attention rested on the Empress. "Any crass person with the means can procure a costly item. But this is a gift without measure: a gift from the heart."

A young man's voice said from the door, "Esen-Temur's loyalty might have been without measure, but can you say the same for his good sense?" A broad-shouldered noble in a rumpled satin riding skirt sauntered in, giving Baoxiang a repulsed glance in passing. "Only an idiot would have trusted that Manji bitch of a eunuch with command of his army. He deserved what he got." He reached the throne and made a cursory obeisance. "Greetings to the Great Khan. Greetings to the Grand Councilor. Greetings to the Empress and the Lady Ki."

The Great Khan viewed the young noble with dislike. The Empress, forgetting Baoxiang, said poisonously, "What important business does the Third Prince have, I wonder, that he dares leave the Great Khan waiting upon his pleasure?"

The Third Prince, the Great Khan's sole remaining son and presumptive heir, rose without apology and flicked his braids out of his neatly bearded face. The pronounced bow shape of his lips reminded Baoxiang of the strange cruel faces of Buddha statues from the southern vassal state of Cham. He was noticeably taller than when Baoxiang had last seen him, a year and a half ago at the Great Khan's disastrous Spring Hunt. A man now, rather than a boy. But, like a boy, still waiting on the cusp: for his Mandate of Heaven; for the title of Crown Prince. The appearance of the Third Prince's Mandate was so notably late that even provincial nobles whispered about how it must mean a Heaven-favored prince was yet to be born. The Empress was young, after all.

Lady Ki barely glanced at her son. Her eyes caressed the Great Khan as she murmured, "I heard the Third Prince spent the morning out hunting. I'm sure the delay was only a result of his efforts to emulate the Great Khan's own successes in that pursuit. Unfortunately the Great Khan has set such a high standard that it makes it hard for others."

"Is that so," the Great Khan said, softening. "It was hardly our intention to make a young man's life difficult. Better we should encourage his efforts." He said in a louder voice, "We bestow Esen-Temur's eagle upon Lady Ki's son, the Third Prince!"

Lady Ki made an elegant seated genuflection as the Third Prince smirked and came over to stroke the hooded eagle on the servant's fist. But he wasn't looking at the eagle. He was looking at Baoxiang. There was a posturing aggression to him that made Baoxiang think of a young buck showing off his first set of antlers. The familiar prickle of danger filled him with anticipation.

"Greetings to the Third Prince," he said, bowing.

"Prince of Henan." The Third Prince's examination dragged over Baoxiang, lingering with naked contempt on all that offended: Baoxiang's hair in its Nanren-style topknot; his long un-Mongol nose and smooth-shaven thin cheeks; his elegant gown and soft scholar's hands. Baoxiang remembered that look finding him during the Great Khan's Spring Hunt. It was almost the same look that other young men gave Baoxiang before they hurt him. But not quite. The Third Prince's boyishly long-lashed eyes returned to Baoxiang's face, bright with disgust. "I remember you."

I'm sure you do. Baoxiang's blackness stirred in satisfaction. *I remember you, too.*

The Third Prince's stroking hand paused on the bird's back. His knuckles had the ungainliness of someone who hadn't yet reached his finished shape. "You really aren't like your brother. But I'm sure you can't be as completely useless as they say. I can trouble you for a favor, can't I?" His cruel young mouth smiled with the anticipation of violence. "Hold the eagle for me while I put on the glove."

All at once Baoxiang was back in his father's mews, twelve-year-old Esen placing the goshawk on Baoxiang's small gloved fist. His nose was crammed with straw dust and the musty smell of dried regurgitated fur. He'd tried to control his fear, but the jerkiness of the bird's movements scared him on some primal level. The more afraid he became, the more the bird danced on his fist in stilted rage. And then it fell backwards off his fist and hung upside down in the tangle of its jesses, screaming in furious terror. He could only stand there trembling as Esen, terse with frustration, soothed and untangled the bird. It had been his own foolishness that had shamed him the most. That he had dared hope for comfort too, as if his terror might matter as much to Esen as a bird's.

"Hold out your arm," the Third Prince said softly. Baoxiang, his eyes lowered in deference, felt a stab of contempt. It was a child's play of cruelty, with a child's lack of knowledge about how transparent he was—and how vulnerable it made him, to be seen. Baoxiang's satisfaction sharpened, gained its own cruelty. *I see you.*

He held out his left arm. He had no protection but his silk sleeve. But there was no point protesting. None of them would intervene. He knew they all wanted this as much as the Third Prince: to see him punished for simply *being.*

The bird, thrust onto its strange new perch, grabbed him in alarm. Its talons were as thick as his fingers. Each point pricked through his sleeve. Not hurting him. Not yet. But he knew what kind of damage an eagle could do with those feet. Despite his best efforts, he felt the first stirrings of fear.

The Third Prince took the glove from Baoxiang's servant and slowly drew it on. He watched Baoxiang openly, intensely, as if the more disgusted he was, the more he was drawn by the spectacle of him. Baoxiang tried to ignore the shift of the eagle's talons and the sight of its open panting beak. He could feel a cold sweat forming. The Third Prince only wanted to scare him, not maim him—but knowing that didn't stop him from being frightened. He was weak and afraid, and ashamed of his weakness and fear. He was everything they thought of him. But underneath the fear was that great sloshing ocean of black anger, rising.

The Third Prince, glove on, let him tremble a moment longer before deftly unhooking the bird from Baoxiang's sleeve. His eyes sparkled unkindly. "Many thanks. This gift well pleases me. Oh, but"—he looked at the rents in Baoxiang's sleeve in mock surprise—"your beautiful gown is ruined. What a shame. Perhaps when you replace it, you should choose a color that suits you better." He said, drawing it out with relish, *"Peach."*

Bitten-peach faggot. It hung in the air as he withdrew, smiling, Esen's eagle on his fist.

Eight pinpricks burned on Baoxiang's left arm. He tucked his hands into his sleeves, feeling his heart slow. As his bright fear drained away, its absence made what lay beneath seem even darker and denser than before.

"Prince of Henan." The Grand Councilor's maroon over-robe, the same worn by the Great Yuan's officials of every rank, was offset by his tone of easy authority. Everyone knew the Grand Councilor was the power behind the throne. "Your gift is well received. What brings you to court?"

It was a welcome return to the ground of Baoxiang's choosing. He bowed over his folded hands and gave a modest cough. "This servant boldly hopes to serve in Khanbaliq in whatever capacity will advance the interests of our glorious empire. Although my skills are unworthy of praise, I have some experience in administration. Before my brother's death, I was the provincial administrator for Henan."

It was a position worth the boast: the highest in the Great Yuan's most important province, albeit an odd occupation for the son of a Prince of the Blood. But then, Baoxiang reflected bitterly, as a half-caste adopted son he'd had precious little of the blood to begin with.

"If the Prince of Henan's estate is in as dire financial straits as his servant's attire suggests, we can hardly regard his skills as exceptional," the Empress sniped. "Perhaps his ignorance extends to the fact that official posts are filled at the start of the year. Or does he think that in the absence of a vacancy, we might create a position just for him?" Her carmine sneer left no doubt about the likelihood.

After a moment's consideration the Grand Councilor said, "But isn't there a recent vacancy in the Ministry of Revenue? The vice-minister position."

Baoxiang smiled internally, without humor.

"The Grand Councilor jests." The Empress's eyes disemboweled Baoxiang. "That one brings shame upon the court just by standing in front of us! How could we possibly permit someone like that as vice-minister?"

Lady Ki turned gracefully towards the Great Khan. The golden phoenix pin in her coiffure, the sign of the Great Khan's favor, caught the light. "Your Majesty, the Prince of Henan is excellently qualified. Indeed, had he come seeking appointment at the usual time of year, he would have been eligible for even higher rank. He is a Prince of the Blood, after all." Her blatant exercise of influence over the Great Khan was shocking. When the Great Yuan had lost access to the Zhang family's salt, it had strengthened Lady Ki: her home state of Goryeo was now the main source of that precious resource. Lady Ki's smile found the Empress. "Surely we should not turn away those who seek to advance the glory of our Great Yuan."

The Grand Councilor glanced at the Great Khan, who flicked a hand in assent. "Prince of Henan," the Grand Councilor said. "Your family's unswerving loyalty and commitment to the defense of our Great Yuan has earned my respect and gratitude. Though my feelings were surely but a shadow of your own, I was deeply saddened by Esen-Temur's death. As you are unable to follow in his footsteps, you may take up the office of vice-minister, and bring honor to his memory by serving the Great Yuan in accordance with your capabilities."

Baoxiang's abrupt fury overwhelmed any joy of success. The Grand Councilor dared think he *understood* how Baoxiang felt about Esen's death.

Shaking with anger, he sank into a prostration of gratitude. The edges of his vision pulsed with the pale flickering that could have been the play of light against the beaten-silver walls. "A thousand thanks to the Grand Councilor and the Great Khan!"

He wished, viciously, that he could show them his rage: the dark, boiling power of it as it surged against the cast-iron inner boundary of himself.

If you saw what I actually felt and wanted, it would wither your pity in an instant.

"Esteemed Prince." Seyhan, Baoxiang's secretary, greeted him as he stepped over the raised threshold of the Hall of Great Brilliance into the shaded colonnade. Even out of the direct sun, the heat obliterated. Baoxiang's lettuce gown was cooking him alive. The hall, which formed the front part of the Great Khan's residence, overlooked an array of dazzling white marble plazas, crisscrossed by staircases heading in every direction. The brightness made his head ache. As he winced, Seyhan slanted his ice-pale eyes at Baoxiang and added slyly in Persian, "Or should I say: Vice-Minister?"

"With thanks to you," Baoxiang said, in that same language. "Was it trouble?"

"A vice-minister? Hardly."

The thought of his deceased predecessor didn't trouble him. It was abstract as a line in an account book: a life, reduced to the modest number of gold taels it had taken to dispose of him.

"A ministerial position would have been easy enough, and more suited to a Prince of the Blood," Seyhan said with grievance. He was a Semu man from Khwarezm in the far west, and his dark beard did much to hide a face composed of an ugly assortment of angles. His hawk nose floated free above any such disguise. As Baoxiang's long-standing right-hand man, he took slights against his master personally. "A vice-minister is a nobody."

They strolled the colonnade at half speed. The heat exacerbated Baoxiang's exhaustion to the point of nausea. Under the sun's searing eye the Palace City's tiled roofs sparkled in a jumble of coral red and jasper green and lapis blue. A high rim of whitewashed wall lay behind the roofs. Khanbaliq, the capital built by Khubilai Khan as a monument to his triumph, was a city of cities. On first approach, the traveler encountered Khanbaliq's sprawling suburbs of mansions and inns and pleasure houses. Next came the massive city wall with its eleven battlemented gates, containing the outer city. At the heart of the outer city was the Imperial City, the imperial family's manicured playground of parks and lakes. And nested within *that* city, like the kernel in an apricot pit, lay the white-walled Palace City, where the Great Khan's residence rose glittering out of a marble sea. As Baoxiang walked in the shadow of the palace, the largest building in all the lands between the four oceans, he thought the proper response would be awe. Instead, he found its newness disgusting. The Great Yuan's azure flags stirred atop the distant whitewashed wall. They were no more noticeable against the hazy sky than a heat shimmer.

As Baoxiang and Seyhan descended to the plaza, they were passed by a knot of maids walking ahead of a roofed sedan chair borne by harem eunuchs. The sedan chair drew level with them and slowed. The Empress glared down at him. Illuminated by the reflection from the plaza beneath, her face was as white as a grudge-holding ghost. "Let me offer you some advice, Prince of Henan. The palace is a very different place to your miserable little province. Go home before you regret it."

The eunuchs bore her away. Palace eunuchs were slaves from vassal states like Goryeo, not Nanren, but with a pang of hate Baoxiang thought of General Ouyang. That wretched cur of a eunuch, the ungrateful recipient of more love and nurturance than Baoxiang had ever had, who'd felt nothing but self-pity as he ruined Baoxiang's life.

"The Empress is a bad enemy to have." The angles of Seyhan's face doubled with concern. "She may not be the favorite, but she has power."

Baoxiang laughed darkly. "How long do I have to find a protector before she sends people after me, do you think? Weeks, or days?"

"Esteemed Prince," Seyhan said, pale and grim. "Why are we here?"

"You don't think I've come to save the Great Yuan from itself?"

The look Seyhan gave him conveyed what he thought about that. "I'm sure the Prince of Henan is more than capable."

Baoxiang said sardonically, "It does seem like they think they can just walk up to Madam Zhang and ask her for her kingdom back."

Of course the Grand Councilor had been *saddened* by Esen's death. Without Esen and his traitorous lapdog Ouyang—without Henan's army to hold the rebellious south in check—the only thing standing between the Great Yuan and collapse was the Grand Councilor's central army: a force that hadn't deployed south in more than a decade. Perhaps the Grand Councilor sensed what peril the empire was in. But as Baoxiang recalled the Great Khan's inertia and his sparring consorts, he thought the Grand Councilor might be the only one.

"A vice-minister is a nobody," he agreed. "But the most dangerous person in a game is the one nobody knows is playing."

After a pause Seyhan said, very carefully, "And what game are you playing, esteemed Prince?"

Baoxiang saw a flash of those contemptuous faces above him, never questioning their assumption that their scorn would be enough to make him wither and disappear. If only they knew how every drop of their antipathy fed the black ocean inside him and made it deeper. He burst out in hatred, "They all look at me and see the worst thing they can possibly imagine. An embarrassment. A mockery of everything Mongols value. *But they have no idea how much worse I'm going to be.*"

He realized his heart was pounding. He had meant to nick the surface but had cut too deep; he had laid open his ugliness for anyone to see. Seyhan's expression acquired another layer of guardedness. Inside he would be recoiling. Baoxiang couldn't blame him. Who would be willing to touch someone else's raw pain, and risk contamination?

He turned on his heel, furious with shame, and headed in the direction of the closest gate out of the Palace City. "Let's find this job I paid so much for."

The Ministry of Revenue, like the other ministries and secretariats, was in Khanbaliq proper. It was on the Thousand-Foot Corridor, the broad avenue that joined the Imperial City's main entrance—the massive Chongtian Gate, on its south side—to the middle gate in Khanbaliq's southern wall. To Baoxiang, whose exhaustion painted the world with a deadened irritation, the ministry building with its blue eaves and gilded roof spines had the same crass, new-built feeling as everything else in Khanbaliq. The phoenix trees standing like orange flames on each side of the avenue were the only part of the capital that seemed older than the Mongols.

"Those trees don't stay pretty for long." Baoxiang jumped. A square old Mongol in an official's maroon over-robe, his gray braids protruding from beneath a lacquered-muslin hat with long outstretched flanges to either side, had snuck up on him in cloth-soled boots. He said in Khanbaliq-accented Mongolian, "In another week, this street will be leaves up to your knees."

Baoxiang took a guess and bowed quickly. "Greetings to the honorable Minister."

"Prince of Henan." The Minister of Revenue took in Baoxiang's Nanren-style topknot caged in a cloud of silver filigree and secured with pearl-ended hairpins; his sallow complexion of the terminally sleepless; and the lettuce gown and its matching shoes. Under his wispy gray beard, the Minister's expression of benign delight didn't change. It seemed a permanent condition, like Ouyang's resting frown. "Our new vice-minister! What a surprise you are. Well, come in. Have you eaten? This heat is too much for this time of year, don't you think? I haven't lived through an autumn like this since I was your age. Let's sit, and I'll get a girl to bring us that drink they like in the south, the one with the red dates and honey. So refreshing! Nanren do know how to handle the heat . . ."

The Minister limped inside, chattering. His chatter gave Baoxiang the impression that capital officials spent their days drinking tea and gossiping, so he was surprised to see that the inside of the building was a busy working office. They passed a library; rooms for account-book storage and rooms for complaints; a room of servants grinding ink, and another of bureaucrats—all Semu men, since Nanren were forbidden from the civil service—who flicked their abacus beads with such vigor that the window-paper buzzed. It was the same as his office back home in Anyang. He felt a painful slice of nostalgia. But the blackness was already inside him, and he had known there was never any going back.

The Minister ushered him along a shaded external walkway and up a few steps into a building with a latticed frontage. Inside was a cavernous private office with a paper-strewn desk and a threatening number of unstable bookcases.

The Minister himself didn't sit. "Rest a moment! This old man had too many cups of tea, and his bladder is weak." His eyes twinkled as he limped back out. "Experience tells me to address it now, so we can sit at our leisure afterwards."

Baoxiang glanced around. A cross-breeze through the doors on either side of the room reduced the heat, but added powerful smells of dry animal dung and grilling bread. After the tranquil environs of the Prince of Henan's rural estate, the city was an assault.

An account book lay on top of the flotsam on the desk, as if it had been shuffled around with everything else and only coincidentally ended up facing him. He flicked through and felt a dull twitch of surprise to see the pages of neat calculations providing the example to be followed, and the blank pages waiting for his answer. He thought of the Minister's disarming chatter, and wondered how many officials had sat in his place without even touching the book.

"You found it! Don't worry too much. Nobody ever passes that test; he designs it that way." A maid had appeared at his elbow with a sweating ewer and matching cups, and a spoke-wheel platter with candied vegetables in each compartment. She gave him a merry glance with her dimples flashing as if in anticipation of his panic, placed the tray on a cluttered side table, and left. Baoxiang regarded the test and felt his lip curl without answering merriment.

The Minister came back swiftly—too swiftly to have made it a fair test. As he limped over to his chair, his eyes darted to Baoxiang's answers gleaming blackly in wet ink. Baoxiang saw the moment his disgust—because, even though he had hidden it better than most, he *had* felt disgust—became respect.

It was the respect that felt like the punch. Baoxiang had wanted his whole life to be respected rather than scorned for his talents. Now this was how easily it came? Yet it was too late.

He said tartly, "Did you think I expected a position with none of the responsibilities?"

The Minister regarded him. "Nobody expects a noble to need a salary, let alone work for one. Especially not the Prince of Henan, whose estate was rich enough to power the Great Yuan's defense against the southern rebels for decades. I assumed you were an incompetent who had let all that wealth run dry. But you do have skills after all. So why leave Henan, Wang Baoxiang?"

The blackness within Baoxiang heaved without breaking, like water right before the boil. "Perhaps I just didn't want to stay."

The Minister's face softened. "Ah. Your father and brother. That was a pity."

Baoxiang was revolted. He didn't want gentleness. He didn't want *pity.* He let his revulsion harden into contempt. A sympathetic fool of a minister was exactly what he needed. Someone who was willing to put aside his disgust for the sake of Baoxiang's talent, and find him useful. "Yes," he said. "A great pity."

The ewer sat in a puddle of condensation. It wet his hands when he poured two cups. He had the idea it was supposed to have been a sweet drink, but it tasted like nothing. He choked it down.

The Minister hoisted himself to his feet. "Well, how lucky to have you take that vacancy! I've had my fill of decorative nobles. I'll have to thank the Grand Councilor for sending me someone who knows what he's doing. What with everything that's been happening to our Great Yuan, I need the help."

"That's what I'm here for," Baoxiang said politely. But for a moment the corners of the room wavered, and whiteness flickered in the corners of his eyes.

Seyhan was waiting for him with their horses when he finally emerged. The sun, hovering just above Khanbaliq's western battlements, slanted through the flaming tips of the phoenix trees and drenched the streets in gold.

When Baoxiang turned his horse down the Thousand-Foot Corridor towards the Imperial City, Seyhan said with surprise, "You don't want to go to the house?"

What Baoxiang felt was too dark for anticipation. "I have someone else to see."

"A member of the imperial family?" Seyhan's eyebrows rose. "Are they expecting you?"

"Not," Baoxiang said, "exactly."

The residence stood in a forested hunting reserve on the far west side of the Imperial City, its shadowed profile punctuated by a golden mulberry rising from an internal courtyard. The residence's head servant stood between the wooden pillars of the front gate to receive them. As the servant opened his mouth Baoxiang said coolly, "If he's not home yet, show me in."

"Whose residence is this?" Seyhan asked, frowning.

The servant said, "The Palace of Abundant Blessings is the residence of His Highness the Third Prince."

To the east was the darkening lake he and Seyhan had crossed on a marble causeway. A pagoda-crowned hill rose from a rocky island in its center. Within its walls the Imperial City had lakes and forests and hunting grounds to rival the wilderness, but none of it seemed quite real. In fact, it wasn't. Baoxiang knew that everything his eyes touched had been shipped in and molded to the imperial family's pleasure, from the earth for the hill to the fish in the lake. The air vibrated with the scream of cicadas.

Baoxiang thought of the Great Khan's expression when he'd looked at his son. It had been the most familiar thing in the world. A father's hatred of his own son: not for what he did, but for what he was. His anticipation gained a sadistic edge that seemed to face towards himself as much as the Third Prince. He thought: *I see you.*

He said to Seyhan, whose face suggested he had reached an unwelcome conclusion, "Wait here."

The servants lit the lamps around him as he waited in the reception chamber. It was a long wait. It was dark by the time there was a murmur outside, and the Third Prince came in.

For a terrible moment, Baoxiang saw Esen. Not Esen as he'd been when he died, but Esen before he started going on campaign: a young man with the gangliness of adolescence still in him, his swagger designed to grant the onlooker the gift of looking.

He wrenched himself up and bowed. "Greetings to the Third Prince."

Rather than return the courtesy, the Third Prince flung himself into a chair. His moue of disgust failed to conceal an interest that pressed on Baoxiang so intensely that he felt an internal pulse in response, like the throb of a heartbeat in a bruise.

"Haven't we already greeted each other sufficiently today, Prince of Henan? Or perhaps you've come to complain about the manner of my first greeting." The lingering smile on his bow-shaped lips suggested he was savoring his role in Baoxiang's humiliation. "Aren't you grateful it was your gown and not your arm?"

Here in the cruel palace, what a gift it was to find someone so transparent. Baoxiang said, soft as a touch, "Did you like seeing me afraid?"

The Third Prince's face flickered. It was so fleeting that Baoxiang didn't think the Third Prince was even aware his body had acknowledged the truth. "Like? It disgusts me to see a man act as you do. But at least I'm willing to give you what you deserve."

"And I deserve it, for nothing more than being afraid?" It came out more bitter than he'd intended. The Third Prince scorned him for his fear because it lived on the surface. But the Third Prince, deep in his glass heart where he thought nobody could see, was so much more afraid than Baoxiang had ever been.

"Don't play dumb." The Third Prince's breathing had quickened. He couldn't wait for the pleasure of bringing blood to the surface, even with words. "Everyone knows about Chaghan-Temur's other son. The son who spreads for men. Poor Chaghan! We couldn't understand how he could tolerate the stain of you upon his house. We thought less of him for it."

His gaze pressed into Baoxiang, seeking the flinch. It was all so pitiable. The Third Prince assumed his words would wound, because all he could imagine was how much it would hurt to hear the same said of himself.

How they'd all hated Baoxiang for his debased desires—for what they thought he did with men—when he'd never had any such desires at all.

He said, "I see my reputation has preceded me."

"You'll just stand there and take that insult?" The Third Prince's forehead gathered incredulously.

"Did you expect me to fight you? If you think I've ever cared for my family's honor, or even my own, you don't know the full extent of my reputation." The thrill was entirely vicious. It was so *easy* to be what they wanted him to be. "Why should I deny it? It's true."

The Third Prince's tan wasn't as deep as Esen's had been. His flush showed readily under his close-trimmed beard. Baoxiang took a step towards him. "I'm what everyone thinks I am. And you knew it in Hichetu at the Spring Hunt, didn't you? The first time you saw me. Even before you heard what they said about me."

The Third Prince said savagely, "You only have to look at you to know the kinds of things you've done. That you *enjoy* them."

"Yes. I really am that debased." It seemed like a thousand

voices from Baoxiang's past were speaking through him. He let their memory stoke his fury. "Think of all the shameful, dishonorable acts any normal man would recoil from, and imagine how much pleasure I must take from them." The Third Prince's eyes were fixed on him. Was his heart racing? Baoxiang's own heart was as steady as it had ever been. His anticipation had none of the excitement that might have made it beat faster. There was only the black density of anger. He said silkily, "Think about what I must want, in coming here."

With a swift step he closed the distance between them and laid his hand in the Third Prince's lap.

The Third Prince stared at him, eyes wide with shock, as his body betrayed itself under Baoxiang's limp touch. Baoxiang felt a rush of sadistic victory. Shame, dealt back upon the shamer. It lasted an instant. Then the Third Prince surged out of his chair and punched him in the face.

Somehow, he kept his balance. His ears blared. His cheek was on fire. It was the most familiar thing in the world: yet another warrior lording his physical supremacy over him as he reeled in pain. Hadn't they all taken their turn? His father first, and every warrior since—all of them, except Esen. And *there* was an irony. Esen had trained his whole life to wound, but he'd never had to hit Baoxiang to hurt him.

Did I give as good as I got in the end, brother, when I hurt you?

"Do you want to die?" the Third Prince spat. His flush had turned into blotchy anger. But that anger was as transparent as the rest of him: it was the violent reflex of someone who needed to convince himself that what had happened was nothing more than Baoxiang's perversity; that he himself felt nothing, wanted nothing. As long as it was Baoxiang's desire, Baoxiang's shame, then it didn't have to be real.

Not that it would change anything. Whether or not the Third Prince acknowledged his inclinations, his father already looked at him and saw something he hated.

Baoxiang sank to his knees. The Third Prince didn't move.

Baoxiang's favorite courtesan in Anyang had been very good at poetry, and made him laugh, but her true talent had lain elsewhere. He remembered the cool brush of her sleeves on his skin as he ached, waiting. Her butterfly touch and lowered head. It seemed impossibly long ago: a fragment from that halcyon life, before the rupture.

But it hadn't been a halcyon life, even then. He held his wistfulness for a moment, then released it into the darkness.

Underneath the pleated skirts of the Third Prince's riding costume, a simple tie held his linen undergarment closed. Beneath it, the evidence of desire. The strangeness of the situation gave Baoxiang a detached feeling. He had the sense of seeing himself from the outside, watching as his kneeling self gradually became indistinguishable from what everyone already believed about him.

The Third Prince sneered, "Look at you, begging to be debased. You really are the worst. If I met you and a dog together on the street, I should kick you first."

Baoxiang looked up at his cruel young visage, framed by the forwards-falling loops of his warrior's braids, and could barely contain his contempt. Warriors were so proud of their tolerance for physical pain, but they couldn't bear an instant of the same shame they inflicted on him whenever they could. *So who does that make the stronger?*

The tie undid without resistance. "That's right," he said. "I am the worst."

Outside, Seyhan offered him a handkerchief. Baoxiang pressed it against the split under his eye as they rode. It throbbed in time with his bruised lips. It wasn't until they reached the western gate of the Imperial City that Seyhan said, in an admirably neutral tone, "So my enemy's enemy's son is my friend. Will he protect you, for that?"

"For one time playing the flute? No." The task itself hadn't excited him, but the pain in his lips and jaw was as satisfying as any accomplishment. "He will, though. He's young, and I'm giving him something he never knew he could have. He just needs to get used to it."

"How long will that take?" Seyhan looked like he was trying to calculate the exact gradient of the Empress's murderous intentions, and Baoxiang's chances of surviving without a powerful protector for one week, or two, or four.

Baoxiang laughed shortly. "I have absolutely no idea."

They flashed their wooden official passes at the gate guards and crossed the moat into Khanbaliq proper. Despite the immensity of the city, its avenues were so straight and broad that, except where the Imperial City interrupted, anyone standing at one wall could see clear to the opposite wall. The nighttime streets bustled with wheeled, mounted, and pedestrian traffic. As busy as it was, the city must have been twice, three times more crowded before it was throttled by Madam Zhang's closure of the Grand Canal. It was hard to imagine.

Baoxiang's new residence was a modest single-courtyard dwelling in the bureaucrats' ward near the outer western wall. The residence's charmless brick enclosure kept the clamor of the food vendors on busy Pingzhe Gate Street at bay. Persimmon trees in the bare courtyard bore a few green-shouldered fruit. Inside, the situation was even more dire. Apart from a few personal necessities, the only items Baoxiang had brought with him were the locked chests cluttering the main room.

Seyhan viewed the chests with dissatisfaction. "You have a room full of gold taels, and yet you're making us live in a house that's uglier than a leper's armpit."

Baoxiang understood the feeling. His residence in Anyang had been a perfect monument to his taste, filled with exquisite furniture, ceramics, paintings. He'd left it all behind. "Feel free to spend your own salary if you'd like it furnished in the style to which you're accustomed."

Seyhan gave him a sour look and went off. Baoxiang's encounter with the Third Prince had antagonized him into temporary alertness, but now as he stood amongst the distilled riches of his estate, his exhaustion swept back with a vengeance. He knew that even if he lay on whatever dismal northern-style bed the residence provided, and managed to slip into sleep, it would be wrenched from him moments later. He wanted just one night's sleep more than he'd ever wanted anything. His endless restless nights wrung him dry, and made his entire existence a torment.

The room was cooling around him. A familiar chill breath swept in from the walls and lifted the hairs at the back of his neck, and all at once he knew Esen was there.

He spun around. The sudden thump of his heart made him nauseous. Esen's presence was always unmistakable, as real and powerful as it had ever been in life, and everything in Baoxiang shook in recognition.

A scattering of ghosts hung behind him, their forms outlined in glowing coronas of dust. Their eyes stared unseeing through the tangled sheets of their unbound hair; their white rags hung as unmoving as statues' clothes. He didn't care about *them.* He scanned their dead faces in a fruitless fury, looking for the one he knew—the one who hid from him.

It was as enraging as having his sleep wrenched from him over and over, until he could cry with it. "I know you're there!" he shouted. His voice bounced back to him, thin with strain. This was what Esen did now, to torture him. How many hundred times had Baoxiang felt his flesh contract around his bones in recognition—how many times had he whipped around, heart clenched like an octopus trap with dread and expectation—knowing Esen was behind him? But each time he turned, the ghost refused him: lingering, taunting, where he couldn't see.

The ghost burst his control. His anger exploded until he felt like nothing more than a skin straining around a black core. That blackness was the new heart of him, reveling in his shame and disgrace. It rose up his throat, and snarled through his throbbing mouth to the ghost. "Did you think I was *finished*? Did you think the hurt I did you was repayment enough? You never did have any imagination, brother! You have no idea how much more I'm going to hurt you."

The hand he held out, shaking slightly with the force of his rage, was thin and pale. A scholar's hand that nobody had ever feared. "Think of everything I am, everything you hate and condemn. Think of how the dishonorable, shameful fact of me sullies everything I touch. And then watch as I become that person everyone worships as the very embodiment of your precious

Mongol empire. Watch me become the Great Khan, and bring ruin upon everyone and every value and every belief you lived and died for. *Watch me destroy the world."*

When he opened his hand, the Mandate of Heaven rushed out of him with a hissing sensation of pure, vicious pleasure. The black flame on his palm wasn't light, but darkness, and it poured out of him until the room was drowned.

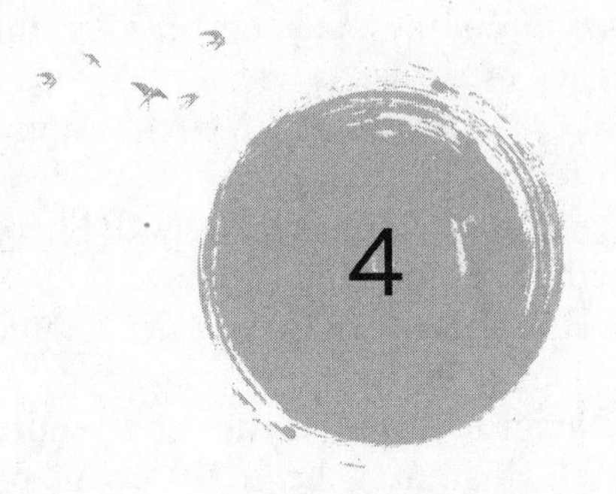

4

BIANLIANG

"The siege units were almost ready, but then they found a number of the equipment carts were mistakenly stored out in the open and need maintenance. So it will be another three or four days," Chu finished, hands clasped behind his back and a nervous look in his eye. "They respectfully ask the General to understand their situation."

"Understand a mistake?" Ouyang paced the splintered floorboards of their command center, the commanders' eyes tracking him warily. He had the vague idea it would be more normal to sit down. Years ago, on a visit to Military Governor Bolud in Shanxi, he'd seen a caged tiger. The animal had paced a furrow in its enclosure on paws that had been bitten bloody. He hadn't thought much of it at the time. But now, he thought bitterly, he understood. Even a beast preferred pain to misery.

An army's initial departure was always—*inevitably*—a headache, which Ouyang theoretically knew after fifteen years in the business. But now every normal delay filled him with homicidal rage. "Find the person responsible for that *mistake,* roll him in a carpet, and make the rest of his unit beat him until he's dead. Then allow them two days to fix the problem. Or I'll have the same done to all of them."

Chu winced and exchanged a glance across the planning table with Geng. Shao, sitting off to the side with his arms crossed and underbite ajar, remained expressionless. He wasn't unhandsome, with his even-toned skin and those round eyes, but Ouyang's powerful dislike made objectivity impossible. It was like being watched by a carp.

To his annoyance, Shao rose and left the room with him at the end of the briefing. Ouyang would have been perfectly content to not have another conversation with Shao until they reached Dadu, or perhaps even longer.

He stopped and said shortly, "Did you need something, Senior Commander?"

Shao gave him a lengthy glance without responding.

Ouyang whirled the instant he heard the sound behind him, sword drawn, but it was too late. The rope was already around his neck.

The last thing he saw as it drew tight was Shao's face, naked in contempt.

*

As Ouyang woke he was already staggering to his feet with a wounded soldier's instinct to get up, get away. His body wasn't ready. A crushing pain inside his head gripped him by the seat of himself, and squeezed. He fell, wavering, to one knee. The animal part of himself cringed from the pain. It knew moving made it worse; it begged him to stay still so that it might stop. But the other part of himself—the part that would do anything not to think or feel—welcomed it. He pressed himself into the white scream, and stood up.

The cell had been unused for so long that it had lost its prison smell. The powdery dirt floor was scuffed where they'd dragged him in. There were plank walls to either side, and an iron-barred door facing onto a corridor with a moist clay wall. He was underground, then. He'd vaguely known the governor's residence housed the constabulary's office. He hadn't bothered paying it a visit. But of course Shao had. Shao always knew where to hide the bodies.

Shao Ge, that traitor. An emotion finally broke through Ouyang's headache. It was pure fury. Even if Shao disagreed with his methods, it wasn't as if he was going to *fail.* How could you fail to achieve your fate? Shao might hate him, but all he had to do was grit his teeth and cooperate. Yet now, for some incomprehensible reason, he was *making everything difficult*. Ouyang's rage increased until it was indistinguishable from his pain. He didn't know how he was going to get out, but when he did: he was going to visit that pain back upon Shao until he screamed.

The wait was interminable. At long last there was a tread in the corridor. Ouyang pulled himself up, a wick inside a flame of agony. At least Shao hadn't taken his armor. He managed to seethe even more at the idea of anyone stripping him—*touching* him—while he was unconscious.

The moment Shao appeared he burst out, *"I would have given you the throne."*

Shao put the tray on the floor. His mirthless mouth was turned down. "That's the issue, isn't it? *You* believe that. But it's been bothering me. If the Nanren rebels have the Mandate, what does it mean that it hasn't come to me, even though I also have an army and the promise of the throne?" He addressed Ouyang's fury with patronizing calm: the rational man lowering himself to address a hysteric. "You *would* give me the throne. But now it's clear to me: you can't. Look at this army! It's on the verge of disintegration under your command. You would have shot nine suns from the sky for Esen-Temur, but you've never given a fuck about anyone you've actually been responsible for. The more I watch you, the more obvious it is. If I want the throne—I'm only going to get it without you.

"So, General. Hand the army over to me, and I'll let you go."

Ouyang found his hands around the cell bars. The fact that Shao didn't flinch filled him with incandescent anger. "Like you let Commanders Yan and Bai go?" His voice was always raspy, the result of lowering his voice to a man's pitch, but having been strangled had increased the raspiness to grotesque levels. "Fuck you and eighteen generations of your ancestors! You think you can *take my revenge from me*?"

"I killed Yan and Bai because I had to, not because it pleased me," Shao said coldly. "Just as I'm not taking your revenge out of spite. And consider: though it won't be by your hand, the Great Khan will still die. So try to see this for what it is. I'm giving you the choice to let it all go. To leave. Live."

Shao had always understood enough about Ouyang to hurt, but never enough to know. If he didn't kill the Great Khan, if he let go of his revenge before it was finished, then everything he had sacrificed for it—*everything he had done*—

Shao's face was a study in contempt. "If you won't hand the army over, then I'll have to assume command after your unfortunate death. With regret, of course. Which gives you two choices." He toed the tray through the slot at the bottom of the door. "Here's the quick way. Try not to choke on your tongue like poor Commander Bai. It's better if it's not *completely* obvious I murdered you. It tends to reduce confidence in one's leadership." His eyes slid to Ouyang's wrist and his mouth sloped with hateful knowingness. "I did think of giving you a knife to cut your wrists with, since you seem to enjoy that so much. But it seemed a poor idea to let you have a blade."

Ouyang thought he'd never hated anyone so much as he hated Shao then. He scooped up the tray and hurled it at the bars. It was only when the wooden bowls bounced to a stop that he realized Shao had already positioned himself out of range.

"The slow way, then. I don't mind waiting. I'm sure it'll be a miserable couple of days. But you've spent your whole life enjoying misery, haven't you?" Shao regarded Ouyang a moment longer. "I'll say a prayer for you when it's all over. I can't imagine many eunuchs have had the privilege of being honored by an emperor."

He turned to leave. "Have a happier next life, General."

"State your business," one of the gate guards said, in Han'er, as Zhu and Ma approached the city wall at the head of the loaded camel train.

Above, Bianliang's twin spires of the Astronomical Tower and the Iron Pagoda thrust into the bronze noonday sky. The wall's pale blocks shimmered behind a layer of exuded warmth. There was no mistaking that Ouyang's army was still in residence. For ten li in every direction the city was ringed by the herds that accompanied any Mongol army. Horses, sheep, goats, and oxen all grazed the pink- and purple-tipped grass down to a uniform flatness, the golden river sparkling low amongst distant reeds.

Zhu watched, amused, as the gate guard stood a little straighter when Ma unwrapped the desert-nomad scarf from around her face. Ma had a Semu woman's ordinary broad features, but there was a luminosity in her regard—a nostalgic, knowing sadness in a face that should have been too young for it—that struck people's hearts, and that they mistook for beauty.

Ma delivered their story in Uyghur, with Zhu translating into Han'er: they were silk merchants from Dadu, and Bianliang was their regular stop on a trade circuit that took them from the north down to the silk-producing regions of the south—Madam Zhang's Pingjiang, and Zhu Yuanzhang's Yingtian—and then across the desert to the western khanates.

Presuming they could get into the city, the rest of the plan was so simple that Zhu hadn't even been lying when she'd said it would be fun. All they had to do before leaving the next day was scatter some of their innocuous-looking silk rolls around the city. Though by appearances they were normal enough, the inner layers of the rolls had been soaked in a liquid explosive mixture invented by Zhu's engineer, Jiao Yu. When the liquid dried sufficiently, which would happen in another day or so, the fabric would start to smolder of its own accord—then burn.

Walled cities were hard to crack. Zhu didn't have siege weapons, and she didn't have six months to starve Ouyang out. But, she thought with satisfaction, if you could make conditions inside the city very miserable, very quickly, you wouldn't have to wait very long at all.

The gate guard came back from his inspection of their loaded camels. "The General allows legitimate merchants a stay of one night. You'll be escorted to a designated lodging house, where you must remain for the duration. If you're not on your way tomorrow before noon, punishments apply."

As they followed their escort inside, Zhu caught sight of leathery shapes hanging from the walls. Surely they couldn't *all* be tardy merchants. But then again, she reflected, wincing at a pinch from her stump, Ouyang had never had much of a sense of humor when it came to punishments.

The bells rang on the camels' bellies as Zhu's Semu men led

them along Bianliang's soft dust roads. In the centuries after the fall of the majestic Song Dynasty, all the grandeur of its erstwhile capital had passed into decay. Faded houses stood amongst fields in what must have once been the bustling heart of the city. Honey locust trees wept showers of tiny yellow leaves over the ruins of temples, and the broken-walled courtyards of grand mansions were filled with ramshackle market stalls. And everywhere the eye rested: soldiers.

Ouyang's army had pressed into every available space inside Bianliang, like mushrooms thrusting up through a fallen tree. It would have reminded Zhu of Anfeng, the former capital of the Red Turbans, if it hadn't been for the horses. Zhu had faced Ouyang's cavalry before, but until now she'd never grasped the sheer scale of horseflesh needed to sustain it. For every man she saw, there must have been five horses. Secured by individual tethers to long lines stretched overhead, the sturdy Mongol mounts were solid-colored and spotted and patched like cats. They ate the hay scattered in the dirt in front of them, and raised their tails and let loose heaps of dung behind. Their presence gave the city a concentrated animal funk that made Zhu's eyes water. Ouyang might have removed the Mongols from his army, but it was still a Mongol army.

"Hold!" A soldier rode up and cut them off, nearly causing Zhu, Ma, and the camel train to pile into their escort from behind. The soldier looked down at Ma and said crisply, "The General gives his greetings to the silk merchants from Dadu. When he learned of your presence in his city, he became curious to make the acquaintance of such esteemed travelers. He would be honored if you would enjoy his hospitality for the duration of your stay in Bianliang."

Ma, forgetting that she wasn't supposed to understand Han'er, glanced at Zhu in alarm. Zhu's mind whirred as she translated. *Ouyang* had extended them hospitality, out of curiosity? If it had been anyone else, she'd have guessed he wanted information: about Dadu, or conditions on the road north. But she knew Ouyang—or she'd thought she did. She would have bet on him being too wrapped up in his own concerns to notice their arrival in Bianliang, let alone wanting to speak with them.

It was strange. More than that, it was a problem. Being under

Ouyang's nose for the evening would make it that much riskier to get out into the city to distribute the silk rolls. And while Ouyang didn't know Ma, and he probably wouldn't recognize any of Zhu's Semu men, there was one face from their party that he was never going to forget.

Zhu caught Ma's eye and silently indicated the lead camel's load. Ma's voice betrayed only the barest hint of her nerves as she said, "How can the General lower himself to be in the company of these unworthy merchants? Please, take this humble gift as a token of our esteem instead."

After a brief one-handed fumble with the saddlebag buckles, Zhu brought out one of the lengths of richly embroidered silk they used for everyday barter. She knew it was a long shot. Taking bribes carried the death penalty in a well-disciplined army. Zhu thought of how Ouyang's men had flung themselves again and again into her ambushes in the valley in Jining. Even if it was out of fear rather than love, they obeyed him. And indeed, as Ma presented the gift the soldier's eyes lingered on it covetously, but all he said was, "The General will be pleased to accept your generous gift in person."

It would be too suspicious to continue to refuse. Zhu could tell Ma was distressed by this deviation from the plan. But though Zhu herself knew how dangerous Ouyang could be—her missing hand and scars from being skewered on his sword were proof enough of that—the knowledge of seeing him again, sooner than she'd been anticipating, filled her with a thrum that was indistinguishable from excitement. She hadn't expected this turn of events, but it would be fine. As long as she managed to avoid Ouyang seeing *her*—which would add an unwanted layer of difficulty to the situation—they would be able to get through the meeting, and then Zhu could start solving the problem of getting the silk rolls where they needed to be.

She had no idea what the solution might be, but she knew there *would* be a solution. There always was.

Without waiting for Ma to speak, she said smoothly, "These unworthy merchants accept the honorable General's invitation with gratitude. Please, lead the way."

⁂

By the time they reached their destination Zhu had managed to switch places with the man at the end of the camel train. Hopefully, given the scarves over their faces, their escort wouldn't notice that Ma's original translator had been demoted.

Zhu remembered, guiltily, that she'd promised to be by Ma's side the whole time they were in Bianliang. It couldn't be helped, though, and besides: Ma was perfectly capable of handling a meal with Ouyang by herself. Ma had actually lived in Dadu, so if that turned out to be the topic of Ouyang's questioning, then all she had to do was answer truthfully. She was a quick enough thinker that Zhu was confident she could brazen through anything else. And Ouyang being Ouyang, Zhu couldn't imagine him staying in the company of guests for any longer than it took to get the information he was after. It would probably be an awkward meal, but at least it would be short.

Ouyang's headquarters was in a sprawling compound ringed by tall spears of ornamental pears, their clattering upper leaves brushed red and purple while their lower halves were still in summer green. From its size, Zhu guessed it must have been the Yuan governor's residence. As they waited, her excitement mingled with a quiver in the seat of her qi. There had always been that strange connection between herself and Ouyang when they came into proximity, as of the natural resonance that occurred between two like substances. Between two people, who were each neither one thing nor the other. She had the feeling of straining for his arrival not just with her eyes and ears, but with that internal aspect that was always casting out into the world with the desire to find something like itself.

An armored figure strode from the gate. And before Zhu even saw the wrongness, she *felt* it. She had plucked a string and there was no answering vibration of a likeness, only the dead air of an empty room. This person's height, the breadth of his shoulders, the masculinity of his features visible even from a distance: none of them belonged to Ouyang, whose bearing obscured the degree to which he was short and slight, and whose woman's face lost its femininity and became uncategorizable the longer it was viewed. This man was a general, but he was a *man*. And he was a stranger.

All of a sudden everything made sense. Ouyang, who would never have paid attention to a caravan of merchants, hadn't. But then, if Ouyang *had* initially commanded this army he'd seized from the Prince of Henan, where was he now, and who was this other Nanren calling himself general?

Though Ma must have been as surprised as Zhu, she made her greetings with admirable composure. "How may we address this honorable general? We had been under the impression that the forces occupying Bianliang were commanded by a eunuch, but clearly we were mistaken."

The unfamiliar general raised his hand to halt the translation. He replied in Mongolian, "I understand Uyghur, but you'll have to forgive me for answering in a language I'm more familiar with." The downwards cant of his mouth gave him a close-guarded look that made Zhu's neck prickle with distrust. "You weren't mistaken, but unfortunately General Ouyang is indisposed with an illness. He instructed me, as his second-in-command, to take charge in the interim. My family name is Shao." He went on, politely, "As you'll no doubt have heard, General Ouyang will shortly be taking us north to Khanbaliq. I was wondering if our honored guests could share any news regarding the current conditions in that city."

It was the obvious reason. But as Shao's eyes alighted on the loaded camels, Zhu caught their predatory gleam, and instantly and unpleasantly grasped his real interest. Any army camped far from home for months on end was under huge financial strain, and Zhu's party had walked into their midst with several thousand taels' worth of pure silk. *Ouyang* wouldn't have cared. But Shao had never had any intention of honoring them as guests. He was going to rob them.

In a second flash of understanding, Zhu realized: Ouyang wasn't ill. Shao had deposed him, and he was already dead. The betrayer, betrayed.

She frowned under her scarf, disconcerted. When she'd ridden away from Ouyang that last time in Bianliang, she'd been sure they would meet again. It had felt inevitable: a continuation of how their likeness seemed to always bend the arcs of their lives towards each other. For him to have died without reaching his fate in Dadu seemed wrong, as if the familiar pattern of the world had been twisted into something Zhu no longer recognized.

But there was no time to dwell. Zhu dismissed her uneasy feeling to focus on the matter at hand. As far as this new general Shao was concerned: he would have been welcome to the silk, if Zhu hadn't been concerned that keeping all the rolls together would only cause a contained blaze, rather than the citywide conflagration she needed.

Her other, significant, concern was what Shao would do with a party of merchants once he'd extracted their goods from them. Ouyang would have let them go. With Shao, she wasn't so sure.

"Please, come inside and refresh yourselves after your journey," Shao invited courteously. There was no matching sentiment in his slashed mouth. "My men will unload your merchandise and take your animals to feed and water."

"The General is too kind," Ma said. Zhu saw she was taking Shao's stated interest at face value. She had no idea about the new danger she was in. "Please let my camel boy help your men handle the beasts. Camels are rather different to your horses, and their bites can be unpleasant." She indicated Zhu at the end of the train. Small, boyish Zhu, whose swathed face hardly drew a glance from Shao as he nodded curt assent.

Zhu watched Ma follow Shao into the compound, her familiar soft beauty made new by the scarf draped around her neck. For a moment Zhu felt a pang at the thought of what Ma might face until Zhu found a way to rescue her. She was well aware that Ma had agreed to participate only because Zhu had promised her it would be risk-free. But there was no point feeling bad about it. Zhu cleared her mind, pleased by how easily she could set aside the distraction. A fizz of eagerness expanded in its place. What mattered now was taking action to get the plan back on track as quickly as possible, and making sure she succeeded at what she had come here to do.

☼

There was no question that Zhu was as much a prisoner as the others. Under guard, she and the unloaded camels had been brought to a crowded field some distance from the residence. The field was scattered with mounds that cast long shadows against the sunset-tinted earth. Ruins, Zhu realized, when she saw an eroded beam poking through one of the hard shells of dirt. Every part of the field that wasn't a mound was overrun by tents and sitting, squatting, spitting soldiers. There were so many horses that the overhead tether lines crisscrossed against the sky with reckless abandon.

The camels cleared a space for themselves by simply existing. Then, satisfied, they sat down like an opinionated mountain range and chewed their cud. Zhu leaned against the warm side of the nearest one and contemplated the situation. The sun set and blurred the tents and horses and mounds into a single mass of shadow. Zhu's guards had gathered around a nearby campfire and were grilling bread and pieces of strong-smelling meat on sticks. Even with the useful darkness, her proximity to them—and the sheer number of other people in the camp—made it impossible for her to slip away unseen.

Something saucered through the air and landed in the dirt by her foot. "Hey, kid. Eat up." It was one of the grilled breads with a bit of greasy meat inside. Zhu picked it up, inspected it, and ate it, unembarrassed by the guards' coarse laughter. Food was food. Gristle crunched between her teeth as she thought. She had to get back to Shao's residence, find and rescue Ma and the others, find the silk, and break all of them out. Time was of the essence. There was no changing the rolls' schedule for ignition, and once they started burning: that would be that. A familiar thread of excitement tightened in her stomach. She spat out the gristle and rose. If there was no way to slip away unobserved, then she would have to do it observed. And figure out the rest of it while she ran.

When the guards glanced up she made an explanatory half-squatting gesture. Once they'd snorted and turned back to their meal, she wandered behind the camels. A nearby mound was just enough to shelter her from prying eyes from the other side. A few paces away a veritable forest of upright poles anchored the ends of the overhead tether lines. Zhu folded herself low and slid across to the nearest pole. A quick inspection showed a tangle of lines snugged into the notches in the base of the pole and knotted in place. Zhu didn't have enough fingers for knots. But she had something else.

Her current wooden hand—this one plain instead of gilded—had been made by Jiao. He'd weighted the joints of the fingers with tiny sliding metal rods, and strung each finger through with thin wire that connected to the palm. By rotating her stump slightly in various directions, Zhu could make the fingers move a little. It was uncomfortable to wear, and didn't look particularly real. But it was a sufficiently hand-like presence to offset the worst of people's disgust at what they most feared for themselves: the mutilation of the precious body their ancestors had bestowed upon them.

Zhu tugged at the hand until the palm section slipped off the metal tang that connected it to the wrist. The tang wasn't bladed along its length, or pointed like an awl, but instead resembled a flat-headed chisel. But that flat head had just enough of an edge to be useful. Zhu sawed through the knots and saw the lines overhead slacken in response. Then she jammed the hand back onto its wrist, eased over to the boss camel, took hold of its lead rope, and waited.

"Hasn't that turtle egg finished taking a shit yet?" A guard, annoyed, came around the camels and startled when he saw Zhu waiting by the head of the lead camel. "Hey! What—"

Zhu kicked the camel into motion, and leaped.

Her foot found the camel's bent knee just in time, propelling her upwards. If she hadn't been so focused on wedging herself between the camel's bare humps, she might have found the guard's horrified shout funny. She knew how uncanny a camel's motion looked: that strange, back-to-front heave as it slowly unfolded to its feet, rising up and up and *up*.

Gathering his wits, the guard lunged for the camel's bridle. It was what you would do to stop a horse. But a camel wasn't a horse. Zhu's camel spat him in the face, shrieked, and lunged at him with bared teeth.

The guard dived out of the way, shouting for help.

The darkness descended into chaos. The other camels unfolded to their feet, startling the nearby horses, who discovered that when they pulled on their tethers they could just *keep going*, and then all of a sudden the field was a torrent of alarmed, tangled animals moving very fast. Zhu clung to the camel's hump and firmly didn't think about falling. Her breath banged out of her with every harsh stride, and she had the sinking feeling of listing to one side. Her heart hammered in her throat.

Soldiers ran alongside the torrent, flailing their arms in a futile attempt to direct the animals without being trampled. A few of the quicker ones had managed to grab mounts, but their horses took one look at the charging camels and decided to keep their distance. Zhu knew her own small clinging shape would be lost in the torrent—for a moment. She hauled on her camel's lead rope until they were running on the outside edge of the pack, and as they passed a narrow side street, flung herself into the air.

It was a much longer fall than from a horse. She smashed down, flopping and bouncing until she came to a hard stop against the front of someone's house. On the main street the torrent rushed away with the soldiers in pursuit.

None of them had seen her fall. Zhu's left ribs pulled, which somehow caused her right arm to twang so severely that she hissed in pain. But pain was only pain. If it was the price she had to pay for what she wanted, then she was glad for it. She turned and hurried, grimacing, through the shadow of the ruined streets towards Shao's residence.

Zhu was already on to searching her third building in the compound, and she still didn't feel any closer to finding her people. It hadn't been hard to get into the compound, what with the gate guards pulled from their posts by the lurid spectacle of horses and camels racing through the streets. But the residence was even bigger than it looked from the street. Dozens of buildings sat inside a maze of corridors and courtyards. To make matters worse, it was a military base in a state of high pre-departure activity: soldiers and servants rushed around nonstop despite the late hour. Zhu, feeling conspicuous in her gauzy merchant's outfit, skulked through the shadows. Her insides fizzed in a ferment of pain and excitement. This was the part she loved, fiercely. The leap from which there was no turning back; the buoyant thrill of knowing that all the threads of action would come together—*had* to come together—into success, even if she didn't yet know how. It was a prayer, and it was faith, but it was nothing like the self-emptying devotion she had learned as a monk. She blazed with desire. She was full with it, and her faith was in herself.

She was slipping through the dark columned bays along the front of a building when a sharp retort made her jump. She glanced up and saw a point of light blooming above the roofs. Her first thought was that it was a signal flare. But then there was another sound, then another, coming faster and faster until they merged into a deafening ripping noise. Sparkling lights shone on the dark roof tiles with a moonlight luster as men ran shouting with surprise into the courtyards, and the air was thick with a familiar dirty, acrid, pickled tang that made Zhu think, suddenly, of her hands blackened with fire-powder residue—

There was no gap between that thought and finding herself sprawled in the middle of the colonnade, a body length from where she'd been. Her vision blazed white and her ears sang a continuous high note. Dislodged tiles spilled over the lips of the roofs into the courtyards beneath, and from the far corner of the compound a pillar of fire jetted upwards into the night sky.

Zhu struggled up, panting. It felt as if every one of her higher-level thoughts had been hammered out of her. Across the courtyard, the window-paper of the facing building hung in shreds, the lattices smashed inwards like broken toothpicks. Inside, two dazed-looking soldiers helped each other up. Only one thing could have caused that level of destruction. *The silk.* She couldn't begin to guess what had made it ignite so far ahead of schedule. Perhaps Shao's men had put it near a heat source, or stacked it too tightly, or perhaps the hot weather had simply dried them faster than Jiao had predicted.

The evening wind pushed the fire sideways, the ragged edge of it spraying red flecks over the compound wall as thickly as sparks from a grindstone. The sparks fell on fertile ground. The clattering-leafed trees in the street were soon peppered with growing spots of red. A few moments later their branches were aflame. Sheets of fire crawled up to their crowns, where the wind whipped them back and forth and showered dripping fire onto the wooden houses below. Zhu's chest glowed with triumph. It was coming together even better than she could have imagined. She'd asked for fire, and received an apocalypse. Bianliang was burning.

The clamor of soldiers rushing through the courtyard brought Zhu back to herself. She still had to find Ma and the others. Luckily, the chaos made it easier to move around. None of the soldiers paid her attention as she darted past them in the corridors. A ghastly orange light filled the corridors, and the warming window-paper gave off a savory, oily aroma like the breath of a wok. Zhu flung open door after door. Nobody was even going to notice their escape, given everything that was going on. It was just as fun as she'd told Ma it would be, and the danger was all part of it. Zhu's life pumped strongly through her body, bringing pain and exhilaration into every nerve, and she thrilled in her own power to keep herself alive. In the moment, as she ran, she felt like she might stay alive forever.

She burst out of the corridor and into another open courtyard. The soldiers seemed to have tamed the fire inside the compound, but now a ceaseless roar washed in over the walls: the burning buildings of Bianliang. Centuries of history subsumed into white ash that whirled up into the darkness, then fell back as thickly as snow. Horses screamed in the distance.

Zhu tightened her headscarf across her face to keep the ash out, and felt her first stab of concern. It wasn't that she *wouldn't* find Ma. It was just taking longer than she'd expected. There were so many buildings, and she'd been searching haphazardly at best.

Think, she commanded herself.

Now that she was standing still, the pain in her ribs had migrated to the pit of her stomach. A deep internal gripe, it was all the harder to ignore for being lodged in the very center of herself. It was yanking her insides, pulling them—

She felt a shock of recognition. *That pain.* It wasn't the pain of a broken rib working its way into her vital organs, but the familiar pain of something yanking on the strings of the universe. And she hadn't felt it since the *last* time she was at Bianliang, as she rode for her life away from—

She swung around and stared at a small building across the courtyard. The door hung agape.

Within the darkness inside, she made out a pale blur. White faces and white clothes, and the dark stare of empty eyes.

Ouyang's ghosts.

Zhu stepped warily over the threshold. She didn't know what the room's original purpose had been, but like everything else it was currently accommodation. Sleeping pallets were disordered from their occupants' hurry to get to the emergency outside, and helmets and water gourds lay scattered about. The room was empty—of humans. The ghosts stood a few paces back from the door in a tight circular formation, like a shoal of fish pressed together by an invisible net. To Zhu's bemusement, the ones on the outer edges had sunk partially through the floor so only their torsos were visible.

A moment later she laughed out loud. They were standing *above* Ouyang. She was seeing the top of a sphere of ghosts. She'd never considered the idea that when he rested, they would contract around him like a cloud. Zhu skirted the ghosts, shivering at their chill, and eased through the detritus to the door at the far end of the room. Underground air breathed up the stone stairs. She pulled her headscarf firmly across her face, and descended.

There was a small vestibule at the base of the stairs with a chair and a rack of unpleasant-looking implements that were, to Zhu's relief, covered in dust. Raised voices rang from the far end of the corridor. Zhu quickly found cover behind the chair and peered ahead. All she could see of the cells was the long row of their front bars stretching into the gloom.

A single guard was down at the end of the row, arguing in Han'er. "You don't get to give General Shao orders! He's the general." He had a hunched look, as if some animal part of his brain knew, and strongly disliked, that he was standing inside a circle of ghosts.

"If the city is burning down then he's not doing a very good job of it, is he?"

Zhu shivered from head to foot in half-delighted recognition of Ouyang's distinctive voice. It was even raspier than she remembered. And for once, the hate in it wasn't directed at her.

A burst of urgent shouting filtered down the stairs, along with the acrid smell of burning hardwood.

"Is that what 'under control' sounds like to you?" Ouyang snarled. "Let me out, you shit-covered stick."

The guard stiffened and took a step away from the bars.

Ouyang said murderously, "*Don't* you—"

But the guard was already hurrying past Zhu's hiding spot. The upper door banged once, rudely, in punctuation.

Ouyang spat a harsh Mongolian epithet. The ghosts standing outside his cell rippled, the force of his rage and frustration blowing through them like wind on the surface of water.

Zhu's eyes stung. The smell of smoke was stronger, now, and the ghosts at the far end of the corridor were indistinct. She slipped out of the vestibule and hustled down the row of cells. The first was empty, and she initially thought the second was as well, until her attention was drawn back with irresistible horror. There was a ghost in the cell—but unlike ordinary ghosts, whose black eyes were empty and aimless, this one's held her own with hate and hunger. Its teeth were sharp, and as Zhu stood there she felt a sickening chill roll through her like contractions of pure dread.

She thought abruptly of the unpleasant-looking tools near the entrance. People tended to die in particularly miserable ways in prisons—ways that might not necessarily leave behind intact corpses—and it seemed like when they did: this was the result. A hungry ghost, that wanted to devour. The stories were full of such monsters, but until now, Zhu had never seen one. She wished she hadn't.

She shuddered violently and hurried on past the third and fourth cells, which were empty, but with the next step she saw who was in the fifth, and her heart swooped.

Ma rushed out of the crowd and pressed herself against the bars with a cry. Zhu's relief was so oddly visceral that at first she thought it was her ribs again. It surprised her. She didn't think she'd been that worried.

Ma's beautiful face was grimy and tear-streaked. "You came."

"Of course I came!" Zhu said, indignant. She grasped Ma's outstretched hand and squeezed it warmly. "I threw myself off a camel for you, Ma Xiuying. A camel! Do you know how tall camels are when you have to fall off one? It's been an adventure. The silk rolls set the compound on fire, and now the compound's set the city on fire. It's worked out perfectly."

Ma's expression didn't seem fully like agreement. She said with some heat, "Please get us out, husband."

"We-ell," Zhu hedged.

"You don't have a *key.*" Ma looked ready to weep with frustration.

Zhu corrected, "Yet."

The upstairs door banged open again, and Zhu dived back into her hiding place. It wasn't the original guard coming back, but a new pair of armored men: one square-headed, and the other large and pink-cheeked, but with a surprisingly feminine step as he hurried after his companion to Ouyang's cell.

"You should be the one in charge, not Shao Ge. Now look what's happened," the square-headed one said briefly. Keys rattled. The other added, "We spoke up for you at the time, but the others overruled us. Here—we brought your sword."

"Where is Shao Ge now?" Ouyang's voice was oddly devoid of gratitude or relief, as if he considered his rescue a natural action of the universe rather than anything to do with the people who had come to do it. He stepped out of the cell.

Zhu stared in shock. She'd expected him to be disheveled, which he was: his armor was dusty, and his looped braids were feathered with loose strands. But his *face.* Ouyang's cold, blank, beautiful face had always been a perfect mask of control that she, alone, seemed able to penetrate. Now, whatever energy had maintained that mask was gone. Ouyang, who had always cared so much about what other people thought of him, seemed to have ceased to care at all. His expression was a rictus of naked rage and pain, and it struck Zhu with the same primal horror as the sight of a flayed man's quivering muscles. He could have been another hungry ghost.

Ouyang strode out of the dungeon, sword clenched so tightly it trembled by his side. His rescuers followed, and behind them the long funeral procession of the ghosts.

As soon as they were gone, Zhu dashed to Ouyang's cell, where the keys were still hanging in the lock.

"Ah, he's always so useful!" she said brightly, unlocking Ma's cell and giving her a brief embrace as she rushed out. Her pang of concern was long gone, so Ma's sob of relief filled her with fond amusement. She savored the moment: it was sweet with all the pleasure and anticipation of knowing she'd won, and all that was left was for the inevitable to unfold. "Don't cry, Yingzi. All's well that ends well. Ugh, I can't wait to get out of this outfit! I'm so covered in camel that I smell like the inside of a water bag. Let's go."

Ouyang forced himself through the chaos outside. He couldn't tell if he was striding or instead staggering forwards like a man with a gut wound. The ground tilted under him, threatening to dislodge him with every step, and his vision bloomed and blotched. How long had he been in that cell without food or water? He supposed it didn't matter. All he needed to do was keep going. His self had shrunk to the locus of pain inside his head, and it put one foot in front of another, again and again.

He was dimly aware of having lost Geng and Chu along the way. The world was full of bizarre things: a tide of bucket-bearing soldiers; gusts of hot wind that dashed embers into his face; a disorienting roaring sound, like water thundering over a waterfall, that seemed to press into his nose and throat as much as his ears until he was gasping for breath. His lurching consciousness produced the flickering thought that this disaster under Shao's watch might have damaged his army so badly that they would never make it to Dadu. But that was impossible. He couldn't believe it.

The door to the command room stood open at the end of the corridor. As he stumbled inside he saw a disjointed flash of his commanders' pale faces turned towards him, their gaping mouths as black as the eyes of the ghosts he saw in his dreams.

Ouyang's sword jerked upwards and bit bone. It was as much a reflex as a predator shaking its head to break a small animal's neck. He didn't realize what he'd done until Shao grunted in agony. Then the world came back into focus, and for a moment Ouyang could only marvel: it had happened so unconsciously that it felt like seeing his wish manifested by some supernatural force. He yanked his sword out of Shao's sternum. The body unspooled a thin stream of crimson as it fell, its carp mouth fixed in a grimace.

The other commanders stared at him in horror. He knew what they thought. They thought he should have heard Shao out. They thought he should have bargained with the person who had tried to take his revenge from him—the revenge he had paid for *with Esen's life.*

They didn't understand. He hated them for that, even more than he hated their needs and their demands and their pathetic, uneasy glances. He was gripped by the fierce urge to hurt them until they *did* understand. Did he even need them? In his mind's eye he saw himself, alone against Dadu's defenders. Fighting on and on, sliced by swords until he was nothing but a raw, screaming mass that still dragged itself forwards, never stopping, until its bloody fingers touched the throne. He imagined the Great Khan looking in horror at him: the flayed, inhuman face of his fate.

For a moment it seemed completely rational, as if the strength of his desire could subvert the world's mechanics and cause it to be.

He said fiercely, "Tell the men to leave off their efforts against the fire."

There was a long silence. Eventually Chu said in a careful tone, "General. The city will—"

"I know. Let it burn."

He didn't need Bianliang. All he needed was an army. All he needed was men who would die, willingly or unwillingly, for what he needed to do.

His fingers cramped around the hilt of his sword. Under the thin sheen of blood it was a plain blade. Other men inscribed their swords with names or meaningful phrases, but Ouyang never had. How could he have done that, when his sword was the instrument of his future treachery? Now that he was free to do so, it seemed pointless. Everything had already ended, and his continuation was nothing more than a pathetic postscript.

"Muster everyone outside the city and finalize preparations for departure," he commanded. "Leave behind everything inessential. We begin towards Dadu at dawn."

Ouyang led his army out of Bianliang, the city smoldering behind him. The evening wind that had whipped the flames had subsided. A column of smoke curved across the sky as if tracing the arc of a burning star. In the end the fire had been contained to the Yuan core of the city. It gave him the idea that ruined Bianliang had been scoured down to its bones, down to the ancient outer walls that had been here before the Yuan, before the Liao, before the Jin. Everything the steppe peoples had brought and built, scrubbed away until all that was left of them was Esen lying deep beneath the burnished grasses. There would be nobody left to sweep his tomb, and when Ouyang passed from the world: there would be nobody who remembered where he lay. It would be his final dereliction of the person he had loved.

"General!" Geng came up beside him. Though Geng and Chu were now jointly occupying the role of his second-in-command, he still only had a hazy sense of them; neither of them had the strong personal desires that had brought Shao so clearly into focus. Probably that was a good thing. Now Geng said urgently, "We're under attack."

Startled, Ouyang wheeled his horse around. In his still-weakened state, the swift motion made his head swim. At first with confusion, then horror, he saw a dark wave of infantry bearing down on the long exposed flank of his travel columns. Yellow banners dashed above the mass. The color left a disorienting blank in his brain. The Yuan's banners were blue; the Red Turban rebels flew red; General Zhang's army, green. Something in the outside world had changed while he had been moldering in his room over the summer. He saw now that the yellow-bannered army had swung around from the city's far side. It must have crept there during the night's commotion, and waited for Ouyang to emerge. But he had no idea who it was.

He shouted furious commands to his cavalry commanders. All his emotions had been subsumed into an undifferentiated pressure that stretched him so hot and thin that he thought he might come apart from it. The commanders *did* respond to his shouts. But it was the response of men who had already been worn down from months of waiting, from punishments, from being roused from their beds by fire and screaming. They were slow—far too slow. The leading wedge of the attacking army punched through his cavalry's meager shield of arrows and barreled into them at full speed.

Ouyang knew what a buckling front line looked like. But something else was happening. As the yellow-bannered army pressed forwards, its mounted commanders were shouting directives at Ouyang's men. And his men: they were curving away from the intrusion like oil from a drop of soap on water. Ouyang stared in disbelief as his men pulled up and dismounted, casting their bows to the ground. They were *surrendering*.

His internal pressure was too much; it was splitting him open. And now he knew what that pressure was. It was his desperation, it was his rage and agony, all of it transformed into a single imperative: *that he not lose*. He heard himself howling as he launched himself towards his dismounting cavalry. He flung himself from his horse and in a single stroke decapitated the nearest man, then grabbed the next by the arm and hurled him in the direction of the enemy. "Get up and keep fighting, or I'll fucking kill you all myself!"

He didn't know what was on his face, but the men around him scrabbled for their swords and bolted in the right direction. None of them made it very far. He saw them fall, folded down beneath the oncoming army like grass stalks. And then the army was upon him.

He fought with rage, with panic, with utter desperation. His body was weak and febrile. It told him firmly how it had nearly been dehydrated to death just hours before. But what was bodily pain compared to his mind's pain? He cut down one opponent, then another. He risked a fruitless glance over his shoulder for his horse. The moment he swung back he realized the glance had been an error. An advancing half circle of the enemy were watching him apprehensively. They were afraid, he thought, and it made him want to laugh in their faces. They *should* be afraid for daring to stand between him and his fate.

A young Nanren commander with a spear said tersely, "Take him."

The first two who came at him fell easily. Then the rest of them broke over him like a wave. He was borne down by the mass of them, even as his sword found armor, then flesh. His face smashed into the ground. The man directly above him was screaming in agony and terror. His blood poured over the back of Ouyang's neck as if it was being squeezed out by the weight of the other men on top of them. He screamed as Ouyang wanted to scream, but Ouyang's breath had been crushed out of him. He struggled weakly, gasping, feeling himself bruise against the disjointed edges of his own armor. He was as powerless as the dead, but with none of the relief of it. At every moment he knew, awfully, that he was still alive, and that while he was alive he had to keep going. He struggled and fought until his muscles failed. Even after that, they held him down. The man above him had finally stopped screaming.

The young commander crouched beside his head and said with grief-stricken fury, "You asshole! You didn't have to kill them. You could have just surrendered." The boy's nose was so large that it seemed unlikely he could ever fully grow into it, and his ears stuck out under his helmet. Ouyang stared dully past him at the blood-slicked sideways world. How young must he be, to still care about men who fell in the field? He couldn't remember ever having cared, himself. At length the boy straightened and said to someone outside Ouyang's view, "Tell him it's done."

They hauled him up. He hung between them, spent, his loosened hair in a curtain across his face and the world graying into blankness beyond it.

At some point he became aware of a figure standing in front of him. A familiar small figure with an ugly face floating above gold armor. The rising sun gilded him from behind.

Ouyang was too exhausted to muster the feeling of hate. All he had was the knowledge of it. "*You.*" The hands on him tightened punitively at his disrespect.

"Me," the Radiant King agreed. "Forgive me for keeping you restrained, but it seems wise to err on the side of caution." His young face wasn't tender, but it wasn't cruel. It shone with a buoyancy that Ouyang couldn't understand. It didn't seem like a feeling he'd ever experienced. "I'd like to keep all my remaining limbs."

Zhu Chongba—that was his name, Ouyang remembered. The monk. He had knelt in despair at Ouyang's feet, his life's blood pouring from the stump of his arm. If Ouyang hadn't been restrained, he would have lunged for Zhu's throat. Lunged, and then fallen, just as Zhu had, to his knees in the blood and the dirt. He realized there was a bitter, unintended mercy in being held.

"It's nothing personal," Zhu told him. "The Zhangs and I have become rather closer neighbors than either of us would like. I'm not strong enough to defeat them alone. But then I thought: if I add your men to mine—" He shrugged. "So here I am."

It took a while to sink in, and even when it did, it didn't make sense. Ouyang had killed Shao, and that was supposed to have *fixed* everything. "You're taking my army." Agony burned through his blankness. *"You're taking my fate."*

Zhu regarded him. Under his wide brow he had a set mouth and sharp chin. His skin, as free of stubble as Ouyang's own, was as brown as an insect's carapace. It was a hard face, but for a moment it softened. "I don't want your fate. I have my own. And I'm not taking your army. I'm just borrowing it, to defeat the Zhangs. Once I've done that, I'll take us north to Dadu to defeat the Grand Councilor and his central army, which was your plan anyway. Then, when I have control of the capital, I'll let you kill the Great Khan." The sun, risen above Zhu's gold helmet, slanted into Ouyang's eyes. "You waited how many years for your revenge? You can stand to wait just a little longer."

Ouyang's every day—his every hour, his every heartbeat—was already unbearable. He was overcome by a terrible disbelief at the thought of how much more it would hurt to wait. It would hurt more than Zhu could ever understand, more than he could ever imagine—because what was happening to Ouyang was the kind of pain that nobody could grasp, or believe, until he experienced it for himself. Ouyang knew that firsthand. He had dreaded and braced himself for what he had to do to Esen, and though every moment of that anticipation had felt like being killed, it had been but a shadow of what it felt like to burn as he now burned.

Ouyang knew, with a certainty that reduced him to a single

incandescent point of shame, that he would have done anything in that moment to get his army back. If he thought it would work, he would fall to his knees and beg Zhu for understanding. He would crawl and abase himself before the combined eyes of both their armies, because compared to his pain, what did his dignity matter?

But he had no power and nothing to offer, and his dignity was worthless to anyone but him.

"I know you hate me for this," Zhu said. His griefless young face shone with the hope and anticipation of someone who had never so much as dreamed that the future might be less than good. "I know you can't believe that I'll win. But I will, because I'm willing to do whatever it takes. Just wait, General, and I'll make sure you get what you want.

"I promise."

PART TWO

5

YINGTIAN

The figure was standing by the boarded-up window as Ma went inside with the tray. The guards with their drawn swords followed her closely. The bare dark room smelled so harshly of new wood that it canceled out all traces of the pungent world outside. Ma's first impression of the figure was of a slight, barefoot Nanren woman in her white underclothes. The translucent window-paper softened and spread the cracks of daylight from between the boards, painting warm yellow bars on the woman's small clasped hands, the loose fall of her hair.

It was strange, the separation between image and reality. Ma's nightmares had been filled with General Ouyang, the Mongols' demonic eunuch general in his shining armor. Every season he'd slaughtered more of her father's rebels and pressed ever closer to Anfeng. They had all known the inevitable that was coming: that when he crossed the wide Huai River, and breached Anfeng's mud walls four zhang high, he would kill them all.

None of them had been able to stop him, or even slow him, not even her father.

None of them, except Zhu.

But how could she pin that history and dread onto this figure who'd been stripped like a woman about to be sold as the spoils of war? How vulnerable she must feel, the intimacies of her bare feet and unbound hair displayed to strangers instead of kept for a lover. Ma's gaze was a violation.

The woman turned from the window, her face shadowed by

her hair. Ma felt a prickle of unease. The way she *moved*—there was something wrong about it, something out of place. The unrecognizability of it stirred a fearful impulse to withdraw, as from a predator encountered in the wild, or a person shouting strange utterances in the street. The impression of womanhood didn't quite break, but rippled: a reflection in unsteady water.

Ma offered the tray with its washbasin of warm water, cloth, and soap ball. "Greetings to the honorable General Ouyang."

"No comb? I'm flattered that they fear me with one." Even that rasp could have been a woman's voice, strained and sanded by smoke or some emotion that had burned so hard it left no traces of itself behind. Though Ma had used Mongolian, the General replied in Han'er. "However, I have no experience fighting with combs. I'm not sure it would be better than nothing."

It was only then that Ma understood why they had taken the General's armor, belt, outer robe, socks, even hair ties. She was suddenly conscious of the two armed guards at her elbows.

The woman tucked her hair behind her ear with another harsh gesture. A gesture, Ma realized suddenly, that was so crude and jarring—that seemed unselfconscious to the point of madness—because it wasn't the distorted rendition of womanhood that she'd instinctively read it as, but a gesture devoid of any reflection of womanhood at all. Not a woman's gesture, but a man's.

He lifted his head, then, and she saw his face. "A shaving knife, on the other hand, could be useful . . . but I suppose I have little chance of convincing anyone that I might need one."

General Ouyang was very beautiful, almost as beautiful as his reputation, but his face wasn't a woman's face. Ma was reminded of the way Zhu's image wavered in her mind in doubleness, in twoness. Ouyang's bearing was a man's, he had a man's mind and manner, and it imbued the delicate roundedness of his brow, the unshadowed fineness of his skin, with an in-betweenness. Not a transient in-betweenness, as of boys in that moment of fragile loveliness before they became men, but an in-betweenness that was fierce and frightening for being permanent, for being other; for being complete in and of itself.

He didn't take the tray. She saw him notice the gold ornaments in her hair, and the expensive metallic brocade of her dress that turned blush or steel, depending upon the direction the fabric fell. "You aren't a servant. Did you come to gawk? Should I expect a stream of visitors, all anxious to see the exotic captive? Perhaps I should plan something to keep them entertained." He glanced at Ma's guards. The assessment in his look made Ma's blood run cold.

She firmed herself. "I came because I wanted to see you. We have a personal connection. Do you know it?"

"A Mongolian-speaking Semu girl, playing at being rebel queen." Ouyang affected consideration. "You do resemble your father somewhat. General Ma, wasn't it? It's hard to remember everyone I've killed. I hope you aren't going to waste your breath in pursuit of an apology."

It hurt, even though she'd expected something like it. She said, "I came to forgive you."

"Forgive?" At first she thought he was surprised; he spoke mildly. "If that's your intention, I should tell you what I did to him. When I met your father on the battlefield that day, I put my sword in under his arm, and I brought it down through his rib cage and split him open. Can you imagine what that looked like? It was like the cut-open side of a pig, with all the white rib-ends showing. He was so shocked! He tried to pull himself back together with his hands. He didn't scream, though, because I'd cut through his lungs. The cut arteries poured all their blood into his stomach, so he started vomiting blood as he stood there. And then when he'd vomited out all the blood in his body, he died: in terror and in agony, while I watched.

"And now here you are. His daughter, done up as a boy king's whore, come to offer not vengeance, but *forgiveness*, to his killer." The mildness fell away. She'd never heard someone speak with such venom before. "Why? Do you feel sorry for me, poor eunuch forced to kill his own people for the sake of his cruel Mongol masters? You must be sorry indeed, if you can forgive me even as your father's spirit screams for justice! Sorry enough to suck my dick, if I had one? Sorry enough to spread your legs for me? That's what women do, isn't it, as long as their families' murderers are handsome? I'm surprised my face could arouse such admiration in a woman, but perhaps when your husband is as ugly as yours—even a half-man presents as an improvement."

She felt as if she'd been struck. Her eyes burned with foolish tears. How could she have believed in that illusion of a vulnerable woman? This *was* the monster of her imagination, and he looked at her the way so many men did: with hate. His eyes forced shame upon her for being herself: for being someone he considered fundamentally incapable of honor, filial duty, loyalty, love.

"*You* might be sorry," he told her. His fists were clenched as tight as beef tendon the moment it entered hot water. "But I'm not. I'm not sorry for any of it."

The contrast between his exquisite exterior and the horror within put Ma in mind of a pearlescent cocoon of silk thread: a coffin for the worm that had been boiled alive.

She'd managed to stop her tears from running over, but her voice shook humiliatingly. "I see the General is indeed a man, despite his appearance. I can tell by how you have no hesitation to put me in my place. I once had a fiancé who used to do the same thing. Perhaps I should describe what happened to him, if you think I know nothing of butchery. But I can see you think having witnessed butchery isn't enough. You only respect the forgiveness of those other men who've performed it." She flung at him, "Perhaps so you can keep reassuring each other it's what you had to do."

There was nothing beautiful about him as he said savagely, "Get out."

The worst thing about being away was how the paperwork built up. Zhu dealt with it at night, in private. She had learned to write with her left hand—after a fashion—but she'd found that the mere sight of her doing so made her officials painfully uneasy. Few were bold enough to stare, but the quality of their attention was evident in the jabs and pecks of their sideways glances: a repulsed fascination with her incomplete body. Her body that offended the ancestors; her body that offended their eyes. They stole looks, then blinked away with pleasurable condemnation. The very fact of herself eroded their respect. Their doubts turned her kingship into something she was forced to earn from them, again and again and again.

As she worked, the servants lowered the brocade bed-curtains, swept the heaped ash out of the censers, and went around the room pinching out the white cocoon-wax candles. The dim light of the remaining lanterns made the palatial surroundings warm and small. Ma entered and dismissed the servants, then after a while came over, with a washed face and in her white underclothes, saying, "You should rest."

Zhu pushed back from the desk with a sigh as Ma unpinned her hair clasp. In her monastery days Zhu's shaved head had seemed as unalterably a part of herself as her black eyes, but now she had to admit: in cold weather, having hair made all the difference to comfort. Though she was perfectly capable of getting undressed by herself, it was nice to feel the care of Ma's hands as she undid Zhu's belt and formal outer gown. Ma worked quietly. Then, with the air of someone who had been ruminating painfully on something, she said, "General Ouyang isn't a very pleasant person."

"You went to see him?" Zhu wondered what Ma had hoped for from that encounter. She hadn't even been to see him herself, her strong feeling being that it would be asking for trouble. "Don't take it personally. Even before I put him in the worst mood of his life, he was the angry type. Not that he doesn't have cause, but I'm not sure he was a sunshine-filled individual even *before* the whole thing with the murdered family and the castration." She added with some outrage, "Still! I'm surprised you couldn't win him over; everyone likes you."

"*You* like me." Ma shucked Zhu out of her gown and draped it over the outstretched arms of the clothes tree, where it would hang all night and startle Ma—though not Zhu, who had developed a robust tolerance to ghostly shapes—whenever she got up to use the chamber pot. "A lot of people have only ever wanted me."

Zhu mentally enumerated the people in Ma's life who had previously wanted her: her dead fiancé, her dead father, her dead friends. It seemed cruel to point out the connection. She joked instead, "When I'm emperor, that's the first change I'll make. I'll put it into law: *everyone* has to like you."

Ma didn't smile. "Be careful of him, Yuanzhang." It occurred to Zhu that Ma had been out of sorts since Bianliang, as if the scare had stayed with her despite everything having ended well. She found it strange how Ma hung on to emotions long after their moment. Zhu herself was afraid on occasion, as anyone was, but that fear always became so wholly transmuted into the emotions that succeeded it, whether satisfaction or vindication or pleasure, that she could barely remember what it had felt like. She had the idea of herself wriggling through life as clean as a snake having shed its skin.

"I suppose you don't know this," Ma said as they settled into bed. "But there's this particular way some men look at you because you're a woman, and they hate you. Usually they desire you too, even as they hate you. But with General Ouyang, there was only hate. I felt like he was making me into nothing, just by looking at me."

Zhu had never been a woman, but once she'd been a girl. She knew all too well the anger and shame of being looked at, and hated, and considered nothing, because of what she was. Still: "I'm pretty sure if I stripped in front of him, he couldn't possibly hate me more than he already does. Anyway! No need to worry. His anger might be burning as high as ten thousand zhang, but as long as I keep him apart from his army, what damage can he do? I'll make sure it stays like that until he's in front of the one person in the world he hates more than me." There was only a little lantern-light inside the bed-curtains. Ma was very beautiful in the soft-edged shadow. Feeling inspired, Zhu slid closer to her under the covers and added, "Besides, the only person with any business knowing what's under my clothes is you."

"I should hope so!" Ma said, suddenly indignant, and Zhu was pleased to see her smiling. "Just try not to get skewered again so that Jiao Yu has to take another look."

Zhu felt her usual powerful dislike at the thought of Jiao: not so much at the fact of his having seen her unconscious body—he *had* saved her life—but at the knowing superiority in his eyes as he'd looked at her, afterwards. She said with distaste, "Well, it's not like he can discover *more* of my secret," and reached for Ma.

She and Ma were both occupied, and Jiao thoroughly out of

mind, when a cough came at the door. "Radiant King, a thousand apologies! Senior Commander Chang is here to see you. He says it's urgent."

Zhu sat up and wiped her mouth. "Oh, Chang Yuchun, king of bad timing! I'll have to leave you to it, Yingzi."

"You dare—!"

Zhu leaned down for a kiss. "Or wait for me, that's good too." She threw on a robe and went barefoot into the corridor.

Chang Yuchun greeted her with a bow that, while appropriately deferential, retained just enough cockiness to remind her that he'd known her since long before she was king. In the time since Zhu had met him as an Anfeng street thief, Yuchun had flourished into a nimble, wiry young warrior. He'd even mostly grown into his eagle beak of a nose—a development that made him, if not handsome, then at least arrestingly unusual.

"Sorry to interrupt," Yuchun said, smirking in a way that made Zhu suspect he'd heard some of Ma's louder noises. "But you wanted to know about developments as soon as they happened. We just got word: Madam Zhang has banned all trade out of her territory. She's cut us off from all our regular suppliers of grain and other goods. We can find alternatives for most of what we need, but the problem is—"

"Salt," Zhu finished. She was displeased, but not surprised. Madam Zhang cutting off the crucial resource that kept Zhu's cities populated, her peasants alive, and her army capable of waging war had been the obvious next step in their hostilities.

"Given how she raised the salt price even before cutting us off, we don't have the reserves to supply our army for a months-long campaign. Which I guess is exactly what she wanted. But perhaps now that we have the eunuch's army onside—could we win quickly enough that having limited salt doesn't matter?"

"Even if we could prove ourselves superior to General Zhang that quickly in the field, there would still be the matter of taking Pingjiang. If we sank months into a siege only to run out of supplies before succeeding, and in the meantime all my cities had run out of salt as well—" That would be a catastrophe, perhaps one impossible to come back from. But there were options other than the one Madam Zhang was trying to force them into, if only Zhu was bold enough to seize them. "I'll think about it," she said, with a sense of thrill. "But first: let me get back to pleasing my wife."

"Well." Zhu poked her head into the cabin of the docked pleasure boat, then came in and claimed a vacant chair around the table. "Isn't this nice!"

There were a few distant lanterns out on the lake—other pleasure boats that had already launched—but not many. Zhu liked it that way. It filled her with wonder to see the lake's vast blackness peel open under the starlight to reveal a mysterious world of gray and blue islets linked by white moonlight roads, the faint music drifting across the water seeming to have emerged from the universe itself.

The other people at the table paused their game. The four of them were pink and loose with wine, piles of winnings at their elbows: hairpins and silver taels and carved jade trinkets. Xu Da gave Zhu a look of amused inquiry, while the three courtesans' frank assessments took in her plain gown, shabby purse, and lack of hair ornaments, and found her wanting. Judging by their dress the women were high-class entertainers, but their poise had melted away: their sleeves were carelessly pinned back and they were leaning comfortably in their chairs. Clearly Xu Da was a favorite client of their establishment.

One of the women said with flirtatious chiding, "Big brother," and Xu Da laughed and went around the table distributing tiles, giving Zhu a pile too.

"Look how bossy they are," he said. "You'll need some money to play."

"I gave it all to you, apparently so you could make friends with expensive women," Zhu said. She took a couple of taels out of her purse and threw them on the table.

"Big brother, who's this?" asked one of the women.

"His *actual* brother," said Zhu, enjoying their disgruntlement at her presence. "What, can't you see the resemblance?"

"So cruel of Heaven to bestow such handsomeness on only

one son," Xu Da said loftily and indicated for the women to begin. "I must have earned some merit in a past life."

"And at the rate you're spending it, you'll be as short and ugly as me in the next," Zhu observed. Xu Da did look well in his aristocratic dark blue gown, or perhaps it was the novelty of seeing him out of armor. It was odd to think how far they'd come from a pair of monks. "Although *is* it merit you're spending?" She raised her eyebrows. "So many women, big brother. A general who doesn't have any yang energy left isn't going to be much good on the battlefield."

The play came around the table and she laid down her tiles, making sure to keep her wooden hand tucked well inside her sleeve. There were only so many one-handed men around, and it amused her to be unrecognized even in her own city.

"I like to believe my semen is an infinite resource," Xu Da said, winking at the women in a way that gave Zhu flashbacks to his cheerful wooing of every girl in a five-li radius around the monastery. "Anyway, look at the eunuch: he doesn't have any semen whatsoever, and he's better in battle than all of us, so I'm not sure it's actually as vital as everyone says."

"Well, if you've got *that* much to spare—" Zhu gave him a jokingly clinical look. "Pity you're not my wife's type. I could do with some offspring." She saw an opening and clapped down her tiles under the reaching hands of Xu Da and two of the women, laughing at their stymied expressions.

"If you want good-looking sons, I'm your man," Xu Da said agreeably. "But it's true, your wife does seem to prefer short little men who look like women—" Then he fell back, laughing uproariously. "Oh, is the eunuch her type? He is!"

"How does that help!" Zhu said, exasperated. "He's not any better than I am for that kind of thing. Also there's the small matter of how much he hates us."

Xu Da smirked. "Hates *you*. Relative to that, I think his feelings towards me might be quite positive."

"*Relatively speaking.* You can always test it in absolute terms by paying him a visit and seeing if he causes you to spout blood from your seven orifices."

She smacked down her tiles and crowed, scooping the pile of

winnings towards herself as the others shook their heads and threw their remaining tiles down on the table in defeat.

Zhu and Xu Da left the women and stepped onto the open deck as the boatman came on board and started winding up ropes in preparation for launch. "Did you hear?" Zhu said. "Madam Zhang has cut off our salt. General Zhang was going to be a formidable enough opponent as it was, and if he knows we're short on resources he'll prolong every encounter to put us under even more pressure. If we're to win, we need to find another source. I want to go after the stockpile in Taizhou." That city, one of the Yuan's last remaining outposts in the south, was the nearest salt-producing region: three hundred li east of Zhu's southernmost city.

Xu Da's casual demeanor fooled most people, but Zhu knew him like a second self: even in the dark she could feel his attention sharpening. "Will you open a second front to the south, just to take Taizhou?"

"I can't hold two fronts," Zhu said matter-of-factly. "No, I want to take the Yuan's salt in a quick strike. That will see us through defeating Madam Zhang, and then we'll have our own permanent supply. We'll go together. Can you put together a team of a dozen of your best men to come with us?"

"All right," Xu Da said. His mouth pulled up rakishly. "In the morning."

"Don't wear yourself out too much," Zhu said, laughing, and jumped onto the shore as the boatman started to pole away. "It's a long ride south."

After the visit from General Ma's daughter, Ouyang received no more guests. The room he was held in was more spacious than the cell in Bianliang, and at least he hadn't been abandoned to die from thirst, but in every respect that mattered—and in truth, there was only one—it was the same. *Someone else had taken his army.* It turned out it was entirely possible to choke upon one's rage and pain without end, never dying from it. Not that Ouyang *could* die. He couldn't, because he had to get out and regain control of his army. And he had to do it before that fucking monk went to face General Zhang and lost.

How long would it take Zhu to mobilize two armies for a major campaign? Perhaps as much as a month. However much time it was, it would be enough. It had to be. Ouyang had a flash of Shao's surprised carp mouth as Ouyang reclaimed what belonged to him. He thought with a burst of such pure, piercing sensation that it didn't seem to be pain so much as fate: *I did it once, and I'll do it again.*

It was hard not to panic, though, as the days passed without sign of any exploitable weaknesses in the room itself, or the many guards assigned to keep him in it. Sometimes, in his worst moments, he wondered whether Zhu had already taken his army from Yingtian without him noticing. What if his fate had already been extinguished in some distant battle, along with Zhu's own futile ambitions? At the same time, he had the certainty: if that happened, he would *know.*

Even in his depths, he couldn't bring himself to consider what might happen to him after that, if he had done it all for nothing.

He was sitting against the wall when, a heartbeat before the door opened, a peculiar—*familiar*—shiver ran through him. It was as if someone had reached out and plucked a string inside him. He only realized he'd sprung to his feet and lunged across the room when a bristle of swords appeared in his face. He held himself in place, panting, feeling like a leashed hound straining after a small animal it wanted to tear to pieces.

"I could have had you killed at any point before this," his captor observed. Wisely, he had surrounded himself with several times more guards than his wife had visited with. He was wearing a floor-length gold gown with a matching gold hair clasp, a gilded hand in his right sleeve. It would have made for a kingly appearance, had it been anyone other than *him.* "I haven't, because I don't want to. But the truth is: I need your army, not you. Don't make me do it."

Ouyang spat, "Zhu Chongba."

"I haven't heard that for a while. I did tell you to remember it, didn't I? Right before you did this to me." Zhu held up the gilded hand, surprisingly without anger. "Our name is Zhu Yuanzhang now, though." He flicked, as if casually, to the royal pronoun.

Ouyang was overpowered by repugnance. Zhu's smallness, the thinness of his neck and the narrowness of his shoulders, the lightness of his voice, the offensiveness of his incomplete body—how dare someone like that wear gold, and believe himself king? Zhu wasn't anything like a leader. He wasn't anything like a ruler. He was an object of contempt who had somehow missed the message, thinking himself worthy based on nothing more than his misplaced belief in himself. "Call yourself whatever you want. It doesn't change anything. You aren't going to win against General Zhang."

Apart from the Yuan's Grand Councilor in Dadu, Zhang was the last great general. *He* was everything a leader should be—a man other men looked up to, and would kneel to, and die for. The kind of man who would embody the honor and dignity of the Nanren people as he sat upon the throne. Ouyang could picture him up there easily enough. Unlike Zhu.

"Why are you so certain I can't?" Zhu asked. He put out his small brown hand, palm up, in a gesture Ouyang recognized. He'd heard that Zhu had the Mandate, but it was still a surprise to witness it: the white, almost transparent, flame. Hardly radiant, he thought scornfully. It didn't brighten the room much more than a candle would have. "Isn't this proof enough that I can do as promised?"

Ouyang seemed to have lost the capacity for even bitter laughter. It came out more like a snarl. "You fool. What does that signify? The Zhangs have it too."

He felt a dull satisfaction at Zhu's unconcealed surprise.

"Interesting." Zhu closed his hand around the flame. "Rice Bucket Zhang has the Mandate? I wouldn't have thought it, especially given what people say about him, but I suppose he does have Madam Zhang prodding him along. Well, it doesn't matter. What is the Mandate but potential? The first person with the Mandate to sit on the throne, wins. And it's going to be me."

Ouyang might have surprised Zhu, but with outrage he saw that he hadn't shaken Zhu's ridiculous belief in himself at all.

Zhu said, "Don't mistake me, General. I believe in my capacities, but I don't underestimate General Zhang. That's why I'm about to head off on a little trip, to ensure I'm in the best possible position before I face him." His gaze traveled over Ouyang, taking in his disheveled desperation. "For some reason, as I was planning my trip, I had the distinct feeling you might do something unreasonable during my absence. I don't want to come back to find that you've burned down the city and run off with your army. I'd have to come get you, and that would be very annoying." He said, "I'm taking you with me."

Zhu was separating him even farther from his army. It didn't matter, Ouyang told himself, though his heart sank. He would find a chance to escape on the road. They could take him as far as the mouth of Diyu, and he would still find some way to get back and do what he needed to do. It had to be possible. Because if it wasn't: Why else would he still be alive? Why would he still be in this much pain? Abruptly, Ouyang could no longer bear it. As if he were only folding his arms inside his sleeves, he ran his fingers along the ladder of burns on the inside of his left forearm until he found the most recent one, and dug his fingernails in.

"Servants are coming with your clothes. They'll get you cleaned up. Try not to kill them, if you wouldn't mind; I think Ma Xiuying would miss them." What was that look of penetrating inquiry on Zhu's hideous little face? There was nothing Zhu might see in Ouyang that he could possibly understand. Nobody could understand what he had given; what he would give, and keep giving, to get what he wanted.

"I'm not your enemy, General. I'm not doing this to torture you. The faster I do what I need to do, the sooner we'll both get what we want."

The strike force that set out for the south consisted of Zhu; his team of thirteen painfully young men, all in drab traveling clothes and riding as well as one would expect of peasants who'd likely met a horse for the first time three weeks ago; Zhu's slightly more seasoned general Xu Da; and Ouyang himself. In addition to keeping Ouyang under watch by rotating pairs of minders, they'd bound his wrists, and put him on a spiritless horse that his minders took turns leading. They hadn't even let him have reins. It was probably, Ouyang thought savagely, prudent. He ached for his sword. He couldn't stop mentally reaching for it, as for a part of himself that was no longer there.

The plan was to cross the plains south of Yingtian, then pass through the Yellow Mountains to Zhu's southern holdings: Jinhua, notable for its many centers of Confucian learning, and the valley settlement of Lishui. After that they would turn east into Yuan-controlled territory, and reach salt-rich Taizhou on the coast. They would cover a thousand li in ten days. Zhu's men were so useless they didn't even realize what an embarrassment that was. Even with a single horse instead of a string, Ouyang could have covered that distance in less than half the time.

Zhu was up ahead at the front of the group, with General Xu. Ouyang glared at his back. He couldn't look away. It was as irresistible as poking a wound. With every li that passed, his longing intensified: to take Zhu by his thin neck and scrub him into the ground until he was a bloody smear in the dirt where he belonged. He wanted it so badly that had Zhu dropped dead right then, he'd have believed himself the cause. Zhu, however, trotted and cantered along with blithe unconcern. He seemed to have forgotten Ouyang was even there.

They ate in the saddle. Ouyang was used to that, but he was less used to what Nanren considered travel food: cylinders of rice inside lotus leaves (unpleasantly chewy when cold), and small hard round pastries filled with some kind of obnoxiously sweetened bean paste. It made Ouyang's stomach hurt, and by early afternoon—even though he'd known well enough to refuse water when it had been passed around—his bladder hurt worse. It was a familiar torment. The first few days of a campaign, before his body adapted, were always spent with a cramping lower abdomen, a blazing dehydration headache, and a vicious resentment of every man who could pull out his dick to piss by the roadside while Ouyang was forced to wait for the evening's privacy. It wasn't even a transporting pain, as the burns on his wrist had been, but a nagging misery that seated him even more deeply within his wretched body than before.

The flat fields directly south of Yingtian had changed to a drier, lightly forested landscape when, to Ouyang's surprise,

Zhu dropped back to ride alongside him at the rear of the group. He took the lead rope of Ouyang's horse, and with a nod sent his pair of escorts trotting ahead. When they were out of sight, Zhu halted by the roadside and jerked his head at Ouyang in the universal gesture: *dismount.*

Ouyang instantly forgot his headache and full bladder. Why had Zhu separated him from the group? Had he changed his mind, and decided Ouyang was too much trouble to keep alive after all? Zhu wore a short saber on his right side—presumably easier for him to handle than the straight sword he'd once fought Ouyang with—though he hadn't drawn it yet. How competent was he, left-handed? No doubt proficient enough to stab a bound, unarmed man. Ouyang flexed his wrists inside the rope, searching fruitlessly for give. If he could take the blade in the meat of his shoulder when Zhu came for him, then he'd have the chance to headbutt him, or smash him in the face with his balled-together fists . . .

"Dismount, and stay over there," Zhu commanded, when Ouyang didn't move. Then, less explicably, "Take off your boots and socks and throw them to me."

When Ouyang stared in venomous incomprehension, Zhu sighed. "I don't want you running away the moment you're out of my sight. Don't you know holding it all day is bad for your kidneys? Give me your boots. There are trees over there. Go do what you need to do."

For a moment Ouyang was so ashamed that the world tunneled in front of him. He had no clue why his unique situation had even occurred to Zhu, but the idea that Zhu had *thought about his body*—about its needs and incapacities—was infinitely worse than suffering through everyone else's obliviousness. The violation of it made him tremble.

He slid off the horse, wrestled off his boots and socks, and threw them hatefully in Zhu's direction. To his regret, they didn't hit him. Even more cause for regret was how Zhu hadn't been wrong about the boots. Ouyang wasn't some filthy Nanren peasant in straw sandals. He'd been raised a Mongol. He rode rather than walked as a point of pride, and he'd never been barefoot outside in his life. Even as he went into the trees, stones and sharp sticks were already gouging his tender soles. His feet wanted to cringe to protect themselves from pain and damage. He forced them not to.

When he was a sufficient distance into the trees, he squatted and pissed, feeling his usual piercing hatred of his body that couldn't even do the most simple thing a man's body should do. He straightened and pulled his clothes back into place. Undid the rope around his wrists.

And then he ran.

As Ouyang ran—stumbled—through the small forest, and onto the scrubby expanse of nothingness on the other side, he was no longer a person but a flame: ablaze in his agony. With some distant part of his mind he was aware of how unnaturally hard his heart was working from exertion and dehydration; how his skinless feet were leaving a bloody trail behind him in the dust. But none of that mattered. The pain took him out of himself. It was no longer his body staggering across the plain, but his disembodied will pressing back towards his army like a haunting. His physical environment had ceased to be relevant. The brightness ahead could have been the sky, or a shimmering lake, or the late-afternoon sun flashing from a stretch of exposed limestone. It was all the same. It was all a blur. A blur that at some point had started spinning around him, even as he pressed onwards. And that didn't matter, either, until with his next step he was caught in the spinning. He went around and around, the world smearing into a featureless streak, and then he was gone. It was all gone.

When he came to, it was dark. The world was stationary, and so was he. The field of stars was cut away by the silhouette of someone's head as they leaned over him.

"Just out of curiosity," General Xu said good-naturedly, "were you actually intending to run all the way back to Yingtian?"

Ouyang couldn't even turn his head away in defeat. With the driving transcendence of his pain gone, his body had asserted itself as a leaden prison. He was too drained to move or think. He couldn't muster a single emotional response. He lay there, blinking.

"If it's any consolation, you made it farther than any of us thought humanly possible. On the downside, now we have to ride all the way back. Here, drink something." He held up Ouyang's head so he could drink the lukewarm water without choking. Then he retied his hands, saying, "If I didn't do this and you were to miraculously recover and steal my horse, I'd be as much of an idiot as you made *him*," patted his shoulder in friendly reassurance—a gesture Ouyang was entirely unfamiliar with, because the people around him usually valued their lives—and picked him up without apparent effort.

Ouyang waited dully for the inevitable comment about his size, but all General Xu said was, "I had to carry him like this after you ran him through and cut off his hand that time. He nearly died, you know."

Ouyang managed to croak, *"I wish he had."*

"Don't you know you can toss a cockroach into the fire and it'll survive?" General Xu laughed softly. He was tall, almost a head taller than Ouyang, with a solidity that set him apart from the wasp-waisted boys that made up the rest of Zhu's team. From his odd new perspective, Ouyang registered his high-bridged nose and the clean cut of his cheekbones. With his handsomeness and easy charisma, he was clearly ten times the man Zhu Yuanzhang could ever hope to be. He slung Ouyang facedown behind his saddle as if he were a dead deer, tied him in place, and mounted. "My brother's a hard one to kill. You weren't the first to try."

It was only early autumn, but the night was cold and still. The starlit road was blue under the horse's hooves. Its every step jolted Ouyang's breath out of him, and so much blood had rushed to his head that it felt like it was about to explode. He couldn't find it in himself to care.

"Do you know how I met him?" General Xu said. "We were novices together, at Wuhuang Monastery. Yes, that same monastery you burned down. I'd already been a novice for a few years by the time he arrived. His family hadn't wanted him. They would have let him die, though they were the ones who died in the end. The monks didn't want him at first, either. Starving children weren't exactly a novelty where we came from. They used to come to the monastery in droves, pleading to be let in. The monks would leave them outside until they died or went away. My brother was the only one who didn't do either. He wore them down through sheer determination. He was so prepared to struggle, to suffer, to do and to endure anything for what he wanted. And do you know what he wanted? Just to be allowed to survive. To be something rather than nothing. To not have to die, for being himself."

There was an intimacy to being alone with someone in the dark, even if they were a stranger; in knowing that their thoughts, the touch of their voice, was for nobody other than you. "The reason I follow him is because out of everyone I've met, he's the only one that when the world didn't allow a place for him as he was, he refused to accept it, and vowed instead to change the world.

"I know you hate him because you think he's ruined your fate. Because you're convinced he'll lose, whether here in Taizhou or against General Zhang, or against the Grand Councilor. But I believe Zhu Yuanzhang can do as he says." General Xu didn't look like any monk Ouyang had ever met, but he spoke with a calm certainty that for the first time made him seem like one: "He'll win. Not in spite of who he is, but because of it."

Taizhou was more of a large town than a city, with a gray storm sky and moist streets pressed into ruts by the Yuan's horseback patrols. The wind whipped the light blue flags along the fortifications. Though the town sat on the shore of a wide brown river, there was something non-riverine about it: a thick mineral taste to the air that filled Zhu with an inexplicable anticipation of something unknown and never before encountered.

Posing as a troupe of masked, costumed traveling performers had made it easy enough to enter town without alerting the Yuan to their presence. As the younger members of the team cavorted on the street in front of a dusty lively Taizhou audience, Zhu watched Ouyang standing rigidly on the sidelines in the glowering demon mask she'd picked out for him. They'd cleaned and bandaged his flayed feet—Zhu had donated her spare chest and stump bandages to the task—but it was astonishing that he could even stand, let alone walk without limping. It wasn't that he was like a leper who couldn't feel pain, Zhu thought. Every line of his body radiated agony. But instead of cowering from the sensation, as ordinary people did, he seemed to be pressing himself into it: there was no space at all between him and his suffering.

The thought of how far he had run—of what he'd been willing to do to himself—thrilled her. Zhu had always known he wanted his fate. But what a pale shadow of the truth that had been! She was filled with a resonance that made her feel like a gong that had been struck for the very first time. Here was someone else who knew what it was to want with his entire self; who burned with his desire; for whom there was nothing else in the world that could ever matter more.

Keeping Ouyang alive had always been an unnecessary risk. Who knew what else he might try if she made another mistake—or even if she didn't? And yet—she couldn't forget the aching wrongness she'd felt when she'd thought he was dead. It had been a hole in the world where something belonged. A canyon she had shouted into, without echo. Now that he was here, his presence filled her with shivering wonder: at this person who was like herself, who wanted as much as she did.

The performance was finishing. When the audience had dispersed, Zhu took the bowl of copper coins she'd gathered and handed it to Yuchun. "Take everyone to that inn we passed, three streets back by the tree with the purple flowers. Get some food for yourselves. The generals and I will take a look around and try to get the exact location of those salt warehouses."

"I'm not sure this is enough to buy food for one person, let alone thirteen," Yuchun said dubiously. He turned the dubious look upon Ouyang, with his bound wrists and the mask that covered his distinctive features. "Are you sure you want to wander around as a group? People are going to think you're one of those Buddhist jokes that don't make sense. Two monks out walking met a demon . . ."

"They are not jokes," Zhu said with mock severity, "they are *instructional koans.*"

"See, there's your problem; people learn things better when they're funny—"

"—I'll be sure to let the monks know that someone who can't read and write has the opinion that an education would be more effective if it were *fun*—"

Still chuckling, Zhu led Xu Da and a silent, grimly unlimping Ouyang down the street. The Taizhou houses with their ramshackle mussel-bed tile roofs grew farther apart, and crouched low under bands of ink-washed clouds, while the trees reduced to shrubs and to waving grasses, and then they crested a sandy rise and saw where the land ended. But beyond it the world went on in such expanse as Zhu had never seen. The river poured into a milky green sea that could have swallowed a thousand such rivers, and rising above it was a sky even larger than the big sky of the plains upon which she'd been born. It was larger than she could have ever imagined. It was a sky without scale. The tiny flecks in it could be birds or dragons; the islands could be as near as her fingertips or as far as she could see. Her heart surged with the thrill of being a human grasping herself in relation to the breadth of Heaven.

"The sea!" Zhu shared a look of delight with Xu Da. Having him beside her reminded her of how they'd sat on the monastery roof as boys, and looked upon the world beneath. But this time he wasn't going to leave her to go out into that adventure while she hid from her fate. What lay before them now, and all the other newnesses the future had to offer, was theirs to experience together.

The long stretch of shore near the river mouth was lined with decrepit open-air eating houses. Men sat on low stumps eating from platters, unbothered by the reek from the nearby mounds of discarded crab shells. Outside one eating house, a man showering wine and sauces into a barrel of still-moving crabs gave the bound demon a startled look as they passed by. "Just can't get him out of character!" Zhu explained, winking.

Past the eating houses was an assortment of moored fishing boats, then a colorful temple that was clearly the only structure on the foreshore that received a regular coat of paint. The usual collection of pitiable characters, banned from entry due to their various diseases and disfigurements, loitered outside.

"Let's ask the monks if they know where the warehouses

are," Xu Da suggested. Then, recalling who he was speaking to, he amended hastily, *"I'll* ask them. You both wait here." He bounded up the temple steps and vanished inside.

Zhu sat down peaceably. After a moment Ouyang followed suit, no doubt only because his feet hurt. She couldn't tell if he still resented being excluded from temples on account of his mutilation. For herself, she didn't mind; she'd been in enough temples for a lifetime. Next to the steps, a large statue of Guan Yin did her secondary duty as patron bodhisattva of fishermen. Zhu wondered if Ouyang knew that Guan Yin had been a male bodhisattva before she was made female. Perhaps that was something only monks knew.

A group of bandit-like people swaggered past. There was something odd about them that Zhu couldn't put her finger on, until all of a sudden she realized: "Women!"

Ouyang surprised her by rasping, *"Pirates."* From the strength of his disgust, Zhu could have believed that pirates had personally pissed in his wine and made him drink it. "Their leader is that degenerate, Fang Guozhen." Zhu knew the name: Fang, an independent warlord, controlled a stretch of coast north of Taizhou. "He's even worse than Rice Bucket Zhang. He surrounds himself with women. Not just in his harem, but doing his business and managing his affairs." He all but spat, "He even has them crew his ships."

When General Ouyang looked at me, all I saw was hate, Ma had said. Zhu realized what had prompted his outburst. It wasn't pirates he hated. It was that they were women.

Zhu liked women, even if she didn't consider herself one of them. She still didn't like how Ouyang had treated Ma. But as she thought of the furious, aching pride with which he held himself—his fruitless challenge to the world to see past his appearance to the man he knew himself to be—she felt a pulse of sympathy. She'd spent long enough rejecting the feminine aspects of her own body to understand how that fear and loathing could have turned into Ouyang's wholesale rejection of womanhood.

When the pirates had gone, Zhu turned her attention to the other temple loiterers. Her eye fell on a group of shabby men with missing limbs who were squatting in a circle, gambling on fighting crickets as they waited for whichever of their fellow fishermen were praying inside for calm seas. Monks, Zhu thought, weren't the only ones who liked to gossip.

"If I leave you here for a moment, are you going to try swimming back to Yingtian just to annoy me?"

"I don't want to annoy you," Ouyang said balefully. She could see his bared teeth through the mouth hole of the mask. They were much whiter and more even than any Nanren teeth she'd seen. Perhaps it had something to do with the Mongol diet. "I want to gut you, get my army back, and go to Dadu."

Zhu regarded him. "It's a mystery how you managed such an epic betrayal, seeing how you always say exactly what's on your mind." Fortunately, Xu Da was already on his way back. From his expression she could tell he hadn't had any luck with the monks. "Well, then stay here with General Xu while I go make friends with those grumpy-looking fishermen. Anyway! I suppose you've already been helpful enough. I might not know anything about fish, or the sea, but"—she waved her wooden hand in his face—"look how much we already have in common."

"They call it Fortress Island." Ouyang listened desultorily from behind his mask as Zhu addressed his men in the inn's dining room. Zhu broke off as one of the inn staff set down steaming bowls of a clear, oily soup with sliced bamboo shoots and red gouqi berries, then resumed, "It's one of those rocky islands you can see from the beach. The Yuan evicted the fishing community that used to live on it, and put their salt warehouses there. They lined all the sea approaches with sheer walls, so now the only way in or out is the guarded harbor where they keep their transport fleet."

General Xu raised a bowl to his mouth, then flinched and put it down again with the rueful look of someone who knew he should have waited longer for it to cool. "An island? That's not what we prepared for."

"Unfortunately," Zhu agreed. "The scouts I sent down didn't make it all the way here, so their information was from people outside Taizhou. When they said 'a warehouse on the shore,' and 'near a harbor,' I was definitely expecting it to be on the shore of the *mainland.*"

What a surprise, Ouyang thought savagely, his scabbed and inflamed feet throbbing with his heartbeat. Zhu's ridiculous expedition was over before it started. They would be returning empty-handed to Yingtian, where Zhu's lack of salt would guarantee his loss to General Zhang. He would have no choice but to find a way out of that closed room. He didn't know how—didn't dare think about how, for the throttling panic that rose in his throat at the memory of those boarded windows and careful guards—only that he *had* to.

Zhu glanced at him. "Even with that mask I can feel you glaring at me. Aiya, so unpleasant! Reminds me of how we used to have to sit in that hall with the demon statues, for death-awareness practice."

He and General Xu exchanged a look and recited in eerie unison, *"My body, eaten by worms; my body, reduced to a blood-smeared skeleton without flesh, held together by tendons."*

For an instant Ouyang saw a body, reduced from the breathing aliveness that Ouyang had known and loved, to bloody bones in the wet ground. His pain flashed over like oil into which someone had thrust a ladle of water. As he felt the beginnings of that excruciating derangement, he knew the misery of his feet wasn't enough to stop it. He snatched a bowl of the soup, pushed his mask up, and gulped.

It was incandescent. It was as if he'd taken one of the hot stones from inside a roasting goat and placed it on his tongue. The thin skin inside his mouth was sloughing off. A tremendous rush of internal pressure squeezed him empty until he felt as though his head were about to float off his shoulders. The memories were gone; the wretchedness was gone; there was nothing left of him but blissful, singular agony.

When he came drifting back, Zhu was looking at him thoughtfully, as if he knew what Ouyang had done, and was trying to figure out why. It was only after Ouyang pulled his mask back into place that Zhu finally glanced around the table at the others. "The fishermen I spoke to were part of the community that the Yuan evicted, so they knew the island well. Apparently the whole island is limestone, and it's riddled with tunnels. Some of the tunnels go all the way from the surface to the sea. If we pay well enough, those fishermen are willing to take us in their boats to the sea entrances."

"What's the catch," General Xu said. He sipped his soup, cautiously.

"Ah, you know me too well! Yes, there's a catch. The reason the Yuan doesn't care about the tunnels is because it doesn't think the sea entrances can be accessed. They're underwater."

"I could be wrong," said General Xu at length, "but I hear the sea's pretty deep. I've never been in water over my head, and I don't think any of the rest of us have, either. I also know for a fact that *you* can't swim, since you spent your entire childhood refusing to get wet." Neither he nor Zhu smiled, but there was something of a smile in the glance they exchanged.

"I know it seems difficult, but it's possible."

To Ouyang's incredulity none of them flinched, or burst out in protest, but instead leaned closer. As if they trusted Zhu to have the answers, despite the manifest impossibility of the situation.

Zhu said calmly, "Because General Ouyang is going to help."

6

KHANBALIQ

The autumn heat was already a memory. Above the scooped roofs of the Ministry the sky was streaked with vitreous dawn, as if a frost high up in Heaven, not yet descended to earth, had fired the celestial surface into vividness the way a kiln transforms a wash on porcelain. Released from the detritus of another night's ruined sleep, Baoxiang felt his exhaustion lighten. Dawn represented failure of one kind, but it still held the promise of all dawns: that the day ahead might be better. He usually managed to hold on to that optimism until early afternoon, when it would be crushed by the realization that night was coming again.

The Ministry's long corridors were quiet. Inside the offices, invisible hands had already lit the braziers and ground fresh ink for the desks. Baoxiang's own office was in the same building as the Minister's, a few doors down. He fell into his work. The flow was soothing: numbers, sums, the clack of the abacus and the stroke of his brush—

He only realized he'd fallen asleep when the sound jerked him out of it. He bolted upright with such force that his teeth clacked together. Though that same dreamed sound fractured his sleep hundreds of times a night, upon waking he could never remember what it was. All he knew was the feeling that accompanied it: a dread so intense it left him shaking, his mouth dry.

"Aigoo, you startled me!" the maid cried.

He stared at her. The presence of another person, while he was possessed by dread, made him feel insane. "I startled *you*?" he managed. "How different the city is to the provinces! It seems a prince is expected to concern himself with the feelings of maids."

Acting the part of himself was the best way of returning *to* himself. To his relief, his racing heart slowed. He was holding his brush with such a death grip that his hand had cramped.

"The Prince of Henan startled this unworthy maid so much that she dared forget he was the Prince of Henan," the maid returned cheerfully. He belatedly recognized her as the merry, dimpled maid he'd met during his test. "A thousand apologies for waking the esteemed Prince, whom she mistook for a hardworking official of the Ministry of Revenue."

Her impertinence was outrageous. She dared intrude into his notice and accuse *him* of startling *her*; she was apologizing without being apologetic in the slightest. Now she placed the tray she'd been carrying upon his desk, and bent down to retrieve a dropped cup. The fabric of her pink-trimmed uniform strained tight over her hip as she knelt, and made desperate cat's whiskers in the curve of her waist above it. Baoxiang found himself watching her profile as she tucked a fall of hair behind a tiny ear. It occurred to him that she was the kind of playful woman he usually preferred. But the thought only served to make him feel ill with exhaustion.

"I didn't call for tea," he said curtly.

She rose with the cup. It wasn't only that her dimples showed when she was amused; each of her cheeks lifted up into absurd roundness. "Forgive me, esteemed Prince. It seemed like you needed it." Her broad face was different to those of the other maids. She was from the northeast somewhere. Goryeo, maybe. "I'll get you a clean cup," she said, gentle, then was gone.

The corridor outside his office filled with the normal bustle of officials and servants and messengers. It was past noon, and Baoxiang was on his seventh pot of tea, by the time someone said, "Ah, for the concentration of youth!"

Baoxiang found the Minister's benevolent gaze upon him. The Minister's robes were as crinkled as if he had slept in them, which made Baoxiang vaguely embarrassed on his behalf. "The eyesight of youth, too! Appreciate it while you have it. I can barely remember what it was like not to have to glue my nose to the page." He deposited a pile of ledgers on Baoxiang's desk.

To save space they had been labeled in characters, rather than Mongolian running script. Baoxiang recognized the Ministry's master account books that were always strictly overseen by the Minister himself, for security. "Take a break from that report. I know you won't have a problem getting it done. Use your youthful strength to carry these for me."

After a pause, Baoxiang said, "The Minister might be the first person to assume I have any strength at all." It had taken him that long to realize it had been a statement of fact and not a veiled insult. He felt oddly vulnerable, as if he had put on armor with a fatal breach in it—and instead of stabbing him, the Minister had reached in and given him a pat.

"Scholars have their own strength," the Minister said. "Have you ever taught young warriors and made them study for more than an hour? How they complain and cry! They're more spent afterwards than if you or I went into battle." His eyes twinkled. "I'm sure you've had enough practice carrying books that your arm won't fall off. Come along, I have to attend the Great Khan's audience with the ministers. If we leave now, we'll have time for a walk beforehand." His whiskered face was conspiratorial. "It's the perfect time for fresh walnuts and persimmons. You're new to Khanbaliq; have you ever had a local persimmon? You must!"

That was how Baoxiang found himself trailing the Minister through the Ram's Head Market, which was on Khanbaliq's east side and not at all on the way to the Imperial City, parasol in hand and a monstrously heavy pile of ledgers—"Don't lose them!"—in the crook of his arm. There was a whiteness to the unclouded sky that Baoxiang had come to associate with the north: as though the sun were shining through an invisible veil that drained the color from it. In the crisp white light the market heaved with activity. Besides the livestock that gave the market its name, there were stalls for books, religious items, trinkets, fruit for eating and fruit for offerings, pornography, songbirds in wicker cages, carved dried gourds for holding crickets, fighting roosters, miniature trees, and interestingly shaped rocks for the garden. The rank animal smell mingled with more appealing ones: roasted chestnuts, steamed buns, griddled breads, all manner of things grilled and things fried in oil.

The Minister darted from stall to stall. His enthusiasm was as embarrassing as his crumpled robes. Baoxiang, protected from jostling shoppers by the spread of his parasol, watched him from a reserved distance. He felt an abrupt stab of loss. It hadn't been so long ago that he had harbored that same spark of interest that found joy in beauty and newness. He couldn't remember how the spark had felt—only that it was gone.

A stick threaded with brown blobs appeared under his nose. "A speciality from my hometown!" the Minister exclaimed. "Grilled chicken livers. Ah, they have everything!"

The Minister ate while he walked, like a peasant. A stream of clear juice ran into his whiskers. Then, with a suddenness that made Baoxiang recoil, he stopped and thrust the stick in Baoxiang's face. "This is so delicious! You have to try."

"I don't—"

"Try it!" The Minister was beaming like a fool.

Between books and parasol, Baoxiang had no hands left. He reluctantly bent his head and tugged one of the livers off the stick with his teeth. Though he made a show of pleasure, it tasted as ashen as everything he had eaten lately.

The Minister was still looking at him. After a moment he said, "Despite what people might think, you're a talented young man. You'll go far, using me."

Baoxiang stiffened, feeling a chill of exposure.

"No need for surprise!" the Minister said. "I know what you're about."

The Minister might act the fool, but if he'd been one he would never have survived long enough to become a minister. Of course he'd be alert to those who entered his orbit for their own purposes. *Fool,* Baoxiang cursed himself. *You were the fool.*

The Minister cut off his protest. "It's normal for ambitious young men to use whatever opportunities are available to them." Baoxiang realized, late, that he'd said it *gently.* The Minister started walking again. "I know you'll exceed me. I don't begrudge it. The time of old men such as myself is done. I'm saying I know, and I'll help you."

Baoxiang hurried after him. He felt as skewered as the chicken liver. The thing he thought he was stealing was being given to him as a gift. It gave him a skinless feeling of shame.

"Be ambitious, Wang Baoxiang," the Minister said. Between one step and the next they passed out of the commercial ward of the Ram's Head Market and into the cold shadow of the walls of the Imperial City. "But be careful. Don't take sides in the imperial family's squabbles. I've seen enough times that when bureaucrats get involved in court politics, it ends badly."

The skinless feeling was painful but irrelevant. Long before he'd met this kind old man, Baoxiang had already seized his fate with both hands. There was no changing it now.

They crossed the moat and were waved through the Imperial City's red gate. "But what use is ambition if you don't take care of your health? I've surpassed more talented men simply because I ate well enough and slept well enough to reach old age. Remember to rest sometimes. Listen to some music in the company of pretty women. Take a nap. Consider a hobby!"

"I would *like* to nap," Baoxiang said blackly. Even the thought of sleep depressed him. "I don't work all the time. Now and then I paint." His mind drifted to the project laid out in the miserable rented house on Pingzhe Gate Street. "Lately I've been experimenting with woodcuts. I've been trying my hand at a likeness of someone I met a few times. He had an interesting face."

"An admirable pursuit! How often I've wished for some artistic talent. Sadly, it was never to be. My horses looked like rabbits and my rabbits looked like pheasants. But I do have some marvelous woodcuts by a young man from Tianjin, I'll show you—"

They emerged through the last gate onto the road that followed the inner perimeter of the Palace City. Pairs of guards stood to attention every few zhang. The high blank walls on either side gave the roadway a trench-like air, and cast the fine white sand underfoot into stubborn blue shadow.

A shout of "Give way!" came from behind, and Baoxiang and the Minister leaped aside as a sedan chair rushed past.

That was Lady Ki above, her gold ornaments swaying. She wore an expression of brutal concentration that was entirely unlike the flirtatious ease she'd had in the Great Khan's presence. It was shocking, like seeing the skull beneath the skin. But, of course: usually when men saw women, they were performing.

Baoxiang thought of Madam Zhang and her immaculate facade. Even his favorite courtesan in Anyang, whom he'd grown close to, had surprised him the first time she'd shown him her real face. He'd had no idea, before then, that she thought and felt and desired as strongly as he did.

"Brace yourself," the Minister said pensively as they followed the sedan chair towards the Hall of Great Brilliance. "Lady Ki is in a mood for blood."

Lady Ki stood out from the officials in the Hall of Great Brilliance like a pearl amongst stones. Even in her youth she wouldn't have been a beauty. Her nose was too long, ears prominent against the sculpted mass of her hair crowned with its phoenix pin. Severe brows, painted mannishly straight, gave her loose-lidded eyes a hooded quality. But without youthful softness to hide the architecture of her bones and the long tendons of her neck, she was a portrait of hard elegance. There was no sign of the rawness Baoxiang had seen in her earlier.

"Your Majesty, this woman dares raise her voice on important matters of state." Lady Ki's smile reached for the Great Khan on his throne. "That traitor Zhang Shicheng and his so-called kingdom are no more than a temporary annoyance. Please, don't consider sending the central army to Pingjiang! To feed him with your attention is more than he deserves. Let him and those other Manji traitors wear themselves to extinction against each other, and harmony will return naturally to the Great Yuan. How could it be otherwise, while Your Majesty possesses the Mandate of Heaven?"

"She's arguing *against* retaking the Zhang family's breakaway?" Baoxiang murmured to the Minister of Revenue. It flew in the face of reason. The Great Yuan, north and south and its constellation of vassal states, was like a spoked wheel spinning with huge force. The loss of a single spoke would spell failure for the whole. Even Esen, who had made it his life's work to quell the rebellions in the south, had known that.

"It makes sense, if you're her," the Minister answered. "Consider: the Empress gets one night a month with the Great Khan.

Tonight is one of those nights. Who's to say she won't conceive a son, this time or the next? If she can produce a better heir than the current one, it will be enough to overcome her family's disgrace. But Lady Ki knows that as long as the Zhangs refuse fealty to the Great Yuan, and the capital depends on Goryeo salt, she can't be discarded." He added in a musing tone, "Lady Ki wasn't always his favorite, you know. He used to prefer the mother of the first and second princes."

Two princes who had died young, as children often did, though one had to wonder. Baoxiang remembered Lady Ki's brutal concentration. Women might desire as strongly as men, but their worlds were narrower. Their desires were circumscribed to fit. Lady Ki didn't factor the fate of the Great Yuan into her decisions. Her world was the palace. All she knew was that she needed to suppress the Empress's threat against her own biggest weakness, which was the one thing outside her power to change.

In the sea of black-hatted officials it was easy to miss the Third Prince in his black damask overcoat. The embroidered silver dragons made it the nighttime mirror of his father's gold robe, as if he really were the Crown Prince waiting for his ascendance. The casual arrogance with which he held himself seemed undiminished by his father's dislike.

"Your Majesty!" The Grand Councilor was incredulous. "How can this situation with Zhang Shicheng be tolerated? He must be punished with swift and decisive military action. It's unthinkable that he who rules the world should not take action against those who offend against his person, and against Heaven itself." All at once he knelt with his head bowed and his hands clasped high in supplication, and shouted, "Great Khan, please consider this old warrior's advice!"

The ministers and their accompanying officials shouted in stentorious echo, "Your Majesty, please consider!"

The round-bellied censers belched clouds that all but hid the Great Khan where he frowned atop the throne. Baoxiang recognized the scent of sandalwood. Even that minor luxury would run out soon: it was yet another southern product that reached Khanbaliq only via the graces of Madam Zhang.

Even kneeling, the Grand Councilor held the room's attention.

A visitor could have seen in a glance where the balance of power lay. Lady Ki, smiling graciously with her sunken eyes promising murder, knew it too. With the ministers all behind the Grand Councilor, she had no chance either of forcing his removal.

Baoxiang thought coldly: *But now you have me.*

The Third Prince stood silently as the Great Khan glanced between his mother and the Grand Councilor. He seemed as uninterested as ever, but as the ministers whispered and the tension rose, his fists whitened in a spasm of shame. Despite the Third Prince's air of arrogance and entitlement, he knew this scene his mother was making was because of him. Because he wasn't Crown Prince. Because he was inadequate.

"Great Khan, please give your command!" the Grand Councilor said, and the Great Khan's heavy lids contracted with a start, like an old man remembering his turn during a board game.

He motioned for the Grand Councilor to rise. "As always, the Grand Councilor speaks sense. How can we—"

Lady Ki gave a cry and collapsed where she stood. There was a shocked silence as the ministers absorbed the spectacle of the fallen, moaning consort; then the room erupted into pandemonium. Baoxiang noticed, idly, that Lady Ki had taken care to fall so her dress presented her to her best advantage: she lay amidst the rippled silk like a maiden in a field of marigolds.

The Third Prince dashed to his mother's aid, only to fall back, ashen-faced, in response to some reprimand. Lady Ki struggled, whimpering, into a sitting position and reached for the Great Khan as he rushed from the throne.

"Call the physician!" the Great Khan shouted, clasping Lady Ki's white hands. As eunuchs and officials went every which way, the Grand Councilor rose, straightened his uniform with two annoyed flicks, and left the hall. He wasn't truly angered. Lady Ki could stall for only so long, and he would have other opportunities.

The imperial physician hurried in with a coterie of assistants. The Third Prince watched with a sickly, yearning expression as they surrounded his mother. It was the hurt look of a child as he saw the center of his world lavishing her attention on someone else; the look of a boy who couldn't stop wanting his mother's love, even though the man he had become knew it would never happen.

"If it isn't the Prince of Henan! Why are you walking? Can't you ride?"

Baoxiang turned as horses came up behind. The Minister had been caught in conversation, but now he regretted returning to the office alone. The sun had dropped during the ministers' aborted audience with the Great Khan, and it shone white and cold on the glittering quartz of the broad plaza that led to Chongtian Gate and the Ministry of Revenue outside. Potted crab-claw mountain trees were scattered here and there, their forms constrained by wire so their gnarled branches reached no higher than Baoxiang's waist. Even in miniature, the trees evoked the dry, hilly landscape of the Great Khan's Spring Hunt. And to complete the picture: the pack of young Mongol warriors pursuing their quarry. The dragons on the Third Prince's otter-trimmed overcoat gleamed with the same drained brightness as the northern sun.

Baoxiang knew this dance. How old had he been, that summer? His hair had still been in braids, so fourteen, perhaps. Fifteen. His father's hunting party had already spread through the forest, their calls coming from all directions. Baoxiang lagged behind, sullen with resentment at having been dragged from his books. It wasn't until he dismounted to retrieve a hare he'd shot that he realized he could no longer hear the calls. The needle-carpeted forest around him crackled softly under its own movement.

That was when Esen's friends came out of the brush. Four young men, trading hot glances between themselves as they swung from their mounts. Their suede boots pressed silently into the needle matting. Baoxiang knew, instantly, what his future held. But worse than the foreknowledge of pain was his powerlessness to control the gush of fear that made his hands sweat and his legs shake. For most of his life, he'd had the idea that Esen and other men were somehow able to master their fear when he was unable. It was only recently that he'd figured out:

they didn't feel it as he did. Oh, they *had* fear. But they weren't conscious of it. They were swimmers in a strong clear current that they never noticed, or fought against, even as it pulled them this way and that.

He dropped the hare and raised his bow. It trembled, but his anger made it the easiest thing he had ever done.

He loosed.

Hitting a target had nothing to do with focusing on the draw or release. It was about desire. You didn't make a shot—it *happened,* because you focused your desire on the target, and your body channeled that desire. And now, alongside his fear, Baoxiang felt the fury-girded strength of pure desire. To hit. To *hurt*.

He desired, and the arrow obeyed. But a warrior, unlike a straw target or a hare, didn't stand still to be shot. The arrow cut through the space where the young warrior had been, and buried itself in the tree behind.

There was silence as the three who were standing, and the one who'd dived to the ground, stared in shock at the vibrating arrow. It was as if they couldn't believe Baoxiang's disproportionate response. But, Baoxiang thought with furious terror, it *was* proportionate. They just had no idea what it was like to be afraid.

Now, ten years later, as another pack of warriors dismounted and advanced on him, he let them see his fear. It was a performance, even as it was also the truth: that he trembled, and the ledgers moistened in his grasp. He knew that seeing his fear gave them the illusion of control. But what they didn't realize was that the insults they hurled—their excitement at the hunt—were new only to them. Baoxiang had done all of this before. *He* was in control, because he knew how it ended.

The first of the young nobles pushed Baoxiang on the chest. Lightly, easily: a predator playing with its food. "Books! Why does a man need so many books? Going off to read them under the moon somewhere?"

The others joined in. They batted him lightly, discovering the game as they played it. Baoxiang's heart leapt as he stumbled. When he recovered, his eyes found the Third Prince. His young, bearded face had the aroused look of someone relishing his own mastery: the hunter who, knowing he can call off his dogs, chooses not to. Of course he didn't want to call them off. He wanted to see Baoxiang punished for his desires.

The young men laughed and pressed close. Their shoves grew rougher, and this time when Baoxiang overbalanced he fell onto the plaza with a cry. His books spilled out in a fan that stopped against the Third Prince's toe.

The Third Prince crouched over the book. Despite his lingering adolescent lankiness, he moved with a warrior's perfect physical confidence. His face shone with interest. But Baoxiang knew it was the kind of interest that, under the eyes of his peers, would kindle into violence.

The Third Prince touched the characters on the book's cover. "Not even poetry! Accounting. How boring."

Baoxiang stifled the first comment that came to mind: *Congratulations, you can read.* Out loud he said evenly, "It shouldn't be so surprising. I'm an accountant."

The Third Prince's color was high. His breath came fast, though no doubt he was telling himself it was disgust. "That's not all you are."

Baoxiang was intensely aware of his own vulnerability. He saw that the Third Prince had excised his own desires from his memory of what had happened between them, so that it had become solely a matter of Baoxiang's deviance. Baoxiang had foisted that deviance upon the Third Prince—had made him feel threatened and uncomfortable—and now he wanted to hurt the source of those feelings. Baoxiang understood the Third Prince's expression perfectly. It wanted what everyone wanted when they looked at him: to eradicate the hateful thing that didn't fit into the world as they had made it.

The Third Prince wore an onyx archery ring on his thumb. He had big, long-fingered hands that were calloused from the sword and bow. Hands made to hurt.

But, to Baoxiang's surprise, the hurt didn't happen. When Baoxiang twisted around to follow the direction of the Third Prince's gaze, he found a sedan chair drawing up.

The Empress looked down at them. Her small mouth pouted in cruel pleasure. "Third Prince! Why are you blocking the road? Please clear the way. It's my night with the Great Khan, and I would hate to hurry my preparations and disappoint him. After all, when you're accustomed to chewing on old bones—you do *so* much look forward to the taste of meat."

The Third Prince's face whitened, though the curve on his Buddha mouth suggested nothing so much as disdain. He rose, Baoxiang's book in hand, and bowed before remounting.

After the young nobles had gone, the Empress turned to Baoxiang. He told himself that she couldn't kill him in broad daylight in the middle of the Imperial City, but his body didn't believe it. He trembled. "I'm surprised you haven't done it yet."

The Empress's smirk was gone. There was no pleasure in what she wanted to do to Baoxiang, only hatred. "Since I have the satisfaction of watching everyone else making your life miserable," she said, "I can afford to take my time."

☀

Baoxiang's uniform hat, with its two flanges that nearly brushed the corridor walls on either side, cast distorted shadows as he passed in and out of the spare lantern-light. Deep inside the private rear wing of the Third Prince's residence, the long corridors of paper-paneled doors branched, and branched again. At each junction the paths seemed to lead identically into darkness. The Third Prince's head servant walked ahead. It was cold inside, even for late autumn. Baoxiang passed under a lantern that washed out his vision, and when it came back: it was there. A figure, rounding the corner at the end of the passage, already gone, even as his heart slammed with recognition.

Gone, but those had been his brother's looped braids, beaded with jade and gold; his broad shoulders in his favorite kingfisher-blue riding costume; his side-split skirts that kicked out with each step to reveal the layered robes beneath, like a bird's secret plumage visible only in flight.

Baoxiang didn't stop to think. He lunged after Esen's ghost, soft boots skidding on the floorboards. He was choking on this feeling; choking on anger; he had no idea what he was going to do when he caught him—

The Third Prince's servant gave him a startled look as he hurtled around the corner. Baoxiang wrenched to a stop, panting. There was nothing there. The abrupt loss of a target for his feelings was dismembering. The servant indicated a door and murmured, "The Crystal Room."

The Third Prince looked up sharply as the door opened. The ledger lay on the desk in front of him. His bowed upper lip curled in a pretense of surprise.

But none of it was a surprise. When Baoxiang had arrived at the Third Prince's residence, there'd been no sign of the jeering young nobles from that afternoon. The Third Prince would have made his excuses to them, book in hand. He'd been waiting for Baoxiang to come.

Baoxiang glided over the raised threshold. *Here I am.* In contrast to the corridor, the Crystal Room blazed with light. Baoxiang had the feeling of having shivered through a membrane through which the ghost couldn't pass. And yet he had brought his anger with him into the brightness, where now it found its new target.

The Crystal Room's harsh glitter quivered on the Third Prince's bare throat, and caught in his silver-beaded braids. Every surface in the room was laden with ornaments of that rarest of materials: glass. Vases and ewers that resembled milky green porcelain had a translucency that made them seem more fragile than any solid substance should be. A crimson reliquary's bloody depths glowed as if it contained mysterious life. There was glass with familiar dragons and phoenixes, and glass infinitely strange: enameled, embossed, shimmering like oil on water, encircled in the gilded script of the western khanates. Goods that had been made and traded generations before the Mongol conquests that had destroyed those traditions forever.

And amongst all those precious pieces: the Third Prince, with his hidden heart of glass. The Third Prince, pretending that he didn't want what he wanted. Pretending that he didn't flinch at his mother's rejection, and the Empress's taunts, and who used his arrogance to hide his fear: that he would only ever be a prince destined for replacement.

The Third Prince pretended, and Baoxiang had his own pretense to deliver. He had the same bright, savage feeling of control he'd had when he'd faced the Third Prince's cronies. He was the only one here who knew how this would end.

The walnut floor was so polished that when he bowed, his reflection floated beneath him as in a night sky. "This lowly one has come to ask if the Third Prince has finished with the book he borrowed."

Third Prince's attention was as taut as a wire. He would have convinced himself that his possession of the book was nothing more than an extension of the afternoon's bullying, even as his body thrummed with hope for what Baoxiang might do. He said to the servant, "Leave us."

Baoxiang added smoothly, "Wait outside. I don't dare take up too much of the Prince's time."

A humiliated blush crawled up the Third Prince's face. Far from extinguishing his anticipation, shame would be winching it even tighter. The thought of someone standing outside, listening, was inseparable from its corollary: of what could happen, in this glass-filled room, that risked making noise.

The door closed. Baoxiang didn't move. He could relieve the Third Prince's tension by going over and doing what he'd done before. The Third Prince might not even punch him first, this time. But he had no desire to be an anonymous mouth that would be discarded at the first pang of denial.

He almost laughed to see the Third Prince finally conclude that Baoxiang wasn't going to offer. Oh, how he must hate Baoxiang for forcing him to acknowledge his shameful desire! Baoxiang saw, with an anticipation so black that it canceled out any fear, that his cruelty was going to be met with cruelty.

The Third Prince rose and came swiftly around the desk. Their boots shushed on the floor as the Third Prince advanced, and Baoxiang retreated, until Baoxiang's shoulders hit the wall.

Baoxiang wasn't short. In a year or two, perhaps the Third Prince would be taller. But for now they were of a height. The Third Prince's eyes were bright with the hunger to hurt. He plucked off Baoxiang's hat and rested his hand lightly on his topknot. "Why do you wear your hair like this?"

Long after Baoxiang had adopted his flamboyant gowns, he had kept his hair in braids. It hadn't even seemed like something that *could* be changed. It wasn't until he was an adult that he'd realized the laws went only one way: they forbade Nanren from wearing braids. Even then, he hadn't mustered the courage to try a topknot until his father had been away. He remembered how self-conscious he'd been as he wrestled his hair up for the first time. But when he'd gone outside, and eyes sliced into him in shock and contempt, he'd felt his self-consciousness transform into a perverse pride. Other men had always thought he dishonored a warrior's braids, but the idea that he didn't crave their cherished status—that he neither respected nor cared about it—infuriated them even more.

He said, cool, "Why hide this handsome face behind hair?"

The Third Prince smiled without humor. Even when Baoxiang was in well-slept good health, his features were too Mongol for Nanren tastes, and too Nanren for Mongol tastes. But they both knew his looks weren't what mattered here. The Third Prince wrapped his fingers around Baoxiang's topknot. Then, in one controlled movement, he wrenched Baoxiang's head against the wall. Baoxiang stifled a sound of pain as he was pulled up onto his toes.

"Look at you," the Third Prince said softly. He wasn't a real warrior as Esen had been, only a soft imperial prince, but it was still easy for him. His fingers dug under Baoxiang's hair clasp and pulled up harder. "You're so weak and afraid. You can't even fight. When they pushed you, you just fell." His gaze traced the line of Baoxiang's throat, with its man's sharp knot and shadow of evening stubble. "How many times have you fallen, and men praised your mouth afterwards, I wonder?"

Baoxiang's scalp was about to come off. But the knowledge that it was *he* who was controlling the Third Prince's reactions transformed the pain into a satisfaction so savage that it verged on enjoyment.

He couldn't fight, but that didn't make him the weakest one in the room. Or the most afraid.

He said into the Third Prince's ear, "Would you like to hear what I was thinking about, when I fell?" The memory was already near the surface, from before. Now he twisted it, in the bitter knowledge that the distortion would be believed more readily than the truth. "My older brother used to have friends just like yours. When I was young, I was fascinated by them. I used to follow them around to watch them spar and sweat, and take off their clothes to wash afterwards. They weren't men yet, but they had men's bodies. When I was alone, I would think about how different those bodies were from mine, and how they made me feel. So when those same young men came upon me alone in the forest one day, I knew what I wanted."

Baoxiang eased down from his toes as the Third Prince's grip slackened. The sadistic impulse gave his voice the same quality as when he spoke with his actual lovers, as if his desire for cruelty had substituted seamlessly for desire itself. "And they knew what I wanted, without my having to ask. They just opened their clothes. And I went down on my knees for them."

For a moment, the memory sprang back to its true shape. How he'd curled on the damp ground, his screams and pleas spurring them to hit harder, kick harder. Even more than pain, the memory was of shame: of powerlessness, and humiliation. Now, as he crafted it into a fantasy that he poured into the Third Prince's ear, he had the feeling of passing on those emotions as intimately as a kiss. Around them, the crystal caught and flung the lamplight in a trembling rainbow scatter across the room.

The Third Prince's throat clicked as he swallowed. The hand in Baoxiang's hair slid to the back of his neck and grasped it in wordless command. *Down.*

It was so pleasurable to refuse. Instead, Baoxiang wormed his hand between them and undid the turquoise-ornamented belt that cinched the Third Prince's sleeveless overcoat. They were so close that he could make out the threads of silvered paper that made up the five-clawed imperial dragons in the heavy damask. Underneath the coat, the Third Prince's robe was silver brocade with braided black ribbons around the waist and a side closure of three knotted buttons.

The Third Prince shuddered and turned his face away when Baoxiang touched him.

Baoxiang knew what it was like to be young and plagued by desire. He'd had ample outlets for his own urges at that age, and their fulfillment had been an ordinary and enjoyable part of life. He could only imagine how intense those urges must be for someone who never had any opportunity. He worked his hand steadily. It would be uneven, a little frustrating, as it always was with someone who wasn't yourself. But it was precisely that frustration that lit up an inexperienced young body with ecstatic astonishment: that it was *real.*

All Baoxiang could see of the Third Prince's turned-away face was an ear and bearded cheek. But the cheek was dark and the neck flickered with strain. He seemed rooted to the spot by humiliation: of being forced to endure Baoxiang's undeniable maleness as they stood body-to-body; of knowing his servant was listening outside the door as he was being broken down within. His distress filled Baoxiang with vicious relish. Whatever Baoxiang had been before, this was where his pleasure lived now: in the cruelty of forcing someone into the most vulnerable part of themselves, where they could be destroyed.

Every so often, back when Baoxiang had been a lanky, awkward boy, Esen had taken him to one of the pleasure houses in Anyang. Esen had never been one for courtesans—he claimed to lack the patience and education to enjoy their flirtatious games—but he'd known what Baoxiang liked. Typical Esen, Baoxiang thought savagely. He could feel the ghost in the darkness beyond the door, watching. Esen had known Baoxiang's preferences, but he'd never had the courage to be honest with himself about his own.

All these fools with their hidden desires. All their denial ever accomplished was to open a door for someone to understand them better than they understood themselves. Someone who would use that understanding to hurt them.

The Third Prince came silently. Baoxiang felt a rush of triumph, and was briefly tempted to try to undo him further. Instead he wiped his hand on the Third Prince's linen undertrousers and edged out from the wall. Anxious as he was to secure protection against the Empress's plans, it would be better to let the Third Prince sit with the encounter—to let the molten edges of it cool to something that could be handled. After that, it would be safe to do it again. And with each repetition, the Third Prince would learn: that if he kept Baoxiang safe, he could keep having what he wanted.

That was the main problem with this approach, Baoxiang thought darkly. It couldn't move any faster than the pace of a human heart. He took the ledger from the desk and left.

❊

The paper in the round lattice window of Baoxiang's living room was so old and browned that instead of reflecting clear lamplight, it glowed as darkly as a peach slice held up to the sun. It had started raining after Baoxiang returned from the Third Prince's palace, hours ago. Now the steady thrum made him feel gently enclosed—separate and separated, in his wakefulness, from those in the slumbering city outside.

A curl of linden wood fell away under his chisel. It was more craft than artistry, what he was doing—at least, with his low level of skill—and it brought none of the joy he'd once had in painting or calligraphy. But there was some satisfaction in seeing vision become form. The woodcut gradually took shape under his hands as the rain continued its rhythm. The chests full of gold taels stood against the wall under the white smears of ghosts.

Baoxiang shook the shavings off the finished printing plate and laid the mallet and chisel next to a pile of bamboo message tubes. He felt gritty with exhaustion. But the idea of going back to bed, only for the sound to jerk him awake several times an hour, filled him with despair. At least when he was working he was suffering *usefully.*

The cut surface of the plate took the rice-paste glue well, then the ink. When he smoothed the paper onto it, then peeled the paper away, a familiar self-satisfied face stared back at him. It was, he thought grimly, a good likeness.

The city's Drum Tower thudded out the fourth watch. Seyhan came in shortly afterwards; it was the month in which he rose before dawn to eat, then fasted until sundown, in accordance with his traditions of worship. "You didn't sleep at all?" Then, seeing Baoxiang's poster, he chuckled. "Rice Bucket Zhang! What's that for?"

The message tubes on Baoxiang's desk were in labeled piles. *Zhang. Zhu. Chen.* Baoxiang took the topmost tube from the fourth pile, *Ouyang,* and tossed it over.

"He's on his way?" Seyhan scanned the message. Baoxiang's embedded spies used a cipher to protect their communications, but Baoxiang had already written out the deciphered text at the bottom of the sheet. Seyhan's colorless eyes widened in astonishment. "He's *not.*"

The taste of blood was in Baoxiang's mouth. He remembered Ouyang striding onto the broken causeway, gloved in it. "No. He'd no sooner left Bianliang than he was blindsided by that rebel who calls himself the Radiant King. Zhu Yuanzhang." How superior Ouyang had always considered himself to Baoxiang! For nothing more than his ability to swing a sword, he'd been lifted out of slavehood and into the sunlight of Esen's regard, and Esen had stared into that beautiful mirror and seen what he valued most in himself. Every martial quality Baoxiang never had; every quality he'd never *wanted* to have. But now Ouyang had been defeated. He'd been hurt, and held down, and tasted the same helplessness that Baoxiang felt every moment of his life. *Look at your cherished general now.*

Of all the people in the world to love, Esen had chosen the only one who could never be anything other than the death of him. And yet he'd been so shocked at Ouyang's betrayal. The bloody taste in Baoxiang's mouth strengthened into an insensate anger that wanted to bite, and bite again, until he reached bone. Esen's pain in that moment had been *glorious.* For the first time in his charmed life, his brother had finally understood how much it hurt to be betrayed.

Ouyang had been the weapon Baoxiang had stabbed into Esen's heart. And even now, he was Baoxiang's to use. His brother's general was good at one thing—and one thing only—and he was as predictable as a messenger pigeon. Baoxiang would use him, and then when he was done—

Oh, brother, keep watching! That will be the best show of all.

"Zhu Yuanzhang defeated General Ouyang?" Seyhan's gaze sharpened. "You knew that would happen."

"Wasn't it obvious? Zhu Yuanzhang couldn't overcome General Zhang's forces with what he had. So he looked around, and there was General Ouyang in Bianliang. Remember, he'd met him before. He knew what the General wanted, and the ways in which his desperation would make him weak."

"So now Zhu Yuanzhang and General Ouyang will take on the Zhangs." The window-paper had brightened, banishing the ghosts. Seyhan looked perturbed. "But with General Zhang's capabilities—he might be able to stand against the both of them."

Baoxiang rose and brushed wood shavings off his uniform. It took him a moment to parse the pressing sensation in his ears. Silence. It had finally stopped raining. "Indeed. Which is why *you,* my dear secretary, are going to print enough of these posters to blanket Pingjiang. Tell our men there to put one up on every street corner. I want Rice Bucket Zhang to see his face every time he turns around."

The vast expanse of the Empire of the Great Yuan, scattered with armies and contenders for the throne, was as legible to Baoxiang as if he were the Jade Emperor looking down from Heaven. Every other player saw only the slice of the game board nearest to himself. It was Baoxiang alone, with his networks built long before he'd become the Prince of Henan, who saw everything. His control felt as fine-edged as a blade fresh from the whetstone. He said, savagely, "This next part is going to be fun."

The rain had turned the unpaved streets of Baoxiang's ward into sharp-smelling yellow mud that flicked up from wheels and hooves. Morning fog sent the ends of the streets receding into a dreary blue distance, punctuated here and there by the blaze of a poplar. Mud-splattered servants and ordinary people parted for Baoxiang's horse without an upwards glance as he made his way towards the Ministry.

His route took him off the main avenues and along the course of the Imperial City's private water supply, which ran in a marble canal that raised it over the common streams and gutters. As he neared the Imperial City, the canal-side path narrowed and weeping larches pressed in from each side. There was the smell of oncoming rain. Above the treetops that marked the line of the Imperial City's walls, dark clouds pressed down on a narrowing stripe of bright sky.

He startled as a girl cut onto the path in front of him. She glanced over her shoulder, saw Baoxiang's horse bearing down on her, screamed and dropped her basket. Persimmons burst out and scattered across the path.

Baoxiang, who would have ridden over the fruit without a second thought, was forced to rein in as the melon-headed idiot dived in front of his horse with a dismayed cry and began gathering up the fruit.

"Would you mind," he said acidly. The girl looked up and smiled with dazzling familiarity. It took Baoxiang a moment to realize she wasn't a stranger after all: she was the maid from the office.

"Oh! Greetings to the Prince of Henan, who has the habit of startling this unworthy maid. I beg the Prince to wait. There's all this fruit, and I only have the one pair of hands." She dimpled at him. "Unless the Prince feels bestirred to help . . ."

The notion that he, a Prince of the Blood, might dismount and dirty his hands for the sake of a *servant* sent an unexpected fizz of humor through him.

The girl laughed at his expression. Her eyes flicked over the rest of him, warm, and her dimples deepened. "I suppose it would be a shame if the Prince's uniform were to become muddy."

Before Baoxiang could muster up a suitably cutting response, they were jolted by a patter of rain. The girl snatched up her basket and dashed under a tree. Peering through the down-slanting branches, she called to Baoxiang, "There's room here for two."

Baoxiang hesitated, wondering if he might make it to the Ministry before the worst of the downpour, but his rapidly softening hat made the decision for him. The tree's skirt of branches hung so low he had to dismount and duck inside on foot.

The rain, intensifying, poured in a circular sheet around them, scything a dark line in the corona of fallen needles. There was a strong resinous smell like a new-made bow. "Your feet have stayed dry," the girl said laughingly, "but I'm afraid the Prince's uniform will get wet from that saddle later. Unfortunate for someone whose job involves so much sitting. Since it's my fault the Prince is caught out here in the rain, perhaps I should offer him my cloak to sit upon."

She touched the neck of her cloak, looking up at him from under her lashes. With a detached feeling, Baoxiang realized she was flirting with him.

She was so much smaller than him. He gazed down at her dimpled smile and the curves that threatened the side seams of her uniform. She was waiting for him, lips parted and breath held. But instead of excitement, a tide of futility swept through him. In another world—in that dead world to which there was no return—he would have leaned down and kissed her. Sheltered from the rain by the tree's branches, they would have fallen laughing to the ground and taken pleasure in each other's bodies.

He *remembered* the joy and generosity of that kind of play. But now there was only blackness where those emotions had once kindled. He had a sharp image of the anguished strain in the Third Prince's neck as he turned his face away. Baoxiang had done that to him. And instead of harboring an answering heat in his own body, all he'd felt at that moment was the desire for destruction. That was the only capacity for connection he had left: for pain and cruelty, given and received. This bright, lively girl liked him, and the only thing it would bring her would be ruin.

He drew back. It was second nature to let his expression twist into disdain. "Do you think you're pretty enough to catch the eye of a prince? If you want to whore yourself out for special favors, better to aim at lower-ranking officials! Even if I liked women, I wouldn't dirty myself with someone as cheap and common as you."

He left her under the tree without looking back. Maybe after everything was over, she would realize he'd done her a kindness.

It wasn't until after he'd reached the Ministry that it occurred to him that it was odd to have run into the girl on that side of the city. Maids didn't live in the bureaucrats' quarter, and the Ram's Head Market, the closest to the Ministry, was in the other direction entirely.

It was a faded afternoon, but the Minister's office was cozy with lamps and braziers. The carpet wall-coverings made it feel like a book-filled ger. It gave Baoxiang a bittersweet feeling. Here, thousands of li from where he'd grown up outcast for his interests, his father's Mongol culture coexisted with the scholarly values of the civilization it had conquered. This blending wasn't even something he'd yearned for. How could you yearn for what you couldn't imagine?

The Minister leafed through Baoxiang's entries in the current ledger of the master accounts. When he reached for the official seal in its box on his desk, Baoxiang couldn't help saying, "Perhaps the Minister might like to take his time to check my accuracy. If there was an error in the master accounts, but your seal was upon it—"

The Minister gave him a crinkled look of amusement as he pressed his seal into the cinnabar, then stamped the page. "No need to worry for my neck, Wang Baoxiang. I haven't found a mistake in your work yet. And if I did find one, my fear would be that it was a failing of my own capacity, rather than yours."

It would have been easier had the Minister been a more unpleasant person. Baoxiang's bittersweetness became acrid, like a pot of sugar forgotten over the fire. "If the Minister has no further need of me—" He rose. "I'll start the accounts for the Bureau of Military Affairs."

"Ah, this silly way that everyone feels they can't leave before I go home! Do you really want to huddle over your desk until your youth withers? If the day's work is done, go. Make a habit of it! I won't be much longer myself, in any case."

With the Empress out for his blood, Baoxiang couldn't complain about the prospect of getting home before nightfall. He bowed gratefully. "I'll leave first, then."

He headed out. It was his most hated time of day: when the long shadows finally overcame his ability to ignore the prospect of yet another sleepless night. The sky above the cedars was the color of despair. It was too early for stars. Without the River of Heaven as a ceiling, he had the stomach-turning feeling of his gaze falling upwards into emptiness. There was nothing to catch on to; there was nothing to stop him from falling forever.

When he reached Pingzhe Gate Street he turned his horse in to his own ward. The hoofbeats of another rider coming through the gate after him made his heart jump. But it wasn't even dark, and there were potential witnesses out and about. The Empress wouldn't try to kill him if she couldn't maintain deniability. If she didn't, Lady Ki would be very happy to use Baoxiang's murder against her. It was reassuring: that as much as the Empress hated him, she hated Lady Ki more.

The rider behind was moving fast. Baoxiang glanced over as the other man drew level. He was an ordinary stranger, his attention on the street ahead. But for some reason Baoxiang's heart jumped again.

It had no time to settle: hands seized him from behind, and yanked.

Baoxiang was a mediocre rider by Mongol standards, but even he couldn't remember the last time he'd fallen from a horse. It hurt when he slammed into the mud, but his primary agony came from disbelief. He couldn't believe the Empress had been so stupid as to act in public. He couldn't believe *he'd* been stupid enough to think she wasn't. He twitched like a smashed beetle as his two assailants dismounted and came over.

One of the assailants straddled his chest. Baoxiang's fear rose, bringing memory with it. Pine-needle matting against his cheek, and his own contemptible cries as the young men's blows landed. It had been an endless moment, one in which his continuously formed hope for an end was continually disappointed. On and on it went, until—it didn't.

Esen dragged him up. He looked stormy to the point of unfamiliarity. Behind him, Ouyang's girl's face wore the same naked contempt as that of Baoxiang's vanished tormentors.

Baoxiang hung in Esen's grip, crying. He was in an agony of humiliation; he couldn't stop himself. And yet he was aware that some wretched part of himself was flaunting his tears at Esen as a challenge. He was taking the ugly truth of his pain and smashing it into his perfect brother's face. How could Esen believe that his refusal to be what everyone wanted him to be was easy, or cowardly, when this was the price he paid?

Esen was silent. For a moment Baoxiang let himself believe that this time, because he was asking for it—because he *needed* it—Esen would see.

Then Esen said in a voice tight with anger, "Pull yourself together."

Of course, Baoxiang thought dimly. That was why Esen had been rough. His anger wasn't at what his friends had done. It was at Baoxiang, for letting them do it. With a curdled feeling, he saw that Esen had waited that long to speak only so he could resist the urge to hit Baoxiang himself.

Esen wasn't Baoxiang's protector. He was a young warrior, like those other young warriors. He felt the same as they did. Stunned, Baoxiang realized: *You hate me, too.*

Now, crushed into the Khanbaliq mud by a nameless assassin, paralyzed by fear and pain, Baoxiang felt Esen's presence. In his mind's eye, the ghost was a little way down the street, invisible to everyone but Baoxiang, watching him with that same stony hatred. The weight on his chest was unbearable. Baoxiang was weak, and helpless, and afraid, and now there was nobody to save him. He heard his own gasps and knew he was about to die.

Happy now, brother? You always wished for me to cease to exist as I am. Now you'll get your wish, and you didn't even have to lift a finger for it. The world has done it for you. It's put me in my place; it's given me what I deserve.

Hands reached for his throat, and the ghost's presence strengthened. It was as if Esen were crouching at his shoulder. The flicker in his peripheral vision could have been the ends of braids. All at once, Baoxiang's detachment collapsed. He had plunged through ice and been swallowed by an enormity beneath. What feeling could possibly be so terrible, or so big? It had to be anger. But instead of delivering the familiar rush of savage, righteous pleasure, this anger was awful and throbbing. It was like being sawn apart. In the grip of that pain, all he could think was how he would never get what he wanted. He would never hurt Esen as much as Esen had hurt him.

But he wasn't strangled. Fingers dived into his mouth, and Baoxiang tasted dirty skin. Before they killed him, *they were going to pull out his tongue.* His wordless howl was pure terror.

"—be very careful, little prince." Through a thicket of panic, he realized he was being addressed. "If you aren't, we'll cut this one off, along with—" He let go of Baoxiang's tongue and grabbed between Baoxiang's legs, squeezing until he screamed. "—this small bird."

The man released him and rose. Baoxiang curled around himself like a shrimp, panting and shivering, as they left. He could barely gather his thoughts about what had happened. If the Empress wanted him dead, why let him go? Was she just toying with him? Or—

Like most people in Khanbaliq, his assailant had spoken non-native Mongolian with the strong inflection of another tongue. But, now that Baoxiang thought about it, that other tongue hadn't been familiar Han'er, or any of the other Nanren languages of the Central Plains or coast, or even the far south where the Nanren sounded more like the people of Cham than they did those in Henan. Baoxiang didn't speak that other language himself. But he knew who did.

His assailant hadn't been one of the *Empress's* men. He'd been Lady Ki's.

And he'd heard that Goryeo accent somewhere else, too. He had a flash of dimples; a basket of persimmons.

In a stroke, it made sense. The Third Prince might not yet know his own mind—but his mother knew. She'd seen how the Third Prince looked at Baoxiang. She must have had reports of Baoxiang visiting the Third Prince's residence. So she'd used the flirtatious maid to test if Baoxiang's preferences were genuine, or if he was only pretending as part of a plot to expose or blackmail her son.

Baoxiang's horror increased. Hindsight showed him exactly how close his escape had been. If he'd accepted the girl's flirtation—which he might have, because he *was* pretending—Lady Ki wouldn't have sent him a warning. She'd have killed him. He'd be dead before the Empress even had her chance to try.

There should have been some satisfaction in having survived. The radiating ache from his balls was already fading, and as far as beatings he'd received in his life, it hadn't even been that bad. But the awful, throbbing anger that Esen's presence had evoked had left him with a wrung-out griminess that felt like the aftermath of tears.

By the time he levered himself up, it was dark. The ghost was gone. A ledger book was lying in the mud where it had fallen out of his uniform. It was ruined—a waste of several days' effort—but he couldn't leave it here. He'd have to burn it discreetly later.

He found his horse in an alley overshadowed by closed-face walls, mounted painfully, and rode home.

7

TAIZHOU

The fishing boat bobbed in the dark. In the shielded lanternlight from the bow, Ouyang could barely make out the half dozen hunkered shapes of Zhu's armored, armed men. The second boat, reduced to a floating point of light that could have been anywhere between an arm's length or one li distant, carried the remainder of the team. The blackness gave Ouyang the feeling of being suspended in the center of an infinite void. Ahead, Fortress Island's seawall rose in a featureless mass against the clouded sky; beneath, the reflectionless water descended.

Back at the inn, Zhu had laid out his plan as though it were completely sensible.

"To get into the tunnels via the underwater sea entrances, we'll need two things." When Zhu leaned forwards over his bowl of soup, everyone except Ouyang unconsciously matched him. "Firstly, if we want to go in at night, the water will be pitch-black: we'll need some way to see where the mouth of the tunnel opens under the surface. Fortunately—and I'm sure this possibility never even occurred to that poor Yuan detachment—I can make a light that shines underwater. Secondly, we need someone who can swim."

On this last point, he had the temerity to look at Ouyang. But whatever quelling power Ouyang's glare had on his own men, either it was ineffective on Zhu or too diluted by the mask. Zhu said, undissuaded, "If I wanted to take my army across a river deeper than a man's height, I'd need barges. But you wouldn't, would you? That time you faced the Red Turbans at Ying River:

instead of having your army cross the bridge to our position, you sent them downstream to swim across to ambush our flank."

Ouyang had a flash of churning black water bearing down through a gorge towards him. He unclenched his jaw enough to grit out, "I *tried* to have them swim across."

If Zhu was gloating, he had the grace to hide it. "So I have a light, and you can swim. If you tow me while I light our way, we can swim through to the dry part of the tunnel and place an underwater line for the others to pull themselves along."

Ouyang wasn't conservative by nature; he'd made his career as a general on the success of a number of risky endeavors. But what Zhu proposed was far beyond the threshold of anything he would have considered. And even apart from that—"You took my army. You're keeping me prisoner. And now you're asking me to *help* you?"

"If I fail here," Zhu answered evenly, "consider that you also fail."

Ouyang thought of the bone-deep desperation that had driven him to run. It wasn't as if he hadn't known the odds were stacked against him. But as bad as those odds had been, how could he have turned down the opportunity when it was better than whatever chance of success Zhu represented? And now—couldn't he still find a way to run again? Couldn't he overpower Zhu and his dozen men, steal a horse, and make it back to Yingtian? If it truly came down to it, couldn't he fling himself into the sea and *swim*?

As if Zhu knew the direction of his thoughts, he said, "Is that really better odds than what I'm proposing, General?"

It was, Ouyang was surprised to discover, a choice. He was suddenly, terribly cognizant of never having had to choose before. There had only ever been the one path. But now a choice presented itself—a choice between two sets of astronomically bad odds—and upon that choice rested either the success or failure of the thing he wanted most in the world. The thing he had done everything for.

The thought that came on its heels was as awful as it was clarifying: *The thing I would do anything for.*

Even cooperate with someone he hated as much as Zhu.

If his best chance to reunite with his army in Yingtian truly was for Zhu to not fail here in Taizhou—then Ouyang would have to make sure he didn't fail.

He *would* do anything, but even so: he had to force the words out. "Perhaps you aren't aware of how unforgiving an environment it is underwater. That far down, any mistake means death. Even a single moment of panic could be fatal. There'll be no turning back and no chance of rescue if something goes wrong."

Had Ouyang himself bent an enemy into acquiescence, he wouldn't have hesitated to rub it in their face for the pleasure of their humiliation. He could imagine other men being smug in triumph, or—worse—callously receiving his cooperation as something to which they felt themselves entitled. But Zhu wasn't smug or callous. He regarded Ouyang with a gravity that felt surprisingly like respect. In that gratingly light voice that should have made him ridiculous, he said, "I'm aware of the risks. If I wasn't willing to risk anything, how could I have a hope of getting what I want? If you know one thing about me, General, then know this: I'll do whatever it takes."

Now Ouyang stood up in the boat and looked down at the black water where it sucked gently at the base of the wall. They had finally unbound his hands. A short line around his waist connected him to Zhu, and a longer line from Zhu's waist connected them to the boat. It made him feel like a sacrifice about to be made. Even though he was ostensibly cooperating of his own free will, the situation was clear enough: if he changed his mind and refused to jump, they would push him. And then there would only be one way forwards that wouldn't let his revenge die.

Zhu stood up beside him. His dark-armored form was abruptly shrouded in an eerie pneuma of flickering pale light as if someone had taken the cover off a lamp. His Mandate. In the otherworldly glow, his determination looked inhuman. Something about that expression sent a peculiar sensation curling through Ouyang, as of recognition. He said harshly, "Last chance for second thoughts."

His answer was a splash. The boat rocked wildly, and he saw Zhu's glowing figure receding from the surface. Then the rope between them pulled tight, and Ouyang went in after.

☼

The water was so cold it felt hot. The pain sent a rush of false heat and life into Ouyang's body, like the fever that made men cast off their clothes in the moments before they died in the snow. The small muscles between his ribs spasmed and fluttered. His eyes stung fiercely. He could make out Zhu hanging below the surface in the center of a ghostly sphere carved out of the blackness. The light found nothing to illuminate except the sheer rock face dropping into the unseen depths beneath them.

Ouyang had learned to swim in the silt-choked rivers of landlocked Henan. Fresh water was straightforward. It wanted you to sink. To his unpleasant surprise the sea was muscular and dynamic, expanding and contracting in internal swells that carried him in every direction. It fought back as he kicked and clawed his way deeper, towing Zhu behind him by the umbilical connecting them. A sharp pain drilled in his ears. He couldn't help thinking about a man he'd once seen executed by having a band tightened around his head. Would his head explode if they went too deep? There was a point at which even a body as hardened as Ouyang's own began screaming warnings: that it was moving too fast, falling too far. It was screaming now as he forced it past what it instinctively knew as the point of no return. Down and down they went.

Then, finally, there was the tunnel mouth: a deeper blackness that resisted the penetration of Zhu's light. There was no time for hesitation. Ouyang kicked strongly to stop their fall, alarmed by the effort it took to counteract the burden of Zhu hanging off him, and swam inside.

The walls were smooth white limestone without any handholds to pull himself along by. Ouyang cleaved to the right-hand wall as he'd been instructed. With his every kick forwards, the line around his waist seemed to yank him back. His lungs burned. Every body length felt like something he was clawing out of rock.

His shadow fell ahead of him over the white floor of the tunnel. If it hadn't been so much effort, it might have been like flying. Zhu's light from behind him bloomed and billowed as Ouyang's passage kicked up fine sediment into bright clouds that obscured and reflected the light by turns.

To their left the wall receded outside the light, and Ouyang had the sense of a vast cavernous openness where it had been.

All it would take was for him to lose the right-hand wall, and they would go drifting into the void. That would be the end of them both. *My body, eaten by worms.* Ouyang remembered the two monks eerily summoning not just the ghost of their own past, but the futures of everyone present. That was his future; that was his rest and reward for everything he'd done and would have to do; and for a moment his yearning for it was as acute as the pain in his lungs.

But that future wasn't here. He kept kicking.

The light dimmed sharply. It returned as he glanced behind. Zhu was still there: a small dark shape floating in the circle of light he cast on the moving clouds of white silt.

Then the light flickered again, more extreme this time: a flash of pure darkness.

Ouyang kicked forwards with renewed effort, refusing to think about what would happen if the light went out. He knew from experience that the painful urge to breathe was only his body's complaining long before it approached its limit. But for those without experience, pain all too easily transformed to panic: they believed they were dying, long before they actually were. Against his will, he felt a moment's grudging admiration for how long Zhu had managed to hold on. But he didn't know how much longer they had.

Each time Zhu's light flickered now, the darkness lasted longer. Ouyang's rib muscles convulsed as he clawed forwards. It was hard to tell what was the light flickering and what was his own vision coming apart from the lack of air.

Zhu's light went out, and it didn't come back on.

Ouyang's lungs acted without his control: they gasped in a huge breath of that pitch darkness. It was only when he heard the sound that he realized what he breathed was air and not water. He had surfaced, and his body had known it before he did. Somehow in that blind, gasping moment he had just enough presence of mind to haul on the rope.

Had Zhu surfaced? All Ouyang could hear was his own rasping breaths and the thunder of his heart.

Then, all at once: pain.

Light.

Ouyang blinked furiously, as if willpower alone could be

enough to focus his eyes that were streaming from salt and the assault of light after darkness. A shape wavered into view: a dark head beside his.

Zhu's eyes were screwed shut in agony as he sucked in air. Ouyang couldn't imagine how there could be anything else in the world for him at that moment other than relief. And yet he had the triumphant look of a man who had pushed himself to his limits without fear, because he had known he was strong enough to endure—to survive.

Zhu hung spent in Ouyang's grasp, a sodden cat held up by the armpits as he towed her through the cavern and dumped her unceremoniously on the small beach at the other end. The white sand glowed eerily in the light of her Mandate.

"I hope my service was to your satisfaction," Ouyang said, looking down at her dourly. He was so completely wet, and so completely displeased with the situation, that Zhu would have laughed if she'd found the breath for it. It would have taken so little effort for him to let her drift off into the void, or for that matter to kneel beside her and shove her face into the sand. The gleam of checked murder in his eye sent a thrill through her. He *could* kill her, but now that he had thrown his lot in with hers at least for as long as they were on this island together: he wouldn't. He was her weapon to wield.

"Always an adventure with you, General." With effort Zhu managed to avoid biting her tongue off as her teeth chattered. She'd never felt her face ache with so many different shades of pain; it felt as though her convulsing muscles were one step from ripping from the bone. "Near death by stabbing, near death by fire, near death by water. I'm looking forward to trying all the variations on the theme." She *had* nearly died all those times. But it wasn't the near-death part she remembered most clearly, but the rush afterwards: the intoxication of pure life that, for a moment, promised that she would never fail, never get old, never die. *Like I'm feeling now.* She knew she was cold and exhausted, but what she felt was warm: with excitement; with success that was close enough to taste.

She sat up, her light dimming with the effort, and hauled on the line around her waist that trailed back into the water. It pulled tight, which was a good sign it was still attached to the boat on the other end. "Are you going to get warmer by glowering? You may as well sit down."

Ouyang's poisonous expression was undermined by the pronounced squish his clothes made as he sat down. A tremor in his jaw suggested that the only reason his teeth weren't chattering as badly as Zhu's was because he was refusing to let them. Zhu had often suffered from cold in the monastery, having less muscle mass than Xu Da and the other novices, and it gave her a strange feeling of kinship to know his small body felt the cold as much as hers. She teased, "Sure you don't want to squeeze out your clothes? You know what they say about sitting around with wet hair. You'll shrink your qi."

Ouyang gave her a murderous look without deigning to reply.

"I've already seen you in your underclothes! I'm not suggesting you get *naked*—"

Zhu's attention was caught by movement in the still water. But the water itself remained motionless. She should have expected it, but even so her skin crawled. Ouyang's ghosts rose silently up through the surface, a white-clad army from the deep. Their feet glided above the sand as they came up the beach to settle in their usual formation around Ouyang. In the yin environment of this dark wet underground cave, lit by the unearthly light of Zhu's Mandate, they seemed as substantial as the living. Zhu had never seen them this close, nor in such detail: they were old and young, their empty-eyed faces turned towards Ouyang as if he were the moon in their permanent night sky. She could barely make out his rigid sitting shape through their encircling bodies.

"They're here, aren't they," Ouyang said tonelessly. He didn't look at her. "I can feel them, sometimes. Around me." Water dripped slowly from the ends of the long pointed daggers of stone from the roof of the cave. "Waiting. For me to finish what was started."

He didn't mean what had been started when he killed the Prince of Henan and took his army, Zhu thought, looking at those dead faces, but long before. How old had Ouyang been when he had first grasped his fate? From his feminine appearance, he must have been cut as a child. Had he been the same age as when she had grasped her own fate? Zhu felt that familiar stirring of resonance inside her. They had been parallel and far apart, but now they had finally converged through the intensity of their wanting; of their mutual desire for their fates that lay together in Dadu.

Bubbles broke on the surface, capturing Zhu's attention. There was a tug on the line; then a shape rocketed from the water with a gasping whoosh. Shards of light danced violently around the cave. Zhu recognized her young commander Lin Ruilin as he lurched into the shallows and slumped to his knees, panting. After a few moments he managed to raise his head and orient towards Zhu's light, like a plant finding the sun.

Then, abruptly, his relief vanished. "Where's General Xu?"

☼

There was a strange suspended feeling inside Zhu; it seemed to live somewhere behind her breastbone. "What?"

The frigid water had purpled Lin's face. He looked like a baby before its first breath. And a baby before its first breath, that never breathed at all, was—

Dead, Zhu's mind supplied, as if from a distance.

"General Xu went first," Lin said raggedly. "There's only one line. How could I have come out before him?"

They followed the line with their eyes to where it entered the water. There were no more bubbles.

"He must have lost his grip on the line," Ouyang said, without much interest. "This one," meaning Lin, because of course he hadn't learned the names of any of Zhu's men, "would have bypassed him on the way."

Zhu thought of the tunnel, filled from floor to ceiling with water. She had known her share of existential terror, but what she'd felt in that black void had been animal, and all but uncontrollable: the awful helplessness of being whittled down to her last moments of life.

But Xu Da was strong. He was still alive down there, waiting for her. Zhu lunged for the knot of the rope around her waist. As she struggled, for the first time she cursed her lack of a hand for her clumsiness, her slowness, when every moment mattered. "I'm the only one who can find him. I have the light. Someone take this rope—!"

"Take it while you do what?" Ouyang was brusque. "Kill yourself, trying to fish out a corpse? Count yourself lucky if he's the only one you lose from this. It's only a pity it had to be the best man out of all of you." He added, "Better had it been you."

"He's not lost."

As Ouyang opened his mouth to reply, the surface wobbled and a figure burst out. Zhu knew instantly, as if it were knowledge that had been transferred directly body from body rather than via anything so slow as observation, that it wasn't Xu Da. In a moment she recognized Yuchun's gasp. And then, in the next, the dark mass he dragged behind him.

She couldn't leave her position; she was still anchoring the line. But Lin was there, helping Yuchun haul Xu Da's limp body to the beach, as Yuchun forced out between gasps, "—found him—floating—"

In the stark white light of her Mandate, Xu Da's familiar handsome face was as gray as unfired clay. Zhu, still attached to the rope, squatted next to him. The suspended feeling inside her had grown into an immense stillness that pressed upon her organs and made it hard to breathe. Lin made a choked sound. But there was no reason for it, because Xu Da wasn't dead. His face was as close to hers as it had been when they'd slept beside each other as boys. In a moment he would open his eyes as he'd always done. Zhu had survived being run through and having her hand cut off, and this wasn't as bad as that. *He would be fine.*

Someone shouldered her aside. It was Ouyang. He knelt over Xu Da with a look of profound distaste. Then to Zhu's astonishment, he took hold of Xu Da's head with an impersonal two-handed grasp, leant down, and kissed him.

All at once, Zhu was convinced she'd gotten it wrong. It wasn't a *kiss.* Horror paralyzed her. Ouyang's chalk skin, his sparkless eyes, weren't those of a human but a hungry ghost, and now he was bent over a helpless sleeping man to eat his lips, eat his liver, feast upon him—

Ouyang released Xu Da and straightened up, looking down at him intently.

For a moment nothing happened.

Then Xu Da convulsed with an awful gurgle. Ouyang rolled him onto his side as he spasmed and vomited onto the sand. The next time Xu Da spasmed he managed to roll himself onto all fours and stayed like that, gasping and retching with his head hanging down.

Zhu barely noticed the tug on the rope as another of their group surfaced. The heavy stillness inside her had gone, leaving a celebratory lightness in its place. Xu Da was fine, just as she'd known he would be. She thumped his back as he coughed, relishing the solid aliveness of his familiar big body.

Ouyang rose. "As long as a person has been submerged in very cold water for less time than it takes to boil a pot of tea, they can usually be revived by breathing air into them. Any longer than that, and it won't work." There was a lingering distaste in him, as if he'd stooped to something he considered as far beneath his station as shoveling out the latrine. Perhaps for Mongols, who trained their armies to ford winter rivers, it *was* that routine.

At last Xu Da pushed himself back onto his heels. As he wiped the hair out of his eyes, he croaked, "We have a huge problem."

"Problem?" Zhu started running scenarios in her head. If he was too weak to fight, she could temporarily leave him here, although then she would be lacking his critical support against the Yuan garrison above—

Xu Da said with great drama, "I'm so handsome, even a eunuch can't resist me."

Ignoring Ouyang's savage look, he laughed until he went into a spasm of coughing, then climbed to his feet, brushing off Zhu's concern. "Enough worrying, little brother. I'm fine. Let's go."

The group, with Ouyang shepherded between Lin Ruilin and General Xu—who still coughed occasionally—emerged out of the tunnel into a ruined village. Masses of heavy vegetation had rounded over the remnants of huts until they resembled tumors or fungi. Ouyang wasn't *impressed* by Zhu's team, but, he thought grudgingly, they exceeded his expectations. He hadn't believed they would follow Zhu on that suicidal dive, but they had. Now their progress was quick and quiet—as if they were, in fact, the elite fighters Zhu considered them to be. Ouyang thought of General Xu's affirmation of his belief in Zhu. It was like they *all* believed. He couldn't fathom it.

The ruined village, which was slightly elevated above the rest of the island, hardly needed to be a mountain to have excellent vantage. The treeless island was so small—no more than three li across, inside its encircling cliff-edge fortifications—that they could make out its major features easily. Those black masses in the center of the island were the salt warehouses, and the floating gleam of light at the farthest point from them would be the guard post above the harbor. The thick marine air made the light bob and twinkle. Ouyang, whose career had been as a landlocked general, found it disconcerting.

"Stay here," Zhu instructed the group, and when General Xu creaked a protest he added firmly, "Rest while you can. I'll scout out the situation down at the guard post. We'll want to make our move while it's still dark, and we only have a few hours, so be prepared to act as soon as we get back." He had let the glow of the Mandate lapse once they reached the surface, and in the darkness all Ouyang could make out of him was the shape of his head. But somehow he could feel the prickle of Zhu's attention turning to him, even before he said, "Come on, General."

Happiness would have been too strong a word for it, but Ouyang would have been content to be free of Zhu's company for a while. Also, the salt water had set his feet on fire. He said sourly, "Worried I'll suborn your men if you leave me here with them?"

"If you had a slightly more winning way with people, perhaps I'd be worried. Mainly, I thought you would have a valuable perspective on Yuan operations. I've never staged a raid on a Yuan outpost before. I don't really have any idea how they organize themselves." He was such a pathetic leader that it didn't even bother him to admit ignorance in front of his men.

Ouyang said with deep loathing, "I don't need a winning personality to turn you in to the Yuan."

He could feel Zhu contemplating him. After a moment he said with a gentleness that wasn't quite gratitude, "If you were going to do that, you wouldn't have saved Xu Da because you were afraid I might lose without him. Let's go."

Nobody had been on this part of the island in years. The vegetation that had overgrown the paths gave beneath Ouyang's weight and plunged him thigh-deep with every step. The waterlogged bandages around his feet were rubbing them newly raw. His only consolation was that Zhu—who had clearly been stunted by his past as a malnourished orphan—was struggling just as much. His lurching progress reminded Ouyang of a hunting dog in waist-high grass, its small head surfacing every few steps to see where it was.

Zhu was probably as relieved as Ouyang was when they finally waded onto more regular worn paths. "There it is," Zhu whispered, as they passed the warehouses and the guard post came into view. The structure was far larger than Ouyang would have expected for an island garrison. With hindsight, he realized pirate attacks probably had something to do with it. He took in the details with a dwindling feeling. They were viewing the rear of a three-story tower mounted on the battlements of the perimeter wall. Torches in the broad forecourt and lanterns behind the post's papered upper windows lit the structure with a magnificent orange glow that obliterated the starlight. The light blinking along the battlements, and its twin in the distance, would be perimeter patrols: the guards' raised torches being eclipsed by the crenellations as they made their way around the island in opposite directions.

"Tell me what I'm looking at," Zhu said quietly. "How many men are we facing?"

Zhu had thirteen men, plus General Xu. He would be facing three to four squads of Yuan soldiers. Desperation tightened Ouyang's throat. What if he turned Zhu in? The Yuan hated him, a traitor, even more than they hated Zhu. They would send him to Dadu for execution. At least that way he would meet the Great Khan, he thought wildly. But to be alone in the capital—imprisoned—unarmed—

Is that really better odds than what I'm proposing, General?

"Thirty to forty men," he gritted out. "The entrance on this rear side won't be guarded, since they'll only be expecting attacks to come from the harbor side. But those lanterns upstairs suggest they work in shifts, perhaps because pirates have attempted night raids before. There's at least one squad on duty right now. And it won't take them long to wake the others as soon as an alarm is raised."

Zhu said, unperturbed, "What are our chances if we simply storm in?"

It was one thing to ask an enemy for information, but—"Are you asking my *opinion*?"

"Why not? You're an experienced general. And I am—"

Ouyang couldn't help it: "—a shameless blight upon this world, completely lacking in honor or experience, *who's never fought a real battle in his life.*"

For a brief instant Ouyang thought he might have hit a nerve. Then: "Why should I be ashamed that I don't have the experience myself, if I can find it elsewhere? I'll use every resource available to me, regardless of what anyone else thinks about it. Look at my men. I know what you thought, when you first saw them. You thought they were useless peasant boys. And they *were*, before I saw their potential. I gave them the chance to realize that potential. To grow, and become what they'd never been allowed to be." Zhu glanced sideways at Ouyang, his teeth showing in a small bright smile. "They're good, General. And, even if you can't respect it, so am I."

"Not good enough."

"No? Tell me why."

Ouyang saw the raid playing out in his head. "The element of surprise will give you an advantage, but not for long enough. The cramped quarters will be to their advantage, not yours. You'll be fighting your way upstairs. Your men will be swarmed and killed." He said viciously, "You'd better have another plan."

"What if we could bring them out of the tower and ambush them here in the forecourt?" There was a muted clink as Zhu opened his oilcloth bag and drew out a round metallic item that gleamed in the dim light. He said blandly, "You remember these."

Ouyang did remember. He remembered very well indeed how his front line had been blown up by one of those unassuming-looking bombs. He was engulfed by the peculiar sensation of being simultaneously enraged and relieved that Zhu had a workable plan. He said with venom, "It won't do any good if you set it off outside, so they come rushing out prepared to deal with a problem. For it to be an ambush, you'll need to get it inside."

Zhu glanced up, considering then rejecting the tower's latticed windows, then drifted higher. "What about the roof?"

"Can you throw that far? *I* can't. And I still have my dominant hand."

"I suppose we can't strap a bomb to an arrow," Zhu mused. "Even if we had a bow. And the roof is curved, so even if we got it up there like that, it would just roll off. We need some way of getting the bombs onto the roof, and keeping them there. Well, then, General." His infuriating smile flashed again. "I hope you're wearing the kind of underwear I think you're wearing."

"Now," Zhu said as the Yuan patrol passed by overhead on the battlement.

Xu Da and Yuchun hauled on the free end of the rope they'd flung around the crenellation, and Zhu, on the other end, walked her feet up the face of the wall as they hoisted her upwards. A childhood spent cavorting on glittering monastery roofs amongst the clouds had all but inured her to a fear of heights. But it was exactly the familiarity of being in the air that made Zhu more conscious of her new physical vulnerability: that now she had only a single hand to stabilize both herself and the overlarge item she was ferrying along with her.

For all his historic clumsiness at the handicrafts required to celebrate the various events of the monastery calendar, Xu Da had done a good job with the project. Ouyang's innermost shirt, as Zhu had hoped, had been made of the Mongols' famous arrow-proof silk. Light and immensely strong, it wrapped around the penetrating shafts without tearing, making arrow removal clean and easy. As a construction material, it was an infinite improvement over the flimsy paper the monks had used to make kites for the new year.

The rope, still soggy from the dive, rasped and stretched against the stone as Zhu rose two, then three zhang up the wall. At last the embrasure came within reach. She pulled herself through the narrow gap between the crenellations, signaled to

Xu Da below to release his end of the rope, then pulled it up and secured it around one of the crenellations so she could descend later without assistance. When she signaled again, Xu Da slipped away to join the ambush position of the rest of the team in the forecourt.

Up on the battlement the wind was much stronger than below. Zhu had to wrestle with the kite to keep it stable as she used an incense stick to light the fuses of the bombs hanging from it. Then, instead of needing to throw the kite hard into the air as she'd done in the monastery, she simply let go.

The sea wind caught the kite so fast that Zhu's hand burned as the string ran through it. It was a much stronger kite than any she'd flown before, and she felt a surge of elation: as if she were controlling something powerfully alive. Within moments the kite was hovering steady, level with the roof, a pale ghost against the black sky.

Although she had deliberately timed her arrival onto the battlements for when the patrols were at their farthest point, her back prickled as the wait lengthened. For as long as it took for the bombs to go off, she was standing there exposed. Her forearm ached from the kite's pulling. How could the fuses not have run down by now? She was suddenly consumed by doubts. What if seawater had leaked inside the bombs and ruined the fire-powder? Would they still work? Surely they hadn't *all* been ruined. The longer she stood there, the louder her doubts became. The prickling in her back strengthened.

Then the weight in her hand vanished. Everything vanished; there was only brightness.

Zhu's consciousness had been cut and restitched without any memory of the intervening period. Even as she realized she was lying several zhang away from where she'd been, she was already curling into a protective huddle as chunks of wood and masonry rained down on her. Whatever sound the chunks made as they smashed down onto the stone battlements was wiped out by a burning crackle in her ears. A pale cloud rose from the ripped-open roof of the guard post. Lantern-light from inside streamed directly up in a trembling pillar, as if a window had been opened up to the black sky.

Zhu scrambled to her feet, casting aside the slack string that no longer had a kite attached to the other end. Yuan guards were already boiling out of the tower into the forecourt beneath, some armored but a larger number clearly having woken and rushed out in a panic. Zhu watched long enough to see her own men snap into action. They were still small in number relative to the Yuan, but with the advantages of surprise and their position surrounding the forecourt: it would be good enough.

Zhu grabbed the rope around her waist, ready to launch herself from the battlements. Even if the patrols had been a long way off initially, they would be coming for her now at a run, and she needed to get out of the way. But . . . there was a strange slackness in the rope. Zhu drew it towards her with sudden dread, and stopped short when she saw the frayed stump. All at once she remembered the ominous stretch in the rope; the way it had rasped over the stone. When she'd been blown backwards, it had snapped. Even if she tied the length that was still around her waist to a crenellation, it wouldn't be enough to lower her more than a body length from the wall.

She cast a grim glance down to the forecourt. Three zhang was more than six of Zhu's body lengths, and the forecourt was paved. What would happen if she jumped without a rope? The pain of injury wasn't a concern—she wasn't afraid of suffering. But could she survive the injuries of such a fall? On the battlefield she'd seen men bleed to death from fractures that broke the skin, and others who'd been crushed by their own fallen horses. She didn't like the odds.

On the other side of the battlements, white foam curled against the base of the seawall. She could choose to fall into the water. But once she hit that black surface she would keep falling, and this time Ouyang wouldn't be there to guide her. That was even less of an option.

And when she looked up, there was the flash of a torch along the battlements: the patrol coming, running.

Ouyang, standing unarmed and unminded at the rear of the forecourt, watched the chaos unfold with a sense of furious, helpless investment.

Zhu's men thrust forwards into the engagement. Torches fell as the Yuan men cast them aside to take on their unexpected attackers, casting the melee into a confusion of shadows. It had been the right decision to save General Xu. Under his unflappable direction, Zhu's youths were acquitting themselves admirably against their far more numerous opponents.

There was something happening on the battlements. Ouyang was surprised to see two Yuan patrolmen closing in on Zhu with drawn swords. Why was Zhu even up there, when the plan had been for him to descend immediately after the explosion? Zhu still had that saber of his. But when it was two against one, Ouyang couldn't imagine him coming out the winner.

Even before he'd grasped his own intent, he was moving. He lunged into the fray of the forecourt, took the nearest fully equipped Yuan soldier from behind and broke his neck, then scooped up his bow and two spent arrows that had fallen nearby. After quick consideration he nocked both arrows. It would be a preposterous shot. Zhu's future assailants were moving with such speed that they were barely more than flickers in the darkness between the crenellations. Ouyang tracked the running pair, feeling his heartbeat slow as his focus sharpened. They were five crenellations away from Zhu. Four, three—

Zhu flung himself from the wall.

He fell, and Ouyang's preternatural focus showed him every detail: the rag-doll flail of Zhu's limbs; the thin white streak looping through the air behind him. The latter surprised him. It wasn't the rope Zhu had gone up with. Before he could identify what the strange cord was, or what might have necessitated its use, Zhu hit the end. He bounced several times, scrabbling against the wall to right himself, as the cord or whatever it was—for some reason he thought of the bandages around his feet, though that couldn't be right—stretched dramatically. Stretch as it did, though, it was still at least two body lengths too short for Zhu to reach the ground.

The patrolmen had reached Zhu's launching point, and were just leaning over to haul him up, when suddenly the ribbon was no longer there.

Zhu plummeted.

Above, the patrolmen gaped over the side. The released end of the ribbon spurted high in the air, then came fluttering down. Zhu must have cut himself loose, Ouyang realized. All he could see of Zhu was a shadow at the base of the wall. Then all of a sudden he sprang up, as unharmed as a dropped ant, and ran off into battle with his saber drawn.

Ouyang stared after him, struck by the sheer unbelievability of Zhu's determination. Had he been afraid as he flung himself from the battlements with nothing between him and death but that slender ribbon? He remembered Zhu's small, resolute face as he stood in the prow of the boat and jumped, knowing that he couldn't swim a stroke. Even if he'd been afraid, he'd done it anyway. Because of how much he wanted.

For an instant Ouyang felt a stirring of something that he couldn't tell himself was hate.

An arrow sang past, startling him out of the unfamiliar feeling. He had moved to save Zhu, he thought with an internal snarl, but he'd only done it to prevent him from losing. After this, all bets would be off again. Because, even with a fully resourced army, Zhu still didn't have a chance against General Zhang. It took more than determination to win a war.

But since he had a bow in his hands anyway, he shot the patrolmen—a trivial task, even the two of them at once, given how they were standing there like melon-headed idiots. And then, because there were more spent arrows on the ground, he gathered them up and made himself useful in ensuring Zhu didn't lose.

Zhu stood at the top of the guard tower, surveying her victory. The forecourt below was a thicket of fallen Yuan bodies. She and her small team had defeated a garrison of forty, and now she had as much salt as she could carry off the island in their commandeered vessels: enough to keep her supplied for as long as it took for her to win against the Zhangs.

And all it had cost her was the lives of two young men. It was an unpleasant feeling, and yet the unpleasantness itself yielded a thrill from how she could bear it without flinching. Had she known in advance that it would have cost her those two youths, she would have made the same choices. She would have given more. She would have given, willingly, whatever it took for success.

Someone came upstairs. It was Ouyang, making his way around bodies with a look of callous distaste. He was unarmed, but Zhu suddenly recalled arrow-punctured Yuan corpses in the forecourt below. Who else could it have been, other than him? There was a pleasing rightness to the idea that he had voluntarily helped her. What she'd told him back in Yingtian had been true at the time: that she only needed his army, and not him. But now that she had him, he was proving quite the asset.

He said dourly, "It seems you got what you wanted." Then he frowned. "Is something different about you?"

Instantly, Zhu was conscious of her breasts. It had been torture up there on the battlements as she'd struggled with the ties on her outer robe and undershirt, then with the bandage around her chest that insisted on becoming tangled in itself. Every fumbling moment had been an agony of frustration for how slow, slow, *slow* she was with just one hand. Even when she'd finally wrenched it free of herself, she hadn't known if it would be enough to save her. If it wasn't strong enough to bear her weight, or if her clumsily tied join between bandage and rope gave way before it broke her fall—

She hadn't known, even as she'd jumped.

Now, as she stood in front of Ouyang in one piece, her breasts were unbound. She doubted he had noticed them specifically. They weren't prominent, especially when concealed by layers of salt-encrusted clothing. And yet it was interesting that he had noticed *something*. He was attuned to other men's bodies in a way that most men weren't. Did he go through the world unconsciously cataloguing all the bodies he encountered, differentiating between those he yearned for and those with which he rejected any similarity whatsoever?

Zhu felt a fierce clench of understanding. All throughout her own boyhood, she'd done the same.

She said lightly, "Who knew salt water would make my hair look this good! If you didn't insist on wearing those braids, you'd see the difference yourself—"

She nearly laughed as he turned away with a snarl.

Through the arrow slits overlooking the harbor, Zhu could see the sea sparkling in the rising sun. It was the milky green of hot mineral springs, of jadeite clouds. The islands floating within it went on and on, and Zhu had an image of herself bounding from one to another all the way to the future.

She said joyfully to Ouyang's slim back, "I know you don't believe. But I got what I want, because I always do. And now you're going to see me take on the Zhangs, and win."

8

PINGJIANG

The Queen sat in the garden pagoda with her neck arched to present her most flattering profile to her male company. The lake breeze, redolent of green weeds and duck feet, whisked over the city walls and into the Zhang family's palace, where it tangled the pearl tassels in the Queen's hair and tossed the foliage of the pistache trees into shivering gold. *Real* gold. Dissatisfied with nature's own display, Rice Bucket had had every leaf painted gold. Guests were stunned first by the dazzle, and again by the headaches that followed. Peafowls roved, crinkling, through the leaf litter. It was as if the trees had rained taels, the Queen thought. It had been about that expensive. She made herself smile.

Her husband the king lounged on cushions with his eyes on the courtesan playing the zheng for their noontime entertainment. It was brighter here in lakeside Pingjiang than it had been in their old capital of Yangzhou, with its deep canals and streets built up with the famous black-and-green pleasure houses. This light tolerated no mysteries. It pointed out the fine dark hair on the courtesan's wrists where they slid from her sleeves, and where her makeup clumped over the flaky skin beside her ear. One would have thought a girl of such average looks and talent would have been better motivated to find solutions to her imperfections.

The Queen, irritated, decided to send the girl back to her house's proprietor with a complaint. She was paying enough for her husband's entertainment not to receive sloppiness. Not that he cared. Rice Bucket Zhang would be pleased with the dregs from the wine jar, as long as you told him they were expensive. Her smile continued, undisturbed. Once, that quality had made him useful, and she had been grateful for it. Now her impatience for the future made her distaste of him all but unbearable.

The Queen glanced across the table at General Zhang as a swirl of servant girls swept in with serving platters. He wore his usual expression of polite interest. Their eyes met like the tap of two bare hands. He didn't smile, but the mournful wings of his eyebrows softened.

Rice Bucket surveyed the platters with a twitch of confusion. The mounds of purple-clawed river crabs must, to him, seem insultingly plain. The Queen laid the very tips of her fingernails against his arm to claim his attention. Half the art of keeping poorly educated men pleased was by offering discreet edification about the flatteries they received, so they knew when they should be pleased. She murmured, "This unworthy woman thought His Majesty would appreciate the opportunity to try the local freshwater crabs. Their season is no longer than that of the night-blooming flower. Every year those in Pingjiang with the means will try to secure two or three to eat at once." The lacquer tugged lightly across her smiling lips. "But even the wealthiest of them will rarely obtain more than one."

Reading and responding to him no longer took her any more effort than breathing. She was both puppet and puppet master, her mind relishing the empty action of her body as it spoke and touched and was touched in turn. On the opposite side of the table, General Zhang's preternatural calm masked his dislike for seeing her caress her husband. Her power thrilled her: that she could control both these men with a single touch.

Rice Bucket had forgotten the zheng player. His gaze upon the Queen was full of self-congratulation, as if she were one of his intrinsic attributes that had brought him to his deserved greatness. He said with satisfaction, "A meal fit for a king, then."

"How perceptive my husband is!" She beckoned forwards the one male servant who had accompanied the girls. "You. Perform your duty."

"Permit this unworthy one, Your Majesty," the servant said, taking a crab claw and breaking it open. The meat within was overflowing with jade-white juices. Rice Bucket watched the poison-tasting avidly. He loved the ceremony of success. And he loved it all the more for having none of the burdens of responsibility.

The Queen stole another glance at General Zhang. How great *his* weariness was, from carrying that burden, though he refused to begrudge his brother for laying it down. Lately they'd barely had time to meet, he was so busy preparing his army to meet Zhu Yuanzhang.

Her annoyance was savage. Zhu Yuanzhang, who inexplicably persisted despite what should have been a crippling deficit of salt. Who had spurned her in the apparent belief that he could control that raging, pathetic animal, General Ouyang, well enough to fling against her. Well, she knew Ouyang, too. And for all the success he'd had so far, Zhu was only a boy. She thought of him standing blithely sunlit on that hilltop, with all of a boy's overconfidence that the world would adjust itself to suit his desires. *I want to be the greatest.*

It was going to be a pleasure, she thought, to see him crushed.

The poison taster departed with a bow and Madam Zhang held her sleeve back and used her chopsticks to elegantly deposit the fattest claws into Rice Bucket's bowl. "Please, husband."

Rice Bucket surveyed his golden garden as he sucked out the inside of a claw. He was dissatisfied again, as if it were the ground he returned to no matter what delights had buoyed him a moment before. "Yue has been bothering me about the delay on the additions to her residence." He tossed the empty claw onto the ground. "Did you tell her she would have to wait?"

Yue, Rice Bucket's newest concubine, was more demanding than a girl of her position had any right to be. And of course Rice Bucket had no idea that the money that fueled his whims came from somewhere, and had better uses than gilding trees and satisfying his concubines.

Yue was a problem. The Queen could feel her presence like a crack in the otherwise smooth ice of her marriage. But that could be dealt with later. She assessed Rice Bucket's level of annoyance. The set of his wide but soft shoulders, chest broadened with self-importance. Men's bodies were so easy to read. It was only mild annoyance, so she cast her eyes down. Demure, undemanding. "Please forgive this unworthy woman for the delays. There was the need to equip General Zhang's army to face Zhu Yuanzhang. But once the boy is defeated, I can prioritize your concubine's residence. I think the new rooms will look most pleasing with a particular mosaic ornamentation I have in mind."

The sequence of his reactions was pleasingly predictable: the softening as he allowed himself to be mollified, followed immediately by the reflexive posturing. "Always asking for more resources, little brother! How hard is it to defeat a boy and a bitch without balls?" He said it like a joke, although of course it wasn't: it was too aggressive, thrown at his brother, who absorbed it as he absorbed everything else that had been thrown his way. He took another crab claw, shook it at General Zhang. "Work harder, little brother, so I can get the Mandate that's our due." For a moment his look shifted inwards, and her senses bristled at that touch of true danger. "It doesn't please me to wait."

In the fractional delay before General Zhang answered, she could feel his guilt that was as strong as a subterranean river. A subterranean fire: that orange fire that was *his* due, she thought with a thrill, not and never his brother's. It had been his ever since he had betrayed his brother for the first time in her bed. His guilt had been exciting and pleasurable then, a sign of her success. But now it had long since curdled into impatience.

General Zhang smiled to cover his guilt, though the sadness grew on his brow. That irritated her, too. *Why must you cling to what's useless? What good is he to you?* He said to his brother, "I hope the expense doesn't inconvenience you too much. Your wife has thought the matter through well."

Rice Bucket scoffed. "You praise her more than she deserves! These women of mine are bothersome with all their demands. Wife, keep enough funds aside to get that residence done soon, so that concubine stops annoying me. And don't slight her. I know what you women are like. Make it as beautiful as yours. Spare no expense."

The Queen bowed her head. "This woman will do as her husband requests." Husband for only a short while longer, she thought. After General Zhang's defeat of Zhu Yuanzhang, it would be time for him to cast aside that guilt and do what they needed to do.

"This woman hesitates to inconvenience her husband, but please let her beg one last indulgence. A guest from upriver will be paying us a visit. Please treat him well. Let him partake of your generosity, feel your status, and show him the scope of our success. The effort will be well spent." The golden leaves rubbed against each other with the scratching sound of pigeon claws on a lead roof. She let her smile touch General Zhang, promising him some intimacy when her husband was occupied with their guest. "Take your time."

General Zhang dipped into the Queen's rooms through the courtyard door. Behind him she saw a rectangle of the black evening garden. Slices of light from the Mid-Autumn Festival lanterns, carp-colored, shone in the cup of each leaf.

He wore a mild expression as he sat familiarly on her couch under the hanging cages of her favorite birds. Zhang Shide wasn't a big man, but there was a purposefulness to his carriage that gave him an air of nobility regardless of whether he was heading into battle or an assignation. It was only because she knew him that she could see the weariness beneath his composure. No matter how delightfully she entertained him, it never quite faded. That was what happened when you turned an honorable man dishonorable. It pleased her to know she had put that discomfort there. And it pleased her even more to know that he would continue to bear it, because he loved her.

"It would have been better for me to come later in the evening," he remarked as she poured the tea. "It's risky, this early. Even if he's entertaining a guest."

The criticism hit a nerve. She put the pot down and said in bad temper, "You might be the general, but trust that I can stay one step ahead of that stupid pig!"

She regretted it immediately. As sick to death as she was of her husband, it was foolish to let frustration slip. General Zhang tried very hard to believe that he could cuckold Rice Bucket and still be a loyal brother, so open criticism of Rice Bucket made him feel guilty. She turned away, telling herself that it was only as a show of discontent that would needle him into placating her, and not because she didn't want to see his reproof. Guilt! What a useless emotion. Guilt was what had him still prevaricating over what needed to be done to secure their future. Was he even now telling himself that there could still be a happy ending? Did he think her shallow, selfish husband, who was sensitive to the slightest insult, would willingly—*gladly*—step aside from the throne for his brother with the Mandate? It made her want to scream.

"To think you used to be so sweet to me at the beginning," he said ruefully from behind her. She didn't reply, so he went on, "I know you're frustrated. It won't be like this for much longer, I promise. When I've defeated Zhu Yuanzhang—"

Not for much longer. Be patient. Soon. She'd heard it a thousand times. His contrition was always genuine. But that didn't make waiting for him to act any easier. Annoyed, she thought of how he would never have cuckolded his brother and gained the Mandate in the first place if she hadn't forced his hand. All those years of longing looks over her husband's dinner table! Another man would have seen her willing, and helped himself. But Zhang Shide would have looked forever. He would have been content with nothing but his own pain and the idea of himself as a good person.

If only she could force his hand again! She could kill Rice Bucket, and give General Zhang no choice but to step up and fulfil his potential. But she knew he would never forgive her for it. In his grief, he would refigure history. He'd remember how his swaggering brother had taught him the smuggling trade and found him his first opportunities, and nothing at all of their slow souring as Rice Bucket proved himself, again and again, unworthy of admiration. He would blame her for ruining a happy future that would never have come to pass. He would cast her as the villain, to separate himself from his guilt.

And if she lost him, she would have nothing.

She turned back and knelt at his feet, clasping his hand. "How dare a woman find fault! Forgive me. I spoke ill-advisedly." It would have been better to have it over and done with, but she could wait until he returned from dealing with Zhu. She would crown him her new king. And then, when he took Dadu and the throne stood before him, there would be neither brother nor conscience in his way.

Her husband never bestirred himself to visit her rooms, so instead of the luxury carpets he preferred—a tripping hazard for unsteady feet—her floors were bare. The press of the hard surface against her knees barely registered as pain. She thought with satisfaction that the bareness made for a pretty picture, the kind that men who thought of themselves as noble, and chivalrous, loved to gaze down upon: the woman's skirts piled in soft drifts against the oil-sheened wood, like a fallen plum blossom; the graceful stem of her body bowed in penitence.

General Zhang's eyes crinkled humorously, as if he knew exactly what she was doing, but at the same time couldn't help himself from liking it. "Why do I get the feeling I should be the one seeking forgiveness?" After a moment he drew her into his lap. The heavy silk of his gown was cold, and smelled crisply of the night air. Even moments like these, when there was friction between them, he touched her as if she might break. Gently. Reverently. She felt mildly scornful. What was he revering? Her made-up doll's face that was no more her real face than her performance of desire was her real self? His gentleness felt like a dismissal of everything she'd accomplished before she'd met him. If she could be broken by an ungentle touch, she'd have been broken a long time ago.

For a while he just held her. There were tiny red leaves in his topknot. They must have caught there when he was ducking through the garden. The new hair at his temples was too short to be pulled back with the rest, and curled wispily away from his head. His gown warmed between them. When she finally felt the flicker of his intention, she pulled back just as he turned his head to kiss her. His frustration filled her with pleasure. She loved withholding what he wanted, knowing how much it increased his desire. But it didn't do to withhold for too long. She slipped off his lap with a little laugh, and pulled him to the bedchamber.

General Zhang always took his time with the business of the rain and clouds. With another man, the Queen would have begrudged the slowness and the need to flatter his efforts to please. It wasn't that there was anything special about him. He was an ordinary man, with ordinary desires, and her body accepted him with the same remote awareness of sensation that she felt when she knelt on hard floorboards, or walked, or ate something particularly hot or cold. But with him it was easy. Over time he had somehow lost his interchangeability with other men and become particular. Instead of having to gather details from his words and bearing to piece together what he was feeling, she simply grasped him whole. He was as familiar as a plant she had tended from seed. Her performance came so instinctively that it no longer felt like work. She embraced his sinewy body above and inside her, and felt a spreading, soft-edged contentment that was as soothing as a warm bath. Here, there was no need for impatience. She was securing her investment, and every moment was well spent.

They lay together afterwards, fingers tangled. Still feeling warm, she said impulsively, "Come moon-watching with me tomorrow night, for the festival. I'll make sure he's occupied."

Her bed, recessed at the back of the room, had fragrant walls of sandalwood on three sides and damask and gauze curtains that could be drawn in front. This time they had only bothered to draw the gauze. The shimmering weave tinged the outer room orange, like the world glimpsed through a flame.

He squeezed her hand in apology. "I can't."

She said, stung, "What, can't?"

"I already promised to take my family to the lake for the occasion. We haven't spent much time together here in Pingjiang. I'd like to build some memories with my son here, too."

His family. His wife, and his son. She'd never met either of them; he'd always taken pains to keep the two sides of his life separate. But now they had intruded into this warm, comfortable space, and it felt as if they were stealing something from her. Not stealing—*damaging.* Damaging what she'd spent so much time and effort building with this man. It was better that he had kept them away from her, she thought viciously. Or else she might have removed them long before. She thought he probably knew that. She felt a fleeting, unfamiliar discomfort at the realization that he'd seen that side of her and believed in it enough to take precautions. She said coolly, "Fine."

He should have dropped it. Usually the way orgasm emptied

a man's head worked in her favor. But to her displeasure, he said, "He's nearly a man already. I enjoy spending time with him. I like him." His face was soft; modestly astonished in the way of a man who didn't realize he had expected good fortune until the world had already delivered.

She hissed, "More than you want to spend time with me."

He was quiet for a moment. Then he said, pained and honest, "You can ask anything of me, you know that. But don't ask me not to love my son."

His honesty struck her with a closed fist. She'd done everything in her power to keep him satisfied. She'd been everything he desired. He *loved* her. For that, wasn't she owed the right to make him do what she wanted? The idea that his love for her had limits made her desperate with fury. Floating in the back of her mind was the unwelcome recollection of how long she'd been waiting for him to act.

"Anything?" She made her incredulity sound brittle, to hurt him. "When you won't let me give you what I want to give you? I could give you a son to love, too."

The Queen had never been careless enough to fall pregnant accidentally, unlike many courtesans. As a young woman, she'd spent more than she could afford on contraceptives and abortifacients. Even then, she'd known it was important to stay free. It was an investment in her future. And it had worked: it had been her freedom that had allowed her to catch Rice Bucket.

But that had been long ago, and freedom had served its purpose. Now it was past time to bind. When General Zhang was emperor, it would be *her* son who took the throne after him. Not his wife's son. Men always claimed they loved their children, but it was really nothing more than the pride of a possession. They enjoyed the status sons brought them; they enjoyed knowing their family names would continue, and that they would be worshipped after their deaths. But, she thought coldly, you could substitute one son for another and to their fathers it wouldn't make any difference.

A spasm of guilt crossed his face. "It's not that simple."

She felt a cavernous violence. She wanted to tear the guilt out of him with her teeth, and spit the soft, bloody mess of it into the refuse. Only men could spend years agonizing over the morality of a decision. They knew the opportunity would still be there when they were ready. They knew their potential would never fade, even if *potential* was all they'd ever had, and never the realization of it. But women didn't have that luxury.

She said with anger, "I don't see how it's not." She pulled her hand away, relishing his hurt silence. Let him be uncomfortable. Let him think about her, his liver punctured and bleeding with misery, while he was watching the moon. "Go, then. Go to your precious wife and son."

There was an enraging rushing sound in her ears. It took her a long time to identify it as her own blood. At length General Zhang put his clothes on, and left quietly.

The Queen swayed in her palanquin as she crossed the darkened courtyard. The moon was full overhead. Her last parting with General Zhang had left her bitter. The thought of him watching that moon with his family caused her bad mood to burrow deep into her stomach, the unique flavor of resentment that she associated only with him. He had the privilege of clinging to his honor and principles, and his feeling of guilt, as though they redeemed him when his actions went against everything he said. As if she were the bad one, for matching thoughts and principles to actions. Her feet hurt more than usual, as if all of her had been rendered more sensitive.

Someone was coming across the courtyard. It was Yue, with a scatter of servants. She was wearing a dramatic, expensive necklace that Rice Bucket had given her. Her demureness demanded attention, with the confidence of a young woman who didn't realize that her currency of youth and beauty would expire. Her husband's concubines had come and gone, and Yue would be no different, but the Queen felt an unaccustomed stab of rage. It was unbearable that the girl dared to look at her and dismiss her with the scornful denial of youth, and think that it would never happen to her. The Queen wanted to boil her down into nothing, to put her in her place, to teach her how it was to be.

The girl was holding a filled bowl. The Queen halted her palanquin. "What do you have there, little sister?"

Yue glanced up. There was a flicker in her face: competition, an eager engagement for a fight. But her voice was demure. "This unworthy concubine greets the Queen. I took the liberty of compounding a most efficacious virility tonic for our husband. As I'm sure you know, sometimes our husband's desires outstrip his capacity." Under its demureness, there was a subterranean smirk of implication. *Perhaps you don't know, because he doesn't desire you as much as he desires me.*

The Queen bestowed a benevolent smile upon her. "How clever! You have our husband's best interests at heart. Weren't the ingredients difficult to find?"

With vengeful relish she saw the girl take the praise at face value, thinking her gibe hadn't been understood. She was so young and foolish, so overconfident in her own capacities. She thought she was winning. The Queen wanted to laugh as the girl puffed up and began listing the ingredients, each more expensive and hard to find than the last.

When she had finished, the Queen said, still smiling approvingly, "Tiger bones? You spare no expense."

Yue, deliciously, took this as her due. "It's the least this unworthy woman can do."

"Tiger bones are full of hot energy. For virility, they say there's nothing better," the Queen mused, lacing her voice with sweetness. She gestured, and Yue came up to the palanquin. She caressed the girl's round cheek, felt the firm juicy tenderness of youth in it that reminded her of the best slices of meat. She delighted savagely in Yue's lifted chin of scornful pleasure, no longer demure even on the surface, as she took the praise while scorning the one who delivered it. "But, little sister. How could you have forgotten that our husband has gout? And you're giving him medicine with more heating properties?" The Queen pinched the girl's earlobe with her long, lacquered fingernails as hard as she could. "What harm are you trying to cause him, you careless, ignorant girl?"

The Queen felt the satisfying popping sound of compressed flesh beneath her nails, even though it wouldn't break the skin. Yue screamed. She dropped the tonic and the bowl smashed on the flagstones. The Queen ground down, thrilling with the sensation of the girl's pain. It made her want to laugh at how helpless she was; how she had to bear it. She held on until her fingers began to ache. When she released the girl, it felt like a release of her own. She could feel it transforming her smile into its true, vicious shape.

Yue staggered away, holding her ear. The Queen noticed scornfully that her feet weren't even that small. She didn't sway, but stumbled clumsily, like a peasant. Tears ran down her face. The Queen saw, with satisfaction, that her eyes and nose were already reddening. She was ruined for the evening. "You should thank me for intervening, little sister. You wouldn't have wanted our husband's taster to have pointed out the same thing. Fortunately for you, I don't see how he ever has to hear about this now." To the girl's servants she snapped, "Your mistress is too careless. Clean it up."

As they scurried to obey, the Queen said, "No thanks? Our husband has more reliable solutions than some quack's harmful tonic." She added scornfully, "Or perhaps you're not so beautiful that he's felt motivated to show it to you already."

It was the Queen who had procured the silver ring that allowed Rice Bucket to continue enjoying his concubines, despite the inevitable impacts on his performance due to his increasing age and excessive lifestyle. It was foolish that men measured their worth as men by their capacity for that one act. But if it was one thing courtesans knew, it was how to satisfy the customer.

Yue said with bitter defiance, "Do you think you still please him so much that he'll overlook anything you do?"

"He owes everything he has to me. I'm his wife and you, poor child, are nothing but a worthless concubine. Don't you know you'll be last season's fashion within three months? I'll select him someone prettier than you as a replacement. I'll keep doing what I want, and he won't even notice when you're gone."

She said to the palanquin bearers, "Continue."

The Queen, waiting in the secluded apartment she reserved for business, stayed seated as her guest stepped inside. The teak floor reflected the peach-tinted lanterns like the nine moons of legend. Heavy brocades lay draped across the couch in sensuous invitation. Save for the absence of music and murmured voices drifting down the corridor, it could have been a room in the green-and-black Yangzhou pleasure house where the Queen had learned her trade.

Those many years ago, Rice Bucket Zhang, young and only dabbling in the illegal salt trade that would later make his name, had swaggered into that pleasure house with no idea of what more he could be capable of. She'd nearly been fond of him for being so perfectly useful. But how long ago that had been, that he had any potential left! For an instant she wondered how it might have gone if it had been a young General Zhang who had walked in that evening, shy and blushing. But that would never have happened. She felt a twist of savagery. Zhang Shide preferred romance, or at least the illusion of it, to purchased pleasures. And he'd never had his brother's overweening confidence or ambition. He would have been less *useful*.

Her guest, Chen Youliang, neither blushed nor barged in like a boor. The Queen was struck by his monumental stillness. He stood just inside the room, hands folded in the sleeves of his black scholar's robe, taking in her domain. And in the center of it, herself: the gem in the display. She saw herself through his eyes. Her glittering, coiffed head turned to bare the arch of her neck; her laced fingers as slender as white onion stems; and tucked into the folds of her hem like pearls in an oyster, her tiny, secret shoes.

"Greetings, Your Highness." Chen spoke with a calm deliberateness that was neither particularly cultured nor particularly crude. It surprised her. From his reputation as a city-conqueror—of Anfeng, which had become the base of the rebel Red Turbans; and more recently of Wuchang, upriver on the Yangzi from Zhu Yuanzhang's capital—she'd expected a brute. "Grateful as I was to enjoy your husband's hospitality, it gives me even more pleasure to make your acquaintance."

His scholar's robes suggested that his bloody past was behind him, but she saw how his bulk was still the kind that crushed. His mass was a weapon; his softness powerful and dangerous. She couldn't tell yet if he was a threat or an opportunity. The weight of his presence assailed her, and she absorbed it with a greedy, prickling curiosity.

"Welcome to an honored guest!" she said, smiling. "Wuchang is far, and the journey too tiring. Please, be comfortable." A maidservant set wine and small dishes of duck tongue, sweet-braised radish, and spiced rabbit on the table between them, then withdrew with a whisper of the door. The gamy, oniony aroma of rabbit, blended with the warm oil of the lanterns, made the room smell like skin.

He ate lightly. "An intimate reception for a stranger! Your Highness flatters this humble person beyond his measure."

"Come now, why so humble? A man should be able to speak of his accomplishments. And from what I hear, my guest is accomplished indeed."

She was grasping his nature already, so she wasn't surprised when he didn't puff at the praise. His black eyes on her were bright and steady. She had the odd feeling that he was absorbing her body, just as she had absorbed his. There was the expected spark of lust in him, but it was controlled. Cold. "Not so much as that. But—" He paused modestly. "—perhaps this person of poor accomplishments and humble desires can be of assistance to those whose ambition outstrips his own. As Your Highness no doubt knows, this unworthy one has some . . . history . . . with Zhu Yuanzhang. It would give me great pleasure to take care of him and the eunuch general for you."

From her removed position on the coast, the details of that particular action had been obscure, but the overall shape clear enough: Zhu had stolen the Red Turbans' figurehead ruler the Prince of Radiance, and won the battle for leadership from Chen. She remembered the arrogant boy-king she had met on that overlooking summit, so full of the confidence of someone who'd never yet failed. Who'd never yet had the world teach him his limits. To have been beaten by him would have been a humiliation indeed.

Perhaps Chen did want revenge. There was something about his calm surface, and the control it required, that indicated hidden cruelty the way a shadow defines a shape. He wanted to defeat Zhu. But, she thought, if the opportunity presented itself: he would hurt him, too.

That, however, didn't mean revenge was Chen's *only* motivation.

Chen added smoothly, "Of course I have full confidence in Your Highness's capacity to put Zhu Yuanzhang in his place. It only seems to me that you would prefer to concentrate your energies on taking the capital, rather than wasting your time with petty nuisances. Why not let me take the garbage out for you? And perhaps when your husband is emperor, he'll look favorably upon this humble servant and his governance in the south."

He did well to paint a picture of himself as a strongman who desired nothing more than revenge and the satisfaction of local rule. His suggestion was plausible. Persuasive. *Use me. I'm no threat to you.* But the Queen remembered how Chen had fled the rout at Bianliang with almost nothing. For him to have rebuilt into a force sufficient to stand against Zhu and the eunuch general—even if he needed her to fund his campaign—was proof of unusual competence and drive. And where there was competence and drive, there was ambition.

He wouldn't let her see the true extent of it, of course. His control gave her the mental image of a layer of thick black oil on water, smothering surface disturbances and preventing anyone from seeing what lay beneath. But then again, she had other ways of learning a man's true character.

She gazed at him warmly, as if she had already decided in his favor. Let him think she had taken him at face value. It would please him to believe it. Men might solicit her support, but in her experience they always came with the base expectation of being accommodated. As if she had neither reason to inform her judgment, nor the power to refuse. "Of course I have to put the matter to my husband, for the final decision. But when it comes to strategy, I find we are usually of one mind."

The long vertical creases in his cheeks deepened in amusement. They reminded her of a tiger's smile. "Of course."

She went on, "But as my husband will have retired for the evening, I fear that conversation will have to wait. And yet we have the rest of the night before us! Perhaps it would please you to hear some music? I have in my employ some musicians whose talents you would surely agree are beyond the ordinary." The lanterns' fleshy glow was as intimate as light seen through a lover's outstretched hand. The Queen felt a voluptuous anticipation. It was a gratification purely of her mind; her body, as usual, remained unmoved. "Or—perhaps there are other diversions my honored guest might enjoy."

Chen's countenance was hooded. For a moment she thought he might refuse. Of course a refusal would still have told her something about his character, though not so much as its alternative. But after a moment he rose and came to sit beside her. He dwarfed her. Again she thought of the tiger and its massive, patient stillness. He didn't grasp her immediately. Instead he touched her dangling earring, setting it into gentle motion, and said very calmly, "How ungrateful it would be of me to decline."

Unwantedly, she thought of General Zhang. How grateful was *he,* that when she had given him so much, he could still turn her aside whenever he wanted? The sensation inside her was a hiss. It didn't fade even as she turned to Chen with her porcelain smile, and drew him down amongst the brocades.

There was so much you could tell about a man from this most intimate of interactions. His fears and his weaknesses; what he thought he was owed, and what he yearned for but believed he would never get. Who he was trying to be. Who he was. She knew Rice Bucket, and she knew General Zhang, and now as she observed their bodies molding together, she knew Chen.

Chen, even more than General Zhang, sought to give her pleasure. He turned and moved her body with precision, finding the places inside and out that caused it to gasp and lubricate and contract. But his was a butcher's knowledge of a body. There was nothing generous about his touch; nothing gentle or coaxing. She'd been right about his hidden cruelty, she thought. His enjoyment came from forcing an experience upon another, whether that experience was pleasure or pain. All his cold calculation was in service of one fundamental desire: control.

He'd wanted her to believe that he would be satisfied with local rule. But as he fucked her, she felt the bloody inferno of his ambition. He would be very happy to take her money to strengthen himself while she wore herself down against the Grand Councilor's central army. And when she was tired, the patient tiger would be ready to take his turn for the throne.

She was able to control Rice Bucket with his greed, and General Zhang with his love. But if Chen's desire was control, then he couldn't *be* controlled. He might lack the Mandate of Heaven, and he might still need outside funding to mobilize the forces he had gathered. But he was dangerous. He was, perhaps, the most dangerous of her opponents. And she knew if she helped this tiger become stronger, he would devour the world.

He looked down at her. As if he was seeing her as much as she was seeing him, he said softly, "Always thinking, Your Highness."

General Zhang knelt on the bed behind the Queen, combing her hair. They were both naked, except for the Queen's bed-shoes. He had come back to her after the festival, of course. That was what made love the most powerful tool, more powerful even than her husband's greed: he always came back. There was a gap between the gauze curtains. Through it she glimpsed them in the imperfect bronze mirror across the room: bracketed bodies blurred into a single curve shading seamlessly from light to dark. When her attendants combed her hair, it was an unremarkable experience. General Zhang combed carefully, but every so often she felt a strand of hair catching against some roughness on his hands. A familiar touch; familiar hands. She held an awareness of them inside her, as if they were her own: the sword calluses across the base of his fingers; his neat square nail beds; the sinewy boniness that had replaced the breadth of youth.

He said, "You like this."

It was a nonsensical statement. It had nothing to do with her. He could style her hair if it made him happy. She would simply get her attendants to undo it later.

He went on, "I can feel you relaxing. Your neck gets soft, here—" His lips touched her neck, before he resumed the rhythm of the combing. "I can feel you turning to meet the comb, resisting it in just the right way. Your body says you like it."

That's my body, but my body isn't me, she thought. *The thing that feels your hands on me, that pleases you, isn't me. My body is for you, it isn't for me.* She resided in her body an inch below the surface, wearing it like a doll, with a sense of ownership and pride, perhaps, but never fully being it. She turned and smiled at him over her shoulder, giving him what he wanted.

Something rueful crinkled in his eyes. He turned her back with gentle rough hands and resumed his work. When he was nearly done, he murmured, "I won't see you again before I leave."

That surprised her. "I thought you weren't leaving until the day after tomorrow." Then, in a spurt of realization and spite, "Ah. You'll spend it with your wife."

"Don't begrudge her time with her husband and son who're leaving for war. Zhenjiang isn't far, but who knows how long we'll be away."

She could imagine his pained, gentle expression. She felt a pulse of savagery at it, that she was the irrational one, the one who was making things difficult. She wanted to pull away from his hands. But overriding her natural instincts was even easier than succumbing to them. "Win easily for me, then," she said. "Save some energy for when we'll have to face and deal with Chen Youliang. He'll have to be put down as quickly as possible." She added, spitefully, "And if he's as skilled with his army as his other weapon, you may find it more of a challenge than dealing with that boy Zhu Yuanzhang."

There was a satisfying silence, so quiet that she could hear the glassine pinging of the coals in the brazier as they fell into ash. "You slept with Chen Youliang?"

His hands had fallen away from her hair. She turned towards him and stretched, displaying her body to him. The body that had been turned this way and that by Chen's butcher hands. And how different were they really, from General Zhang's own hands? "Come now, are you jealous? It was just business."

"I'm sure it was." He withdrew. "But you're telling me because you want to hurt me."

Hurting presumed too much of an attachment to him; that was something for true lovers, romantic lovers, young people, people they would never be. She said, cruel, "Some men like the idea that a woman has been with others. They pay extra to watch a woman they like with another man."

"You don't need to talk like that." She heard his distaste, and relished it. Romantic that he was, how he must love to forget her true origins, what she was, what she had always been.

She purred, "How can you know if you haven't even tried?"

For a beat she thought she'd succeeded in rousing anger from him. A man cross-legged, naked, on a bed, the softness and vulnerability of his body out of its prime, the thinness of skin that showed the hollows between still-strong muscle and bone in the way that didn't show on young men, should have been silly. But he had a dignity to him. And the look he gave her was a true penetration. He said, "I'm sorry I hurt you."

She recoiled. He thought he had *hurt* her, as if she cared enough for him that she could be hurt, when she was just using him? An unidentifiable hot paralysis swept across her. She needed him to love her, and for him to think she loved him, so why with him was it so strangely unbearable?

Whatever he saw in her face made him take her hand and say, gently, "Let's not part like this."

What was that hot feeling? Hate, she thought. She hated him. She hated him for his concern, and she hated his face with its pity, and sorrow, and understanding, that had nothing to do with the truth of her at all.

"Like what?" She laughed, her voice brittle in her own ears, and slipped her hand out of his. It was the same motion that in another time and place would have been playful, but now it was as savage as her heart. "You haven't hurt me." She touched him lightly on the face, teasing, although her heart was a heaving tumult of spite and anger. Did he look at her and think he *understood*? She thought violently, *Everything you see I've designed for you to see.*

Their hands on her body, thinking it was their hands on her. There was no difference between them: Rice Bucket and General Zhang and Chen Youliang. They were all pieces for her to use at the right time, to serve her own purpose. And when they'd reached the end of their usefulness, she would discard them. Some sooner than others. That was what she'd done her whole life, and it had never failed. She was a courtesan and a queen, and one day she would be an empress.

She refused to look at him as she rose and put on her robe. "You had better leave now, or you'll be seen."

❋

The parade was over. General Zhang had left, marching under their flags in the direction of Zhenjiang. The Queen was barely aware of her husband in the carriage next to her. She could still see in her mind's eye the receding flags under the mounting pillars of dust, and the aching feeling as of a string pulled tight between her and that army marching away. A strange feeling, kindling a discomfort that seemed like fury. It wasn't attachment. It was just caring about making sure he won so she could execute the next part of her plan.

The carriage jolted to a stop. The Queen's teeth clashed together and her hair ornaments swayed forwards and then back again, their resettling sending an unpleasant murmur through her. Her impatience with the servants felt like a burning nugget beneath the surface. Their performance reflected on *her.* By performing badly, they were visiting a violence upon her that she would have to wait to visit back upon them.

Rice Bucket's impatience had no such checks. His skin was so thin that the slightest frustration became an unbearable thorn that he had to rage at. He raised the curtain of the carriage and stuck his head out, and to her discomfort she saw him go rigid.

"Husband—"

It was as if she didn't exist. He threw open the door and lunged out.

The Queen called a servant sharply to help her down from the carriage. She wasn't sure what could have pulled her indolent husband into action when nothing short of several beautiful women could compel him. Her unsteady feet took her across the rutted dirt road, more slowly than her eyes, which had already risen to the wall to take in what Rice Bucket was gaping at.

At first she couldn't even tell what it meant, it was so unexpected.

It was a woodblock-printed poster, of surprisingly good quality, in two colors. A caricature, recognizably of Rice Bucket himself, in an artist's fine hand. And atop Rice Bucket's head was a cuckold's green hat.

The hat beamed from the poster in that luminous, violent green. The sickening color, leaping off the page, reached into her and touched her with a strange cold knowledge that she recognized as the awareness of mortal danger. So many people knew. Trusted servants, and people she had shown for good reason. But never, never Rice Bucket. She had never worried overmuch. He would never have cared to notice. He *would* never have noticed, unless it was shoved in his face. Unless it was made a public humiliation. Unless someone made it so that he had to care.

Her body, the body that wasn't her, was shivering with tension like an animal. But that body had forgotten that it couldn't run.

Rice Bucket scrabbled at the poster, but it was glued down. He let out a howl of rage. He must be shredding his fingernails. Eventually he managed to tear off a strip right down the middle of the caricature's face.

He turned, brandishing the strip, and his contorted, reddened face seemed like a demon's. For a moment it fixed on her with incinerating hatred, before it was dragged away to something behind her.

She turned and saw another poster in the distance. And then another, and another, jumping as if joyfully from wall to wall of the city, across the street and down side alleys, on the sides of official buildings, high in a tree: that luminous unnatural green like a glowing lichen scraped out of the world's disgusting places, screaming Rice Bucket's humiliation to the world.

A column of slender printed writing ran down each poster to the side of Rice Bucket's leering caricatured face: *If brothers are loyal, the family's hearts will rest at ease.*

"You whore." Rice Bucket loomed over where the Queen knelt, bound awkwardly in her thickness of finery that wasn't made for kneeling. He hadn't dragged her out of the carriage into his rooms, he had let her walk with the servant holding her elbow, but she had read his intention in every furious step. The terrified animal part of herself had stilled; it had finally accepted that it couldn't run.

His emotions, like his attention, were short. But they were intense. She thought, distantly, that he would probably hurt her body very badly, though perhaps she could still appease him. Looking at him now, she didn't know how much it would take to satisfy him. The veins in his neck and forehead bulged; even his eyes seemed reddened.

He spat down at her, "With my own brother? So this is what you two have been doing behind my back? Did you think I wouldn't notice? Did you think I wouldn't *care*?"

She knew he cared. There was only one thing Rice Bucket truly valued, save his pleasure in the moment, and that was his reputation. He wanted to be esteemed, he demanded it from the world, and the poster had turned him into a laughingstock he couldn't ignore.

General Zhang wasn't here. But even if he had been, what would it have changed?

She felt briefly furious with herself for thinking of him, as she cried, "It's not true! This unworthy woman would never bring shame upon her husband."

"You expect me to believe that?" Rice Bucket brought a bamboo cane down onto her back. In their mutual fever pitch she didn't feel it; it seemed to glance off her surface. "Once a whore, always a whore! And my brother, always thinking he's better than me. Is he laughing behind my back too?"

He hit her again and again. The impacts sent sensation through her body; something told her it was pain, and something about it made her body scream, even though her mind held itself distant. "No, my husband, I beg you! We're innocent, it's a slander. Someone is trying to hurt us!"

She sheltered herself with her hands that were almost as tiny and useless as her feet, as the cane whistled and bit into her, and she heard her own voice screaming as strange and unrecognizably as when she performed pleasure.

"Who would do such a thing if it wasn't true?" The exertion made him heave and blow. But there was enjoyment in it, as if he relished the swing of his arm and the thud of the cane. He owned her; he controlled her; and he thrilled in the exercise of his power and the catharsis of his rage through each blow. It was the most honest work he'd ever done.

"It's Yue!" she cried. "My husband, she's trying to make you jealous. She wants to drive us apart. She wants to hurt us both;

she wants what I have." She flung herself forwards and grasped him around the waist. Pressed her head against his belly, his crotch, and felt the sweated dampness of his clothes; smelled his rage. Her mind was clear. Her body was her armor, absorbing the blows while keeping the pain from her. "She knows she's not practiced at pleasing you. She knows she can't compete with all these years that I've kept you happy. Don't fall for her tricks, husband! You know what we women are like!"

He looked down at her. His belly heaved under her face as she mashed it against him, her makeup smearing, as supplicating as a dog. "So there's no truth in it." His voice was vicious with disbelief.

"None!"

She had always thought him stupid, but he was as cunning and vicious as a wild boar; she knew he could kill. He took her by the throat as she knelt there, and said with soft venomous hate, "Who can believe the words of a whore?"

He strangled her until she realized, distantly, that she had urinated. He gave a grunt of disgust and threw her down. He withdrew the silver ring from his purse before undoing his belt. When his gown fell open, he came for her: stabbing at her with his spongy penis until it was hard enough to jam the ring on. It would have been more effective to keep beating her, but he wanted to hurt her this way: to show her her place, as all men inevitably wanted to do.

He twisted her ear until she arched and screamed, then managed to thrust into her. Of course he didn't want her limp: that wouldn't have hurt. "How dare he take what's mine, when I'm the elder? I've given him everything he has. Without me, what would he be?"

She tried to look away, but he took her head in his hard fingers and squeezed until she cried out. "Look at your husband, you bitch."

She stared at the beating pulse of the veins in his face. Let him fuck her, let him make her look at him; what he couldn't do was make her feel. She was suspended inside herself, an apricot kernel surrounded by its shell. Safe, even as her body pissed and bled. She wanted to spit at him: *Do you think if something like this could destroy me, there would have been any left of me when we met, to make you who you are now?*

He left her there when he was finished, splayed like a broken thing. But she wasn't in her body. She simply had an awareness of how it lay, its head turned to the side, bruises on its jaw. One of her shoes had come off, displaying a triangular foot, and it seemed completely alien: not like something that could have belonged to a person at all. She felt no pain, no shame, even as her servants came in—how convenient for them to have waited until Rice Bucket left—and started screaming.

Well, she thought, dry-eyed inside her shell, he was the fool. General Zhang was going to win, and return. *And soon, husband: there won't be any room for you.*

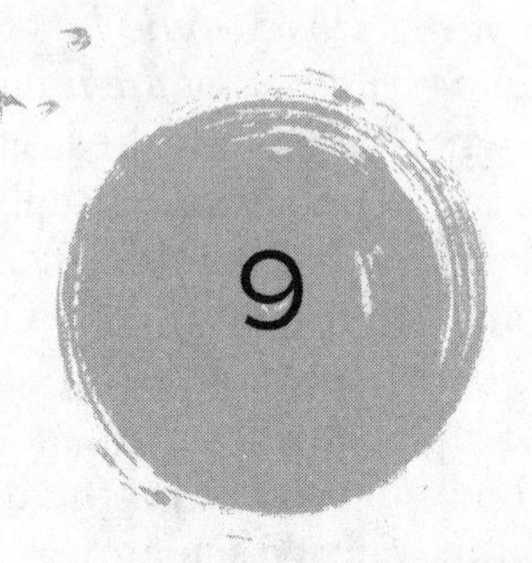

9

BORDER OF THE KINGDOMS OF ZHU YUANZHANG AND THE ZHANG FAMILY

Zhu's young commander Chang came into Ouyang's prison tent, saying, "The Radiant King wants to see you." Through some mysterious process of convergence with his leader, Chang was almost as short and ugly as Zhu himself. He had brought several guards with him, and they all waited pointedly until Ouyang stood with bad grace. His body creaked like a rope under strain. The powerlessness of his ongoing captivity wasn't just driving him mad with rage and despair, but had put him in such a constant state of tension that his bones seemed fit to crack. Chang added with a scowl, "Don't try any funny business."

Outside, dawn crept over the plain that lay between Zhu and Ouyang's armies on one side, and General Zhang's on the other. The past days of battle had flattened what had once been a sea of fluffy pink grasses, and now the autumn frost turned the trampled stalks into an endlessness of silver billows.

After they'd returned from Fortress Island, Zhu hadn't spent enough time in Yingtian for Ouyang to come up with another escape plan, let alone implement one. With ruthless speed and efficiency, Zhu had gathered up his and Ouyang's men and marched them east to the border between his and the Zhang family's territories. The goal of the current fighting was the Zhang family's key town of Zhenjiang, which lay across the pink grass plain at the intersection of the Grand Canal and the Yangzi River.

If Zhu took Zhenjiang, then Madam Zhang in her capital of Pingjiang—south of the Yangzi—would be cut off from her cities north of the river. And without those cities, her fall would be all but assured.

And yet, as Ouyang had known would be the case: Zhu wasn't winning. All of Zhu's previous victories had been the result of overwhelming action, and he had clearly hoped to win the same way again. But General Zhang was experienced in dealing with brash young upstarts like Zhu Yuanzhang. He had dug his heels in and was forcing Zhu to expend his men—and, by extension, *Ouyang's* men—in near-daily engagements that yielded minimal progress. In Ouyang's opinion, General Zhang would be well able to keep up the resistance until Zhu wore himself out. Then the question would be whether Zhu would withdraw—yielding the eastern portion of his territory to General Zhang—or whether he would stay put, and be annihilated.

As soon as Ouyang had seen what was happening, his fantasies of escape had gained a new register of desperation. But even if he broke out of the prison tent, what then? In Yingtian, his army had camped outside the city together with the horses and herds of livestock that were essential to its function. If Ouyang had been able to get back to his army there, he could have convinced his commanders to overthrow Zhu's own, and wrenched back control.

But here on the pink grass plain, there was no such separation between his and Zhu's armies. In terms of supplies and logistics, and even where they made camp, the two armies had become one. Tents and gers stood side by side, and the comet tail of Ouyang's herds and spare horses reached all the way back into Zhu's own territory. There was no way of physically extricating his own forces to take them to Dadu. It made him sick to think about.

A gold banner hung from the peak of Zhu's command tent, its fingers pointing limply downwards in the morning stillness. Chang lifted the tent flap and went through, holding it for Ouyang—who, catching a glimpse inside from over Chang's shoulder, stopped in shock. His hand was still raised to receive the tent flap. His heart made an urgent motion in his chest that made him cough.

Zhu, clad in his golden armor, was standing with his back to General Xu, who was combing his hair. Perhaps they were speaking; Ouyang had no idea. He could only stare. In keeping with his size, General Xu had big hands: they made Zhu's head look small as he gathered his hair together. His practiced deftness was the same as that of men performing all those small, ordinary, masculine tasks that stood alongside the larger work of warfare: cleaning armor, or mending tack. Fletching arrows.

But it wasn't any of those tasks to touch another man intimately, to address his bodily needs, as if he weren't a general but a—

Ouyang's cheeks burned with such vicarious shame that he thought he might go blind with it. He would have *welcomed* blindness. Since Zhu was still growing out his hair, it was shorter than that of most adult men and oddly squared-off at the ends. General Xu twisted the length of it around twice, then slid the golden hair clasp over it and fixed it with the matching pin.

It was worse than seeing two people fucking, because *men didn't act like this.* Men didn't serve each other, they didn't touch each other, and yet Zhu and General Xu let everyone see it without shame. As if it had never even occurred to them that it made them objects of derision.

Chang glanced around when Ouyang failed to take the tent flap from him, then, puzzled, followed the direction of his attention to Zhu and General Xu. "What's up?"

He had no idea how wrong it was. None of them did. Zhu smiled easily at General Xu before moving away. It was an affection that couldn't have existed in Ouyang's world. But here in Zhu's world—a world led by a man who looked nothing like a leader should look—everything was different. It was worthy of nothing but Ouyang's contempt. But as he watched Zhu pat his general's arm in gratitude, what he felt wasn't contempt, but an uprooting sadness. It took several breaths and clenching his hands so tightly that his fingernails cut into his palms, before he could follow Chang inside.

Zhu turned as Ouyang entered and said courteously, "Thank you for coming, General," as if Ouyang had had a choice. For a moment his insect gaze, eerie and unjudgmental, rested on Ouyang's white-knuckled fists. "I wanted to consult you about a matter. As I'm sure you've noticed, I'm not making the headway against General Zhang I would have hoped for." At least, Ouyang thought with scornful despair, he was self-aware enough to recognize that much. "There's no possibility of me gaining additional reinforcements in the short term. You've fought alongside General Zhang before. You know his capabilities. So tell me: What are the chances we'll prevail in this current situation?"

Zhu, and Commander Chang, and even General Xu: in Ouyang's eyes, they were nothing but children. Like children, they didn't know yet what they were capable of—but, equally, they had no idea what they *weren't* capable of. Ouyang said flatly, "You won't."

Drums sounded outside, gathering the men for the day's useless battle. It was curious how Zhu not only solicited Ouyang's opinion, but seemed to actually listen to it. On the other hand, that opinion didn't seem to have squashed him as it should have, because he went on, "What if I asked you to devise new tactics for me? If I can't win it, could you?"

The sheer naïveté of it was so boggling that Ouyang had to take a moment to collect himself. "You melon-headed *idiot*. Do you think Madam Zhang would have had a fraction of her success with someone other than General Zhang leading her forces? It's hardly a surprise that he's better than you and your commanders combined. *But he's also better than me.*"

It was nothing more than the truth. Ouyang's willingness to throw endless numbers of conscripts at his problems had obtained him results for a long time. It had worked until it hadn't. He'd never cared enough to be a good general the way General Zhang was good. General Zhang didn't have to whip his army to gain their obedience. He knew and trusted them, and they gave him their blood and sweat and pain because they trusted him not to throw them away carelessly. He said bitterly, "I can beat General Zhang in an individual fight. But I always knew that if I went against him as a general, I would lose."

It hadn't bothered him, because he'd never thought it would happen. But now Ouyang couldn't separate his army from Zhu's.

Both his and Zhu's armies were going to be shredded against General Zhang, and there would be nothing left to take them to Dadu. But Ouyang wouldn't accept that. He couldn't.

Ouyang had spent some pleasant times with Zhang Shide. Apart from his mystifying decision to dedicate himself to a conniving, ambitious whore, Ouyang respected him. Liked him, even. But now he knew, awfully, that his respect was like a candle flame against the howling wind of his desperation. There were no longer any limits to what he would do.

"If you want to stop a man with a good and noble heart like General Zhang, don't stop his army," he said. "Stop *him*. Hurt what he loves even more than those whom he fights for."

An alien shine appeared on Zhu's small face: not that of a friendly companion cricket, but a mantis that could kill something as fast and beautiful as a hummingbird. "And what's that, General?"

There was only one thing men loved more than their brothers or their lovers. One thing that contained all their dreams and desires for the future, their hopes and their honor. One thing that, when lost, shattered not only a future, but a family.

The hot seeping sensation between Ouyang's fingers was as unstoppable as the tide of his emotions. "His son."

"How sure are you that his son will actually be in Zhenjiang?" Zhu spoke indistinctly as she used teeth, hand, one foot, and the other elbow in her attempt to cram the last of the mission supplies into a large woven shoulder pack. Then, victoriously: "Hah!"

"I'm *not* sure." Ouyang watched her contortions with disdain. He was prepared for their journey in nondescript Nanren-style clothing, with a triangle hat pulled low to hide his face. Zhu wouldn't be the only one-handed man in the region, but it was distinctly possible that Ouyang *was* the only eunuch. If General Zhang's men were to realize who exactly it was wandering around Zhenjiang, it wouldn't bode well for the plan—or for them. "You asked what I think. That's what I think. General Zhang likes to install his son somewhere behind the front lines. Safe, but close enough that he can call him to the front to observe certain points of the campaign. Perhaps in a year or two, when the boy's education is more complete, he'll keep him alongside the whole time. But right now he's still young. When I visited Yangzhou last spring he wasn't as much as thirteen or fourteen, if I can judge such things."

He sounded hostile, as if the whole concept of pubescent boys offended him. Zhu could understand. She knew what it felt like to be an outsider in the midst of boys' changing bodies—even if, in her case, she'd never desired what her fellow novices *had,* so much as she'd hated her body for changing in a different direction entirely. But Ouyang's body wouldn't have changed at all. How much of a torture must it have been to watch everyone else effortlessly attaining what you wanted, but could never have?

As Zhu hoisted the overstuffed pack, Ouyang said scathingly, "You look like an ant carrying a grain of rice. Perhaps you'd prefer to take a donkey wagon instead of a horse. It would suit your peasant style better."

"Ah—about that." She should have known how he'd expected to travel. "Since General Zhang has checkpoints set up on the main roads into Zhenjiang, it doesn't make sense for us to go that way. But there are plenty of hill trails that the peasants use to get from their hamlets into town for market day."

"*No,*" Ouyang said, seeing where this was going, as Zhu confirmed, "We're walking."

Several hours later, when they were not quite halfway to Zhenjiang, she paused and glanced back at Ouyang's unfamiliar behatted shape trudging tensely up the moonlit hillside. Though by now his feet would be healed from his escape attempt, they were still the soft, tender feet of someone who'd never walked a long distance in his life. She remembered how narrow and pale they'd been when she'd glimpsed them in his prison room in Yingtian. And yet, since an aristocratic Nanren woman's feet would have been bound, she'd been struck by how they were the most clearly masculine part of him.

"Does it hurt?"

"Did it hurt when I cut off your hand?" Ouyang said viciously, not-limping past her without stopping.

Zhu hurried to catch up. "I'm not sure those two things are comparable. Your blisters versus my life-threatening amputation." The amputation *had* hurt—objectively, it had been the worst pain of her life—but she would have happily paid several hands as the cost of getting what she wanted.

"Once it gets past a certain point, all pain is the same," he said. "Whether it's a blister or a *life-threatening amputation*, which I also happen to know something about. There's nothing interesting about pain. The only distinction is in degree. The higher the degree, the more it erases you. Until it hurts so much you aren't there at all." After a moment he added, shortly, "That can be a good thing."

It was a strange idea. Zhu couldn't imagine ever wanting to erase herself. For a moment her thoughts drifted back to that long-dead boy who had been the original bearer of the name Zhu Chongba. He had lain there in bed and breathed out his life along with his fate of greatness, and let her seize it. He hadn't been strong enough to bear the suffering that desire engendered. But Zhu was.

"Well, maybe I'm tired. Maybe *my* feet hurt. I guess we should rest awhile," she announced. There was a solitary tree a short distance from the path that had protected the ground beneath from dewfall. "This looks like a nice spot!" After checking first for buffalo dung, she plopped onto the ground. Ouyang, outlined against the dark crest of the hill in a corona of moonlight and ghost glow, made a picture of reluctance, but after a moment he came back and eased stiffly down beside her.

The moonlight changed, filtered through the bodies of Ouyang's ghosts that had gathered around him once he stopped moving. Zhu took off her boots and socks, as if she only wanted to stretch her toes, then left aside her socks when she put her boots back on. After a moment, without looking at her, Ouyang took the socks and pulled them on over his own.

They rested, listening to the squawks of the night herons as they headed to the river. The translucent ghosts that were clustered around Ouyang cast a pale haze of distance over him, though he was only an arm's length away. It made Zhu think of the first few times she'd seen him. He'd been as remote as the beautiful moon, even as their connection had pulled her as irresistibly as gravity. It felt strange but right to sit beside him now, as if after all her downhill rolling she had finally settled where she belonged.

He surprised her by breaking the silence. "The ghosts. The ones that follow me. Do they look like the people they once were?"

Zhu saw her father and brother, transformed into their death-selves, standing on the other side of a moonlit grave. For so long she had felt attached to her brother by fear and fate. Now that she'd become her present self, that attachment had faded. The memory of those ghosts felt like a story someone had told her about strangers. "Yours look like people," she told Ouyang. Perhaps it was better not to tell him about the distorted wretched monsters who had been denied their rest and lingered on, ravenous, in the crevices of the world.

His face was turned away from her, invisible under the hat. He was silent for so long that she thought that was all he wanted to know. Then, in a rasp so terrible that she couldn't tell whether it was something he wanted or didn't want, he said, "Is Esen-Temur there?"

Esen-Temur, the Prince of Henan. More than ten years ago, Zhu had sat on the monastery's swooping green roof and marveled at a young Mongol lord whose braids had tossed in the wind like the mane of a horse eager to run. His identity hadn't meant anything to her at the time. It only now occurred to her to look back and think about him as the son of the man who had killed Ouyang's family. As the one who had been Ouyang's lord and master, until Ouyang had betrayed and killed him that day at Bianliang.

Based purely on the circumstances, Zhu could have believed that Ouyang had spent a lifetime regarding Esen-Temur as his enemy, his hate hidden beneath servitude. And yet, now that she knew Ouyang somewhat, she couldn't fathom it having been like that. Ouyang wasn't the kind of person who could successfully pretend for a moment, let alone years. He had spent a lifetime by Esen-Temur's side. They had ridden together, fought together, entrusted each other with their lives. The only way Ouyang could have done it was if it had been real. If, until that very last moment, his loyalty had been true.

She heard an echo of Xu Da's voice from that long-ago rooftop: *They say he cherishes him even more than his own brother.*

But what Zhu remembered most clearly about that day wasn't Esen-Temur himself. It was how the Abbot had forbade Ouyang from accompanying the others into the hall because he was a eunuch. Esen-Temur had made a brief protest. Perhaps he really did cherish Ouyang. But in the end even he had left him behind to stand alone in his shame.

Zhu looked at the ghosts drifting around Ouyang where he sat with his knees drawn up, the dark eye of a whirlpool. Death rendered princes and peasants alike into white raggedness, their hair tangled around their shoulders as if they were in mourning for themselves. But of the dozens of dead faces in that eerie congregation, none that she could see were Mongol.

"He's not there." Even to her that seemed an unsatisfying answer, so she added, "But one of them is probably your father. If you can tell me what he looked like—"

Nothing about his appearance changed, but she had the strange conviction that for a moment he froze. Then he got to his feet, saying tightly, "No. That's all I needed to know."

She watched him making his way up the hillside, the ghosts trailing in a slow stream behind him. She found herself thinking of the blood she'd seen between the fingers of his clenched fists when he came into her command tent.

It can be a good thing. To be in so much pain that you were erased from yourself.

ZHENJIANG

In busy, prosperous, riverside Zhenjiang, it was as though a war weren't happening at all. Zhu strolled, and Ouyang limp-marched, down the main street, taking in the sight of the rich mansions, the bustling shops and teahouses. Ouyang's face was hidden by the hat, but his posture was so rigid he might as well have still been wearing armor. It would have been less conspicuous for Zhu to have brought Xu Da or Yuchun, but Ouyang was the only one who'd met General Zhang's son. Accidentally abducting the wrong thirteen-year-old boy would be unfortunate for everyone concerned.

As if Ouyang could read her thoughts, he said dourly, "I'm interested in your plan to locate an individual in this place where we know no one, and to which neither of us has previously been."

"Well—" Zhu said, turning brightly from her perusal of a meat stall where a boy of about thirteen (the incorrect one) was making a desultory effort to keep flies off the silver-membraned slabs of buffalo meat.

He'd already walked past. "I'm not actually interested. Just get on with it."

Zhu went to open her pack, but was distracted by a woodblock-printed poster brushed onto a nearby wall. It was a caricature of a man's face under a bold green cuckold's cap. It had been the Yuan's practice to put up posters for wanted criminals, but these days there were few Yuan-held towns left in the south, and Zhenjiang certainly wasn't one of them. "Huh."

Ouyang came back and looked over her shoulder. "That artist has some talent. It's a good likeness. That's Rice Bucket Zhang."

"I've never met him." Zhu memorized his face. "Perhaps I should, though! They do say the best way to look handsome is to stand next to someone ugly."

"Are you sure you're the one who'd look handsome in comparison?"

Zhu mock-scowled. "I suppose I can console myself with the idea that I'm more competent, and my wife more loyal." She read the small characters running down the side of the poster and laughed with scandalized delight. "*General Zhang* is the one fucking Madam Zhang? I thought you said he had a good and noble heart! Or is she really so beautiful that even honorable men can't resist? I should have pressed harder for a look that one time I met her."

"Even the ugliest whore has her tricks," Ouyang said with more than his usual spite. "Men are—"

"Fools, yes, with little thought of consequence beyond their own pleasure. Whereas the women I've known all seemed quite attuned to the matter of consequence. And for all that General Zhang seems a well-formed figure of a man, Madam Zhang didn't strike me as the type to risk a jealous husband's wrath for anything as useless as either lust or love—*ah*." The truth filled itself in. "When you said I wasn't the only one with the Mandate. You didn't mean *Rice Bucket*. You meant General Zhang." She looked hard at Ouyang, or at least at his hat. "You let me assume."

Ouyang's shoulders, she'd discovered, were as easy to read as those of a furious cat: *I let you assume, because you're holding me against my will, and also: I hate you.*

It made sense that Madam Zhang would hitch her cart to the strongest man in the family, even if it wasn't the head of that family—or her own husband. "Does Rice Bucket know? He doesn't, does he." A petty, jealous man might be willing to let his brother show himself competent on the field, but would never tolerate him having been chosen for the throne instead of himself. "What a scandal! All this time poor Rice Bucket hasn't been ruler of his own bed, let alone his army or his kingdom. The thing that surprises me the most is that she hasn't already deposed him and taken outright control, with General Zhang by her side."

"I don't doubt that's what she wants. But General Zhang *is* honorable. He finds himself in the difficult position of loving his brother, and also loving his brother's wife."

"Even having the particular brother he has," Zhu noted ironically. She hadn't felt that torn to let the original Zhu Chongba die, but she supposed she was hardly a good person. "Do you think this poster is from the Yuan? A campaign of public humiliation against an enemy seems creative for them."

Ouyang shrugged. "I wouldn't have thought it the Grand Councilor's style, but even an old warrior can learn new tricks. Who else would it be?"

"Well," Zhu said, frowning. It was true that the only parties with a particular interest in bringing the Zhang family down were herself and the Yuan, but she had a niggling feeling. "I suppose it must be."

They'd reached that lull time of the morning, when household servants had finished their most pressing tasks and were thinking of sitting down for a cup of tea before preparing lunch. Zhu put aside the matter of the strange poster, opened her bag, and waved a small dried gourd under Ouyang's hat. The gourd was buzzing loudly. "Time for business!"

"You're purveying . . . fighting crickets," he stated with utter derision.

"You didn't fraternize much with your soldiers, did you?" Zhu laughed, then laughed even harder because although she couldn't see his face, she *knew* he was rolling his eyes. "General Zhang won't have left his boy without a couple of guards, some servants, perhaps even a tutor or two, and I bet they're all bored out of their brains." She hustled over to the nearest mansion and knocked on the front gate. "Gambling on crickets is a great way to pass the time. Ma Xiuying isn't a fan, though. She thinks it's cruel. She wants me to ban it when I win—apparently since I'm going to come back as a bug in my next life, she thinks I'll be doing myself a favor—"

She brandished the gourd as a servant opened the front gate. "Crickets?"

"How many houses," Ouyang said, "are we going to do this at."

"As many as it takes," Zhu said cheerfully, accosting a servant coming out the front gate of the next house. "Crickets?"

By afternoon Ouyang was footsore and fantasizing about single-handedly razing the whole of Zhenjiang as a more pleasant and effective means of flushing out their quarry. He'd never in his life stopped to consider how many houses there might be in one (large) town, and apparently the answer was *far too many*. His already low faith in Zhu's plan had reached such a baleful nadir that when Zhu knocked on the gate of a nondescript mansion near the center of town, and several uniformed guards rushed out to buy every last cricket, it took him a moment to realize what had happened.

As Zhu all but bounced away from the mansion, Ouyang gritted out, "Even if that's the place—"

"Even!"

"—don't you think General Zhang will have ordered him to stay inside?"

Zhu paused outside the pair of teahouses that faced the mansion from the other side of the street. "You weren't much fun as a child, were you."

Ouyang said with the finality that used to terrify entire battalions, "I was a slave."

Zhu, however, not only refused to be terrified, but had an annoying tendency of never letting Ouyang have the last word. "Nobody could accuse a monastery of lacking discipline, but even monks knew the futility of trying to keep spirited boys inside. He'll come out. We just have to watch and wait. Let's get a table."

But when Zhu stepped into the open frontage of the nearest teahouse, the proprietor's gaze shot to the wooden hand without even seeming to register the person it was attached to, and without so much as a word he spat directly onto Zhu's boot.

Ouyang was surprised by the totality of his own rage. But he *knew* that look. It was the look he'd received his entire life: the one that told him he wasn't even a person in other people's eyes, but a thing. If he hadn't been wearing the hat to conceal his face that so offended people with its refusal to be one thing or the other, that same disgust would have been flung at him. Ouyang had mutilated Zhu precisely because he'd *wanted* him to be spurned and shunned. He'd wanted him to feel the exact shade of misery that came from being beneath the world's contempt. But he didn't realize he'd taken a threatening step towards the proprietor until Zhu grasped his wrist and towed him outside.

"No need for a fuss!" To Ouyang's furious astonishment, Zhu seemed unbothered by the stain upon his honor and, more visibly, his person. He dragged Ouyang into the neighboring teahouse, pronouncing cheerfully, "Oh, look! This place is better, anyway. They won't kick us out when it gets late, so we'll be able to sleep at the table until tomorrow."

Ouyang had no idea how Zhu had gathered that from a glance. To him, one teahouse was much the same as any other. They settled at a table at the open front of the establishment, which gave a clear view of the mansion across the street. An unsmiling but polite proprietress brought over a plate of acceptable cold sliced drunken chicken. It was only after they'd been sitting for some time that it dawned on Ouyang that all the other patrons of the teahouse were women. They sat mostly in groups, though some alone, each with a lantern in front of her. One was playing the flute, while others played games or chatted. Now that Ouyang was paying attention, he noticed a man approach one of the groups. After a brief exchange, one of the women took up her lantern and led him off into the night. He abruptly realized how Zhu had known this teahouse wouldn't close all night. "They're *whores*."

Zhu turned from observing a pair of guards who had just returned to the mansion with a jar of wine. "They're lovely girls. I haven't been spat on once since we got here. I'll have to leave a tip."

Just thinking about the spitting incident brought Ouyang's rage rushing back. He found himself recalling all the times he'd seen people turn from Zhu in the street, here and in Taizhou. The way even street sellers hesitated to serve him, and stared at him from the corners of their eyes when they did. And yet the offense rolled off Zhu as readily as water from a straw raincoat. "How can it not bother you, to be treated like that? He didn't even greet you like a human! You could see it in his face: had a dog crawled into that teahouse at the same moment as you, he wouldn't have hesitated to kick you first."

Most of the time, Zhu's facetiousness gave him a screened quality, as if it were a second eyelid he had drawn across his inner workings. But for a moment the screen fell away. "It does bother me. Do you think it didn't? Nobody feels good about being hated. But this is who I am. It took me a long time to become this person. Someone who not only can, but will, get what they want. And now that I'm who I need to be: I'm not going to hide myself so that others don't turn away from me, or spit on me. If the world's judgment is the price of what I want, then it's a price I'm willing to pay." The whore's flute had a thin, strangled sound that set Ouyang's teeth on edge. Zhu said softly, "I'm willing. And I'm strong enough to do it. But it can be hard. To swallow the insult, and endure the world's contempt. I think you know what that's like, General."

Ouyang, staring at that small, ugly, hated face, was pierced by a twang of uncanny recognition. It was as if he'd glanced into the bronzed depths of a mirror and found that the image there wasn't of his hateful body, but his self. It wasn't a pleasant feeling. When all he wanted was to be free of Zhu, it seemed to pin them together, as if their two wriggling bodies were impaled on the same spear. He jerked back from the table, hissing, "Why does that untalented bitch play so loudly? Does she think it's her skills with a flute that will impress the customers?"

As diversions went it was transparent, but to Ouyang's relief, Zhu let it pass. "I think many men find expertise on the flute quite desirable."

He said it so seriously that at first Ouyang didn't get it. Then he did. His mind first delivered him the image of General Xu with his hands in Zhu's hair, then a permutation of that same image that made his body flush so hot with vicarious shame that it seemed a miracle he didn't combust. He ground out, "Is General Xu good at the flute?"

The moment he saw the sharp prick of curiosity in Zhu's eyes, he realized with a sinking sensation that the only person he'd exposed had been himself. But all Zhu said was, "Honestly, I don't think Ah-Da has a musical bone in his body. Have some more of this excellent chicken." He looked across the street with a thoughtful expression. "Did you see how those servants went out to tend to the horses stabled down the street? I bet tomorrow we'll see the boy go out for a ride."

He got up and went over to the flute-playing whore. Ouyang's confusion grew as they chatted at length, money exchanged hands, and then Zhu came back and put the flute and two small pots on the table.

"What a nice girl! So helpful." Zhu opened one of the pots, sniffed, and made a face. "Did you know if you mix these two kinds of makeup together, your face will blister right off and you'll die horribly?"

"I did not," Ouyang said, "know that."

Zhu gave an enigmatic Buddha smile. "My wife told me.

Women know all sorts of things." He handed a chopstick and his belt knife to Ouyang. "Sharpen it to a point."

When Ouyang had done it, Zhu fitted the sharpened chopstick inside the flute, put his mouth over the end, and gave it an experimental puff. The chopstick shot out of the flute and embedded itself into the nearest woven wall.

"Seems I have a natural talent for the flute," Zhu said, and laughed to himself.

He retrieved the chopstick and smeared the end with the contents of the two pots. "Do you find the idea cruel? I know how much you Mongols love horses."

"Fortunately for you," Ouyang said, "I'm not a Mongol."

Zhu's insect eyes glittered. "Good."

The small riding party that Ouyang had watched mount outside the gate of the mansion had just diminished down the street when Zhu trotted up to the teahouse leading a broken-down horse and a two-wheeled curtained carriage. "Did you get it done?"

"No," Ouyang said with scorn. "Somehow I missed hitting an entire horse from a distance of less than twenty paces, so I went across the road in full view of our intended target and his pair of guards, and stabbed a poisoned chopstick into its leg with my own two hands." After a night spent slumped over a teahouse table, he felt sandy-eyed and unpleasantly unwashed. His blisters throbbed. "I hope you didn't pay too much for that nag."

"I definitely paid too much for it," Zhu said cheerfully. "But when you're a king, your generosity should be broad enough to sail a boat in. Let's go."

They caught up with the group where they had come to a stop at the edge of town. All three of them had dismounted and were looking in dismay at the lathered, distressed horse. As Zhu led the carriage past, Ouyang slid out and neatly broke the first guard's neck from behind. When his companion turned in alarm, Ouyang ducked under his flailing arm and elbowed him in the face. The man fell to the road, where Ouyang knelt and broke his neck, too. Then he rose and advanced on the boy, who was making useless noises and trying to back away. With two quick jabs to the pressure points, he was unconscious.

Zhu was there in a flash, opening the carriage door so Ouyang could sling the boy's limp body inside. "Good work, General." He dived into his bag and pulled out a wadded bundle of fabric. "Now all we have to do is—"

He was still talking. But the moment Ouyang saw the dress in Zhu's hand, the world fell away. There was only the pulse of his rage and shame. How had he even come to expect anything different? Somehow he'd become lulled when he should have known better. His entire life had taught him the lesson. Whether Mongols or Nanren, people were all the same: they wanted to humiliate him, even as they used him.

"General. *General.* It's not for you. It's for me. *I'm going to wear the dress.*"

It was the urgency in Zhu's voice, as if he actually *understood* what Ouyang was feeling, that broke through his haze. Zhu had even taken a step forwards, as if he'd thought of grasping Ouyang's arm in some kind of—what? Reassurance? Solidarity? Ouyang abruptly recalled how Zhu had offered him the opportunity to take a piss in privacy. Zhu hadn't only realized Ouyang's unique lack, but he'd even (foolishly) taken the risk of extending him a consideration. None of the other men he'd known, Ouyang thought awfully, had known what it was like to be different. They'd never had any idea how it felt to struggle with something they took for granted, or to be spat upon by strangers for how they looked.

With effort, Ouyang unclenched his fists. He didn't have to look to know his palms were bleeding. "I can get us through General Zhang's checkpoint. Nobody needs to—demean himself."

"It's manned by more than a dozen soldiers." Zhu was already stripping to his undershirt and undertrousers. "I know you're good at what you do, General, but that's too much for even you to handle." He smiled crookedly. "Besides, I don't mind. I know who I am. Wearing a dress doesn't change that." He wrapped the dress around himself, then bent his head down so he could hold one of the pair of side-ties taut with his teeth while he knotted the other one around it, one-handed. He pulled out his hairpin and clasp so his hair fell loose over his shoulders. But then, taking a ribbon from the now-empty bag, he frowned. "Hair is hard with one hand." He held it out to Ouyang. "Can you tie it for me? Twist it behind into a single bun, like a married woman would wear."

Ouyang recoiled. He tried, unsuccessfully, to avoid thinking about General Xu's strong fingertips tracing the curve of Zhu's head as he gathered up his hair. "I'm not going to *serve* you."

"I'm not ordering you to serve me," Zhu said, exasperated. "I'm asking you to *help* me. Whose fault is this, anyway? Take some responsibility. You could have blinded me in one eye, or carved an insult into my forehead, but no: it had to be the hand!"

"When they check the carriage, it's not going to be your hair that's the problem," Ouyang fired back. "You really think anyone's going to believe someone as ugly as you could be a woman?"

Zhu rolled his eyes. "Ugly women exist. What a peculiar life you've had, to have only met beautiful ones. That's what you get for growing up in a palace. I'm a perfectly plausible woman. Anyway, we don't have time to argue." He jumped into the carriage and pulled the unconscious boy onto his lap like a concerned mother of an ill child, and swept the curtains closed. "Start walking."

The checkpoint, when they reached it, was a small wooden barricade across the road. As Zhu had said, it was amply manned. General Zhang clearly had no intention of letting troublesome enemy spies, saboteurs, and provocateurs move freely between the front and the Zhang family's territory.

"Halt and state your business." A soldier came forwards to meet Ouyang as he approached.

"My wife and I are returning from a visit to the town physician with our ill child," Ouyang said stiffly, in his best imitation of Zhu's southern accent.

The soldier blinked in confusion, which made Ouyang wonder if he had given a rendition of a peasant, a monk, or something else entirely. But all he said was, "We'll check your vehicle and you can be on your way."

Ouyang felt a growing trepidation as the soldier went to the carriage. It occurred to him that when his own men were on similar guard detail, they had a tendency to examine women's chests with more rigor than mere diligence would have deemed necessary. What were the chances the soldier would notice that Zhu's chest was flat? He could hear Zhu speaking indistinctly from inside the carriage. With visceral repulsion, Ouyang realized Zhu had raised the pitch of his already light voice until it sounded genuinely female. But if anything, that only served to make Zhu's performance even more laughable. Who in his right mind would think a woman's voice matched that small stringy body, that brown face with its sharp chin and bony, bulging brow?

But to Ouyang's surprise, the soldier came back, saying, "Go through." As the other soldiers pulled open the barricade, he added, "Wouldn't have thought your wife was old enough to have a kid that age. I guess when there's a shortage of girls in your hamlet, it's either marry a ten-year-old or start trying the cows and bitches—"

Ouyang couldn't leave this disgusting discussion fast enough. Finally the barrier was open. "We'll take our leave."

Too late, he realized he'd forgotten the Nanren accent. Suspicion flashed across the soldier's face. "Where did you say you were from?"

After that, it seemed to happen very slowly: the soldier drew his sword, placed the tip beneath the brim of Ouyang's hat, and lifted it up.

They looked at each other. The soldier recoiled. "You're—"

Zhu had been right, back in the teahouse. Ouyang knew exactly what it was like to have to swallow insult. He'd done it over and over, even when it felt like filling his belly with red coals. But now, for the first time in his life, he did exactly what he'd always wanted to do when someone recoiled from his face.

He took the soldier's sword off him, and gutted him.

The other soldiers came at him. General Zhang kept his forces to a good standard, so they were reasonably skilled. But they were only ordinary men, whereas Ouyang had trained his entire life for a single purpose.

It didn't take him long.

When he was done, he cast the sword onto the heap of corpses and stalked back to the carriage. Zhu had come outside, a ridiculous sight in his flapping skirts, and was staring at him with his mouth open. Ouyang realized that Zhu had only ever seen him fight from a distance, or when he was half dead from thirst after being imprisoned, or when he was drawing out a fight to toy with someone (before maiming them). It was grimly amusing. Even Zhu, who had that uncanny understanding of him, hadn't known what he was capable of.

Ouyang wiped his bloody hands on his equally bloody clothes and took the horse's lead rope.

"It would have been faster if we'd just done that straightaway. Let's go."

"A man's greatest treasure is his sons," Zhu said dryly to the boy bound to the chair in the middle of her command tent. He was an ordinary-looking child, his hair tied boyishly with a ribbon and his body already taking on the bean-sprout proportions of adolescence. "And what a treasure you are, young master Zhang! But rest assured: I have no interest in dragging out this situation, and I'll venture your father will be equally pleased by a quick resolution. You'll be home before you know it." She patted his trembling shoulder, then tugged the ribbon out of his hair.

Xu Da came over to take it. "I'll send it to General Zhang now?"

Just then Jiao brushed into the tent in his usual curt way, bearing a slender leather sleeve of instruments and two bowls of different sizes.

Xu Da stiffened. He towed Zhu away and said in an undertone, "Is the ribbon really not sufficient?"

Though Xu Da didn't go so far as to issue an outright objection, his hesitation was reasonable enough. The idea Zhu had come up with was unpleasant, but then again: "If all we do is cause General Zhang some worry, he'll just fight harder instead of surrendering. That won't do us any good. Now that we have him on the coals, we have to light the fire." She put her hand over his and squeezed to tell him that, even if she wouldn't change her mind, at least she understood his feelings on the matter. "I wouldn't do it, if it weren't necessary. I won't make it worse than it needs to be."

Jiao Yu, who had knelt to take the boy's pulse in his left wrist where it was bound to the chair, called over, "A strong, healthy young man."

Even with the knowledge that this was the only way to victory, Xu Da could never have done this. The fact that Zhu *could* wasn't because she didn't have any sympathy for a terrified child. It would have been easier if she didn't, she thought wryly. Unlike her old rival, Chen Youliang, who flayed men alive for personal satisfaction, she didn't have an interest in cruelty for cruelty's sake. It was unpleasant to witness suffering. Distinctly so. But the reason Zhu was king, and the reason she would one day be emperor, was because she was strong enough to bear the consequences of what had to be done.

She said to Jiao, "Continue."

The boy had gone pale with horror. As Jiao tied a tourniquet to the boy's upper arm he bit his lip until blood showed, but he didn't cry.

Zhu saw the fixed direction of his stare. She shook her sleeve down to cover her wooden hand and gave him a reassuring smile. "Don't worry, little brother. We're not cutting any bits off you." *Yet.* "This won't hurt."

Jiao drew a needle from the leather sleeve. He had a cold, interested focus, no different than if he were tooling a piece of metal in his workshop. Zhu briefly wondered whether that might be worse than Chen's pleasure. Jiao slipped the needle into the crook of the boy's arm, placed the small bowl, and loosened the tourniquet.

Xu Da said steadily to the boy, "Don't look."

But the boy hadn't heard: he stared in horror as a thin runnel of blood spurted from the end of the hollow needle into the bowl.

When the small bowl was full Jiao handed it to Xu Da, then tightened the tourniquet so the needle dripped blood more slowly into the larger bowl. He had marked the inside of the bowl with numerous horizontal lines. As they watched, the blood crept towards the first line. The boy let out a whimper before he caught himself.

Zhu remembered the delighted astonishment she'd felt the first time she'd seen Jiao's water clocks. But this was a clock of blood, and it measured out the heartbeats of life. She clamped down on a creeping sense of horror. This was the best approach, with the best possible outcomes, and she wasn't going to squander it to squeamishness.

"Jiao Yu tells me that most healthy young people can tolerate losing a quarter of their blood without ill effect," she explained to Xu Da. "About the amount that the large bowl holds. Send the messenger with the ribbon and the small bowl you have there. Have him tell General Zhang that if he surrenders in time, the boy will suffer no permanent harm."

She turned to Jiao. "How much time?"

Jiao cast his eye at the lines on the bowl. "Until Snake hour." He added, unemotional, "It could vary somewhat, depending on this particular individual's physiological characteristics."

Zhu said to Xu Da, "Go."

There was no longer any pink grass on the plain, only churned earth. Zhu, in her gold armor, rode triumphantly from her lines with Xu Da and Ouyang following. The sharply angled autumn sun was already burning off the overnight rime, sending up a rippling white mist that rose as high as their horses' chests and caught the light on its surface in a blazing layer.

General Zhang came to his surrender alone. Behind him the line of his army seemed like a fleet on a sea of clouds. The sun on their distant armor threw a fire of bronze and gold.

It was the first time Zhu had seen General Zhang up close. The winged curve of his hair as it swept back into his topknot reminded Zhu of geese in flight; it had the same sorrowful shape as his heavy eyebrows. The weight of his brows gave his black eyes a lowered, inwards quality of weary dignity.

"Greetings to my esteemed opponent, the Radiant King." He wasn't handsome, but the depth of his feeling—open, and yet in its detail unbreachably private—drew the eye as powerfully as symmetry. Zhu saw he wasn't angry or embarrassed at the position she had forced him into, but resigned. Regretful. Directing his voice over Zhu's shoulder, he added, "And greetings to you as well, old friend. I never thought we would meet again like this."

To Zhu's surprise Ouyang said stiffly, "I ask your forgiveness, Zhang Shide."

General Zhang dipped his head in acknowledgment. "We each have our duties to uphold. Which man amongst us doesn't understand that? I always knew you were prepared to fulfil your duty. I don't fault you for it."

The muffled quality of the air eased as the mist burned off. Birds called in the trees that stood at the edge of the plain, where it started its gentle roll into the Zhenjiang hills.

"My son—how is he?"

"Unharmed. We stopped the clock as soon as we received your surrender." Because she thought it would please him, Zhu added, "His courage does his father credit."

It did please him. "I underestimated you, Zhu Yuanzhang. When you defeated General Ouyang, of course I attributed to you a certain degree of military competence. But now I see you also possess the qualities I most strongly associate with my own Queen."

"Dishonorable qualities?" Zhu asked wryly.

He took it in good humor. "I mean no offense. I refer only to the quality of seeing opportunities that other leaders might hesitate to take."

"I suspect your Queen and I have a surprising amount in common. It's a shame we got off on the wrong foot. I hope you can smooth things over for us, General."

"I—"

Zhu's horse spooked as a shape shot past it from behind, and in the instant before Ouyang launched himself from his saddle and bore General Zhang to the ground, Zhu saw an arrow drop through the empty sky.

Xu Da was already tearing towards the trees. There were no more arrows. One had been sufficient. Zhu gathered her horse and rode forwards.

Ouyang sat inside a circle of ghosts, General Zhang across his lap. The arterial blood splashed on General Zhang's jaw was so bright it didn't look like blood. Zhu thought of a girl's red lip paint; the flash of a woodpecker's red collar. The arrow point and a handsbreadth of shaft protruded from the side of his neck.

"Well," she said, exasperated. "That didn't come from *us*."

"It was Rice Bucket," Ouyang said with flat certainty, and Zhu remembered a taunting poster; a cuckolded brother. "The shame was too much for him to swallow. This is his revenge."

Zhu supposed Ouyang would know about both shame and revenge. She regarded the body. It seemed shrunken, as if General Zhang's last breath of outrushing spirit and qi had left a collapsed space behind, though he wore the same weary expression of sorrow. "He has the face of someone who remembers all the tragedies of his past lives. I guess he didn't break the pattern with this life, either! He should have gotten rid of Rice Bucket earlier."

In Zhu's opinion, General Zhang hadn't been the paragon of nobility that Ouyang had seemed to think he was. Perhaps his heart had been unwilling to betray his brother, but his flesh had been willing enough. The very first time General Zhang had fucked his brother's wife, he'd committed both himself and his brother to a path upon which one of them would die. Any further hesitation after that point didn't make him *good*. All it showed was his reluctance to take on the guilt of being the one to act first.

He'd desired, without having the strength to bear the suffering produced by that desire. The cost of not having that strength had been his life.

Xu Da returned, breathing hard. Zhu noticed a smudge of blood on his lip, and made a note to find him some lanolin for the crack. "I couldn't catch him. And . . ."

Zhu followed his glance towards General Zhang's army and grasped his meaning. All they could have seen from that distance was their general collapsing. Of course they'd be assuming that Zhu had broken parley and killed him. Which, she reflected, was hardly an unreasonable assumption. Between Ouyang and herself, they did have something of a reputation for backstabbing.

"Even if we didn't get the surrender, I suppose it wasn't for nothing. Without General Zhang leading them, we should be able to force a win. Lead the charge," she instructed Xu Da. "If you can take advantage of this confusion and their leaderlessness, their lines will break and you'll be able to get them into retreat. Do it now!"

Ouyang laid General Zhang down. Before he rose, he touched the armored shoulder and murmured, "I'm glad you didn't have to know who killed you."

Did that matter? Zhu wondered, looking at Ouyang's empty-eyed ghosts. Dead was dead. It was only the living who cared. It was only the living who felt, and desired. It was only the living who chained themselves to the past, and told themselves it was for the sake of the dead that they did what they did.

Ouyang's well-trained black mare had stayed close even after his leap from the saddle. Her ears flicked as if she were tracking her master's swirling ghosts. As he remounted, Zhu said to him, "General Xu will handle the charge. I have another job for you. Come with me."

☼

As Ouyang dismounted outside Zhu's command tent, something flew at his head. He caught it reflexively: a sheathed saber. Zhu's expression was matter-of-fact, but Ouyang realized he'd become accustomed to seeing humor in that insect face, either on the surface or underneath. Without it, Zhu was suddenly chilling.

Zhu said, "Now that his father is dead—"

He didn't need to elaborate on Ouyang's behalf. "I know."

After Zhu had finished with the boy, he'd been moved to a prison tent on the outskirts of camp. Ouyang found him sipping one-handed from a bowl of medicine, pale-lipped but seemingly in good health. His other hand had been tied to the tent frame. Though the boy had his father's features, they lacked that mobile expressiveness that had so held the eye. His skin had already lost the preternatural clearness of childhood, and had a shiny, lumpen quality.

Ouyang untied him wordlessly. As the boy relaxed in relief, Ouyang could see his thoughts: the torture was over and his father had struck a deal for his return. Everything would be fine. Ouyang felt an abrupt stir of irritation. The boy had fallen into this predicament because he'd left the Zhenjiang house against instructions. He'd played around, only to discover that there were, indeed, consequences to his actions. Where was his shame at having dishonored and disappointed his father? Where was his guilt about what he'd done?

Ouyang had been ten when he'd taken on the burden of his family's honor, knowing his suffering would be rewarded with nothing but scorn and contempt. Ten, when he'd had to go on alone. And yet this boy, older than Ouyang had been, had never taken a step without his father there to shelter him. What good was there in letting a boy go about in a dream, protected from pain and responsibility? Ouyang's irritation sharpened into savage impatience. It was the same urge he had to tear a stuck bandage from the wound of a soldier who whimpered uselessly about the possibility of pain. *Of course it would hurt.* Just as it hurt when a boy had to step up and become a man, unless he wanted to remain a child forever. The world was unfair and full of pain. Everyone had to learn it eventually.

The boy followed Ouyang unquestioningly into the stand of bamboo that fringed the camp. His boots were so new that their still-white soles slapped awkwardly against the soft fallen leaves. When they had gone a short distance, Ouyang stopped. The boy looked around in search of the men he assumed his father had dispatched to receive him. But there in the whispering green tunnel, there was nothing. No approaching horses, or the flash of familiar uniforms through the trees. There were only the two of them.

"Esteemed General. Aren't you—returning me?" The boy's voice had just begun its adolescent cracking. Even if this hadn't been the boy's end, Ouyang thought bitterly, that respectful demeanor—the demeanor of a child who hadn't yet learned to make the crucial differentiation between a man and a eunuch—wouldn't have lasted much longer.

He said, "Your father is dead."

He saw the exact moment the words punctured the boy's dream. It was satisfying to have ended that privileged innocence about the world's cruelty, like a minor revenge.

"But he was surrendered!" The boy's face whitened. "Was it you? Did you kill him?"

What else would anyone assume of a known traitor? Ouyang lied, "Yes."

It was better this way. What good would it have done to tell the boy that his father had been assassinated by his uncle? There was nothing the boy would be able to do about that before Ouyang killed him. He would die like a helpless child, an unwanted kitten, and there would be no meaning—no honor—in that death at all.

He extended the sheathed saber to the boy. "Here."

The boy didn't move. To Ouyang's disgust he saw that his face was already crumpled and snotting. "Why?" the boy cried. "Why would you kill him? He liked you. He respected you."

"I had to," Ouyang said with frigid control. In a way, it was true. Had General Zhang been standing between him and his fate, he would have cut him down regardless of his respect and affection. *What barrier would that pose for me, given what I've already done?* He had a terrible awareness of a tsunami of pain trembling on the periphery of his consciousness. He found himself clutching desperately at his disgust for the boy, as if it might save him. "I had to, just like you have to do this. Or do you want me to cut you down, dispose of you, as if I were taking out the trash? *Take the sword.*"

But the boy seemed to have lost the ability of speech. He shook and cried as Ouyang stared at him with hate. Didn't the boy see how he was giving him a chance for his death to have meaning? He should be *grateful.* Was he going to fritter away the last scraps of his life in fear and dishonor, refusing the task of being a man?

He felt a sudden, savage desire to crush that fear until it oozed like a snail out of a broken shell. "You bring shame upon yourself and your family! Will you not have the courage to do what needs to be done? Will you let your ancestors look down and see their name dishonored by someone so pathetic he couldn't do his duty? I'm giving you the chance to avenge your father. *Stop crying like a child and try.*"

The wind rubbed two overlapping bamboo trunks together with an irregular squeaking that set Ouyang's teeth on edge.

The boy slowly looked up, and with vicious satisfaction Ouyang saw the shame had worked. He was glad. It wouldn't have been right if General Zhang's son had died like a mewling infant.

The boy took the saber, though his hands trembled so violently that he had to try several times to draw it. Ouyang stood before him: unarmed, unarmored. The only thing his vulnerability made him feel was a virulent self-hatred. Being unarmed meant nothing when you yourself were a weapon.

The boy lunged.

He had gathered himself admirably, in the end. He had poured himself into this one last effort: not to survive, but to do everyone proud. To be the man he was expected to be. And in the end it had been a good effort. General Zhang had trained the boy well.

But all Ouyang had ever done was kill.

He looked down with the blank feeling of having briefly absented himself from his own body. The bloodied saber was in his hand. The boy was on the ground.

As Ouyang watched him writhe, all at once the situation seemed squalid. It was harder to see honor and purpose when the thinking human parts were gone, and all that was left was meat. He knelt and finished the situation. Another dead son, of a dead father.

Had anyone asked Ouyang, when he first started on his path of vengeance, whether he would forget his own father's face, he couldn't have believed it. His father was the reason for which he'd done all of this. But over the years his drive for revenge remained, while the memory faded. Zhu had asked him what his father looked like. But Ouyang no longer knew.

It was only when he went to gather up the body that he noticed the slash on the inside of his left forearm. The blood had already sprung up between the cut edges of his sleeve. He stared at it, fascinated. It seemed to have had nothing to do with the boy: as if it had simply appeared as part of his own wishful thinking.

All at once, the pain struck. An exquisite scream ran through him from head to foot. He was a tree hit by lightning, his self blinking out in that world-ending flash of brightness.

He came back to himself, pulse by pulse. He was still kneeling in the same spot. The pain had been exactly what he needed, but even that hadn't been enough. If only it could have lasted longer.

He rose with the boy his arms. At least he could lie alongside his father there on the edge of the plain. In time the grass would regrow, and their twin graves would overlook that shimmering sea as it changed from pink, to white, to pink again, under the endlessly turning seasons.

Against his will, Ouyang remembered the lonely tomb on that other grassy plain.

If only he could cut himself so deeply that he didn't have to feel this feeling. If only he could hurt himself enough that it lasted forever.

Zhu dismissed the messenger who had come bearing the latest news—the Zhang army was in retreat, after being routed by Xu Da—and eased off her wooden hand with relief. She'd had it on continuously since she and Ouyang set out for Zhenjiang, and her stump ached from the longer-than-usual confinement.

She'd no sooner laid it down than Ouyang came in with her sheathed saber. She found herself noticing his fingernails as he wordlessly laid it on the desk in front of her. His fingernails must have been much the same size as her own, but as seen on another person they suddenly struck her as incongruously tiny. There was dirt beneath them. He'd killed and already buried the Zhang boy, she realized. If she'd given that task to Xu Da or Yu-chun, they would have balked. They'd have argued that a mere boy was harmless. That was exactly why she'd sent Ouyang. Who knew better than him what could happen when you didn't tie up loose ends, and left alive a boy who believed you had a role in his father's death?

Zhu's thoughts drifted to her own loose end, Chen Youliang. Could it have been him behind the poster campaign that had caused the Zhang family's implosion? She knew he'd been trying to establish himself in Wuchang, but with his current resources he was years away from posing a threat to her western border. Still, Chen had a political mind. She could imagine him using underhanded methods to strengthen his position against the other actors in the region. But given the grudge he bore her for usurping the leadership of the Red Turbans, why would he have engineered General Zhang's death if all that did was help her towards the throne?

That throne, her goal, was as clear as the brightness at the end of a tunnel. But for a moment Zhu felt a stir of unease, as if there was some movement she was failing to see in the shadows to either side.

As she returned her attention to Ouyang, it occurred to her that he was more bloodied than she would have expected from the disposal of an unarmed, unsuspecting child. Upon closer inspection she found the source of the blood was a long slash on the inside of his left forearm. The tight satin of his Mongol-style sleeve was already saturated from wrist to elbow.

"You fought him?" So much for how it was better not to see it coming.

"I did him the kindness of letting him die with honor," Ouyang corrected. After a moment he added rigidly, "He understood. He died bravely. His father would have been proud."

Was it really bravery, though, if the reason a boy raised a sword was because an adult's expectations had made him believe there was no other avenue?

"I've always thought honor must be cold comfort to the dying. Given the choice, I'd prefer not to die. Roll up your sleeve."

Ouyang glanced at his wound as if it hadn't even occurred to him that it might be cause for concern. "Why?"

"Do you want it stitched or not?"

"By you?" His surprise was disdainful. "If I want a one-handed botched job, I'll do it myself."

"It's not going to be a botched job," Zhu said tartly. "It's not like monks have servants. Unlike you, I've spent most of my life mending my own clothes. I know how to use a needle. *Also* unlike you: I've had some practice doing things with one hand." She dragged her desk chair to the middle of the tent. "Sit!"

When she came back with the supplies, she was mildly surprised to find that he'd obeyed. She knelt by his side, prompting him to make a strangled sound of disbelief. "No man I ever respected would lower himself the way you do."

The icy distance in that harrowed, beautiful face seemed as reflexive to him as breathing. "I don't think it's lowering to help, or to ask for help."

"So I've seen," he said with disgust. But after a moment he yanked up his sleeve, heedless of how it stuck to the wound.

It was a deep wound, with yellow fat visible through the oozing blood, but that wasn't what caught Zhu's eye. It was the bracelet Ouyang wore around his wrist, of jade and gold beads.

Ouyang wore similar beads at the end of his own braids. All Mongol warriors did. But as soon as Zhu saw them, she knew whose beads they'd been.

She remembered the awful desperation in Ouyang's face when she'd met him that time in Bianliang before his betrayal of the Prince of Henan, and the agony in his voice as he'd asked her if Esen-Temur was amongst his ghosts. And now he kept a part of that dead man around his wrist, in an intimacy that wasn't for friends, or even for brothers.

He had loved Esen-Temur, she thought with a shiver. He had loved him, but even that hadn't been enough to stop him from killing him.

He didn't flinch as she started stitching. He didn't even comment disdainfully about the way she had to hold the end of the thread with her teeth as she tied off each stitch, as she'd half expected him to. She glanced up, thinking she'd see him gritting his teeth against the pain. But to her surprise his expression had gone inwards, smoothed by a strange relief.

Just that morning, she'd seen Ouyang kill a dozen men without effort. Now, somehow, he'd fought a child and been wounded. On some level, could he have wanted it to happen? In her mind's eye she saw his flayed feet, his fists clenched so tightly that blood from his cut palms squeezed between his fingers. *It can be a good thing.*

He wanted that pain, she realized, because it was the only thing that could burn away the agony of what he'd done.

The resonance that Zhu always felt in Ouyang's presence increased until it threatened the steadiness of her hand on the needle. Ouyang had willingly killed the one he loved and plunged himself into a living nightmare. For the sake of what he wanted, he'd been prepared to do anything. To give not just anything, but everything.

Like me, Zhu thought. The rush of recognition was so strong that she shuddered. She'd always known she and Ouyang were alike. But now the truth vibrated not only within her flesh, but the currents of her qi: here was the person who was the most like her in the entire world.

She bent her head to bite off the thread of the last stitch. Instead of the natural scent of his skin, all she could smell was blood. As he rose to leave, she said, "Wait."

She brought his sword from the chest and held it out to him, balanced flat across one palm and one stump. He didn't reach for it, but his eyes went to it with a yearning, desperate hunger that reminded her of someone gazing not on an object, but a dislocated part of himself.

She kept the sword outstretched between them. "I know you're intent on going to Dadu and facing the Grand Councilor alone. But if you do that, there's no guarantee you'd win. You could well lose, and then everything you did and gave would have been for nothing. Before you met me, you had no other choice. But now let me give you another option." His blood on her fingers was drying into a brownish wash that reminded her less of battlefield gore than the tidal stains between Ma's thighs at that time of the month. "Take back command of your army. Instead of me holding you captive, and using your army against your will: take it back, and lead it voluntarily alongside mine to defeat Madam Zhang. And when that's done, march together with me to Dadu. Fight at my side as we take on the Grand Councilor, and win.

"I'm making you this offer because we want the same thing. Because we both want it so much that we'll do whatever it takes—endure whatever suffering is required of us—to achieve it." As she spoke she felt like she was channeling not just belief, but a pure distillation of their likeness. "Work with me, General. Because together: nobody can stop us."

His jet-beaded braids, fraying out of their teardrop loops, brushed the sides of his down-tilted face as he looked at his sword. After a moment he took it, and drew it. In the hand of someone whose armor had so boldly pronounced his identity on the battlefield, it seemed unbefittingly plain: without either adornment or inscription.

And yet, despite its plainness, it was the sword Zhu would have known anywhere. Her right hand flickered into existence as she reached for the blade and wrapped her fingers around it as she'd done when it pierced her. It was the sword she'd held inside her; it was the sword that had made her who she was. As the oscillating note of likeness between them surged, his eyes flew wide. Zhu remembered how, long before he'd known who she was, he'd turned to look at her as she knelt in that line of gray-robed novices. He could feel the connection between them, as she could. But unlike her, he'd never grasped what it meant: that, in this world that hated him, he wasn't alone.

"Our fates lead to the same place, General. They're entwined. Don't you feel it? They always have been. Because we're alike." It was his sword she held, but their sameness pulsed together as intimately as if she'd thrust her ghost hand inside him and grasped the slippery beating flesh of his heart. Their chests rose and fell in rhythm. She asked him, "Will you help me?"

His expanded pupils had entirely swallowed the flecked amber of his irises. They were the black pools of a dead man's eyes. As Zhu looked inside him, she had the feeling of seeing all the way down to where that burning, tormented self twisted in the awfulness of what he'd done. He rasped, "I will."

Even after she released him, her body sang with its understanding of the only other person in the world who knew what it was to want something as much as she did.

As he lifted the tent flap to leave, his small figure once again completed by the sheathed sword in his hand, she couldn't help calling to him, "What was he like?"

He turned back. There was such unbearable rawness in his look, as if he'd been excavated down to the seat of his grief, that she thought he might not answer. Then he said with sad bemusement, "Nothing like you."

10

PINGJIANG

The Queen's attendants stood frozen around her. She knew this tableau of their arrested bodies would be burned into her memory forever, the way a plunging star shocks the earth into glass that holds the shape of its impact. Her own shock was painless. All she had was the sense of having experienced some acute but unidentifiable bodily derangement.

"How?" she demanded. No thought, only reaction. "How?"

The eunuch stood in front of her with his head bowed. It was as if the Queen had shouted at the unspeaking trees. Her question was gutted of meaning by its own stupidity, its own irrelevance. Because it didn't matter. Nothing mattered outside of the fact that had already been stated.

She was suddenly furious. *How dare he.* How dare he make a mistake, this one unfixable error, and ruin everything she had tried so hard to bring to fruition? She could see his eyes, dark and apologetic under that furrowed brow. It made her want to scream. He was always so apologetic, endlessly apologetic. But she didn't want his apology. She didn't want the quiet way he absorbed the wounding words she flung at him. Next time he came to her rooms, she would make him flinch. She would overfill him with viciousness until he *hurt*—

That painless but deranging shock, again.

No. It wouldn't happen. He would never come to her rooms again. She would never get to castigate him for this particular mistake.

She stumbled, catching herself against the edge of the dressing table before she fell. She realized, then, what was happening to her. Not from sensation, but from the learned pattern of it: how this sense of internal disorder accompanied her observation of crushed bones moving in her feet, or her limbs bending too stiffly the day after a beating. *My body is in pain.*

General Zhang was dead. She was astonished at how it had disarrayed her as violently as a blow. Zhang Shide himself had only been useful. He had been a man with the combination of attributes she needed: strong of body, noble of mind, and infinitely foolish of heart. She could have used any such man. It had been him only because he was *there.*

But she thought, violently and abruptly, that she had loved him. It was the kind of thought that needed confirmation from the world. It needed her pain, so she could know it was real and not just a wish. But her knowledge of her body's dysfunction seemed as distant as a scarp on a cold desert horizon. She had no idea how to turn that knowledge into feeling.

As she stood hunched over, clawing at the censer, she heard her husband in the corridor. Coming *here,* where he had never come before. It was revolting. To have him in her inner sanctum, violating not just her space but her memory—

A new emotion flashed over into anger before she could identify what it had been. She had the idea of her emotions as water draining through a maze of channels that all led to the same place: her endless well of anger. But she was grateful for the anger. It was, at least, something to feel.

When Rice Bucket Zhang came in, the Queen was standing elegant and upright, smiling.

As soon as she saw his face, reddened with victory and self-congratulation, she knew the far worse truth of the situation. Whatever the "how" of it, there had been nothing accidental about General Zhang's death. It had been her husband's doing.

Her smile didn't falter. It was as separate from her self as the paint on the surface of a vase.

You killed him.

That was why he had come. He wanted her to know. He wanted to see her pain.

It was an exchange she would have made. To allow her loathed husband to possess that truth of her, in return for being able to feel what she was supposed to feel.

She made a reverence, saying, "This woman has heard the sad news. Though her words are surely too unworthy to comfort her husband in his time of grief, she dares offer her humble condolences."

He was too close. His personal smell, massage oils mixed with the bitter whiff of the medicinal, assaulted her. She had a flash of him thrusting into her, silk carpet rucked up underneath her from how her body had skidded when thrown, then saw it as if from the outside: her empty face, disarticulated white limbs, and the servants looking on blankly as he punished her; as he crushed her to pieces.

"Your *condolences.*" How she hated his face, alight with boorish cruelty. It excited him: this viciousness that he thought could squeeze pain out of her. He was too stupid to know that porcelain didn't bleed. "But, my loyal wife, you should be congratulating me."

He took hold of her face, his fingers digging into her jaw. For matters of cruelty alone, he was capable of thinking ahead. Or perhaps it was only instinct. He knew the keener pleasure came not from forcing torment upon a person, but in feeling their struggles against it.

She denied him any reaction as he thrust his other hand before her face. She had known, of course, what would be in it. But her sense of internal disorder intensified. It was only when she saw his triumph that she knew she was shaking. He had come for her pain, and now he had it. His victory filled her with a fury of frustration. He'd stolen what she couldn't even feel for herself. She wanted, savagely, to slash open the caul that separated her from herself, and spill out the viscera of her feelings. But neither desperation nor anger could cut; the weight of them did nothing but cause her lungs to gasp in mechanical reflex.

"Did he have this while he was fucking you? Did he think it could be his?" The orange Mandate of Heaven reared up from the creases of Rice Bucket's palm. She was always surprised by how it burned without sound. All light made noise, save that of the sun. "Zhang Shide dared cast his ambitions up! When everything he was, everything he accomplished, was owed to this family. To *me*."

It was as grotesque as if he were holding General Zhang's heart or liver in his hand. How could it be that *he* was alive? It defied her sense of the natural laws of the world. He had killed his own brother, the uncomplaining engine of this family's success. And for this ruination that he considered his victory, he had been granted Heaven's recognition. It was too bitter to be possible.

At the same time, she knew what a fool she had been to believe that a good man might win.

Rice Bucket turned her face from side to side, looking for her pain, as if she were an object under a collector's scrutiny. "I should kill you too, you lying bitch."

His hand slipped to her neck. She knew his intent. Her pain had whetted his appetite, and a glutton ate without restraint until there was no more to be had. She wondered if her body was experiencing fear, and if he could feel it. Inside that vessel, she was cold and still: she felt nothing.

After a moment he said, "You're lucky I'm a generous person. I'll forgive you, for now. But after I defeat Zhu Yuanzhang, take Dadu, and become Emperor, you'll have to prove you're still worthy of being one of my concubines." He squeezed lightly, so the blood congested inside her head, then let her go.

Perhaps only unconsciously, he knew he needed her. Zhu Yuanzhang was marching to lay siege to Pingjiang, and they no longer had a general. Despite the manifest challenges of the situation, she thought he could still succeed to the throne if she willed it so. But the idea filled her with disgust.

When he left, this time she didn't collapse. It seemed like yet another failure. She had never given Zhang Shide anything true, and now that he was dead she couldn't even give him her grief. For a moment she was gripped by the strange idea that she wasn't even a person, but a ghost that had taken possession of a body it had seen while passing by. Perhaps it had only been because Zhang Shide had the Mandate of Heaven, which allowed him to see the spirit world, that he had been able to see *her*.

Her maids hovered in her peripheral vision. They knew her coldness better than anyone, but she could see that even they didn't believe she felt nothing. They thought she had only been holding back her true reaction in refusal of Rice Bucket. They were waiting for her to cry.

In a surge of anger she snatched a bottle from the dressing table and smashed it to the ground. The spike of pleasure, savage and immediate, made her reel. She seized the priceless glass bottles, the mother-of-pearl boxes, the stoppered porcelain flasks, and hurled them to the floor in a frenzy of destruction. She was a glutton in this, just like Rice Bucket: she reveled in the spray of liquid and knife edges, and the sparkling cloud of pearl flakes and perfume oil. She smashed and smashed, until her scrabbling hand came up empty.

She stood amongst the wreckage, her ribs pressing bellows-like against the inflexible silk that wrapped her. Her maids were cowering. The sight of them filled her with hate: that *this* shocked them, when they had observed the same violence inflicted upon her with blank interest.

She sat and picked up her hand mirror. Her makeup was smeared in big, ugly streaks along her jaw, the reddened skin showing beneath. Tomorrow's bruises. She felt that savage urge again: to spray her anger out into the world. Addressing the mirror rather than the maids, she said, "Come fix me."

She drank down the silent pulse of their dread: of what would happen when their weight pressed their soft-soled shoes into that glittering field. Worthless shoes, with worthless feet. The thought of those big feet, with their spread bones and grasping toes, disgusted her. Let them be chopped like meat, as they deserved.

Against the rising pleasure a thought came, unbidden: *He hates me when I'm like this.*

Her hand shook so hard that she could no longer see her face in the mirror. She was abruptly overcome by such an annihilating fury at her body, at the *fact* of it and its uncontrollability, that if she could have destroyed the world that contained it she would have.

She dashed the heavy metal mirror to the table with such force that it bounced. To the maids she said, sweetly, "If you take too long, I'll make you crawl."

Days passed. She had a sense of her body moving through them. She smiled, and danced, and was fucked. But within the flawless ceramic skin that the world saw, her self had only a ghost's disinterested awareness.

Until this.

She read the letter again, following the thin strokes of the calligraphy that brought to mind the elegant twisting of reeds in the wind. The hand had been familiar, even before she had encountered the writer's courteous reintroduction. She remembered him. Lord Wang Baoxiang, the cool-eyed scholar she had done business with many times when he was the administrator of the Prince of Henan's wealthy estate. He was the Prince himself, now.

She could feel the threads of the universe twisting them together as neatly as his calligraphy. It was her own doing that had removed Esen-Temur and allowed him to take the title. And now here he was with his offer, in her time of need. How well informed he must be, to know of what had befallen General Zhang from as far a distance as Dadu.

A normal person would have hurt. Wang Baoxiang had taken her loss, turned it into marks in a ledger, and transformed it through bloodless figuring from a negative into a positive. Instead she felt herself welcoming the logic of it, accepting into herself what she had tried to make herself believe. *It doesn't matter that he died, and that I can't feel grief.*

If what Wang Baoxiang claimed was true—

She thought, coldly, *I would do business with him again.*

11

KHANBALIQ

Baoxiang lay clamped in a state of dread. Drafts rifled the bedcovers. The window-paper thrummed as violently against the lattice as his heart against his ribs. Outside there was thunder, but it was the other sound that had wakened him. That sound was the trip wire in his dreams, waiting to eject him back into sweating, terrified wakefulness. He was sick to his stomach with exhausted frustration. It was his own mind refusing him sleep, as if it were always turning away from something unbearable within, but he couldn't imagine what could be worse than this torment of unrest.

The thunder came closer. So far there was no snow in dry Khanbaliq, but its storms didn't lack ferocity. It had been a long time since Baoxiang had outgrown his fear of thunder, but each crash sent a residual vibration through him, like the hum of storm-warning in metal.

Once, his father had tried to force his fear out of him. It was one of those early memories that stood alone like a sea stack, unattached to anything before or after. He wasn't sure how old he'd been. Old enough, he knew, that he shouldn't have been afraid.

The birch-tar sealant between the floorboards of his father's residence oozed in the summer heat. Baoxiang, bored, lay on his stomach and picked at it with his fingernails. It gave off a burned metallic smell like a freshly sharpened knife. Now and then he came across a stuck ant. He rescued them all, though none turned out to still be alive. He hoped Esen would be home soon. Then there would be someone to be bored with. But Esen always took forever on his afternoon rides, and all Baoxiang could do was wait.

The first crack of thunder caught him by surprise. Baoxiang had always found thunder uniquely upsetting. It was overwhelming. Even with his hands over his ears, the sound would push in through his skin and the soles of his feet and froth him up until he wanted to scream. But now as the thunder began in earnest, Baoxiang's discomfort was eclipsed by a terrible sense of catastrophe. *Esen* was out in that storm. There was no shelter on the estate's flat roads and wide-open fields and pastures. Esen would be hit by lightning on his way home; he would be killed. The more Baoxiang thought about it, the realer it became. With every crash of thunder he knew Esen had died. He sobbed in agony. Esen being wrenched from him wasn't an abstract absence, like that of Baoxiang's mother or the man whose name and blood he carried. It was an absence in *himself,* a bleeding and carved-out space where something vital had been, and he knew he would never survive it.

His father found him weeping hysterically on the floor. Chaghan was startled. Disapproving. But not disgusted or contemptuous—not yet. Back then, he'd still thought Baoxiang could be fixed. "Baoxiang! What is this? Get up."

But he couldn't obey. In his frenzy of misery, all he could do was scream and scrabble at the floorboards in an attempt to escape the source of his terror. He was dimly aware of being lifted by the collar and hauled, stumbling, through the residence and into the windswept courtyard.

"Listen to it!" Chaghan shouted to be heard. The courtyard was a scissoring terror of light and noise, and Baoxiang thrashed and wept in his father's iron grip. "It's just a sound! What reason do you have to be afraid? Stand, and learn to master your fear!"

Years later, long after Chaghan had given up on him and they were set in mutual opposition, Baoxiang had wondered if it had ever been possible for him to be what his father wanted. Now, remembering Chaghan's frustration as he screamed himself insensible, he knew it never had been. His fear had been irrational, but it had been real because he *felt* it. How could it not be a part of him, a truth of him? Even as a child without the words to express it, his deepest self had demanded that those who professed to care about him should understand what was true to him. And if they couldn't—if they *wouldn't*—then he would not split himself for their approval.

It seemed inexplicable to him now, how an unformed child could harbor such a stubborn refusal to let elements of himself be stripped away as flawed and undesirable. And yet, he thought with an astonished, vicious pride: even then he had been himself.

Through the sound of the storm, Baoxiang caught voices at the front gate, then a sudden flux of people going in and out of the house. He was dressed by the time Seyhan knocked and came in with a rain-splattered lantern. Baoxiang was never sure whether it was the dramatic angles of Seyhan's face that made his expressions so readable, or whether his people used their faces with an incontinent openness, but he saw instantly that Seyhan was unsettled. His secretary said without preamble, "There's a message from Madam Zhang." Then, at Baoxiang's impatient gesture for a scroll, "No. Come and see."

A neatly dressed maid was standing in the residence's main room, her face downturned as she made a reverence. Ghosts stirred in the shadows behind her.

Baoxiang ignored the ghosts. "Your mistress sends her reply?"

When she didn't respond, Seyhan murmured, low, "She can't speak."

The use of a mute messenger, who couldn't be bribed or forced to spill more secrets than she'd been authorized to convey, showed that Madam Zhang maintained her usual shrewd control over her affairs. Baoxiang remembered the first time he'd met her, years ago. Despite her reputation, he'd found it hard to believe that the woman standing beside Rice Bucket Zhang was anything more than a glossy shell—until the moment her husband left the room, and she turned to him with the swift animation of a dried flower blooming in a teacup. He'd been attracted, certainly. But even then he'd recognized that what he saw was no less a performance than the face she wore in front of her husband. She was merely giving him what he wanted.

Her head still bowed, the maid proffered a letter. Baoxiang read aloud with a mounting sense of victory, "'The Queen of Salt thanks the Prince of Henan for his most worthy letter and offer of assistance. On the condition that he can demonstrate proof of his claim to the Mandate of Heaven, she will be most grateful to accept the offer.'" All he had to do was show the mute girl the flame? Easy enough. But the letter continued. "'The Mandate is much claimed by those who do not actually possess it. Moreover, people are easily deceived by what they see. So I sent someone unable to be so deceived. If the Prince of Henan truly has the gift he claims, he will be able to confirm by return letter a particular fact about my maid that can be ascertained by no other means.'"

The girl raised her head. There was no mistaking her closed eyes for a moment of repose. The injury that caved in her eyelids was so recent that exudate still crusted under her lower lashes. As Baoxiang watched, disturbed, fresh liquid ran and left a pinkish trail down her face. She was crying: silently, blindly.

Seyhan said, "Your future ally is a harsh mistress."

The slow movement in the darkness behind the girl was as languid as a drowned corpse's clothes in the current. The ghost drifted forwards, drawn by Baoxiang's attention, and as if she could feel its presence the Queen's maid opened her mouth—that terrible tongueless void—and gave a gurgling howl of grief that raised the hairs on Baoxiang's arms.

No historian had ever recorded the other strange ability of the Mandate of Heaven. Emperors didn't speak of it. Baoxiang hadn't even told Seyhan. But Madam Zhang knew. She knew, because General Zhang must have had that ability as Baoxiang did; as Zhu Yuanzhang did; as did all of them whom Heaven deemed capable of the throne, even if only one of them would reach it.

He said shortly, "She was a twin."

All at once, the girl's grief repulsed him. He'd sought something from Madam Zhang. Now he had it. All it had cost was the lives of these two maids? There was nothing easier. He'd spent a lifetime struggling to preserve some truth of himself against his family's resistance. It had always been so hard, as if he'd been a salmon jumping upstream for years on end. But now that he'd surrendered; now that he'd stopped fighting; now that he'd let himself become what they always thought of him: it was all easy. It was easy to be cruel, to destroy, to fill the world with misery for the sake of what he wanted. It was so easy that it felt like fate.

But as Baoxiang looked at the two girls, the dead one's intact face no longer mirrored by her living sister, his triumph darkened and sank, as if it were being borne down by a rock-weighted net into bottomless waters. It was a familiar sinking feeling of dread. He knew it, because it was the only thing he ever brought back with him from those unremembered dreams: the awareness that something awful had already taken place, and that, having happened, it could never be undone.

The storm had only worsened by the time Baoxiang battled his way to the Third Prince's palace after work. This time the Third Prince wasn't in the Crystal Room. Baoxiang found him in the rear of the palace in a training room. But the Third Prince wasn't drilling swordplay: he was lying on his stomach on the couch along the back wall, socked feet crossed behind him. When Baoxiang came in he shoved something under the couch cushion and sprang guiltily to his feet, then relaxed when he saw who it was.

"You were reading?" Baoxiang asked in surprise.

The Third Prince flushed violently. "Read? I'm sure *you* do. There are better things to be found on a page than words."

Baoxiang had a good idea of the kind of printed entertainment that circulated in groups of young men. But in the same way Esen had been able to tell a deer from a horse on the horizon, Baoxiang knew the difference between flimsy pornography and a proper book. A warrior who read alone for pleasure! Even the concept was bizarre. Baoxiang thought of the Third Prince retreating into books as his friends pulled away from him, the loneliness of his unacknowledged, unfulfilled wanting as repulsive to them as his desires would have been.

Baoxiang abruptly wished he hadn't seen the book. He'd already known everything he needed to know about the Third Prince. His plan didn't need *sympathy*. It didn't need this entangling web of emotion that drew together this hurt boy and Baoxiang's own younger self, who understood.

"I was in the mood for cheap pleasures," the Third Prince mused. "But, how fortunate! The universe has delivered something even cheaper to my door. What kind of fun shall we have on this rainy evening, Prince of Henan?" His gaze found the blunt training swords and spears on the wall, and then, on the table beside the couch, his own sword with the turquoise-inlaid dragon swallowing the hilt. "Useless as you are, even you can hold a sword, can't you?"

Baoxiang had seen enough warriors sparring over the years. As much as they thrilled in the violence and exertion, he thought their greatest pleasure was the intimacy of touching, and being touched. If he didn't set the tone of this encounter, the Third Prince would crush him into the wall or floor while telling himself that the physical contact was nothing more than the ordinary bonding of brotherhood. He would make it excusable, deniable. And that was exactly what Baoxiang couldn't let it be.

He pulled his rain-damp over-robe over his head and let it fall. The gown he wore underneath, being his own clothes, was better quality. It didn't puddle but stood up around his ankles where he dropped it.

The Third Prince's mouth fell open at the sight of Baoxiang in his underclothes. Gathering himself, he said incredulously, "What are you *doing*?"

Baoxiang didn't answer. As he undid his undershirt, the Third Prince's surprise transformed into unguarded ravenousness. Did he know how he was leaning forwards, his whole body signaling desire? Baoxiang paused, shirtless, his skin prickling with cold and anticipation. He wanted this, too, even if it wasn't what the Third Prince wanted. He undid the waist tie of his undertrousers, and let them fall.

The Third Prince's breath came quickly as he stared. Only a boy could have found ordinary nakedness erotic. The undeniable fact of Baoxiang's maleness made him feel strangely powerful. His thin chest with its few hairs around his nipples, his angular flanks and soft penis—everything he thought of as neutral—excited the Third Prince.

Baoxiang's cruelty coalesced. It was like the sullen, barely visible fire simmering on the black charcoal in a brazier. This time he wasn't giving away anything for free. It was time for the Third Prince to admit that what was happening here was because *he* wanted it. He said silkily, "If the Third Prince has instructions, he'll have to provide them."

The Third Prince said, strangled, "You *dare*—"

What a world of difference between having something done to

you, and having to ask for it! But even as the Third Prince shuddered between shame, anger, and even deeper shame, he couldn't look away from Baoxiang's naked form. How strange to be the object of desire, Baoxiang reflected. His body had the power to wound, when before it had only ever been an invitation to be wounded. He could feel it pressing against the Third Prince's shame, like a knife against a gauze screen. Was this how a courtesan felt when a young man came to her, quailing and ashamed of his bodily wants that were inexpressible except through fumbling?

Burning with shame, the Third Prince willed Baoxiang with his eyes. But he was only a child, and Baoxiang had fought with his will his entire life. He said, as if with generosity, "Whatever the Third Prince needs."

The storm outside had dimmed the training room. It made Baoxiang think of those tender moments of seeing a lover's body in the half-dark. But now he was seeing someone clothed, but flayed: stripped down to the shimmering vulnerability of what should never be seen. The Third Prince choked, "I—"

Baoxiang glanced down at himself, and felt the Third Prince's gaze follow. He didn't angle himself, or let a hand graze his genitals or buttocks, which would have been patently ridiculous, but let his glance offer his body and all its possibilities.

He'd never had this quality of attention on him before. Usually his interactions with others involved the playing of familiar roles: himself as disgraced son, or pathetic scholar, or faggot; his opponent as castigating paterfamilias, disapproving brother, domineering warrior. But the Third Prince had forgotten to play his role. This was his raw, naked self pressed against the invisible shield of Baoxiang's performance. Rain lashed the roof in waves. Drafts shuddered the room.

"I want—"

Skinned down to the bare bones of his desire, the Third Prince was so young. His face was heavy with color. Baoxiang watched him teetering on the edge, and willed him to fall. His desire for that fall suffused him, the way sexual desire suffused the Third Prince. A thrum of connection pulled them each towards the other, who could fulfil what they wanted.

"Third Prince!" They both jumped at a servant's cry from the other side of the door. "Third Prince, the storm has downed a tree over the stables—"

The spell had been broken. Whether or not the Third Prince was really needed to catch a horse, he bolted to his feet with a wild look and was out the door.

Baoxiang was left alone, naked and furious. He'd been *so close.* He seemed fated to be abandoned for horses. He remembered, with a drowning sensation, the last time Esen had left him. Books burning; a screaming horse. And a traitor slipping in the door, as Baoxiang at last realized what he wanted.

Drowning, the honorable mode of execution for Mongol aristocrats, was said to be an unpleasant death. As the expanding darkness inside Baoxiang filled his lungs instead of air, and his anger turned to panic, he could see why it might be so unpleasant. How many more attempts would it take to secure the Third Prince's protection, and how much longer would that take? The Empress might not have felt any need to rush, but she wouldn't wait too much longer for her gratification. He was suffocating, and he didn't have *time.*

"Still here?" The Minister poked his head into Baoxiang's office from the corridor outside. Baoxiang was startled to realize how dim it had grown. Aside from his single lantern, there was only the dull red glow of the brazier, and a few slivers of light from the brighter corridor lanterns that bent and twisted their way up the stepped mountain of ledgers on his desk. It was oddly hushed for midafternoon. Now that the days were short, many Ministry officials hurried home early to their families and warm houses. Even Baoxiang would have preferred to leave before dark, out of fear of the Empress, had he not had his own reasons for staying.

As the Minister limped in he called over his shoulder, "Girl! Bring some of those leftover snacks from my office."

A moment later a maid came in, bowed silently, and deposited a plate of savory fried mung-bean fritters on the edge of Baoxiang's desk.

The Minister eyed her as she left. "Damp as a squib! Shame how that other girl had to go back to the country to look after her parents. She had a liveliness, don't you think?"

So the Minister had noticed her flirtations with Baoxiang. Despite his kindly demeanor, he was a sharp-eyed old man. Baoxiang said noncommittally, "I don't really remember."

"A young man should better pay attention to the pretty girls around him, than work all the time," the Minister chided. "Don't think I haven't noticed! You've been the last one in the office every night for the last half month or more."

The fritters' aroma of wild onion and stale oil turned Baoxiang's sleep-deprived stomach. "The Minister shouldn't waste his time paying attention to such a lowly official."

In lieu of reply, the Minister took a fritter and ate it with all apparent enjoyment. Since nothing else seemed forthcoming, Baoxiang returned to his task. Even deadened by exhaustion, he still took pleasure in forming each crisp character. He'd just found his concentration when the Minister broke it again. "Did you hear the Grand Councilor had a private audience with the Great Khan? He managed to persuade the Great Khan to let him retake the east coast. He plans to march on Pingjiang as soon as the army can be readied."

Baoxiang recalled the glimpse he'd had of the Grand Councilor at a foreign dignitary's visit a few days ago. In his lacquered black ceremonial armor, each scallop edged with gold like dragonscale, the Grand Councilor had appeared as distinguished as the khans of old. Anyone who fretted about the future of the Great Yuan needed only to look upon the Grand Councilor for his heart to fill with certitude: that the Zhang family and the other southern rebels would be crushed, and the empire returned to wholeness and glory.

"I can't imagine Lady Ki was pleased."

"Indeed! We're in for interesting times, before the dust settles between them. We can only hope the Grand Councilor finds a quick victory, so Lady Ki doesn't have too much time to stir up trouble while he's out of the capital. But those Zhang merchants are strong, I'll give them that! They might hold out for longer than we'd like. I suppose we'll just have to see."

But, without General Zhang, Madam Zhang was no longer as

strong as the Minister assumed. Once, she could have matched the Grand Councilor. But not now. Not unless something changed.

A hiccup of emotion ran directly from Baoxiang's brain to his brush hand, and the next stroke came out wrong.

The Minister watched Baoxiang black out and redo the character. "You know, Wang Baoxiang: even of those born with particular talents, only very few are fortunate enough to find the perfect match between their occupations and their aptitude. I'm glad you're one of those."

Another hiccup threatened. Baoxiang lifted his brush before it blotched. "Ah, then the Minister should have met my brother, the Prince of Henan before me! *He* was someone fitted to his career. There was no greater a warrior in the whole of the Great Yuan. Even people who never knew him mourned his death, as the loss of all that was good and worthy in the world." For some reason, a bamboo tocking sound from outside—a roaming tea vendor, calling for customers—suddenly jolted him into heart-pounding awareness, as if he'd fallen asleep midsentence and awakened in a cold terror.

"Esen-Temur was well known for his talents. But do you really believe yourself to be nothing in comparison? What I see when I look at you is a young person full of a promise I haven't seen in years, who has finally found a place where *his* particular talents fit."

"Don't say you didn't also think of me as others do, when you first saw me," Baoxiang bit out. He found himself reflexively exaggerating the mincing intonation of his speech. It was that old push and provocation, that old insistence on being seen, even if all that came from it was hurt. "You chose to look past my appearance and—*predilections*—because I have these talents you value. But Esen was a warrior. He didn't value scholarship. There was nothing for him to see in me but my flaws. To him, and everyone like him: What am I, but entirely worthless?"

There was a very long pause. The Minister's long gray eyebrows, drawn together, shadowed his eyes like two palm-frond fans. He said, finally, "My son is a warrior, a commander of one of the Grand Councilor's battalions. I have no doubt he would have found a kindred spirit in your brother, had they ever met.

And it's true: his accomplishments as a warrior bring me a great deal of pride. But I like to believe he would have brought me no less pride had he been born disabled, and not able to walk or ride a day in his life. Just having him is pride enough, to carry my name and pray for my spirit when I'm gone.

"Your brother might have been a warrior. But he was still your brother. I'm sure he—"

Baoxiang was overcome by such fury that for a moment all he could see was blackness. He spat, "He *what*?" Had been as open-minded as the Minister, and it was only that Baoxiang had been closing his eyes to that side of him all along? "No. I hated him, and he hated me. We were two people for whom understanding was impossible."

The Minister was wise enough not to continue. At length he rose with a groan at his stiffness, clasped Baoxiang's shoulder, and said only, "Go home, Wang Baoxiang."

He limped away down the corridor, and Baoxiang heard doors open and close and the distant voices of servants as they brought the carriage to the front. Then the Minister was gone, and silence fell over the Ministry as thoroughly as snowfall.

Each day, that was the moment Baoxiang waited for. When he was finally alone in the Ministry. As he made his way to the Minister's office, he saw his own behatted shape cast against the corridor windows, like that of a villain in a shadow-puppet play. He went to the bookcase he had gone to so many times before, and took the relevant master account book. Back at his own desk, he drew out its twin, already half-filled from the night before, and resumed his patient work of copying.

Baoxiang stood with the Minister in the twin lines of officials that flanked the plaza in front of the Hall of Great Brilliance. Unlike in Henan, where the winters were crisp and clear, mingled dust and coal smoke smeared Khanbaliq's sky like yellow bean paste darkening in an emptied bowl. Above, the Great Khan waited to receive the foreign envoy. Lady Ki posed at his side. Today was her moment. For the annual ceremony of Goryeo's tribute payment she had donned the short ribboned jacket and cup-shaped skirts of her people, and she looked alien and magnificent. It was impossible to tell if she felt any ambivalence about how her personal power was derived from her country's submission to the Great Yuan. Goryeo's tribute payments bought her the Great Khan's favor, but its cost was her own people's impoverishment and shame.

The tribute procession made its way through the plaza. First the all-important blocks of snowy salt, followed by chests of gold and ginseng; horses and hunting birds; textiles; wagons of common barley and more luxurious wheat; and finally the long train of well-scrubbed young eunuchs and maids in the bleached white, underwear-like garments habitual to the people of Goryeo. Once upon a time, Lady Ki had been one of those tributes: a girl torn from her family and consigned to a strange land where she had neither kin nor language nor status, and only her will to save her. Now, elegant and ornamented and the mother of a prince, she gazed upon the tributes with detachment.

The Goryeo envoy, who had as much Mongol blood in him as did Baoxiang—or, possibly, more—knelt at the foot of the stairs. "Ten thousand years to the Great Khan!"

As vast as the Goryeo tribute seemed, it was no real substitute for what the Great Yuan had lost to the Zhangs. When the Grand Councilor retook the east coast from Madam Zhang, and the usual enormous volumes of salt and grain resumed their passage up the Grand Canal to Khanbaliq, the Goryeo tribute's significance would return to what it had always been: a token. Lady Ki's moment of power would be over.

"We are well pleased by this gift from the King of Goryeo," the Great Khan pronounced. He turned to Lady Ki and added indulgently, "Shall we send a gift in return, to acknowledge your native land's generosity?"

The Empress had been standing in the colonnade with the Grand Councilor and the Third Prince. Now she stepped forwards before Lady Ki could respond. Against the hall's stark white stone, her towering hat and camellia gown had the semblance of a bloodstain. "Please, Lady Ki, don't bestir yourself! I've taken the liberty of organizing a gift for the King of Goryeo on behalf of my husband the Great Khan. I have the immodesty to believe it will be well received."

Lady Ki could have been one of the dragons capping the balustrades, such was her motionlessness as she assessed this unexpected turn of events. The Empress was the highest-ranking palace woman. Though her action was wildly irregular, given Lady Ki's connection to Goryeo, it was technically within the Empress's remit to organize gifts for foreign dignitaries. Lady Ki could make a fuss, and hope the Great Khan would disregard the harem's rules to chastise the Empress, or she could concede and hope to match the Empress in whatever game she was playing. At length she said coolly, "My sister the Empress has thought of everything."

The Empress smiled savagely. But it didn't seem to be directed at Lady Ki. Baoxiang felt a sudden, nebulous unease. "What could be more appropriate for the King of Goryeo than a personal gift that will touch his heart? Fortunately, since he was raised in this very court, his tastes are well known to all of us."

Even a provincial like Baoxiang knew what she meant. Crown princes of the Great Yuan's vassal states were fostered in Khanbaliq until they ascended their native thrones, so for years the current king of Goryeo had been a member of the imperial party at the Great Khan's Spring Hunt. Baoxiang remembered a coquettish prince who overcame his mediocre looks by flaunting the most fashionable court styles, and whose honor guard consisted of a dozen suspiciously beautiful young Goryeo men. He was exactly the kind of man Khanbaliq condemned amongst its own, but was more than pleased to permit upon the throne of a subordinate nation.

"I did consider a more traditional gift of a bow or horse," the Empress mused. "But then I remembered how *very* fond he was of beautiful items of a scholarly nature. Art, literature, calligraphy—all are amongst his interests." Baoxiang's unease became icy dread, but there was nowhere to run. "I fancy that you and he have much in common"—the Empress flung her voice into the crowd, where it found him like a falling arrow—"Vice-Minister of Revenue."

As he stood frozen, a pale flicker ran down the side of his vision. Not ghosts, but the dispassionate faces of the officials in the opposite line as they turned to stare. *Too soon* was all he was able to think through his horror, as the Empress's eunuchs ran from the wings and placed a low writing table at the foot of the steps. He wasn't ready. He hadn't had enough time. In the shadows of the colonnade, the Third Prince's face was unreadable.

"You're known for your artistry, Vice-Minister, are you not?" the Empress purred. "I'm sure it will be no stretch of your talent to produce some calligraphy suitable for the King of Goryeo. Please: I have prepared everything."

The distant table, laid with ink and brushes, seemed the only object in the plaza. Baoxiang had always imagined the Empress would dispose of him in some ugly, backhand manner. But, oh! She had poetry in her soul, after all. He had humiliated her brother in front of the Great Khan, and now she would do the same to him before finding some flaw in his work—some insult to the dignity of the Great Khan—that would result in his exile or execution.

This was the one dream he couldn't wake from. He was fetched by the eunuchs, despite his protests, and guided down the long plaza to the table. Then he was kneeling, shaking, with the brush in his hand. "Quickly!" The Empress lapped up his fear like wine. He had never seen her so pleased. "Don't bore the Great Khan."

Baoxiang was light-headed from terror. But when he clawed for his anger, it came. It was a saturation that washed the fear and trembling clean out of him. Did the Empress think he would give up before he started, and doom himself to a mistake, rather than fight with the full force of his talents? Did she think he'd defied the world for the sake of something *he wasn't even good at*?

When he touched brush to page, the calligraphy flowed out of him in such a stream of fury and feeling that it was as if his Mandate itself were pouring onto the paper. In those twisting, angular characters was the truth of himself laid bare—his black heart, his blacker intent—but none of them were masters enough of the calligraphic art that they would be able to read that deep. All they would see was his work's superficial appearance:

Flawless.

With savage triumph he ascended to the second landing of the steps and knelt with his head lowered, thrusting the paper overhead so those above could see. "Ten thousand years to the Great Khan!"

During the silent perusal that followed, he imagined the Empress's face souring as she realized he'd slipped her trap. He didn't have to wait long for a verdict. The Great Khan said with clear disinterest, "A fine piece. Well done, Vice-Minister."

The Great Khan was already waving him away when the Empress laid her hand on his arm. "Then, my Great Khan," she said sweetly, "should he not be rewarded?" Without pausing, she called, "The Great Khan honors the Vice-Minister of Revenue with a cup of wine!"

Baoxiang startled. A eunuch was already scuttling up the stairs with a jade cup of wine on the tray. He realized, as he brought himself back under control, that his initial impression of the Empress had been correct. Why bother with the poetry of humiliation, when you could cut straight to the kill? She had prepared everything, indeed. He knew what was in that cup, besides the honor of ceremonial wine. His death. And it would be so slow that when it finally happened, nobody would connect it back to the Empress.

She smiled at him, full of laughter.

The Third Prince's gaze darted between Baoxiang and the Empress, then skittered away. Baoxiang was suddenly overpowered by anger. The dark wave of it snatched him up; it held him like an unbreathing jewel within that sheer obsidian wall that climbed ever higher with its promise of pure devastation. His fear was a bright spark, far below; he couldn't even feel it. The Third Prince saw what the Empress intended with that cup of wine. It wouldn't cost him anything to intervene, since he was already her enemy. And yet, for no more reason than being afraid of what it would mean about himself if he acted, he was going to let Baoxiang die.

The Third Prince had a *choice,* and he was choosing to turn away. But Baoxiang had never had a choice. He'd always had to be himself.

As he reached for the cup, he let the calligraphy fly free. As if directed by his rage, the wind snatched it and slapped it against the Third Prince's shins. The viciousness of Baoxiang's thoughts seemed capable of transcending the air, transmitted as directly as sound through bone.

Look at me. See me.

The Third Prince retrieved the wayward paper. When his eyes found Baoxiang, they were resentful. The Third Prince had known that turning away and letting Baoxiang disappear, as if he'd never existed, wouldn't end his unwanted desires, but he'd allowed himself the fantasy. Baoxiang's refusal to play along made it hopeless. Their gazes shivered against each other, hate meeting hate, and Baoxiang's anger rose in furious challenge. *Acknowledge me, if you aren't too afraid.*

He raised the jade cup. "Ten thousand years to the Great Khan!"

On the Third Prince's broad face, with its high Buddha cheeks and cruel mouth, surrender looked like grief. In a few strides he was down the steps. Baoxiang's fingers sang from the blow; the cup, jetting out its contents in a clear ribbon, inscribed a long elegant arc over the descending staircase before kissing marble and bursting into a cloud that wafted up, glittering.

"What is the meaning—!" the Empress cried.

The Third Prince's sneer was seamlessly in place as he turned to the Empress. "I'm sure the Empress didn't mean to insult the King of Goryeo by sending him a gift with such a careless error." With a brutal flick he swept open Baoxiang's calligraphy for display. "How can this be anything other than trash, when the wrong character has been written!"

The Empress flushed red as her hat. Baoxiang abruptly recalled the Third Prince reading the characters on his ledgers. Esen had never bothered to learn any script other than Mongolian, and now in a flash of understanding he saw that neither the Empress nor the Great Khan had, either. Only the Third Prince, poised in seemingly cruel victory above him, knew that Baoxiang's work was perfect.

The Third Prince said something in a foreign tongue that provoked a shocked murmur from the Goryeo delegation, then switched back to scornful Mongolian. "Don't tell me you believed the Vice-Minister's reputation as a brilliant scholar! He falls short in this arena, as in every other. Look at him! One glance could have told you he was incapable of upholding the honor of our Great Yuan. I question your judgment, Empress. Even from the outset, your idea of a gift was less than fitting." He swiftly unbuckled his belt and held out his sheathed turquoise sword across his palms to the Great Khan. "We are a warrior nation, and the King of Goryeo was raised in this court. He is as skilled with a sword as any ruler should be. Surely this is a more appropriate gift than useless ink on paper." He didn't look at Baoxiang.

After an agonizingly long moment, the Great Khan gave a terse nod.

The Empress burst out in a fury, "Then punish him for his incompetence! Great Khan, your officials dishonor you with their carelessness. Banish him!"

"Why reward insult with such easy punishment?" the Third Prince sneered. "A degenerate such as the Vice-Minister would clearly thrive outside the Great Yuan in the company of his fellows. If you want to punish him, do it properly. Thirty strokes with the heavy bamboo, here in the plaza of the Hall of Great Brilliance, so everyone can witness what it means to dishonor the Great Khan with weakness and incompetence."

It was well done. The Third Prince was giving the Empress a good enough taste of Baoxiang's suffering to satisfy her, while at the same time making sure the beating was such a public spectacle that she had no opportunity to have him "accidentally" beaten to death.

And yet . . . even a nonfatal beating by the Great Khan's skilled practitioners was likely to be as painful as a death by poison. Baoxiang's fear, until then submerged by his anger, burst its restraints. From the contempt on the faces above him, he knew they saw it. But even as he shook, and a sour taste flooded his mouth, a deeper part of himself vibrated with perverse anticipation. Let them make him low, and unperson him with pain and fear, and paint him with humiliation and disgrace and shame.

Then think about what kind of person I am, when I'm the one sitting up there and you're all prostrate beneath me.

The Empress snarled, "So be it. Make him scream."

❋

Baoxiang reclined with drugged languor in the round bamboo bathtub that had come with his house, medicinal leaves and sticks bobbing around him.

His beating that afternoon had drawn a hearty crowd. It had been the perfect spectacle to satisfy the Empress, and he hadn't even had to perform to give it to her. Even if he'd wanted to, he couldn't have. His thoughts had fled at the first stroke of the bamboo. In place of performance he offered the truth of his pain, and the Empress with her wet-lacquered scarlet mouth fed upon it as greedily as a hungry ghost from a nighttime traveler. It had been a relief when the pain, having increased to agony, finally passed into unreality: his self beaten so thin that it dissolved even as his flesh endured and went on, separate from himself, screaming.

The medicine Seyhan had poured down his throat afterwards had mercifully absented the pain. But with it had gone all clarity. Baoxiang had once been an eagle capable of seeing every thread in a brocade laid out six li beneath, but now a cloud had consumed him. Even the black knife edge of his anger had spread and faded until it was as smooth as twilight. He had a dim recollection of panicking as the medicine took hold, and of how he'd gripped himself in desperate refusal to let himself slip. But now that was all in the past. He floated.

The Third Prince came in. Baoxiang observed this fact without surprise. He said carelessly, "There you are."

Instead of his usual lapis earrings, the Third Prince was wearing blue kingfisher feathers clasped in silver. Something about the color set Baoxiang adrift. He had the idea that it should have caused pain, but all he felt was a nebulous stirring, as if the medicine had numbed his heart as well as his body.

"I see you made it through in one piece." Under his scornful veneer, the Third Prince looked uncomfortably self-conscious. Baoxiang remembered his moment of surrender: his grief, as he'd finally given up his dream of being as he should be. The blotches on his cheekbones were dappled pink and white like an upper arm bared to the cold.

"No thanks to you."

The Third Prince laughed incredulously. "It's *entirely* thanks to me."

"The next time you want to give the Empress ideas about how to punish me," Baoxiang mused, "I have some suggestions."

"You're complaining about thirty strokes? You didn't even get all thirty." The Third Prince had taken off his boots outside the bathroom. His bare feet were puppyishly large on the slatted floor. The bathroom only had three walls—there was a hanging screen of bamboo strips in place of the fourth, as was usual for older residences—but a battalion of braziers fought the cold. "Were you too out of it to remember? The Minister of Revenue took five for you. Said you were his responsibility. And I tell you what: he took them without a sound! You can tell he's the father of a warrior."

Baoxiang saw the Minister's lined face; his white-clad body laid over the bench. He hadn't asked him to do that. He'd never *asked* him to be kind. His new soft-edged consciousness transformed whatever his original emotions had been into a slow, painless bloom of feeling.

"I suppose I could have had you thrown in the dungeon," the Third Prince reflected. "But once you're in, there's no getting out. My father doesn't do pardons. You'd have ended up like that Manji traitor who's been there since before I was born. You're half-Manji, you could have made friends with him! Or maybe not. Like father, like son, right? If he's anything like that dour little bitch of a eunuch, I can't imagine he'd be good company." He smirked. "Though I'm sure your brother would have begged to differ."

Now *that* would have been a shock, under normal conditions. The dead coming back to life. Baoxiang felt like he was watching a play. He'd still had his hair in bunches when the elder General Ouyang was defeated and sent to Khanbaliq, where he'd—*allegedly*—met his end at the hand of the Great Khan. It had been the rippling repercussions of that one death that had shaped his whole life, and the lives of everyone around him.

He realized he was laughing: weightlessly, terribly. It poured out of him like the uncontrollable flow of a bodily fluid. When he flung his head back there was no pain, only pressure, where the lip of the tub bit his neck under the wet fall of his hair. *It could have all been different.* He said, panting, "But this is good, too. For the end. It'll make it even better."

He was a sponge; his pupils felt wide open enough to swallow the world. The Third Prince said accusingly, "You're *flying*."

"Seyhan gave me something. It's very effective. I don't feel *anything*. It's wonderful. It's awful." But if he couldn't feel, if he couldn't follow his razor-edged anger and viciousness towards his fate, where would he be? Lost, he thought.

"Seyhan? Your Semu man outside?" The Third Prince tensed. "Will he—"

Baoxiang lolled back. He saw the Third Prince's eyes fall to his chest, to the dark red coins of his nipples. "Don't worry! He doesn't care what I do. Foreigners are different. If I were in his homeland, he'd hate me as much as the next person. But it doesn't hurt his pride to serve me here. In his eyes, we're all as depraved as each other." Thinking of foreigners made him add, "I didn't know you spoke your mother's language. That was what you were speaking, wasn't it? When you saved me. You're not as stupid as you look."

"People think a lot of things about me," the Third Prince said, "but they don't actually think I'm stupid. It's just you."

"Yet there you are, with your clothes still on."

The Third Prince's throat worked. After a moment he opened his clothes, hands trembling on each of the three layers. His chest was whiter than Baoxiang's, mottled with the same pink flush as his cheeks. His muscles had a stretched juvenile flatness over the knobbly points of his lengthening frame: sternum, ribs, hips. A strong body, but so vulnerable in its state of exposed desire. Women could conceal their wants, but there was no hiding for men. The Third Prince had been stripped to honesty. To the truth. The kingfisher feathers slipped between his braids as he avoided Baoxiang's eyes. With another of those strange blooms of feeling, Baoxiang understood nobody had ever seen him like this before. He was the first.

The Third Prince said, low, "I didn't want to save you."

He still thought of it as weakness, even though he'd found the courage to admit what he wanted. So many people never did. Baoxiang told him dreamily, "You're braver than him."

A chill stroked his exposed skin as he stood up, sheeting water, and turned around. His inner blooming had filled him with tender lassitude. His body throbbed intensely, without pain.

The Third Prince stepped into the bathtub behind him. Baoxiang's cold-pricked flesh yearned instinctively towards that other nearness, that warmth, that other body. Instead of pain, there was only sensation. His internal throbbing was as sweet as arousal.

The Third Prince's trembling hand grazed Baoxiang's buttock. It stalled there, as if that single touch was already too much of the forbidden. Baoxiang's pulse beat beneath it. He felt softened, receptive, incapable of causing hurt.

"I've never seen a man bruise so easily. It's like you're made differently from the rest of us. The way you're so thin; how you can't stop fluttering your hands and swishing your hips like you're desperate for us to touch you." The Third Prince's breathing was rough as he took himself in hand. "You have a dick, but can you even get it up? Or are you different that way, too, so you can only take your pleasure like a woman, on your back with a man—inside you—"

His knuckles brushed Baoxiang's lower back as his hand shuttled frantically in the narrow space between their bodies. Between bodies that weren't actually different—or at least, not in the way the Third Prince was imagining. Baoxiang didn't know how it was for men who desired other men, but he knew there was nothing intrinsic to his body that would give him pleasure from being fucked, presuming the Third Prince could find the courage to do it. It would just be another painful humiliation. But in this dream where neither pain nor fear existed, for once the thought didn't bother him.

The Third Prince came with a gasp. Warmth splashed Baoxiang's back, then dripped between his buttocks. There was no mistaking any of it for being with a woman, he thought lazily. Nothing about a masculine voice or the penetrating pear-blossom smell of semen stirred him. And yet, even in the absence of his own arousal, the basic familiarity of another person's release left him floating in satiation.

As he drifted, his eye fell upon the soupy surface of the water. He was so captivated by the peculiarity of his reflection—pale face with its bruise-ringed eyes and irises eaten by pupil; wet hair plastering his chest—that it took him a long time to notice the ghost.

Esen's bearded face swayed in the water. He was in his

kingfisher-blue gown. His down-sloping eyebrows gave his upper eyelids a soft goosewing curve; his mouth followed the lowering line of his moustache. Baoxiang stared at the face. Every detail of it was familiar, but he couldn't read its expression. He knew that beneath the surface of that becalmed ocean inside him, a storm must have been raging. He couldn't feel it. He needed to speak to the ghost, he needed to call it—curse it—but the medicine had stolen his savageness, it had separated him from his heart-pounding self, it had taken away everything he was. Being lost was so unbearable that he wanted to cry. But he couldn't.

The Third Prince stepped out of the tub, breaking the face into ripples. Baoxiang sank back into the water as the Third Prince put on his clothes and left. The ghost's presence rang like an echo in an empty room, but long after the water had stilled again, the only reflection there was his own.

Baoxiang refused to take any more of Seyhan's medicine. The pain was only bearable in that he bore it, all the while feeling as malevolent as a mink. At work he found himself mentally daring someone to comment on the cushion he sat upon, just so he might have the pleasure of incinerating them with a response. Even better if it were someone who had *watched* him being beaten. But any official who had made it this far had already learned to keep his gibes inside trusted corridors, so Baoxiang's irritation had nothing but itself to feed upon. Even as his body throbbed, though, the part of him that had already lived the moment of his vengeance a thousand times over in savage rumination could appreciate how it made everything easier to have become twice as vicious as before.

The city pulsed as furiously as Baoxiang's bruises. Baoxiang had played his own role in organizing the Prince of Henan's forces for their southern campaigns, but what he saw in Khanbaliq, as the Grand Councilor prepared to mobilize the central army, was of a different scale entirely. The streets were jammed with soldiers on horseback, soldiers on foot, servants, tradesmen, and Semu merchants leading strings of horses fresh from the steppe. A river of officials rushed between the ministries and bureaus in the southern and eastern quarters of the city, and the marketplaces burst with every provision a conscripted soldier's family could buy him to ensure his survival.

It was just as frantic within the Ministry of Revenue. Requisition requests poured in, and receipts, and demands for reimbursement, and every one of them had to be approved. Baoxiang spent whole days on his cushion in a state of transcendent fury, stamping documents while some hovering minion breathed down his neck, ready to whisk them to their next appointment.

And amongst all that chaos, an opportunity was growing. Baoxiang could feel it like the point of an acupuncture needle against inflamed skin: an awareness that wasn't yet pain or relief, but would soon be both.

The Minister gave a rueful smile as Baoxiang minced stiffly into his office. Behind an obscuring mountain of paperwork, he was sitting on his own cushion. A foul-smelling medicinal tea steamed on the desk. Even five strokes was enough to remind one of the fleshy animal nature of one's body for weeks on end. "Headed home, Vice-Minister?"

The sight of the Minister's pain spurred an uncomfortable memory of those soft clouds of feeling that had bloomed in him under the influence of Seyhan's medicine. But he hadn't been himself. Now that he *was* himself, as sharp as a filleting blade, it was the work of a moment to excise that false feeling and let the blackness rush into where it had been.

Baoxiang laid a limp hand on the mound of ledgers. It was so large that he experienced a moment of true awe. "This is too much for you to do, Minister. You need to delegate."

"I would, were it not a requirement for it to be conducted by the Minister's own hand." The Minister sighed. "Unfortunately I don't have enough hands, nor hours in the day."

"The rules take no consideration of the fact that the one expected to abide by them is human. If you try to do it all, and sicken yourself with overwork, it will make matters worse," Baoxiang pointed out. He was keenly aware of this being the moment. He had gained the Minister's trust; he had made himself indispensable. Everything was in place. The sesame-black ocean had filled every chamber of himself; there was nowhere hesitation could have fit. "Let me help you do the authorizations. I can do them overnight, and bring them back tomorrow morning, and nobody will know."

The Minister sighed again. "You're right." He rested his hand possessively on the carved paulownia box on his desk for a moment, then handed it across.

Inside, the Minister's seal nestled in velvet. Its handle was worn smooth, its ivory face stained red with cinnabar. As the supreme authorization for all matters financial in the Great Yuan, it could never be apart from the Minister. It could never be used by any other than the officeholder, on pain of death. The Minister said with a small smile, "Just don't lose it."

Baoxiang flipped the lid shut. But when he looked up, his reassurance died in his mouth. A maid stood in the shadows behind the Minister. Behind her ragged fall of hair, the black sclera of her eyes stared at him unseeing. There was no dimpling pleasure in that pretty face now.

Back to the country to look after her parents. Baoxiang realized he'd let himself believe it. He'd refused to know what he'd already known. In having found out Baoxiang's sexual preferences—or at least what he'd told her about them—the laughing maid had, by association, learned too much about the Third Prince's. Of course Lady Ki had killed her.

Baoxiang had conceived of his rejection as a kindness, but instead he had killed her. He thought of the blind tongueless girl and her twin. So many dead. So many ghosts. And so many more to come.

"Wang Baoxiang?" The Minister was looking at him with concern.

Baoxiang relaxed his white-knuckled grip on the box. "I won't lose it," he promised. "I know how important it is."

12

OUTSIDE PINGJIANG

"So much for Pingjiang being a jewel amongst jewels!" Zhu said. "I've never seen a city that looks so much like a turd." Lit by orange torchlight, the stone walls of Madam Zhang's capital were shaggy with a recent plastering of lake mud. Swoops of netting hanging from the crenellations gave the appearance of a fruit tree festooned with nets to keep the bats off.

"Mud and nets spread the force of projectiles across the structure, lessening damage to the stonework," Jiao lectured from his horse beside her. "Stone-faced walls with a compressed earth core and these additional preparations are highly resistant to traditional ballistics. That's why the Mongols use incendiaries."

"We do," Ouyang said coolly. Now that Zhu had given him back command of his own forces, he was once again that haughty, untouchable general in darkly gleaming mirror-plate armor. The leather flaps hanging beneath the rim of his helmet enclosed all but a moon sliver of his face, as if what he wanted to be seen was his armor and not himself. But, Zhu thought with a lingering shiver of recognition: she had seen him. He had donned his shell again, but there was no returning him to that looming, mythic figure who had faced her from across the battlefield. He was a person like her. Beside her. He continued, "Another option is to take the local population, herd them towards the walls to absorb the city's defenses, then fill the moat with their bodies. That one works quite well."

Zhu winced. "Is it really ruling if I don't have anyone left to rule?"

There was a faint glow on the underside of the night clouds behind Pingjiang: Zhu's original army, led by Xu Da, which was closing in on the city from its more distant eastern flank, while Ouyang's forces approached from the nearer west. In the weeks since General Zhang's assassination, Zhu and Ouyang had used a series of coordinated pincer movements to sweep through Madam Zhang's territory and take city after city. Zhu had been well aware of the extraordinary risk she was taking by putting Ouyang back in command. If at any stage he'd decided to take his army and leave, she'd have been hard-placed to prevent it. Now, though, their serial victories made for an exhilarating proof of concept: that together, they were unstoppable.

Madam Zhang, having finally run out of room in which to retreat, had withdrawn into Pingjiang and locked it down in preparation for a siege. Zhu knew she was hoping to hold out until the Yuan's Grand Councilor arrived in the south. If he came and found his original target clammed shut—but Zhu and Ouyang milling around outside—it was a good bet he would take the opportunity to crush them instead, even if it meant he would have to address Madam Zhang at a later stage.

But if there was one thing a Mongol army was good at, Zhu thought with satisfaction, it was cracking open Nanren cities. With Ouyang's help, she'd be in possession of Pingjiang long before the Grand Councilor made it anywhere near the south.

"Or we could tunnel under," Ouyang was saying.

"Tunnel next to a lake? Don't be stupid." There was an extra bite to Jiao's dismissiveness that Zhu recognized all too well: that of a man speaking down to his natural inferior. To someone who wasn't a man. Jiao was bold enough that, ever since discovering Zhu's secret, he didn't hesitate to let slip directly to her face his fundamental lack of respect for her capabilities. Each time she proved him wrong, she had the feeling that all she'd done was create a one-time exception. It never changed his mind.

"Oh, can you not? The Yuan's engineers were able," Ouyang said in tones of frosty murder. "But, then again, they were Semu men from Khwarezm and Khorasan. The technical understanding of the people in the western khanates is certainly superior."

A squeaking stream of bats flew over, en route to the lake.

"I didn't say it was impossible," Jiao returned stiffly. "I suppose those engineers used timber props at the digging face, with brick reinforcement for the completed sections . . . and then, yes, they would have needed pumping capacity to keep the ground drained . . . but the labor requirements would be extreme . . ."

"Fortunately for the matter of labor, my men are conscripts. Unlike *his* men"—Ouyang didn't deign to look at Zhu—"they're well used to harsh treatment. Order them to dig, and they will dig."

"A single tunnel won't be enough," Zhu told them. "We'll need several, or we won't be able to get enough men into the city simultaneously to seize control. And we'll need to provide a believable excuse for why our armies are sitting outside without attacking. Perhaps if we were to arrange for your army to *seem* to be constructing siege engines—" She turned to Ouyang and asked, "How long does it take to put together trebuchets like you had that time at Bianliang?"

When his face flickered with pain, now she knew why: he was remembering Esen-Temur's death. The leather vambraces he wore over his forearms covered the wound General Zhang's son had given him, but she caught the way he flexed his left hand to squeeze relief from the injury. Eventually he said in that eerie tone of detachment that meant he'd managed to erase himself, "Half a month, if materials are already to hand. You could stretch it to a full month, to allow for inexpertise and incompetence."

Zhu didn't consider it her business how Ouyang chose to manage his emotions, as long as it worked. "Then by all means, let's embrace my incompetence. Engineer Jiao! Don't spare any effort on this task. I want those tunnels completed within the month."

The three of them had come to scout Pingjiang in advance, which made for a long ride back to where Ouyang's army was slowly making its way towards the city along the shore of Lake Tai. They were still some distance from the night's camp when the track they were following converged with another, and brought them upon a messenger riding in the same direction.

"Is that a message from General Xu?" Zhu called to him in her king voice, and nudged her horse to catch up with him. "Since we're already here, you may give it to us directly."

As Zhu drew up alongside, she saw a flash of the messenger's shocked face as he recognized who it was that was hailing him. Before she'd had a chance to react, he'd already wheeled his horse around. In another moment he'd vanished back into the darkness at a gallop.

"Well!" Zhu peered after him as his hoofbeats faded. Had it been daylight, Ouyang could have ridden him down, but under current conditions even his superior horsemanship seemed unlikely to prevail. She said ironically, "What are the chances that *is* actually General Xu's messenger, but all of a sudden he remembered he left the message behind and so now he's on his way to fling himself into Lake Tai with embarrassment?"

Or, more likely: there was a spy in Ouyang's camp. Zhu scoured her brief glimpse of the messenger for clues. His horse had been lathered. Had his clothes been dusty, too, as if from days on the road?

If she was right, that made him a long-distance messenger. That ruled out Madam Zhang as the person responsible, even if she was currently the one with the most vested interest in knowing what Zhu and Ouyang were up to. Did that mean it was the Yuan? Zhu didn't love the idea that the Grand Councilor might know more about their activities than they did his. And if he discovered how rapidly they planned to take Pingjiang, he would hardly stick to the plan of trying to win back the eastern seaboard. He would stay in Dadu, and prepare to defend it against Zhu and Ouyang when they came.

He might even, if he had a long enough lead time, call some allies to his aid.

No, Zhu thought. She couldn't allow that to happen, especially if it might mean that even she and Ouyang together might not be strong enough to take the capital. If the Grand Councilor had placed a spy to discover their plans—then she had no choice but to dig him out.

Ouyang's army, now settled firmly on Pingjiang's western doorstep, was a hive of activity. As Ouyang rode with Geng and Chu to check on the progress of the decoy trebuchets, he had to rein his horse around so many donkey carts and men carrying baskets of dirt on their heads that if someone had told him Zhu had ordered his men to build a city instead of digging under one, he'd have believed them. To make the situation even more unbearable, the men were burning green bamboo on their cooking fires—also Zhu's idea—to help obscure their activities from watchers in Pingjiang. The fact that it was working perfectly was exactly what made it a nightmare: the smoke, pressed down by a layer of damp lake air, created a choking blanket that made everyone's eyes and noses run as badly as if they were shoeless street urchins in winter.

Ouyang's entire focus, since being taken captive by Zhu, had been to get his army back. Now that he had it back, everything that he'd once found normal had the deranged quality of a fever dream. His men in their Yuan uniforms; the gers interspersed with the tents; the horses—they all belonged to the world he'd left behind. Every moment of familiarity triggered a cascade of memories. Out of desperation to escape, he'd begun leaving his vambraces off so he could dig his fingernails directly into his wound. But even that method was less effective than it had been. He'd disrupted the wound's healing so many times that even though the granulated pink scar tissue with its weeping red split was uglier than ever, it was growing numb to the repeated abuse. Somewhere in the back of his mind he knew that by tearing deeper and deeper into himself to get what he needed, he was risking doing more than just hurting himself. But he couldn't stop.

"A good harvest, this year," Geng observed, as a line of supply wagons rolled past. "Finally, a good year after five bad ones."

Geng's interest in farming officially qualified him as the most boring man Ouyang had ever met. He supposed that a boring second-in-command was better than a sly and cunning one, as Shao had been, or even one whose presence irritated him for no particular reason, like Chu.

His attention drifted as Geng droned on about crop yields, the importance of irrigation, and his hopes that at least a new emperor would placate Heaven enough to put a stop to the ceaseless natural disasters that were making ordinary people's lives a misery.

"Are we sure that emperor's going to be Zhu Yuanzhang?" Chu interjected. "I didn't always agree with Shao Ge, but at least I could imagine him on the throne. Zhu Yuanzhang is—well, he might have the Mandate, but he's the size of a bug! His voice is less broken than my fourteen-year-old cousin's, and I can't even bear to look at that deformed body of his." His round face shone with concern. "Can someone like that really win?"

It occurred to Ouyang that, had he wanted the throne himself, Chu could have listed the same concerns about his fitness for the role. It made him think of the radiant seriousness in Zhu's small, ugly face as he'd offered Ouyang's sword back to him, and insisted upon their likeness.

We're alike. Ouyang had spent his entire life believing he was the only one who felt and breathed as he did. There was nobody who understood what it was like to be him, or who could even imagine it if they cared enough to try. Even Esen, who had spent a lifetime with Ouyang, hadn't been able to look past his surface to his true self. And yet—Zhu understood.

Ouyang hadn't looked in a mirror since adolescence. But as Zhu stood in front of him that time, he'd found the mirror image he'd run from. Everything he found so unbearable about Zhu—his repulsive smallness, his light voice and physical incompleteness—made them the same. Zhu had held Ouyang's sword out to him, and told him their fates were entangled because they were alike.

And Ouyang had known, with a shuddering certainty that was as strong as his desire for what he wanted, that it was true.

"Zhu Yuanzhang may not be the picture of regality, but from his victories I'd say he's proven his fitness to win," he snapped at Chu. "Trust that I'm only cooperating with him because I believe he's our best chance of achieving our goals. If that ever ceases to be the case, I assure you: we'll go alone."

As he rode on in bad temper, he wondered about Chu. As unpleasant as Shao had been, his ambition for the throne had always been a clear reason for why he'd joined Ouyang. Geng's motivation was equally apparent. As he'd told them all at excruciating length, all he wanted was a return to stability so he could go home and farm his precious millet (or whatever it was that he farmed). But what did Chu want? Insofar as Ouyang had ever thought about Chu's motivations, he'd assumed he was a believer in the cause of Nanren freedom. But now he couldn't help wondering if Chu's doubts about Zhu were really about his capacity. Did Chu want the throne for himself?

Not that it mattered. All that business of who would win the throne lay beyond Ouyang's own end—the end he anticipated like a blade poised above the skin. *Together, nothing can stop us.* He'd let himself believe it, and yoked his fate to Zhu's, and now all he had to do was keep going for a little while longer. Soon, he and Zhu would take Pingjiang. Soon, they'd take Dadu. Soon, Ouyang would make everything he had done worth it, and then, finally, the pain would stop.

Ouyang stood in the tunnel, trying very hard not to think about the way the roof over his head was sagging between its timber supports like tofu skin hung over rods to dry. Both he and Zhu—unlike almost everyone else they commanded—could stand up straight inside the tunnels, but it was a close enough fit that Zhu's topknot had gathered a crown of yellow clay from scraping the ceiling.

They had come down during the lull between night work shifts, so the tunnel was empty apart from the two of them. Where they stood at its farthest point, the walls were still bare earth instead of brick, oozing and ridged from the shovel. Instead of the tomblike stagnancy Ouyang had been expecting, the tunnel's breath had a surprisingly deep, rich freshness, like the crushed-moss fragrance of a first ride along a forest path after rain.

Zhu had lit their way with his Mandate. Now, when he raised his glowing ghost hand to touch the blank face at the end of the tunnel, the stronger light from his hand interfered with the diffuse corona from his body and sent a play of shadows racing back along the walls. Ouyang's brain protested.

"Nearly there," Zhu said with satisfaction. He spoke quietly. The tunnel had reached the outer edge of Pingjiang's wall, and although nobody knew how clearly a voice might rise through the ground, none of them wanted to find out. The week before, the collapse of one of the tunnels had left them convinced of discovery for several hours. But in the end they'd been lucky. Instead of the sound traveling upwards into the city, it seemed that most of it had been puffed out of the tunnel's mouth like air from a blowpipe. Pingjiang had stayed asleep, and Zhu, with some reluctance, had diverted resources to have the trapped men dug out: "A mysterious rumble is one thing, but twenty men yelling for help isn't something even Rice Bucket Zhang is likely to attribute to nature."

Zhu's ghost fingers moved like flesh as he touched the wall. "Incredible, isn't it?" he murmured. "Our success is just on the other side of this. In a couple more weeks, we'll be in Dadu. We'll have everything we wanted."

A traveler had once told Ouyang that far to the north of the Mongols' old steppe capital of Karakorum, above the blue ice of the Northern Inland Sea on the edge of the world, the night sky danced with the breath of celestial dragons. Was that the same as this light that Zhu poured into the darkness? Zhu's small face had gone inwards as he dreamed of his future. His was a visage that would never be anything other than ugly. But for a moment, there in the unearthly, shimmering radiance of his Mandate, the intensity of his want captured Ouyang's eye as powerfully as beauty.

For all that they were alike, Ouyang knew that this was a chasm between them: Zhu could cherish his idea of the future, while for Ouyang it was nothing more than the hope of an ending. He said with a pang of bittersweetness, "It must be pleasing indeed, to imagine yourself so powerful that you can make the entire world that scorned you, and trod upon your head with contempt, kneel before you."

He had a dim memory of the satisfaction he'd had from exacting petty revenge upon those who'd slighted him. If what Zhu was after was that same satisfaction, but magnified to match the scale of the whole world that lay under Heaven, then no wonder he relished the idea of it.

"Is that why you think I want power?" Zhu regarded him curiously.

"Isn't it why anyone does?" Ouyang was fairly sure it was

why Shao had wanted power. Probably Madam Zhang too, given her start as a common courtesan.

Water pattering from the ceiling mapped the contours of the small space around them. At length Zhu said thoughtfully, "I spent the first part of my life being told I was nothing. The world, never seeing my value, would have thrown me away without regret. I'm sure you know the feeling. Even though you had your revenge to cling to—when the world treated you as a thing, didn't you dream of being a person, as I did? You and I, General: we were both denied a chance to live freely, let alone be great or have our names remembered, for simply being who we are." The tight confines of the tunnel made it sound like Zhu was speaking directly into Ouyang's ear as he murmured, "Nobody would lift a finger to change the world for us. To make a place for us. What choice did we ever have, but to do it ourselves?"

It was disconcerting to be included in Zhu's vision, as if Ouyang were cooperating with him not merely to get to the end, but to build some kind of continuing future. For as long as he'd known his fate, Ouyang had looked ahead and seen that the world ended with his revenge, because he himself ended. For him there'd never been a future. There was only the blink of nothingness that would at least be a respite from the pain, however brief, before it began all over again in his next life. Without a future, what he had now wasn't so much a life as it was a suspended death. Sometimes he had the idea that, at the moment of Esen's death, he'd followed him across the barrier between worlds, and the only reason Zhu could see him now was because he could see ghosts.

But, Ouyang thought, Zhu *could* see him. It was as if Zhu were standing on the other side of that burning barrier, his phantom hand outstretched. As if Ouyang might be able to take it with his own dead hand, and step back into the world of the living—into Zhu's new world that existed past the end.

Was that world even something he wanted? Ouyang couldn't imagine what kind of degraded, upside-down world it would have to be for it to have a place for someone like him. And even if he *did* want to join Zhu there, could he? What more effort would it require, when he was already giving everything he had just to keep going?

He didn't know. But as he stood there in the dripping underground, invisible life crawling through the composting soil around him, for the first time he wondered if it might be possible to continue, after the end.

The mouth of the tunnel was on the periphery of the camp. Zhu, with Ouyang behind, emerged into smoke that was as thick as a blanketing fog. It trapped the light from the torches, transforming it into bright currents that ribboned around the looming shadows of dirt mounds and timber frameworks. A few men hurried between tasks, their silhouettes wavering indistinctly through the murk.

They were making their way back to the center of camp when Zhu's idle glance snagged on an indistinct outline in the haze. Two mounted men in conversation, perhaps, though it was hard to tell from this distance. There was nothing too suspicious about it. Ouyang's army was large enough that it was often more convenient to ride from one part of camp to another, and there was no curfew preventing men from wandering around between work shifts. But Zhu's instincts pinged. Her mind went to the Grand Councilor's messenger. Since she'd prevented him from delivering his message that first time, wouldn't he try again? Now here were two men, meeting during the quiet time between shifts, on the deserted outskirts of camp—exactly as a messenger and his contact might.

Zhu grabbed Ouyang's tiny wrist and pulled him behind a stack of buckets. When he shot her an outraged glare for her presumption, she indicated the direction of the men and mouthed: *Spy.*

Though he didn't stop glaring, he caught on quickly. When she edged out from behind the buckets and dashed to a mound of dirt that was a stone's throw closer to their target, he was close on her heels. The smoke was a double-edged sword. While the thickness of it masked their approach, they'd have to be almost on top of the men if they were to have any chance of identifying the spy.

Several more scurries between hiding places delivered Zhu

and Ouyang into the lee of a small pile of rocks that was no more than ten chi from the men. From this short distance, it seemed likely they'd be able to make out faces. Zhu felt some sharp edge of Ouyang's armor digging into her shoulder as she craned her neck over the rocks. The smoke didn't only reduce visibility, but also muffled sounds: even at this close range all she could hear was the murmur of voices, without being able to make out what language they were speaking. To Zhu's disappointment, both men's faces were still too hazy to make out. She squinted determinedly. If there were just one eddy to thin the smoke—

When it happened, she could have sworn that neither she nor Ouyang had made a sound. One of the men's horses spooked. It seemed to have come out of nowhere. Its rider exclaimed as he tried to wrestle back control. The pair's movements stirred the smoke, and it was only then that Zhu saw what the horse had sensed: the white shapes drifting through the smoke, as barely visible as falling snow against a mother-of-pearl sky. She could have cursed in frustration. Ouyang's ghosts.

Even worse: it wasn't only the horse that had been spooked. Zhu saw the other man's head turning as he scanned the smoke. Some horses *did* just spook at nothing—Zhu, who had grown up with placid monastery buffalo, had little faith in the common sense of horses—but clearly the man wasn't willing to take his chances that they were still alone. He bolted. His horse's muffled hoofbeats receded deeper into the camp, and in another instant even they too were gone.

The remaining rider gathered his horse. He milled uncertainly, cursing to himself, then came to some decision and urged his horse into a canter. Zhu hurriedly fell back behind the rocks as he neared. She'd just taken in the fact that Ouyang was no longer there, when a jumble of movement off to the side concluded with a thud. The now-riderless horse careened away into the smoke.

Zhu said with energy, "I know you can't help yourself, but it would have been more useful if he were still alive!"

Ouyang crouched by the fallen body. To Zhu's regret, she saw it was the messenger they'd seen before, not the spy. "If you have a problem with the way I do things, next time *you* fling yourself in front of the horse." He rummaged through the man's clothes and brought out a piece of paper. "At least now we have this."

Zhu took the note, summoned her Mandate for some extra lighting, and peered at the elegant handwriting. It was the Mongolian script, which she'd learned in her monastery days, but now for some reason she couldn't make out any familiar words. "Yes, so useful!"

"Give it to me, peasant." Ouyang snatched the letter as Zhu protested, "It's not that I can't *read*—" and then said, vindicated, "See!" as Ouyang glared at the paper.

"It must be a cipher," he said, with a distinct lack of grace.

A cipher, in the Mongolian script. That made sense, if the spy were working for the Grand Councilor. But—"If it's from the Yuan, why can't you decipher it?"

"It's not from the Yuan. I've never seen anything like this before. It must be from someone else." Ouyang's frown increased as he examined the flowing handwriting, as if chasing some elusive recognition. But eventually he shook his head, defeated, and handed the note back.

Zhu chewed the matter over as they resumed their walk back into camp. If the spy wasn't working for the Yuan, then who? She felt a return of the unease she'd had in Zhenjiang. It was stronger, now: a sense that all these hints of movement in the shadows—a poster, an assassination, and now a spy—added up to *someone*. Someone who knew them, and was watching them, but they didn't know him. She didn't like the feeling one bit.

Zhu dropped Ouyang off at his ger. Then, instead of heading to her own command tent nearby, she made a short detour to the part of camp where the few dozen men seconded from her own army were staying. In the most odoriferous of the tents, she found Jiao already awake (or perhaps not yet slept) and prodding at an array of dubious pots upon a brazier. Zhu marched in and thrust the note under his nose. "Here's a fun little present for you." There was nothing Jiao enjoyed more than showing everyone how smart he was—and, conversely, nothing more likely to drive him wild than a problem he couldn't solve. She could practically hear the crackle of his interest as he realized what he was looking at. If anyone could crack a cipher, it'd be him. "See if you can get anything out of it, and let me know."

"Buddha preserve us!" Zhu exclaimed as Xu Da doubled over coughing, and thrust a cup at him. "Are you dying? Drink something."

Xu Da gave her a streaming-eyed look of reproach. "How are you all *living* like this?"

Zhu had stopped noticing the smoke, even when sitting next to a campfire that was actively belching it in her face. After having steeped in it for the better part of a month, it had come to seem to her like a natural part of the environment, like incense in a monastery.

"The difference being that incense *smells delightful.*" Xu Da and a handful of Zhu's commanders had ridden across from his eastern position to join Zhu and Ouyang for the briefing. "This smoke, on the other hand, is made from bamboo and dried horse shit."

"But think how delicious we're becoming!" Zhu said longingly. "Superior even to Jinhua ham: smoke-marinated men from Zhenjiang—"

Xu Da had finally stopped coughing by the end of the briefing—during which they'd received an update from Jiao on the tunnels; had a spirited discussion on whether they should use the (functional) decoy trebuchets during the assault; and refined their plan for getting several hundred men through the tunnels as fast as possible—but he still gave Zhu a dark look as he rose. "We better be able to act soon, because if I have to come back here again I'm going to rupture something. Anyway, I'm off—"

A pair of guards barged out of the smoke and startled Zhu with salutes. "Informing the Radiant King that we apprehended an unauthorized person approaching the camp with a message. Please give your orders!"

Zhu felt a spurt of excitement. Since losing the spy that night, she'd asked Ouyang to tighten his camp security with just this result in mind. With a live messenger in their hands, they'd be able to persuade him—nicely, or less nicely—to give up the spy's identity. It was slightly odd that the messenger had chosen to make his approach during the daytime, when he would be more easily caught, but perhaps it was related to the timing of the briefing. If the spy was one of Ouyang's regular soldiers, it would make sense for him to have chosen a time to meet when all the senior members of camp were occupied.

Zhu rose and said sharply, "Bring him to my tent."

The guards saluted again. "Obeying the Radiant King's orders! Does the Radiant King also require the message? It's . . ." The guard faltered. ". . . large."

On the camp's fringe, the messenger had been separated from his message. Zhu, Ouyang, and Xu Da regarded the handcart and the enormous earthenware jar lashed to it. The jar was as large as a person, and wearing a loose thatched lid like a straw travel hat. A strong odor battled through the smoke.

"A message, or a winter's supply of pickled cabbage?" said Ouyang, with the disdain of someone who'd never stooped to eating a vegetable.

"I don't know!" the messenger—a local peasant, by appearances—was protesting. "I didn't know him. He just paid me, said you were expecting it, so I came—"

As Xu Da reached for the lid, the cured-pork smell of firepowder suddenly flashed through Zhu's mind. "Don't touch it! Someone fetch Engineer Jiao. It could be a bomb."

"Not with a loose lid like that, it isn't," Jiao said when he arrived. As usual, his opinion came with a supercilious air. "And in that volume it won't be poison, either."

"Fine, get it down," Zhu instructed, feeling slightly foolish, and then as the guard leapt into action, "Wait, not like that—!"

But the guard had already slashed the rope, with no regard for how a heavy jostling item might have tightened its restraints over the course of a long journey. The rope parted with a bowstring twang; the cart lifted a wheel off the ground as the jar considered its options and everyone else considered whether they could catch it or be crushed trying; and before they could decide, the jar took matters into its own hands and dashed itself heroically to the ground. The contents flooded out.

It wasn't a message from the cipher-writer. This was a message that wanted to be read.

There, spread on the ground in a wave of pickling juice: hands. Men's severed hands, women's hands, children's hands, lapping at their feet like so many beached starfish.

One of the guards retched, which made those around him visibly think about following suit. Zhu shooed them away. The smell of pickle juice, considered separately from what it was pickling, was unobjectionable, but that was without adding vomit to the mix.

Jiao said with a cold clinician's eye, "They're amputations, rather than taken from corpses. Observe this discoloration around the cuts, which we can take as an indication of bleeding—"

A single arm poked through the tangle of hands. With a powerful look of displeasure, Ouyang used the point of his sword to fish it to the surface. It was a man's forearm, cut below the elbow at the same point where Zhu's own arm ended, its flesh incised with characters that opened colorlessly in the dead flesh like gills.

Chen Youliang sends his respectful greetings from Nanchang.

Nanchang, Zhu's southernmost city. For a moment she was too stunned to make sense of it. While she'd had all her attention on the Zhangs, her old enemy Chen had launched himself out of Wuchang in the west and taken her city. He'd done *this* to her people, and now he wanted her to know.

But how had he done it? Chen might have been building up his forces, but he hadn't been anywhere near posing a threat to her. She'd been sure of it, or she'd have never turned her back on him. He shouldn't have had the capability to move against her, let alone *win*.

However he had managed it, the fact of it stood. Zhu had been on the verge of winning Pingjiang, but now she had no choice but to withdraw to take care of Chen—before he took care of her. And now everything she'd achieved since General Zhang's death was going to go to waste.

This was exactly the sort of thing that happened, she thought with deep aggravation, when you didn't tie up loose ends.

It was as if Zhu knew exactly how he would react, Ouyang thought in fury, as he reached Zhu's command tent and found it newly surrounded by multiple rings of guards. Not Ouyang's men, but Zhu's own, that he must have called over from General Xu's position directly after receiving the message from Chen. Commander Chang thrust his sheathed sword horizontally to block Ouyang from entering. "General. Before you enter, I'll have to trouble you to give me your sword. The Radiant King's orders." Ouyang glared at him, but Chang only said, "Please don't make it difficult for me."

Zhu was standing inside, waiting for him, as Ouyang strode in and snarled, *"Tell me you're not withdrawing."*

"What other choice do I have?" Zhu asked bluntly. At least, Ouyang thought in a spasm of agony, he'd spared him any softening nonsense. "I can't take and hold Pingjiang here in the east, while simultaneously marching north to take Dadu *and* defending my rear from Chen Youliang. I have to deal with Chen first."

"You don't! Dadu is what's important. Dadu's our goal, isn't it? We need to take Pingjiang quickly, then march on Dadu. *Then* once you have the throne, you can come back and retake those cities from Chen Youliang!" In some distant part of his mind, Ouyang knew that once Chen took cities there would be nothing but ashes and corpses for Zhu to retake, but that didn't matter. Nothing mattered, but *continuing*.

"We're going to get to Dadu," Zhu said with such gentle force that it felt like he was trying to press his reality directly into Ouyang's flesh. Ouyang, staring into that small mandibular face that was on the same level as his own, had the urge to step back. "We'll get there, I promise. Chen Youliang attacked me with a fleet, so we'll need a fleet to face him. We're going to get that fleet. We'll destroy him. Then we're going to come back here and take Pingjiang, and *then* we're going to Dadu. If I have to, General, I'll imprison you again, use your army without your consent, and do it all myself. But I would much rather your cooperation. I know you can see that we're stronger together. I'm still your best chance of getting what you want. *So let's do it together."*

But even if it was true, and Zhu represented a better chance of success than Ouyang would ever have alone, what did that matter in the face of the pain he couldn't bear even as it was?

As if Zhu could read his mind, he said, "Just hold on a little while longer, General."

It *was* true that Zhu was still his best chance. It was also true that once he got to the end, all the suffering and pain and everything he'd given would be worth it. But to keep waiting—

He said with an anguish that forced his voice into a high register of absolute desperation, as if it had been ripped from his guts without any moderating consciousness, "*I can't.*"

He cringed at the sound of his own voice, but to his surprise, Zhu didn't. "You can. But you don't have to do it by yourself. Pull up your sleeve."

Ouyang looked at him without comprehension. Zhu had stitched the wound there, but he didn't know what that might have to do with this present situation or the pain he was in. At his hesitation, Zhu said, "Shy? I've seen it before, General."

Ouyang reluctantly tugged up his left sleeve. The bracelet of Esen's beads sat at his wristbone; beneath it, the pink slash with its weeping, darker red fissure down the middle ran nearly the length of his forearm. As Zhu inspected it with a peculiar, intense curiosity, Ouyang suddenly realized: Zhu *knew* what he did to himself in order to continue. All at once he grasped, with an anticipation as keen as yearning, what Zhu meant to do. He would curl his fingers over Ouyang's scar, pressing lightly there for a moment. And then he would dig his fingernails in. He would tear and claw and rend, until Ouyang hurt.

But if that *worked,* Ouyang would have done it himself. He'd already done it too much. The wound no longer responded. And as much as he trembled with anticipation, he knew with despair that it wouldn't be enough.

Zhu nodded as if, having assessed the situation of the wound, he'd decided on a course of action. Then he took Ouyang's hand. Ouyang was briefly surprised by how their hands were the same size. It felt like holding his own hand. Then Zhu raised Ouyang's hand and took two of his fingers into his mouth.

It was the most bizarre thing Ouyang had ever experienced. He had no idea what was happening. Zhu had the appearance of hardness—he was all angles and lines—but his mouth was soft, his tongue quiescent under and against the tip of Ouyang's fingers. Not sucking, not licking. Just holding him inside. His gaze was frank. A faint sense of ridiculousness hovered next to a stronger, ritual-like solemnity that Ouyang didn't know how to answer.

With a peculiar flood of heat, he suddenly remembered the last time he was inside Zhu: the intimacy of their bodies joined by his sword; their faces together at the same height; the way Zhu's dark eyes had been fixed on his. The stillness of the moment, just like this one.

Without breaking their gaze, Zhu bit down.

Ouyang made some sound. He had no idea what. The world shrank first to his fingers, then dissolved. He'd never felt a fire like this: a concentrated pain that simultaneously embraced the entirety of him. Somehow Zhu had known exactly how to undo him. He had never welcomed any sensation so much.

He had the distant awareness that his body was still in the same position. It would have been a better representation of how he felt, he thought dazedly, if he had collapsed to his knees and laid his face upon Zhu's boots, and clasped them in breathless, helpless gratitude for the gift of this pain.

He heard the rasp of his breath. It should have been a humiliation to be taken into his place of need and held like this, but his capacity for emotional response had already left him. He could only stand there in surrender to that ecstatic redness while Zhu relieved him of his pain, his thoughts, and then, finally, himself.

Once Ouyang left, Zhu returned to her desk. The taste of his blood lingered on her tongue.

She could still see his voluptuous engagement with the pain as it moved through him like internal weather. His eyes had been dilated, lips parted around unvocalized agony, as he'd stared at her. Was that how she'd looked at him, when he'd held her open with his sword? Her mouth had flooded with the taste of him as his involuntary trembling turned into deeper, sharper spasms. She could feel how he was holding himself still around them, even as the pain rose. And when it peaked she held him there on that clean bright edge: where agony and relief merged into one.

It would be enough to keep him from leaving. She'd seen the moment the physical pain had eclipsed his anguish, allowing him to set aside his desperate impulse to rush alone to the end. She'd given him what he needed to stay with the plan—to stay with her. And if he needed it again, she would give it to him.

The idea filled her with a rush of satisfaction, sweet and powerful.

The doorflap swished as Jiao came in. After the vulnerability of the moment Zhu had shared with Ouyang, Jiao's smug dislike grated even more than usual. She wondered if he'd crossed paths with Ouyang outside her tent. Given his lack of respect for her, he'd probably enjoyed the idea of Ouyang storming in to challenge her authority. She gave him a hard stare. *If I could master* him, *think about what I could do to someone like you.*

Jiao smiled slightly, as if to remind her of what they both knew: that she needed him. He handed her back the ciphered message. "I can't decipher it. Not without the key."

She hadn't really thought it would work, but she had to allow that perhaps she'd *hoped.* "There's no other way, even for an exceptional man like you?"

There was an ironic flicker in his eyes, as if he were taking pleasure in her predicament. "My apologies for having disappointed the Radiant King with my inadequacy."

Zhu didn't like the idea of letting the spy continue his work, and she liked it even less that she'd made Jiao aware of the situation without getting a solution in return. But now there was nothing for it other than to keep security tight and wait for another opportunity to catch him in the act.

As Jiao went to leave, he stopped as if caught by a moment's idle curiosity. "Chen Youliang took Nanchang with a navy. But you only have a land army. Your Majesty, where are you going to get a navy from?"

His mildness didn't fool Zhu. She knew what he was really asking. Could she still win? For a moment her dislike flashed over into hate. She was sick of playing along to Jiao's game where he asked her to prove herself to him, over and over. But she couldn't just cast him aside, much as she might like to. His technical expertise, including his innovations around fire-powder weapons, was one of her biggest strengths. She said repressively, "Fang Guozhen has ships."

"Why should that pirate cooperate with you? He's hardly known," Jiao said, "for his philanthropic spirit."

Was there something more challenging in his tone than usual? But then again: Jiao was always in a foul temper whenever he felt a puzzle had eluded his intellect. "Any man of good sense will cooperate with the one who'll rule him in the future."

Jiao's creased, wispily bearded face had never been kindly. Zhu hadn't thought of her father in years, but the annihilating judgment of Jiao's look flashed her all the way to the beginning: to where she had been pressed into that small shape of worthlessness that would have killed her. She bristled as Jiao looked at her like she was nothing and said, "Aiya, I hope you have a better reason than that."

13

PINGJIANG

The Queen stepped into the banquet hall just as the poison taster exited. Rice Bucket sat alone at the vast sweep of table with the dishes drawn in towards himself, like a sea anemone surrounded by the detritus of many successful dinners. He didn't look up as she approached. He was gouging at the cheek of a jellied whole pig's head with what she recognized as fretfulness rather than true appetite. Ordinarily, the Queen would have felt it in her interests to soothe whatever was bothering him. But that time was well past.

She made a reverence. Without straightening up, she said, "My husband is to be congratulated on the withdrawal of Zhu Yuanzhang."

She thought he might make her stay there, bent in submission. But after a moment he glanced sidelong at her, mouth open and chewing, and jerked his head for her to be seated opposite.

The servants laid chopsticks and a bowl of rice before her, and, at her instruction, a small portion of vegetables glistening in the red-oil braise that was commonly used on fish. No doubt the concoction tasted well to others. In her own mouth it produced only the usual faint repulsion.

"Zhu Yuanzhang! He who dared come against me. Did he think he defeated me at Zhenjiang? I threw him a bone, that's all." Diverted from whatever plagued him, Rice Bucket leaned back and flung his arms across the backs of the neighboring chairs, red-oiled chopsticks dangling from his fingers. He regarded her with a humorous expression that could have been that of any benign patriarch, had it not been for the hardness around his eyes. The hardness that allowed for no feeling for anyone save himself. It was that fundamental disinterest that had always made him slow to provoke, slow to react. But how she had underestimated the danger of that reaction! *I threw him a bone.* Her chopsticks rattled, surprising her. Her fingers had gone numb. They had always been as white and fine as lengths of spring onion, and now they seemed the exquisite possession of a stranger. But her mind was as calm as a clock.

"It wasn't as easy as that little fuck thought it would be, was it, when he had to dig in outside this city. These strong walls of mine! Did he think I would crumble at his posturing?" He scoffed. It was only because she was listening closely that she caught the hitch in his next breath, as if the force of his derision had sent some fractional agony through him. But he recovered swiftly. "One taste of my power, and now look at him roll home to his mother's cunt!"

It hardly surprised her that he had no idea about Chen's role in Zhu's withdrawal. Someone whose world consisted only of himself would always believe that the smoothness of his path was the result of his own hands. She thought coldly: *Nothing you've accomplished has ever been due to you.*

He gave his wheezy laugh that had as much good humor as a saw blade. "And you, wife. What the fuck have you been doing this whole time? The city is no longer under threat, and you've been sitting doing nothing? I want a force ready to send to Dadu. It's time I took what's mine."

There was a rancid tang in the air, like hard tofu that had gone slimy with age. It rose up powerfully, though Rice Bucket didn't seem to notice. She replied coolly, "The largest force we can muster is unlikely to be sufficient to overcome the Grand Councilor and his central army. You can be sure he will not hesitate to give his utmost to Dadu's defense."

Rice Bucket slapped his thighs as if greatly amused. But between one slap and the next the laughter dropped from his face with an abruptness that bespoke danger. Her eyes went to his raised hand. "Why does it sound like you don't believe me? If I say they'll win, they will win. Unless—someone stands deliberately in my way and sabotages me. Betrays me." He said, softly, "Will that be you again, wife?"

She saw the moment the next flicker of pain passed through him, sharper this time. He dropped his hand as his attention went inwards. The first traces of sweat stood on his brow. "Is your stomach bothering you again?" the Queen asked.

She turned towards the servants waiting at the wall, but he interrupted her loudly, aggrieved, "Do you think I don't know what indigestion feels like? This is different. There's something wrong with the food." His voice rose further, with a trace of panic. "There's something wrong with it! I'm being poisoned."

"How could that be?" the Queen said calmly. She held up a forestalling hand to her husband's bodyguards, who had started forwards. She said clearly, for their benefit, "We would have been alerted had the poison taster shown any symptoms. Not to mention I've eaten the same dishes and I'm in no ill health. Husband, please be calm. I'll send for the physician."

Rice Bucket suddenly cried out. "Ah, it's an invasion of cold qi, I feel it down below." He scrabbled at his gown with hands shaking in fear, wrenching it from its fastenings and thrusting down his white underclothes. "It's attacking my source of yang. I can feel it retracting, coming into my body. If it comes into my body I'll die!"

When the Queen came over, under the swell of his bared abdomen she saw that his genitals were pale and waxy-looking as though frostbitten. His scrotum was so hard and constricted that it had pulled the purse of his testicles right up against the entrance to his body. He was trembling, groaning, pale and sheened with sweat. His misery made the Queen think of a beggar's monkey she had seen in the street, being beaten savagely by its owner. She remembered the cruel disconnected pleasure of seeing its little screwed-up face in pain and distress, its terrified defecating that disgusted her and at the same time elicited in her a savage joy that wanted the entertainment of more.

She laughed, bestowing it with all the lightness she could muster. "Oh, husband, relax! The number of men with such complaints who visit the pleasure houses . . . truly there's nothing to be worried about." She pulled up his underclothes and closed his gown, murmuring solicitously, and called to the guards, "Go, all of you. Instruct the physician to prepare the medicine for the dripping disease, and to come with all haste."

"How long will it be?" he groaned, as she shut the door behind them and returned to the table. "The pain increases. Ah, it's unbearable!"

"Is it so very bad?" she said, with a flicker of interest. "It's unfortunate, of course, that the physician will find a shortage of the exact herbs he's looking for, and he'll have to call out for more. And of course since he'll have been very busy attending to your concubine, it will be some time until he arrives, I think."

He looked at her without comprehension. "My concubine—?"

"Ah, the poor girl! She was only looking after your best interests. When I heard she was asking around for a medicine to smear on that ring you use, to enhance your lovemaking, I had someone make a little substitution. Do you think her maids were too embarrassed to let the physician know where the complaint started? She was a pretty girl, wasn't she? I suppose nobody is pretty as they die."

She saw the moment, after some time, when he realized what she meant. In a great surge he lunged out of his seat towards her, a wounded bear with a shout forming in his throat, but it died as the color rushed from his face and he fell back into his chair. He braced himself on the table, trembling, his mouth open as if to groan but with no sound issuing. His belly heaved, but he seemed unable to draw air. The Queen was trembling, as if her body were balancing on unsteady stilts instead of legs, but she said with deep contempt, "What a shame, husband. It seems the bucket has run empty of rice."

"But I—have the—"

"Did you think it guaranteed you success, even knowing what you yourself did to Zhang Shide? You fool. You're not the only one who has the Mandate."

She hadn't been sure, when she first read the offer, at how Wang Baoxiang would make good on his promise to break the siege of Pingjiang. She thought back to her meeting with Chen. She had refused him, but it seemed he had found a willing patron after all. A patron who had been waiting for an opportunity to use him. For a moment, it occurred to her that Zhang Shide's death had created that opportunity perfectly.

Rice Bucket's head was hanging low as he gasped. She ran her fingers lightly down his face, then placed the tips of her fingernails under his chin. She dug them in, levering him upwards so he had to lift his head. She felt the urge to keep digging them in all the way to his brain. He looked at her with eyes bulging with panic; she wasn't even sure if he could talk anymore. "I have my choice of emperors. So I'm choosing someone better than you. I *will* take an army to Dadu, but you, Zhang Shicheng: you're not part of the plan."

His breath was a terrible labored wheeze. The old-tofu odor increased, along with the sharp smell of fear. It disgusted her. She wanted to scrape him out of her body, to close herself to him, like a polished stone that had bludgeoned but was still shining white under the gore. "Dying as you lived. How amusing! I never thought you and your brother had anything in common. But he also died as he lived. Perhaps this might be a more uncomfortable way to die than by arrow on the battlefield. Perhaps you should have lived a more useful life."

But as she watched her husband straining for air, his lips turning bluish and a pink froth appearing at the corners of his mouth, she felt her horror grow. Speaking of it had brought it to mind: Zhang Shide's last moments on that battlefield. If the murderous arrow had pierced his lung, would he have struggled like this, every attempt to breathe only collapsing his lung further until he suffocated? Was this what his last breaths had sounded like?

She realized that, before this, she had believed he would have thought of her in his last moments. She had needed to believe that despite her last harsh words to him, he had died knowing the truth: that she had lied in that moment to hurt him, as she always did, and he would have forgiven her. But now, as she watched Rice Bucket, she saw pain replacing his humanity. Dying reduced him to an animal without speech, without higher-level thoughts, only the dimming awareness of himself. Zhang Shide, dying on the battlefield, wouldn't have thought of her at all.

She had imagined herself staying until Rice Bucket's end. She had even taken pleasure in the idea. But her lungs were heaving, her heart pounding; her bodily sensations were overcoming her, and she felt a sharp terror of the knowledge that she was porous to them. She would be breached.

She was stumbling, in this nonfunctioning body that had been broken so it couldn't run. The floor pitched beneath her at steep angles. She lurched wildly, catching herself unfeelingly on a censer and then a hot brazier, and wrenched the door open and fell outside. Her lower back was spasming: her grief piercing her kidneys, her liver, her spleen. She couldn't bear the way her body was asserting itself over her, thrusting relentlessly through her barriers.

Inside that room her husband was drowning in air. Through the roaring in her ears she heard him scrabbling at the table, like live turtles being steamed in a covered wok: the sound going on and on.

The pain was pressing onto her. She was cracked beneath it, she was pieces held together with the wire of her self. Every message from her body was trying to tear her apart, and all she needed to do was let go. She *wanted* to feel the pain, because people who loved, who had been loved, felt it. But even as her body spasmed; even though she strained to let go; she couldn't. Each throb of desire to let go came with a stronger, answering pulse of resistance from some deep place within her. She thought, randomly, of a courtesan she had known long ago, who had tried to kill herself by holding her breath. But the girl's will had never been as strong as the reflex that forced her to breathe and kept her alive. She had only overcome it, eventually, by casting herself into one of the canals that flowed outside Yangzhou's green-and-black pleasure houses. She had transformed her reflex to breathe and draw in air and life into drawing in water and death.

At length, the Queen became aware that the sounds from within the room had stopped.

A long while later the physician came running. He saw her on the floor in the corridor, and cast her a look of horrified recognition as he rushed past her into the banquet hall. Recognition, rather than suspicion, because in her crumpled figure he'd seen what made perfect sense for the situation: a woman, grieving.

But it was all an illusion. Porcelain wasn't a person, and it neither felt nor grieved.

She picked herself up. The throes that had racked her body were gone. Her mind was cool. She went back into the banquet hall, where the physician had come too late.

14

KHANBALIQ

For weeks on end the scraped blankness of the sky had promised snow, but never delivered. The whole of Khanbaliq was learning an insomniac's despair for what was withheld, even as they continued to exhaust themselves with the final preparations for the Grand Councilor's campaign. The army and its herds and supplies and siege machines gathered upon the plain to the south until it was all that could be seen even from as high as the fifth story of the Imperial City's lake pagoda, the Palace of the Moon. Flags flew over the winter-yellowed grass. Within the city and without, the lakes were freezing solid. This was the season for war, when the cold spread its fingers into the south, and in just a few more days: the Great Yuan would ride.

Baoxiang was in his living room contemplating his money chests when Seyhan came in, remarking, "So few people have lived the saying, 'May your wealth fill a hall.'"

The interior of the house's roof had presumably once been a neat interworking of dark and pale woods. Over the years the two woods had warped at different rates, and now the pattern bulged as if it were being viewed through the shifting thickness of the ocean. "It's time," Baoxiang told Seyhan, who lifted his bony brow in acknowledgment.

"Would you like to keep a reserve, in case Chen Youliang needs more?"

"I might have helped a hungry tiger, but I don't need to keep hand-feeding him for the rest of his life," Baoxiang said darkly. "Send it all."

The moment of action, when it had come that afternoon, had been as ordinary as the Minister hailing Baoxiang in the corridor. "Vice-Minister! There you are." The Minister, looking harassed, shuffled through the stack of papers he was carrying and extricated an account. "We need to pay this vendor of saddles; in fact it should have been done already, except for our oversight, and now he writes in complaint. Will you send a courier with the funds?"

Nobody else would have seen the potential in that simple request. Indeed, without the other elements Baoxiang had already put in place, there would have been no such potential. But it was a thread that, if pulled, would bring down an empire, and it had drifted into Baoxiang's hands as softly as a filament of spiderweb carried by the breeze.

For a moment, he hesitated. He could still let go. The thread would float away tracelessly, and only he would know it had ever existed.

But why should he? His rising anger sliced the uncertainty from his thoughts, leaving pure darkness beneath. The Minister had trusted him, and been kind to him, but where had he been when Baoxiang had been worthy of affection? Where had he been when Baoxiang needed it? Had a single person intervened, when the world was teaching him its brutal lessons about who it valued, it could all have been different. But there hadn't been even that one person. And now it was the whole world, and everyone in it, that would suffer the consequences of him doing what it had driven him to do.

When he took the paper from the Minister, his hand was steady. "Consider it handled."

Baoxiang sat naked on the edge of the Third Prince's bed. Semen cooled on his thigh. His jaw clicked as he eased it open. He could tell there would be finger marks on his face. Over the course of a handful of encounters since the bathtub, the Third Prince had learned to take his pleasure with increasing confidence, but his grip was always too hard: as if he were in a terror of failing to mark the difference between a warrior like himself and a weakling like Baoxiang, even as he rutted against Baoxiang's stomach or between his clamped thighs.

In contrast to the imperial grandeur of the rest of the Palace of Abundant Blessings, the Third Prince's bedroom was a wholly personal space. It was also wholly a mess. The dusty wall-carpets appeared to have been hung continuously since last winter—or perhaps even the winter before—without being taken out and beaten over the summer. The floor and every flat surface was a topographic upheaval of books, bowls, gowns so crumpled they looked like someone's discarded attempt at folded paper, armor, gourds, string tied with varying degrees of aptitude into decorative tassels for a sword or spear, two hats, a pouch of frankincense and cloves for freshening the armpits, an extravagant foreign steel belt knife, and too many dingy undergarments. Under it all was a suspicious animal odor, like a fur collar left in the sun, that Baoxiang recognized with regret as the lingering rankness that young men left on their sheets.

"You have *servants*. You're aware their job is to clean." He plucked a discarded undershirt from the clutter and scrubbed his thigh with it.

The Third Prince lay sprawled naked on the rumpled covers with his knee cocked to the side like a wading stork. He tensed when Baoxiang glanced across at him: being looked at by a man, especially when he was in a defenseless state of postcoital softening, was a different proposition from looking *at* a man. But his discomfort passed readily. Baoxiang's perpetually limp dick hardly threatened anyone's manhood. The Third Prince smirked and said without malice, "You're the one who likes being on his knees. Clean it yourself, if you're that bothered."

The sole of the Third Prince's foot, pressed into the side of his opposing knee, drew Baoxiang's eye to the flesh beneath it. Even on a man's hard body, that part was tender; its softness, depressed by the balls of toes and heel, seemed the body being cradled unselfconsciously by itself. For a moment Baoxiang had the urge to lay his hand there in marveling acknowledgment: that this part of another's body, that went unseen and untouched and unconsidered in the course of ordinary life, was within his reach.

It was a foolish urge. Baoxiang shook it off and hunted for his clothes on the floor. All that mattered was that he had the Third Prince where he needed him. The rest was superfluous. He said, casually, "Do you have your normal standing appointment with your mother tomorrow night? I won't come, then."

"Just come a bit later. She usually cuts me short to answer the Great Khan's summons, anyway." The Third Prince fiddled with something small and round that he'd found in a bowl. He continued, in a mocking tone, "Do you know how they prepare women for my father, Vice-Minister? They're stripped naked and delivered to his quarters like meat wrapped in blankets. Don't be fooled by my mother's elegant appearance! You should see how eager she is to go fuck the Great Khan, as if she's no better than a whore." The mockery was self-directed, but his act teetered as violently as an acrobat who was already lost to the fall. "If effort was rewarded by results, she would have replaced me a dozen times over by now. How disappointed she must be!"

The Third Prince's pain made Baoxiang remember how long it had taken for him to believe that the approbation and acceptance he yearned for would never come. He'd been older than the Third Prince by the time he reconciled himself to the world as it was, and killed the part of himself that clung, against all evidence, to the belief that he could be loved.

He felt an uncanny ringing sensation. But the only ghost in the room was that of his younger self, seen in another's face.

Something flew at him. It was too late to duck. Baoxiang exclaimed as it caromed off his forehead, "Son of a turtle!"

The Third Prince gave a brittle grin. "Careful about whose father you insult."

Baoxiang retrieved the missile from the floor: a peeled chestnut. He didn't mind chestnuts, but he'd never found the work of peeling them to be worth it. A single slip would send a dagger of heat-hardened shell under his fingernail, and then it'd be misery for a week. But for Esen, doing battle with the chestnut had been half the fun. Sometimes during the winter, while their father was away, they would sit in the quiet residence with a roasting pan on the brazier while the snow fell outside: Baoxiang reading, and Esen handing him peeled chestnuts, one by one.

Suddenly the thought of that sweet mealy taste made him want to gag. He abandoned the chestnut, and sorted through the mess for his clothes.

The Third Prince watched him dress. He said, diffidently, "It's late. You could. Stay."

Baoxiang had never asked for the Minister's kindness. But now it occurred to him, with a curdled feeling, that he *had* asked for the Third Prince's vulnerability. It had been given to him, and now he cradled it in his hands as would a lover, safeguarding his beloved's heart.

But Baoxiang wasn't the Third Prince's lover, and he had come here for a reason.

"Next time." He made a show of regret. "I need to get back to the office. This afternoon the Minister asked me to make a payment for one of the Grand Councilor's vendor accounts. So I sent a courier with the funds, but now it's bothering me: I can't remember an open contract for purchases from that vendor." He could feel Lady Ki on the end of the thread; a puppet poised to dance. "I wouldn't normally be concerned, because there are so many contracts. I can hardly remember all of them. It's just that with a sum that large, I feel like—I *would* have remembered." He saw with satisfaction that the Third Prince was watching him with a new sharpness. "I'm sure it's nothing. But if I didn't check, I'd be up all night."

The thread, pulled.

He didn't go back to the office, of course. And he would be up all night regardless. As he rode back to the house he wished, savagely, for it to snow, but the sky refused to grant him relief.

The Minister stuck his head around the corner of Baoxiang's office. "You're here! The Great Khan has called for an audience with the ministers. Will you come? The timing's a pity, what with the Grand Councilor still here and so much to do. But there's no help for it. We can only hope it doesn't go for too long—"

It was a single pulled thread snarling other threads; a whole structure, beginning to distort. It was all as it should be. It was all as Baoxiang wanted it to be.

"Is something the matter? You don't have to come, if you don't want," said the Minister, quizzically.

"No." Baoxiang rose, smoothing his uniform. "I'll come."

It still hadn't snowed. The sky ached for release. As they hurried through the archway to the plaza beneath the Hall of Great Brilliance, the Minister startled: the open expanse was already filled with the massed maroon gowns of officials. "How come—are we late?"

The snowless light turned the Great Khan's golden gown the tea-steeped brown of a monk's shawl. The Grand Councilor, in contrast, seemed even more regal than usual in his dragonscale armor. Pulled from his preparations, he looked impatient. The Empress, at his elbow, was stiff with wariness. It was clear neither of them had any idea why Lady Ki had called this meeting. Because of course it had been her.

"Good of you to come, Minister of Revenue," Lady Ki called. Her shimmering ermine cloak was the color of the snow that hadn't fallen. Of ghosts and mourning. Beneath her on the plaza, the black-hatted officials were as static as lines of text on the page. "Perhaps you can clear up a matter for us. Approach the throne."

The Minister shot Baoxiang a surprised look. Baoxiang reflected it back, savoring the performance. As he watched the Minister limping slowly down the plaza, his sense of his own reprehensibility was as sordid and satisfying as a bruise. There was no such thing as an act so despicable, it seemed, that it exceeded his ability to find pleasure in it.

Lady Ki said sweetly, "Minister of Revenue. Is it true that yesterday, under your instructions, the Ministry of Revenue dispatched a courier bearing a significant sum with which to pay a vendor?"

All Baoxiang could see of the Minister was his uniformed back, but he could hear his bemused frown as he replied, "Noble consort, many such payments are made each day in the course of the business of the Ministry of Revenue."

"The payment to which I refer was allegedly for the purchase of saddles." Lady Ki looked over the heads of the gathered officials. "Come."

An imperial courier, his uniform still dusty and streaked with horse lather, came trembling down the center aisle. He was followed by a stream of eunuchs. Lady Ki said, "Perhaps the Minister can assure us of the ordinary nature of this particular payment."

She'd engineered it for maximum dramatic suspense: each eunuch bore only a small bag, so that as each tossed his bag at the Minister's feet, the pile grew to immense proportions. The last eunuch opened his bag and turned it upside down, letting taels shower out. There was no mistaking the peculiar thud of soft gold against the plaza stones.

"Personally," Lady Ki observed, "I would have said it to be far out of the ordinary. This is gold sufficient to buy a kingdom—or two. Imagine how many saddles could have been purchased with it! But then: It was never for saddles, was it?" She turned to the Great Khan, relishing the performance. "Great Khan, this courier was intercepted on his way to the steppe tribes. That he was carrying this quantity of gold makes it clear what the situation is. The Minister of Revenue has been skimming funds from the imperial coffers to buy support for his patron's future treasonous actions against the Great Khan." She smiled, drawing the moment out. "Did you expect anything less from the Grand Councilor, than ambition for the throne?"

Even before Lady Ki had finished, the Great Khan was thunderous. There was no need to make him believe: every word Lady Ki said fed into his worst fears about the man he relied upon, and whose indispensability he so resented. Lady Ki knew him well.

The Grand Councilor recovered quickly from his shock. "The honorable consort has gone too far!" he flung at Lady Ki. "I hope she has considered the consequences of being unable to furnish proof of such outrageous lies. I cannot say where the gold came from. But I can say with confidence that it would have been impossible for anyone, even the Minister of Revenue himself, to have stolen such a sum from the imperial accounts without it having come to attention. How could such a theft be hidden, when the entire system of the Ministry of Revenue is for the purpose of keeping track of every tael spent?" He stared in furious challenge at Lady Ki. "My loyalty to the Great Khan is, and has ever been, unquestionable. I deny the accusation utterly. It is baseless slander of the worst order!"

"Baseless! If not originating from the imperial accounts, then from whose hidden pockets has come this wealth enough to purchase armies? There is no such person in the Great Yuan, Grand Councilor! As for proof—indeed, you are correct that the Ministry of Revenue *does* keep track of every tael spent."

The eunuchs came once more into the plaza, this time their arms full of books. The Minister, registering what they were, flinched.

Lady Ki smiled down at him. "Yes, Minister. The master ledgers from the Ministry of Revenue. Do I have your assurance that what is contained in these books is the true record, audited by no hand other than your own?"

After a beat, the Minister said, firmly, "I have nothing to hide. The books will show the truth."

"Indeed." Snow-scented wind blew over the plaza and ruffled the ledgers, which the eunuchs had laid out, open, in sequence. Somehow, without previously realizing it, Baoxiang had become so cold that he felt paradoxically as if he were burning. But why was his body reacting so strangely? He couldn't fathom it. This was what he wanted, and he'd known since the beginning that this was where his plans led.

"I must commend you on the precise nature of your bookkeeping, Minister," Lady Ki said. "It took but a moment for skilled accountants to find that the system has furnished its own evidence. But please, see for yourself."

The Minister's shoulders tightened, then in a rush the old man went forwards, as if drawn, and fell to his knees turning the pages.

"I think you'll agree that there's a distinct pattern of money being skimmed from official purchases and placed in a special reserve. The balance of which just so happens to be identical to the sum found with the courier." Lady Ki said lightly, almost curiously, "How very long you and the Grand Councilor have been planning to overthrow my husband the Great Khan!"

The Minister had stilled over the books. He looked as if he

were prostrated there, begging to be found innocent. But there was no possibility of that.

The Great Khan said terribly, "Is that your seal, Minister?"

The seal Baoxiang had taken and used on those master ledger copies into which he had inserted all his careful falsehoods. Even had the Minister not already known that Baoxiang had borrowed his seal, he would have known who was responsible. Who else had the skill to create a paper trail that simultaneously created money and stole it?

And it was in Baoxiang's pocket that all the unspent income from the Prince of Henan's estate had gathered. Lady Ki was right: it was wealth enough to buy kingdoms. It had been more than enough to buy the destruction of the last true defender of the Great Yuan.

Everyone present could tell that the Great Khan had already been convinced. The Minister, too, knew that protest would be useless. He answered the Great Khan with dignity, "It is my seal."

Neither man had to be dragged away to his execution. Each placed the accoutrements of his office in a folded pile at the foot of the steps—the Grand Councilor his sword and armor; the Minister his hat and over-robe—and followed the Great Khan's eunuchs from the plaza.

The Minister paused as he passed Baoxiang. Though his face was more crumpled than Baoxiang had seen it, he was calm. With a jumpy, vicious feeling that was like spoiling for a fight, Baoxiang realized he didn't want calm. He wanted blame. He wanted to hear the Minister speak the truth of what he had done. He wanted to be named aloud as the kind of person who had not just done those things, but delighted in them. *Because I'm the worst.*

He said, cruel, feeling the performance crackle through him, "You should have trusted your first impressions of me. That revulsion you felt, the first time you laid eyes on me: Why put it aside? It was telling the truth. I've always been as bad as everyone says. You just refused to believe. And that's why this happened to you. You made a mistake."

But to his dissatisfaction, the Minister didn't match his anger. His face was shaded with some grave emotion that Baoxiang should have recognized, but somehow couldn't. "I never had any doubt that you could achieve whatever you set your mind to, Wang Baoxiang. I don't know what your ultimate goal is. But I hope, for your sake, that when you do achieve it, it'll prove to be what you wanted."

He left Baoxiang seething. Of course it would be what he wanted. He'd visualized his moment of triumph so endlessly that it seemed realer, its emotions purer, than anything he'd ever experienced. He looked up at Lady Ki gloating with victory at the top of the steps. She didn't see that a thread had been pulled; that the world was unraveling. She didn't see how her victory was the beginning of the end, and how every step she took from now on was only securing Baoxiang's ascent to the throne, and his twisted dominion of blackness and despair that was all he'd ever wanted.

The executions, taking place the next day, were public. Baoxiang didn't attend. He sat in his slowly darkening office until the time was well past, staring at the ministerial seal in its box upon his desk. His seal, now. It unsettled him how the Ministry's work hadn't so much as paused. How many times had a minister been deposed—betrayed, replaced—that it could be met with this air of routine? Pairs of officials, separated by the width of their hat-horns, strolled the corridor; someone nearby had a fresh pot of roasted-buckwheat tea. Servants cleared baskets of papers out of the Minister's office next door. Wrongness crawled up Baoxiang's throat. He realized he'd been waiting for some kind of special awareness of the moment. For the rush of satisfaction—of victory—that came from having imposed his will upon the world. But the Minister's personal apocalypse had left no more of a ripple than a stone slipped into a dark pond. And in place of satisfaction, Baoxiang had a sinking feeling he could only identify, inexplicably, as wretchedness.

From the street outside came the falling intonation of bamboo sticks banged together. A hollow, mournful sound. It was only the call of a roaming vendor of fried pastries, but some eerie quality of the sound amplified Baoxiang's wretchedness into shuddering dread. For an awful moment he couldn't tell whether he was awake or asleep. He was on the precipice of something unwitnessable—something so terrible his dreaming self couldn't help but turn from it—

And yet even as Baoxiang's body shook, he felt a kindling impatience at himself that rapidly approached fury. Was it this same impatience, this anger, that Esen had felt whenever he'd witnessed Baoxiang's weakness? Baoxiang suddenly understood. Whatever this pathetic internal quailing was, he couldn't stand it. He wanted to gouge it out of himself in chunks. It didn't even make sense. Hadn't everything gone perfectly? By only making himself as dishonest and dishonorable as the world already thought him, he'd achieved exactly what he wanted. He'd laid the foundation for everything to come. It should have felt *glorious.*

He wrenched himself from his office. The snowbound clouds ached like eyes that couldn't cry. Eyes that couldn't sleep. His wretchedness and anger ratcheted one another tighter and tighter, his desperation for relief mounting with them. He was nearly at his destination when he passed a carriage going in the opposite direction. Lady Ki, leaving. Her cool gaze through the curtains presumed to know where he was headed. What he wanted. *This time,* he thought viciously, *you'd be right.*

The Third Prince was standing amongst the formal furniture of his receiving room, toying with a wine cup. A whiff of Lady Ki's perfume lingered. When he noticed Baoxiang in the doorway, a grin split his bearded face and he exclaimed, "Oh, a ghost! I heard the Minister of Revenue had been executed, and yet here he is before me."

For a moment Baoxiang was pinned by the obscene brightness of it: that the Third Prince was *happy.* It didn't seem like an emotion that could exist in the same world as himself. And yet—the Third Prince's happiness wasn't fully real, either. He was happy because his mother was happy—because she had poured her exultation and her triumph into him, as if he were a glass vase to be filled. She had sat in this same room, overflowing with satisfaction—the same satisfaction that Baoxiang, from whose hands that victory had been delivered, should have had.

"A day of double happiness, indeed!" He couldn't disguise the contemptuous edge. He wasn't sure he wanted to. His anger was a black flood about to break its banks. "Not only does Lady Ki see her enemy brought down, but in celebration she even bestows a single visit upon her son."

The gibe failed to puncture the Third Prince's good mood. "I've never seen her so pleased. Did you hear?" He strutted over, draining the cup. When he tossed it aside, it didn't break, but rolled vigorously across the carpet. "She petitioned the Great Khan to change the executions to death by slow slicing." His flash of white teeth was boyish: a child's impersonal delight in cruelty, like ripping the wings off a dragonfly. "She wanted to see the one who held himself so pridefully—who dared wear that black armor around the palace as if it were *his* to rule—put in his place. She said the results were even more spectacular than she could have wished. The executioners have such skill at slicing off pieces, without causing too much blood loss, that the Grand Councilor screamed for half a day before he fell unconscious. Apparently it was like watching a master fillet a fish." He added, entertained, "He might still be breathing, if you want to go take a look, not that there'd be much of him left by now."

A face flickered in Baoxiang's interior blackness—it might have been the Minister's, screaming—but instinct wrenched his inner eye from it so efficiently that nothing lingered.

"Now that the Grand Councilor's gone, my mother said she'd give me command of the central army." An army that Lady Ki had no intention of using. The ultimate decorative position, for a decorative prince. The Third Prince said, smirking, "You may have secured your own promotion out of this matter, *Minister*, but it seems I still outrank you."

Baoxiang said, silky with rage, "Indeed. I should show my respect to the Third Prince in his new elevation." He said to the servants, "Get out."

The Third Prince watched with pleasure as Baoxiang disrobed, then followed suit. Even with the servants gone, it felt like an exposure to stand naked in this wide-open main room. But if the Third Prince didn't care, Baoxiang cared even less. Whatever vulnerability he might have felt had been sucked into the black whirlpool that was the heart of him. The Third Prince palmed himself in anticipation. His broad-knuckled hand all but swallowed his erection. He said, smiling, "You're always so desperate for it."

But when he pressed forwards, Baoxiang stopped him with a hand to his chest. The eager heat of his young skin sent a jolt through Baoxiang's own contracted, permanently cold body. He had the urge to curl his fingers into that springy flesh, to sink them in until the blood welled up. To make the Third Prince scream as the Minister had screamed. He said pleasantly, hand flat, "Do it properly this time."

Baoxiang caught a flicker of uncertainty under the Third Prince's smirk. It was as vulnerable as the soft spot in a baby's head; as a gap in armor. His cruelty sharpened. Inevitable though this moment was, he realized he'd always been afraid of it: of the pain; the particulars of the degradation. But now he wanted it. He burned for it: to finally hit bottom.

"You can, can't you? Fuck." Baoxiang paused delicately, spear poised. "Unless fucking me isn't what you really want."

They were as close as two people locked together by a sword-thrust. But there was a new, invisible opaqueness between the surface of the Third Prince's black eyes and his inner thoughts. He'd learned something, after all. He wasn't as transparent as he used to be.

"Perhaps what you want," Baoxiang went on, his tone as sleek as the skin over beating organs, "isn't to fuck, but to be fucked. Is that it? You're always so quick to point out how different we are. But when you're alone in the dark, with your hand on your dick: Aren't you dreaming of being the one bent over, the one being fucked? In your secret thoughts, you're so debased that you take your pleasure from the shame of having another man do that to you. Do you think you can hide it forever? It's written all over you. One day they'll see the truth. That you're just like me."

The spear had gone in. The Third Prince's hectic flush had risen as fast as a slap. He was no longer smiling. But to Baoxiang's surprise, he didn't lash out immediately. There was a discomfiting awareness in his eyes as he held Baoxiang's gaze. Somehow

Baoxiang always forgot he wasn't stupid. He had been so easy to manipulate, at the beginning. It had been like winding up a toy. But he'd changed. He was learning, growing, and even now the person Baoxiang understood him to be was only the ghost of a future self: of the man he would become.

"I didn't know we were going to be so honest with each other. But since you've given me the opportunity—" The Third Prince's cruelly bowed top lip was paler than his bottom lip. His beard didn't reach all the way around his mouth, but left thumbprint-sized patches to either side: soft stretches of bare skin that, had he been someone else, might have held crescents of laughter. "I met your brother, that one time in Hichetu." He said softly, "Is it a coincidence I look exactly like him?"

While Baoxiang reeled, he took him by the wrist, twisted it around, and slammed him face-first onto the carpet. Baoxiang cried out, and then again as the Third Prince spat into his hand and thrust into him. The Third Prince might never have done this before, but he knew how to use his body like a weapon; like violence was his inheritance. He forced himself inside Baoxiang with a stuttering series of shoves that hurt just as much as Baoxiang had imagined. He bit back another cry. The Third Prince laid his entire heavy body over Baoxiang, then placed his lips against Baoxiang's ear. "Did you love him? Did you want him to do this to you?"

Baoxiang's fury was consuming. It was a welcoming fury, a greedy fury, that crackled his nerve-ends into a state of heightened sensitivity. This was the pain and degradation and humiliation he'd come for. It wasn't what he'd wanted from Esen—he'd never looked at his own brother with lust—but it was what he wanted to *give* him. For Esen's sake, he would be fucked, lowered as far as it was possible to go, be ruined beyond repair. This would be his gift to his perfect, sanctimonious, empire-worshipping hypocrite of a brother, and he wanted it with all his heart.

His hipbones ground into the floor. The Third Prince's knees were dug into the back of Baoxiang's knees, as if they were nesting tables. Their flesh dragged and stuck. It couldn't have been any more comfortable for the Third Prince than it was for Baoxiang. His breath rasped out with each impact. His bodily agony was a wild paroxysm. He was being screwed into the dark awfulness of his soul, and he knew, furiously, that if only he could find it, there would be pleasure in the pain. Somewhere inside there would be the righteousness he had come for—the vicious satisfaction, and the twisted, cruel joy of knowing he was about to plunge the entire world into his own living nightmare of pain and suffering. He was groping for the pleasure, clawing through the darkness for it. It was at his fingertips; it was slippery, elusive, threatening to dissolve into wretchedness. With a last, monumental straining effort, he forced himself upon it. His trembling relief, that what he'd wanted *did* finally feel good, somehow felt as desperate as terror.

Water was leaking out of his smashed-flat face onto the carpet. What did it matter what he'd once wanted from Esen? This was what he had now. It was exactly what he wanted, and when the rest of it was finished: it would feel just as good as this. It would make everything worth it.

Lady Ki's carriage waited on the rocky island base of the Palace of the Moon. From the center of the frozen black lake and its cobweb of marble bridges, the pagoda thrust glittering into the blackness. A carapace of mirror mosaics multiplied the light from the strings of lanterns hung along the pagoda's serried balconies: a thousand new stars for the starless sky.

Lady Ki was in the ground-floor shrine, kneeling before a floor-to-ceiling gilded Buddha, when Baoxiang entered. Her crimson hooded cloak draped around her with the thick static folds of a frozen waterfall. Despite the cold, she'd been waiting for him the whole time he'd been at the Third Prince's residence—knowing that when he left, he would find her here. It was hard to believe anyone ever bought her performance of a swooning flower. If the strength of a person's will could be measured by how far they had risen, then Lady Ki's ascent from tribute woman to the Great Khan's consort signaled a determination even greater than Baoxiang's own.

He knelt beside her, accepting the lit cluster of incense sticks from the shrine attendant. As he raised the incense and bowed three times, the loud throb between his legs was as if the Third Prince were in the room with them.

"Praying for the former Minister of Revenue?" Lady Ki inquired, after the attendant had withdrawn. "I'd be careful if I were you. Being seen to honor a traitor tends to raise doubts about a person's own loyalties."

He wondered if she knew he'd framed the Minister, or if she only thought he'd informed her about an existing plot. He couldn't tell. He said coolly, "The strength of my loyalty, once given, might surprise those who see the particular forms of its attachment as dishonorable."

Lady Ki glanced at him sidelong. It was strange seeing her up close. He'd only ever seen her before from below, as if she were a looming statue. Inside her crimson hood her face was a cool oval, her nose pinkish in the cold. Her lips were thin and graceful; her neck swanlike. In face and form, the Third Prince followed his father. Perhaps that likeness had contributed to his father's hate. When faced with a copy of your own youthful self, alike except in one crucial matter, that difference might become all you could see.

"Do not mistake me, Minister. Had I the power to force my son's heart to see clearly, so that he might look upon you with disgust and shun your company as unfit for any man—let alone the heir to the throne of the Great Yuan—I would. But," she said, suddenly raw, "it seems not even a mother has that power."

The tail end of her words had peeled her face open. Baoxiang thought, in a moment of blank surprise: *She cares about him.*

As he recalled the times Lady Ki had spurned the Third Prince so she could lavish affection upon the Great Khan, he felt his perspective revolve. Like everyone else, he'd assumed Lady Ki only protected the Third Prince because he was her route to power. But perhaps . . . Perhaps she protected him because he was her child. Perhaps, as a foreign woman alone in the court of the empire to which her own nation lay subordinate, she had been forced to protect her deficient, vulnerable son by the only means available to her: by cultivating the Great Khan's favor. Perhaps she was afraid to show how much she cared, because she knew how it would be used against her.

There was a pain in Baoxiang's chest: a frozen blade in his heart, slicing it when it dared beat. Lady Ki might care. But what difference did it make to the Third Prince's sadness whether he was unloved, or simply believed himself to be? A connection between two people existed only because of their shared belief in it as real. There was no such thing as a connection with only one end. There was no such thing as love, alone.

Lady Ki's flash of openness had gone. "I was surprised when, yesterday, my son conveyed to me information about the former Minister's activities. I wasn't sure if I should trust the source. But in the end, it proved extremely advantageous." There was no warmth in her address at all. "It seems that the connection I had previously taken to be a disadvantage for my son, can be of use."

Baoxiang didn't need warmth, and he could tolerate her unconcealed disgust of him. He was as cold as she was. All he needed was for her to keep thinking of him as useful.

"Stay loyal to us, Minister," Lady Ki said as she rose, "and I'll reward you when I'm Empress." Baoxiang stayed in place, throbbing, as she swept out. Now that the loss of the Grand Councilor had left the Empress vulnerable, Lady Ki would be eager to rid herself of her rival. She might not be able to scrub the deviancy from her son's heart—but she knew if she could guarantee that he was the only son in line for the throne, he would *have* to come into the Mandate. If Khubilai Khan's descendants had held the Mandate in unbroken sequence since the founding of the Great Yuan, what other possibility could there be?

For a moment Baoxiang felt the quiver of the Third Prince above him, inside him. It wasn't just the touch of another's body against his own, but of another vulnerable human spirit, with its own chains of insecurities and desires that led it forever into suffering.

Baoxiang pushed the thought away. He didn't know why that aspect of the encounter had been the one that surfaced. The whole point had been his own pain and humiliation—his personal ruination—that had transformed him into this pitch-black self that would finally enact the end. Because it wasn't Baoxiang who was useful, but the Third Prince and Lady Ki who would be useful to him.

He rose, and left.

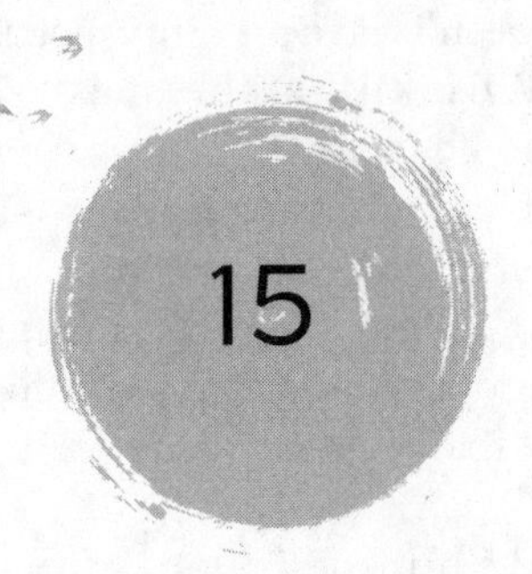

15

YINGTIAN

"I can see Chen Youliang asking Madam Zhang for help to build his navy. But why would she agree?" Ma asked Zhu, who lay beside her in bed. Zhu was only back for a night—having brought the armies back to Yingtian to rest and resupply under Xu Da's supervision, she would be leaving immediately for Fang Guozhen's pirate base in Qingyuan to secure herself a navy. It was hardly the victorious homecoming Ma had dared let herself dream of. The thought of what Chen had done to the people of Nanchang was enough to make her feel sick. The thought of Zhu facing Chen directly in battle was even worse. "You'd think Madam Zhang would be the last person to nurse a starving tiger, even if it promised not to eat her. And besides that, she didn't know she was going to lose General Zhang and end up besieged. Why would she have thought she'd need his help? It doesn't feel right. Don't you think there's something else happening?"

It felt cozy and safe there under the coverlet, their heads propped together on the square pillow. Zhu smelled different, as she always did when she came back from traveling, but the familiarity of her presence made Ma's entire body relax. Ma couldn't help wishing she didn't have to leave so soon. She'd thoroughly disliked accompanying Zhu to Bianliang, but it was almost worse to be the one always left behind to wait, and worry.

"I think you're right. There's something we're missing." Zhu stared up at the bed-curtains swooping overhead, her brow furrowed in thought. "But even if that's true, and there's someone else playing this game—how much of a worry is it, really?

Whoever he is, he doesn't have an army, because we know where all the armies are. What kind of threat can someone without an army be to me, when I have two?"

Ma had been unpleasantly surprised to learn that Zhu had restored Ouyang to command. In her opinion there was a major difference between merely having goals in common, and the trust necessary for real cooperation. Zhu's gambit had been successful so far, but—"Is it really a good idea to rely on General Ouyang so much?"

"You really dislike him, don't you," Zhu said, cracking a wry smile. "If you want good company, or an audience for a joke, I agree: he's not your man. But when it comes to killing people—if he came in second place, who would dare be first? He's been very useful. Anyway, no need to worry. I know how to keep him under control. I understand him. After all: we're alike."

Ma remembered Ouyang standing alone in his prison room in his white underclothes, his eyes black with hate and his hair tangled over his face like a ghost. Even though he was someone who'd done what he considered the worst thing possible, he didn't regret it. He was someone who was willing to do whatever it took to get what he wanted, regardless of sympathy, morality, or the simple fact of the connection between two human beings. And he did it because he believed it would be worth it, at the end, regardless of the pain it caused for him or anyone else. She said, chilled, "Don't be too alike."

QINGYUAN

The sea at Qingyuan was as brown and flat as a river, poked through with what seemed like a thousand dragon-hump islands. Fang Guozhen's home base, at the northern end of a stretch of harbor-riven coastline that ran all the way down to Taizhou's salt warehouses, was dense and secretive: a haven for the ships that filled its every nook and cranny, and speckled the open sea like a festival of kites.

"It does make you think, doesn't it, that if a rock can be reincarnated as a person for good deeds, then a bad person might come back as an inanimate object," Zhu said, staring at the ships anchored in the shallow water. The ships stared back at her with the fiercely painted eyes on their prows, promising all manner of murder and pillage. "Do these ships carry people, or eat them?"

"Three masts, two decks, cargo capacity beneath the waterline, keeled for stability," Jiao observed. "Classic pirate vessel type, designed to raid and run. They wouldn't be any good for carrying heavy artillery, or direct engagement with Chen Youliang's warships." According to reports received from around captured Nanchang, Chen's three-story vessels towered over ordinary river craft the way Chen himself towered over normal people. His flagship vessel's cannons had crushed Nanchang's walls like peppercorns under the pestle.

"So what?" Yuchun asked belligerently. "Bigger isn't better. If they're small and fast, we can use a strategy that plays to those strengths." Yuchun, who was only a handspan taller than Zhu and had a similarly wiry build, prided himself on being one of the faster—if smaller—men on any given battlefield. When Xu Da had stayed in Yingtian to supervise the armies' resupply logistics, Yuchun had taken it upon himself to accompany Zhu, Jiao, Ouyang, and Ouyang's two commanders, saying, "Maybe *you* didn't see the look in the eunuch's eye when he first heard you were going to withdraw from Pingjiang, but I did. Someone should stand between the two of you in case he loses it again. And since I don't see Jiao Yu sacrificing himself for anyone, I guess it should be me."

It was true that Ouyang's pain was always building up inside him, like blood filling a socket where a tooth used to be. It was equally true that the more pain he was in, the more he was driven by instinct rather than reason. It could have been cause for concern. But, Zhu thought with pleasure, now she knew how to release that pain. She'd learned how to control him.

As satisfying as it'd been to bite him that first time, it had been excessive. His hand had swelled up like an inflated bladder and stayed that way for days: impossible to hide; even more awkward to explain. After that, Zhu had restrained herself. Now, as

Ouyang looked pensively out to sea, to everyone else he must have seemed as pristinely untouchable as ever. Only she knew how his sleeves covered a ladder of marks she'd made. Only she knew what he looked like as human sweat was forced from that perfect jade face, and what he sounded like as he surrendered to the pain.

And it *was* pain. Just because he wanted it, didn't mean it hurt any less. What Zhu gave him was the kind of injurious pain that ordinary people wouldn't have dared inflict on someone they knew, even if begged. What they couldn't have understood was how good it felt. Every one of Ouyang's agonized reactions was a pure physical expression of their connection—their mutual wanting—that pulled them into the future. To the place where they would end together, as they were meant to.

"If you have some heretofore undemonstrated expertise in naval strategy, Commander Chang," Jiao was saying, "now would be the time to share it. Saying the word 'strategy' does not will it into being." He added in a veiled tone, "It's interesting how Fang Guozhen hasn't yet allied himself with either the Yuan or any of its enemies. I'd be surprised if you were the first to approach him."

"Fortunately for us, I'm very persuasive," Zhu replied coolly. His skepticism reminded her sharply of the other time he'd doubted, before the first time she'd faced Ouyang at Bianliang. It wasn't a wholly unwelcome reminder. That time had, after all, been a success.

The town of Qingyuan was well populated, despite its air of disrepute. It was also, Zhu noticed with amusement and Ouyang with visible distaste, as female as a nunnery. From shop owners to street urchins, merchants to street porters, and the pirates who thronged the streets with their strong creased faces and rope-roughened hands: eight out of ten of them were women, and Zhu wasn't convinced the remaining ones weren't, too. "He's made the *whole town* his harem?" Yuchun said, marveling. "I can't believe I've been wasting my youth in camps full of gross men when this was an option."

"Are you interested in joining the harem, or having one?" Zhu inquired. "You're not pretty enough for the former. As for the latter, I hate to break it to you, but: the best way to become the kind of man who has a harem—a king, for instance—is to spend a lot of time in camps full of gross men."

"Don't front, everyone knows Ma Xiuying would cut off your balls if you took a consort," Yuchun said spitefully, which, Zhu reflected, was true in spirit if not anatomy.

At their lodging house she prevailed upon the nearest visibly unoccupied member of the group—Chu, the rounder and more bearded of Ouyang's two senior commanders—to carry a note of introduction across to Fang Guozhen's residence, then trotted down the rickety stairs to the aural accompaniment of creaking sails and seabirds, and the chamber pot smell of the canal that let out directly onto the foreshore. A single large pig frolicked in the brown water.

The dining room was full to the brim. But as Zhu joined her party, she was curious to see that they were the only group. The other diners were all women, though less weathered than the pirates outside, and appeared to be traveling alone. They wore trousers and short plain robes instead of skirts, and ate in silence.

"This uncle's honorable establishment sees a lot of pilgrims," Zhu noted, when the proprietor came over with chewy sweet potato noodles speckled with cubed yam, pork and scallions, and a sweet bean sauce. "Are they heading to Mount Putuo?" It was one of the four sacred Buddhist mountains, out on one of the dragon-hump islands. Seemingly every second monk who'd visited Wuhuang Monastery had a tale of nearly having his neck broken by reckless sedan chair bearers on one or another of the sacred mountains. Zhu, who'd climbed several hundred mountains' worth of monastery stairs on her own two legs—while carrying buckets—had felt a distinct lack of sympathy.

"Those women?" The proprietor slapped the bowls down, making the noodles jump. (He was clearly a man, Zhu reflected, though perhaps one like Zhu herself: there was something about the timbre of his voice. Ouyang, sitting across the table, curled his lip in derision.) "They're not pilgrims, they're here for the competition. Aren't *you* pilgrims?" It was a fair enough assumption. Since Zhu hadn't wanted the world to know the Radiant King was seeking an alliance with Fang Guozhen, her group were dressed even more plainly than the women. The proprietor explained, "Fang Guozhen hosts a celebration every year on his birthday. The highlight is a fighting competition for women who want to join his crews for the year ahead. He only chooses those who prove themselves well. The woman who wins the entire competition gets to make a request of him. Anything they want, within his power to grant. That's a rich prize, coming from someone as powerful as Fang Guozhen. Women travel from afar to compete for it."

"Can't be much of a competition, if they're women," Yuchun laughed.

"You'd be surprised, young man. Take some time to watch before you continue your journey, you'll be impressed by their skills."

"Women are found in all sorts of unexpected places these days," Jiao said, and smiled faintly when Zhu gave him a hard stare.

"I'll warn you not to bother them, unless you want to experience their skills personally. We had a man killed here last year for touching one without her permission. Of course, if they approach you . . ." The proprietor chuckled. "Well, then it's your lucky day."

Yuchun said breezily, "Since this table consists of an old man, an ugly man, a man so boring we've probably lost him twice already without noticing"—this was apparently a reference to Ouyang's other senior commander, Geng—"and someone who isn't a man, I like my chances." Then, at Ouyang's glare, "What? Don't be offended with me for just saying the facts."

"You were such an unattractive child," Zhu mused. "Your body and your ego have both grown magnificently. But I hope your other weapon has kept pace, or the women might be disappointed."

Chu slipped back into the dining room and handed Zhu the reply from Fang.

Zhu opened it, not failing to notice how it had already been opened—and presumably read—then immediately put that aside as she focused on the much larger problem at hand.

"What does he say?" Yuchun was oblivious to her reaction.

Zhu did her best to feign unconcern as she tucked the letter away. "As expected. He'll meet to hear my proposal. That's all we needed at this stage."

It was technically true. And it wasn't that she'd come expecting Fang to welcome her with open arms. But what she *had* expected was for him to receive her promptly, with the courtesy befitting her status as a major power. Instead, all she had was his insolent offer to meet several days from now, with the implication that she was less important than his petty birthday celebrations. And what *that* meant was that he wouldn't be coming into this meeting with a willingness to be persuaded, as Zhu had let herself hope, but quite the opposite.

She was aware of Chu's inscrutable gaze across the table. He'd read the letter, she thought sharply. He knew how bad it had been. Jiao, too, was watching her, less inscrutably. His expression was pure knowing superiority. *I hope you have a better reason than that.*

But even if the challenge was greater than it had first seemed, she wouldn't fail. How could she? She wanted too much for that to ever happen.

❋

"Senior Commander Chu saw the note from Fang Guozhen," Geng commented. The slatted bamboo blinds of Ouyang's bare inn room rattled in the icy breeze. It hadn't snowed yet in Qingyuan, if it ever snowed at all, and the smooth brown foreshore stretched out with a skim of bubbled brightness on its surface. "It was an open insult. He has no intention of agreeing to enter into an alliance with Zhu Yuanzhang."

Ouyang wondered if you could walk on that bright surface. Perhaps you would sink. There'd been no opportunity for Zhu to hurt him on their trip down from Yingtian, and his pain was an ever-expanding cloud that pressed against his every crack from the inside, threatening to burst him apart. *Just a little while longer. Hold on.*

"Are you listening? Zhu Yuanzhang has no navy and no

prospect of getting one. Chen Youliang is going to destroy him. You promised we'd go alone as soon as he wasn't our best chance."

He couldn't stop thinking about Zhu pouring that other kind of pain into him. Pain that was pure bodily sensation. Pain that was mercy. Pain that flayed out of him everything that was unbearable, every torment of mind and memory, until all that was left of him was a fleshless seed suspended in the relief of perfect, burning, weightless agony. Why couldn't Geng stop bothering him and leave? His craving was sharper than hunger. All he wanted was for Zhu to come, and deliver that blessed relief.

Geng said, "Or have you forgotten why you're doing this?"

It connected like a slap, as intended. Ouyang snarled, "*Forgotten?*"

With monumental effort he managed to stem the sudden irruption of memory. Of everything he could never forget. Even in death, he thought savagely, he would remember.

Geng, unintimidated by the snarl, merely waited. There should have been no need to explain himself to someone whose role was to obey him without question, but when Geng showed no evidence of leaving, Ouyang ground out, "When Zhu Yuanzhang makes his offer, Fang Guozhen will come around. Zhu Yuanzhang can be . . ." He paused and groped for the right word, then said, feeling dire, ". . . convincing."

"Zhu Yuanzhang," Geng said with artificial patience, "doesn't have anything to offer."

"He'll find something. It will work out. It always does, for him." If it hadn't been true, it wouldn't have felt so bitter. Zhu drove towards the future as though it were realer than the present—the sheer strength of his belief and determination somehow forcing the world around him, and everyone in it, to make way. "Besides, even if we did go, what about the Grand Councilor? If we march alone and fail—"

A chill ran through him at the thought. He couldn't imagine what that would be like, to die without achieving his goal, in the knowledge that everything he had done had been for nothing.

"I wouldn't worry about the Grand Councilor," Geng said with a strange ease, as the blinds clacked out a windchime tune.

"He always had a lot of enemies in court. I doubt he's even in command anymore."

"You *doubt* he's in command?" Geng couldn't be serious. Did he really want Ouyang to make the most consequential decision of his life based on nothing more than a guess? He said in a tone that he hoped brooked no argument, "I meant what I said about leaving Zhu Yuanzhang. I'll do it the moment he can't give me what I need. But as long as he can get himself a navy and prove himself capable of taking on Chen Youliang, then there's no reason to."

"I see." Geng's square face was opaque. For a moment, Ouyang wondered what he was thinking. Was he really so invested in his farm that he wanted to get to Dadu as soon as possible, regardless of the risk? His fleeting curiosity dissolved into impatience. This was *his* mission; his fate; his pain. Geng and Chu had only ever been there to help him succeed, and they mattered even less than Shao had mattered.

"It's a waste of time to wait," Geng said. "But I suppose you'll change your mind once he fails."

Zhu was ascending the steep inn stairs towards the rooms when she bumped hard into Senior Commander Chu, who was descending.

"Both in too much of a hurry!" Zhu laughed, then, "No, don't bother," as Chu, full of apologies, tried to wedge past her to rescue her leather packet of medical equipment from where it had fallen to a lower stair. Zhu put aside her kingly dignity and crouched to retrieve it, along with a stray paper that had fluttered down.

"This yours?" Zhu glanced at the paper curiously. "You write in Mongolian?" She'd only ever heard Chu speak Han'er, even to Ouyang, and although his Henan accent had northern inflections that were unusual to Zhu's ear, it was still a Nanren accent. She realized she'd been thinking of him as much the same as her own men, when of course he'd been years in a Mongol army.

Ordinary people's handwriting somehow never resembled the neat Mongolian script Zhu had learned to read as a novice monk. She read the note laboriously. It was a requisition list. She handed it back.

"Mongolian's what I'm used to, for military matters. I wouldn't know the characters for most items of equipment," Chu said with a rueful shrug. "That's what happens when you get conscripted by the Mongols at sixteen. I was just discussing some ideas with the General about what we'll need for the final march up to Dadu. The Radiant King should let him know if you have any additional equipment orders, and I'll action them when we get back to Yingtian." He flattened himself against the wall and they squeezed past in opposite directions.

Zhu continued up the stairs, pondering. Chu could read and write Mongolian. Perhaps that was common to all Nanren commanders in a Mongol army. But then: Chu had read Fang's reply. Was he just curious, or did he have another motive for wanting to know?

When she and Ouyang had come upon the spy and the messenger, the spy had spooked when he'd realized that the messenger's horse was reacting to Ouyang's presence. It was common enough knowledge within Ouyang's army that there was an uncanniness about their general that made flames flicker as he passed, and animals snarl or flee. So it wasn't surprising the spy had made the connection. What *was* surprising was that the spy's own horse hadn't reacted. Horses did eventually become used to Ouyang's ghostly parade, Zhu knew. He could hardly ride if they didn't. Did that mean the spy was someone close enough to Ouyang that this horse had already become accustomed to ghosts?

Ouyang didn't have friends. He didn't have a trusted inner circle of confidants within the senior ranks of his army. As far as Zhu could tell, there were only two people Ouyang considered worthy of his time: the two Nanren commanders who had been with him since the beginning of his plan to betray the Prince of Henan.

That was interesting. Zhu reached the top floor, but instead of heading to Ouyang's room as she'd been intending, she went to the room at the farthest end of the corridor, tapped the door open with her foot, and went in.

Of the three split-bamboo pallets on the floor, only the middle was occupied. Yuchun bolted upright, the blanket falling down to reveal his bare chest, then relaxed when he saw who it was. The naked woman beside him glared at Zhu and hissed, "Do you mind!" Zhu had the impression that she knew how to kill a man in many different ways, and was considering putting one into action.

"Well, if that's how you feel about it, put something heavy in front of the door before you start! Do you think I wanted to see you practicing qigong with my little brother?" Zhu's eye fell upon some distinctive items of clothing on the floor. "Wait. Are you one of those martial arts *nuns*?"

When the woman scowled, Zhu said hastily, "No offense. I love nuns! Monks think they're the toughest, but tell you what: we all know nuns have them beat in that department. And even if you have to wear black all the time, isn't it nice that they let you keep your hair! You're very pretty, you know. I would have said it was a waste on a nun, but—well, it seems you're as fine with breaking *that* part of your vows as some monks I've known in my time."

"We're not a celibate sect," the woman said witheringly. "*Obviously.*"

"I'm guessing you didn't come to Qingyuan to join the pirate crews, if you're already in a sisterhood," Zhu mused. "Did you come to win the favor? How do you know Fang Guozhen is good for it? He wouldn't be the first man to promise the world to a woman, only to kick her out of bed with a single copper cash."

The woman frowned at Zhu. Like a typical nun, she didn't seem to have much of a sense of humor, which made it doubly bizarre that she had chosen to hop into bed with Yuchun, of all people. "Fang Guozhen's word is his bond. One of my sect-sisters won the favor four years ago, and he delivered on it. She asked him to go against the Goryeo pirates that raided her home village when she was a child, so they would never terrorize the coast south of Qingyuan again. And he did, although it took a year and the resources of his full fleet."

"Well, that certainly puts him in the running for the most honorable man in the Great Yuan," Zhu said, impressed. "Not that I'm sure who his competition would have been. Tell me who hasn't broken his word once or twice in these troubled times, and lived to tell the tale." She spoke flippantly, but she could feel an idea forming. She'd been bothered by Fang's rude response to her overtures. Her reputation as the Radiant King, and her almost complete capture of Madam Zhang's territory, should have earned his respect. Not to mention that now that General Zhang was dead, Zhu alone had the Mandate of Heaven. How could Fang fail to recognize the inevitability of her success? But . . . it wouldn't hurt to have some insurance up her sleeve.

"Little sister, please trust that I wouldn't say this to just any woman I was meeting for the first time. But as you don't seem the shy type—" Zhu took the purse from her belt and hefted it enticingly. "How much for your clothes?"

Perhaps she wasn't as humorless as all that, because the nun burst into laughter. "Don't tell me *you* have your eye on that favor, little man. Perhaps you'd fit into my clothes! But if you're thinking of entering the competition, I'd reconsider. A female disguise won't fool Fang Guozhen. Men have managed to sneak into the competition before, but they've always been discovered. And as honorable as Fang Guozhen is to his friends and those he's given his word to, he's ruthless to those who seek to take advantage."

But she didn't try too hard to press the point. In addition to being tough, nuns were eminently practical. At length the nun sauntered out in her white underclothes, clutching a handful of Zhu's silver.

"I can't say I've ever paid a woman so much to give someone *else* a good time," Zhu commented, hanging her purse back on her belt.

"Your own fault for carrying such big denominations." Yuchun, whose hopes for a continuation of his amorous encounter had been dashed by the nun's departure, was unsympathetic.

"Say what you like about the Mongols, it's a pity that paper-money thing didn't work out," Zhu mused. "So much more convenient for travel. Though I suppose having a monstrously heavy purse on one side does balance out the lack of arm."

Unlike Zhu and Ouyang, who had both insisted on private rooms for reasons that neither wanted to disclose to the world at large, Yuchun was sharing with Chu and Geng. Zhu regarded Chu's belongings where they sat atop the rightmost pallet. "You get along with Senior Commander Chu well enough, don't you?"

"He's a pretty good guy." Yuchun lolled back in his blanket nest. "Can take a joke, unlike that frigid boss of his. And he gets a hilarious lisp when he's drunk. Why?"

Zhu gathered up the nun's outfit and tucked it into her armpit. "Take him out drinking with you somewhere in Qingyuan tonight. Then on the way home," she said, "kill him."

Zhu was amused to find that somehow it was Ouyang who had ended up with the nicest room in the inn. Instead of a pallet he had a three-sided bed against the wall, and his floor was blissfully splinter-free. There were even split-bamboo blinds that clacked in the bracingly kelp-scented breeze. When she went in, shutting the door behind her, he was cross-legged on the bed, honing his sword with a smooth rectangular stone. Zhu had become so reaccustomed to seeing him in armor that his return to ordinary clothes—not even layered Mongol satin, which he wore like another kind of armor, but a soft short robe in the Nanren style—made him seem unfamiliarly small and vulnerable as he focused on his task.

They never spoke about what Zhu did, when she came to him. But when his head came up, and he saw she was alone, his sharp awareness of her felt like a spark jumping to bridge the gap between two bodies.

"There's something I need you to do for me." Zhu tossed the bundle of clothing onto the bed beside him. "Fang Guozhen's competition. I need you to enter, pretending to be me, and win it."

It was cruel to request that of him when he'd been hoping for something else. Ouyang held himself rigidly at the best of times, but she sensed his instantly increased tension as his eyes shot to the bundle. The silence stretched. Then he said with frighteningly flat affect, "You want me to pretend to be you, pretending to be a woman, fighting against women."

It suddenly seemed like a bad idea for him to be holding a sword. Zhu, perhaps uniquely, knew exactly how much she was asking of him. Other people might wonder why he should be so bothered by the idea of being mistaken for a woman, since they essentially saw him that way already. But for Ouyang, to be seen as a woman—to be all too easily believed as one—would be to admit that his lifelong, prideful efforts to be recognized as himself had been a failure. It would be to admit that the world had never truly seen him as a man, but only tolerated him in the role on sufferance. By putting him in a dress, Zhu would be forcing him into a mold he had always refused to occupy, because it wasn't who he was. She would be forcing him to inhabit his shame, in front of everyone.

"I'd do it if I could. You know that, don't you?" She felt as if she were pressing her sincerity against unyielding jade. "You've seen me do it before. I'd be happy to do it again. But even if I did, what I can't do is fight well enough to win. And I *need* a win, General. I need that favor from Fang Guozhen.

"I'm not trying to humiliate you. I'm asking because there's no other choice. Yuchun is the right size, and he has the skills to win, but he's—" *too obviously masculine.* She swallowed the observation before she ended up making the situation worse. "The only one is you."

His lip was curled in visceral repulsion, his refusal evident in every line of his body. She said, because she knew it would hurt, "I thought you would do whatever it takes for us to win."

She'd stabbed him, and the raw pain that flashed to his surface was more than seemed humanly bearable. His fist white-knuckled on the hilt in his lap. For a moment, Zhu found herself hurting with him, as she watched him struggle: with what he knew had to be done, even as it was yet another thing he didn't want to do.

His moment of collapse was almost too private to witness. He must have known she could see it, because he turned away. At length he rasped out, "If you need me to do it—" He seemed to grind to a halt around some internal obstruction. Then, in a spasm of self-hate that seemed just as much a hatred of her, he said in a rush, "Then *make me do it.*"

Zhu's sympathy was an unfamiliar knot in her chest. It was the closest he'd ever come to asking for help. She drew out the leather packet she'd dropped on the stairs, and flipped it open to show him the array of hair-fine needles. "On our way here, I asked Jiao Yu how I could make someone hurt without damaging them. He told me to try these. I think he thought I wanted to torture a confession out of someone." Naturally, the idea hadn't bothered Jiao's conscience. "Since you can relieve pain with acupuncture, you can reverse the techniques to cause it. Although it takes a skilled practitioner to produce the peak of sensation, even those with a basic knowledge of the meridians can make a person scream."

"I wouldn't scream," he said, his eyes latched onto the needles. It was almost more intimate to see someone imagining their release than seeing them in the moment of it. It was to see them quivering on the pinnacle of aliveness, daring to let themselves thrill with want, even though the object of their longing could still be denied to them.

She said softly, "Open your clothes."

He hadn't thought about what would be necessary for it to happen. She saw him realize, saw how the prospect of the humiliation colored his wanting without providing the mercy of erasing it.

It was a long time before he placed his sword on the bed and stood up. He didn't look at her as he untied his outer and inner robes, and opened his undershirt and let it fall.

He was so tense that the tendons stood out on the sides of his smooth throat, where there was neither a man's knot nor the shadow of a beard. Zhu knew immediately—instinctively—that she was the only person who had ever seen him like this. The immensity of his surrender filled her with an awe that made her breath catch. She'd already seen the fat and blood and muscle inside him, but this was the true violation, and it breached some boundary between them that would never be restored.

What Ouyang concealed beneath his men's clothing was the same as what Zhu concealed beneath her own. It wasn't a sameness of the kind that could be seen in a mirror, but a sameness of substance: that both of them deviated from what the world believed their bodies should be, according to the roles they performed within it. Zhu had the feeling of their likeness binding them so tightly that their hearts and lungs moved as one. If they touched, how could it be the ordinary touch of two bodies? It would be a fusion of selves: the transcendence of perfect acceptance, because they understood each other's feelings and physical existence. Because they were the same.

She hovered the tip of the first needle over his skin. Even before it touched him, the nearness of her hand made the all-but-invisible hairs there rise towards her. Her answering shiver felt like an echo in flesh.

She knew about their likeness, but he didn't. She was seized by a sweet, powerful urge she had never felt before: to open her clothes and show herself to him, so he could understand why she knew how it felt to be him. Somehow she knew it would be deeper than merely revealing herself. It would be giving herself. Sharing herself, in the completeness of who she was, to the only person she had met who could understand.

Before she could pursue the urge further, he said desperately, *"Do it."*

As if they were rolled together by a wave, the hair distance between them was bridged, and the needle slipped in without resistance.

Ouyang stood in the row of female competitors. Bamboo poles twice the height of a person, their tops arched over to suspend beribboned, basket-woven globe decorations that leaped and shimmered in the damp seaside wind, had been planted to mark out an oval in Qingyuan's sandy dirt. The cold conditions hadn't quashed local interest in the competition. The crowd was a cacophonous mass jostling and elbowing for position: roving food vendors, squealing children, dogs, chickens, some men, and more women than Ouyang had ever seen in his life. They were here for a show.

He was wearing a satin-collared black robe belted above a fluttering, sheer split skirt; lightweight black trousers tucked into soft high boots; and a black half veil. His hair hung loose save for a small ribboned knot behind to keep it from swinging into his eyes. Twisted-up rags had changed the shape of his chest into something he couldn't bear to think about.

He couldn't have done this at all if Zhu hadn't used the needles on him. At first he'd been disappointed at how painless the insertions had been. But then Zhu had placed one last needle, and it had turned him into lightning inside. He hadn't screamed. It hadn't been a matter of willpower: he'd simply forgotten how. He'd forgotten he might want to. The pain, intensified by the humiliation of exposure, was overwhelming sensation. At some point he'd become aware that he was gasping and shuddering on all fours at Zhu's feet, his dripping sweat darkening the unwaxed floorboards. He'd been beyond pride, beyond caring. He didn't know why it was Zhu who could do this, or why it couldn't have been anyone other than him. But for what Zhu gave him, Ouyang would have knelt forever.

Even now, as he waited on the competition sand, his nerves crackled with leftover lightning: a glorious, singing agony that made everything, for the moment, bearable.

Above them, Fang Guozhen sprawled on his pirate throne. He was fat: masculine and magnificent with it, a tooled silver breastplate and fur-edged pauldrons increasing him to even greater proportions. A lion's-head belt buckle as large as Ouyang's two fists rested on the mound of his stomach. Beneath it the groin flap of his armor lolled between his loose-trousered legs. His unbound hair was as uncouth as a bandit's. On any number of other men, that same sprawl and armor would have been worthless peacocking. But to Ouyang, who knew warriors, the power of Fang's body was as perceptible as gravity. Fang could play at crassness with ease, because he knew he could prove himself where it counted.

Fang called lazily, "Let the games begin!"

Ouyang's first opponent faced him across the oval and bowed her greetings. She was about the same age as Madam Zhang—old for a woman—and had two short swords of the kind Ouyang normally disdained. But now, with his sword in his left hand and his right immobile in a wax cast that made it look wooden, he felt inside out and at a disadvantage. He didn't bother to return her bow.

The woman made a face at his rudeness. "If that's how you want it," she said, and struck.

Ouyang fell back, but she didn't leave him a moment to settle: she was on him immediately with a bizarrely unpredictable sequence of slashes. He hadn't realized how reliant he was on being able to intuit his opponent's intention before a move was made. But he'd never fought a woman, and to his displeasure it was *different*. She was so small and fast he could barely find her, and there was something about her springy flexibility that he was constantly misjudging. He flung himself into the air to avoid a low sequence, leaving a flutter of severed skirt behind him, and was irritated to land off-balance. He'd never fought anyone like her except—

Zhu, he realized, surprised, but then again he'd only fought Zhu once: perhaps he was imagining the likeness.

"I don't want to hurt you, little sister," his opponent said in his ear the next time they clashed. "But I'm here to win the favor. Do you just want to be picked for the crews? If so, it'd be better to save your energy so you can put on a good show against the other girls—"

Ouyang flung her off with the extra force of disgust, and she sprang up from the sand with a snarl. "Oh, is that how it is? Young and arrogant and needing a lesson?"

Anger gave her wings: her left sword nicked him on the shoulder, then her right sword skimmed close enough to ruffle his veil. There was a sound like surf, except this flat brown sea was barely capable of raising a ripple. He realized it was the crowd cheering.

"Hacking around like you're chopping wood," the woman mocked. "You have that lithe little body, but you don't have any idea how to use it. Was your shifu a man? You'd have better success if you didn't fight like you think you're stronger than you are—"

But Ouyang was already striking again. Women *did* fight differently, but he wouldn't have been the best swordsman in the Yuan if he hadn't been able to adapt. His opponent's eyes flew wide as she desperately threw up both swords to catch his descending blade.

He felt a silent, grinding satisfaction as he bore down and felt her shudder and buckle. All those years of training where he'd forced himself to do everything that whole men with bigger bodies and longer limbs could; all those repetitions that had honed his efficiency and wrung every possible strength from an inferior body: because of all those, he wasn't pretending to be strong. He *was* strong. And even left-handed, he was stronger than her.

She broke away with a hoarse cry of effort. His strength hadn't just surprised her; it'd roused her suspicions. This time as they drove past each other, she flung at him, "Can someone with so much talent really be so shy as to need to wear a veil?" She struck again, missed. "Or do you wear a veil because you have something to hide? I've never fought a woman as strong as you. You don't fight like a woman, and you haven't spoken a word." She sneered. "Let me tell you something about the last man who entered this competition. Fang Guozhen made him eat his—"

Ouyang *could* have avoided the kick he saw coming. He simply chose not to. He let it land exactly where she'd aimed it: between his legs. It hurt, of course—scar tissue was sensitive—but what it didn't do was crumple him as she'd been expecting. And it was all the opportunity he needed. He caught her extended leg between his thighs, grabbed her suddenly flailing arm by the wrist, then twisted her around and slammed her face-first into the sand.

She screamed with rage, still resisting despite his knee in her back. He found himself welcoming the chance to punish her for daring to think she knew anything about him. He wanted to scrub her out like a stain. He *wasn't* a man—his body and everything about how other people responded to it made that abundantly clear—and he wasn't stronger than her because he was one. He was stronger because he'd stood up under the yoke of the world's scorn, and worked harder than any man had ever had to.

He twisted her arm tighter, relishing her weakening struggles. It was an effort to stop when she finally went limp. He leaned down and said into her ear with savage disgust, "Fang Guozhen made him eat his balls? I hope he enjoyed the taste. But that's hardly going to happen to *me*."

He was so caught up in self-loathing that he barely noticed his other opponents. Woman after woman, all of them less strong and less determined than he was. And then he was standing there panting, his left hand aching from the unusual exertion of holding a sword, and he realized: the sun was on the horizon. It was over.

A wooden token came spinning out of the air. He caught it automatically, and when he looked up he found Fang gazing down at him from the dais. "Congratulations to this fearless competitor! I never did believe a physical impediment should be an obstacle to brilliance. I haven't witnessed such a strong performance in years." His eyes were heavy-lidded with lingering interest. "Come see me at your leisure, my champion. I'm very much looking forward to granting your request."

Ouyang was shocked to realize the implication of that lingering look. Over the years he'd been the subject of innumerous sexual gibes, but none of those who'd mocked and speculated and spoken their fantasies aloud at the edge of his hearing had actually believed he *was* a woman. He'd never been undressed by a man's look before, even if what was being undressed was only a figment of that man's imagination. For some reason it made him aware of the thickness of Fang's body; the huge difference it had to his own; its intent that held him like a threat.

He clenched his left fist around the token hard enough to bite. It wasn't enough to erase the peculiar curl inside him, a stirring that was probably only residual pain from scar tissue, but that seemed to originate in a part of himself that was missing and always would be. He thought, dreadfully, *I would have done anything.*

But anything wouldn't be necessary. He'd already done his part. Whatever came next would be up to Zhu.

"The Radiant King! Nobody warned me you'd be such a shrimp," said Fang, as he absorbed the spectacle of Zhu in her gold robe and gilded hand. But he had made her stand below, as if he were the king. Behind his throne-like chair a circular window of pure white paper transmitted Qingyuan's cold winter light unaltered. His robe, collared in silver marten fur, strained across his powerful belly; his legs were spread as if to encompass the entire room between them. The population of Qingyuan was proof enough that his boldness had its admirers. But the amusement in his eye was as cold as the window, and it held Zhu outside. "So you want me to help you, on account of you being the one who'll win. But why should I believe it? There's no shortage of strong, ambitious men with their eyes on the throne of the Great Yuan."

"True enough," Zhu agreed. "But I alone have the qualification. Of all those who would contend for the throne, tell me: Who else has the Mandate of Heaven? The proof of my future success is incontrovertible."

Fang smiled, but it was mocking. "But do you really have it, Zhu Yuanzhang? Stories of the Radiant King's divine Mandate have indeed spread as far as Qingyuan. But stories are easily manipulated to benefit the teller. In these troubled times of ours, I make it a policy to never trust what I hear from a distance. Let me see this so-called proof of yours."

Zhu held out her gold hand with its carved palm faceup, and let the splendor of her Mandate rise from it: a white light that was whiter than the window-paper, as white as the eye of the sun in Heaven. It was the light that had struck conviction into the hearts of a hundred thousand other men. Now it caught the motes of dust in the hanging swaths of jasper silk that separated Fang's reception hall from his other chambers, and turned them into stars; it illuminated the substance of the briny coastal air until the room swam with a glimmering whiteness like fog, or milk, or the qi that spilled from a body in the fluids that made life. It was a sight she'd seen countless times, and still her heart thrilled. "Can you deny it, Fang Guozhen?"

"It seems I can't deny that you have it." Zhu's surge of vindication was abruptly quenched when he went on, "But what I *can* deny is that it's proof of anything. White?" Fang raised his eyebrows. "Hope you didn't pick such an inauspicious color yourself! Your little light trick isn't special, Zhu Yuanzhang, and neither are you. Surely you didn't think you were the only one with the Mandate. Or did nobody tell you about General Zhang?"

Madam Zhang and General Zhang had approached Fang, and been refused? Zhu frowned. She hadn't known that. She didn't like the idea that Fang was in the habit of refusing alliances. "General Zhang is dead. It seems you can't trust everything you hear at a distance."

"Is he?" Fang was manifestly unconcerned. "That's a shame. Nice fellow. I had my money on him. The other one, though: he's definitely still alive and kicking."

Zhu had walked right into that one. She said, terribly, "What other?"

"Ah, that one was a good color! Fortuitous, prosperous, dramatic. An enduring classic." He lounged back, a deliberate affront to Zhu's formality, and said, smiling, "Red."

Red had been the color of the old Mandate held by the Red Turbans. Zhu was relieved. For a moment she'd wondered if Fang meant the invisible hand that reached from the shadows to pull a string here, a string there, to no discernible purpose. But if that Mandate had been red—

Zhu remembered the eerie child the Prince of Radiance, spilling his bloodred light across a stage. "That Mandate's long gone. I ended it."

"Did you? Well if you did, you didn't do a very good job of it. I saw it just the other month. Its bearer came to me, just as you do now, and tried to convince me into an alliance."

All at once Zhu knew. She saw severed hands; a message written with a knife into human skin.

"That's right," Fang said, reading her expression. "Chen Youliang's the one you need my navy to defeat, isn't it? Fortunately for you I refused him, just as I refused the Zhangs. I'm sitting this one out. I don't care who brings down the Yuan, and I'm honestly not sure it'll be either of you. If there were three Mandates, who's to say there might not be more? Work it out amongst yourselves. I'm sure I can be helpful to whoever ends up on the throne."

Zhu felt like she was trying to burn the belief into him. *"It will be me."*

But Fang just spread his hands. "Will it? Come to me again if it happens. Then we'll talk."

The edges of the wooden token bit into Zhu's clenched fist. She thought of how she'd forced Ouyang into that place of bared, trembling humiliation, all so she could make him do something he didn't want to. But even before entering his room, she'd known he would. For the sake of what he wanted, he'd do anything.

So would she.

"If I win," she told him, "I'll be the emperor. You'll come to *me.*" Fang was still grinning when he caught the token. When he saw what it was, the grin slid off with satisfying rapidity. Zhu said in a carrying voice, "I claim my request."

"That was you?" Fang wasn't casual now; his full focus was on her. Zhu's skin prickled in response to the imminence of physical danger. "The left-handed fighter in the veil? How did you make it this far without discovery? Other men have tried before, but the women usually find them out." The floor-to-ceiling drapes around the periphery of the room stirred heavily, less enclosing than imprisoning. "As you well know, the competition was only for women. I pride myself on honoring the requests made of me. But I won't have my hospitality abused." In his anger, Fang was soft-spoken. "I won't be made a fool of." He leaned forwards to take up his sword from the table.

Zhu's robe was fastened with a ribbon instead of her usual heavy golden belt. She'd planned for the contingency without allowing herself to dwell on the details. In her opinion it wasn't so different from killing an innocent boy, or torturing one: not something she wanted, or that she would take pleasure in doing, but something she was strong enough to do. She would never not be strong enough, she thought ruthlessly. That was why she would never be defeated.

She undid the ribbon, letting her king's gown fall open to reveal what she had left deliberately naked beneath. "I competed legitimately."

Fang paused with his hand on his sword. She couldn't read him at all. Then, just as she thought she'd made a mistake, he roared with astonished laughter. "*That's* why you're such a shrimp, with a voice like that! I thought it must have been because you were fifteen. Oh, yes! I like this much better."

His surprise modulated into a look of deep interest. It was a horseflesh look, but with an aspect Zhu had never experienced directed at herself: male desire. It felt wrong, as if the world were being inverted. Without breaking eye contact, Fang called to whichever servants loitered on the other side of the drapes, "Nobody enter!"

To Zhu he said, "You didn't have to cover your face, though I can see why you might be shy about your looks. I've never been interested in useless, pretty women. I like a woman who can keep up with me." His interest sharpened. "You have a woman's body. But you have the Mandate, and you walk and talk and fight like a man. How much of a woman are you really?"

For a moment Zhu saw herself through his eyes. His look coalesced her into flesh against her will; it pressed her into the fact of her ugly cricket-brown face, her body with its sharply pointed hips and lean muscled legs, her small breasts. She hadn't imagined how unpleasant a feeling it would be.

Fang undid his gown and threw it off. He was naked underneath, as if he went through the day ready to avail himself of the women's bodies constantly surrounding him. His cocky grin had returned, but there was a challenge in his eyes. Zhu took in his big crude body, where the softness of a luxurious life masked but didn't conceal the utilitarian solidity of his breadth, the powerful width of his thighs as they spread over the chair, his rising physical interest.

Fang might see her one way, but she wasn't what he thought she was. All at once she had the feeling of having broken out from under the pressure of his gaze with a resurgence of herself. Nobody could make her anything other than she was, she thought fiercely. Nothing about what she looked like, or wore, or did, would change her.

She stepped out of her puddled gown. The stiffness of the gold brocade kept it standing half upright like an empty shell: a cicada's abandoned husk. Her bare feet shrank from the cold stone. It was only a drop of suffering into a cup whose meniscus ballooned further the more it was filled, so that it was infinitely capacious. *I'm strong enough to bear anything.*

"Don't worry," Zhu told him. "I can be woman enough for you."

☼

It was nightfall by the time Zhu returned to the lodging house. Her triumph more than outweighed the unfamiliar, objectively somewhat unpleasant, twinge between her legs. Fang had laughed in friendly surprise when Zhu had risen from the bed they'd (finally) ended up in, and he'd seen the smear of blood amidst the larger stains where he'd spilled. "Don't tell me you were a virgin!"

Zhu ignored that. "So I have use of your fleet, then," she said briskly, as she dressed.

Fang lolled in the rumpled sheets, unperturbed. His expansive confidence had translated into a generosity in the business of the rain and clouds. Zhu had no doubt the women he usually bedded found it enjoyable. Although she'd personally found it about as exciting as cleaning her teeth, it hadn't been entirely devoid of interest: there was always something to learn about a person during physical intimacy, whether that be sparring or fucking. *Or giving pain.*

"Ah, Zhu Yuanzhang. You have the distinction of being the most expensive fuck of my life. But yes, I'm a man of honor. You have use of my fleet."

"You also have the distinction of being the one and only person who's fucked an emperor-to-be," Zhu pointed out. "When I have the throne, come make your request of me. I'll make sure to grant it."

"Generous," Fang said, amused. "What if my request is to fuck you again?"

"Request what you like. But, food for thought," Zhu said as she strode out in her gold gown, "I'm not so honorable that I wouldn't order you made a eunuch afterwards. Now *that* would be a distinction: the emperor as the last fuck of your life. I'll let you judge whether it would be worth it."

Once Zhu was back in her room, she called a servant and ordered a bowl of warm water to wash with. She was pleased at how well it had all turned out. With Fang's ships and crews to carry her and Ouyang's armies, she could stand against Chen. Meanwhile, Madam Zhang would spend herself uselessly against the Grand Councilor, weakening him in the process. By the time Zhu finished with Chen and headed to Dadu, what obstacle would be left between her and the throne?

Someone had come in the open door while she was immersed in her thoughts. When she glanced up, she had a surprise: instead of the servant she'd been expecting, it was Ouyang.

He was shaking. That was the first thing Zhu noticed, even before her mind supplied that he was furious. His clenched fists were bloodless from pressure.

Ah. Zhu had all but forgotten about her unilateral decision to get rid of Ouyang's commander Chu. She felt a guilty start at the thought of how she'd just walked through a dining room full of women—they were much friendlier now that the competition was over—but there'd been no sign of Yuchun. Was he holed up in his room, cleaning his sword and dwelling on what Zhu had made him do? He had always been a callous child, hardened by life in much the same way as Zhu herself, but even he wouldn't have found it trivial to kill an unsuspecting member of their own, spy or not.

Ouyang was right to be annoyed that she hadn't consulted him, but she was taken aback at the strength of his reaction. She hadn't thought he'd cared much about either of his seconds.

"The spy was Senior Commander Chu," she explained. "He was the one sending those ciphered notes. I couldn't have him giving away our plans, especially once we head to Dadu."

"Senior Commander—" he repeated emptily as his gaze raked her with furious disgust.

Her skin crawled at the intensity of it. She realized: *This isn't about Chu.*

When he threw something at her, she ducked, even as the crumpled note was already fluttering down between them. Zhu didn't have to look to know what he'd discovered about her. Even as she couldn't believe that it was happening, she knew. Nothing else could have caused him to react like this.

His rasp barely sounded human. *"I should have known."*

She'd felt Ouyang's disgust before, but at least that disgust had acknowledged what she was. This was a disgust she'd only seen him aim at others: a disgust that stripped everything from her, and made her an object.

Gulls shrieked outside. He was colder than Zhu had ever seen. "My eyes told me, but I put it aside. I *made* myself believe in you, though the truth was right there in how you looked, how you behave. It was so obvious. You were so willing to lower yourself for men, serve them, kneel for them. Did you let Fang Guozhen fuck you? You did, didn't you." His throat worked violently, as if he could barely force the words out. "How could I have been stupid enough to believe, knowing a real man would rather die than be as you are?"

He stepped close; as close as they'd once been. But there was no promise in that closeness, now, only threat. She could feel him cataloguing her parts, comparing them, reducing her to the specific shape of her flesh. And it wasn't just her he was recontextualizing in light of his new knowledge, but everything she'd done. Everything she'd done *to him.* She could see the moment his violent new desire was born: to erase the fact that she'd seen him at his most vulnerable. That would have been the most unbearable part of it for him: that he had placed himself in the power of exactly what he most reviled and resented and endlessly measured himself against.

"How you must have laughed to see me out there dressed as a woman! Did you enjoy lowering me to your level? Did you enjoy taking my pride from me? I debased myself in front of you. I let you *see* me. You asked me to give everything, and I gave it, because I believed you when you said you could get me what I want. I believed you, because you were always telling me how you understand me, how we're the same, how we want the same thing." It was strange to hear feet tramping normally outside in the corridor. The sounds of merriment still rose from the dining room downstairs. And yet everything was coming undone. *"But you're nothing like me."*

The sameness between them had been something precious. Now he'd smashed it with a hammer, and it hurt more than she would have thought possible. In an instant Zhu had been transformed from someone Ouyang respected to someone he thought didn't deserve to exist. She wanted to gasp from the pain. Nothing she had done, or been, mattered in the face of the one thing he couldn't forgive: her femaleness.

He was caught in his own terrible reality, and she knew she couldn't reach him there. She tried, anyway. Her voice sounded strange in her own ears. "What you've found out has nothing to do with who I am. The only thing about me that's changed since yesterday is that now I have everything I need to win. Fang Guozhen gave me his ships! We just have to stay together, stay the course—"

"Nothing to do with you? What you kept from me is how your failure has been written in the stars from the beginning! For whatever reason, you've deluded yourself that you'll win the throne. But don't you get it?" His eyes were wild. "*You're not a man.* You'll never be able to give me what I want. You never could have.

"Emperor? You?" He laughed harshly, incredulously. "You're just another whore."

The maid came in behind Ouyang with the bowl of water. The sheer violence of his startle made Zhu think that if he'd been armed, he would have cut the girl down where she stood. The maid cried out as he whirled on her, and dropped the bowl with a smash.

Ouyang snarled and shoved his way past Yuchun, who'd appeared panting in the doorway behind the maid. Yuchun's head turned as he tracked Ouyang's passage. "There was yelling—"

Zhu was shaking. She realized she'd been shaking the whole time, as if the vibrating connection between them had finally shaken them both to bits. She'd opened herself to the only person who could have fully understood her. And he had reached into that most tender and vulnerable place, and hurt her.

They'd been going to win. They'd been going to win *together*. But now—

So this is what betrayal feels like.

She could barely breathe from the pain of it. But she was Zhu Yuanzhang, and she was strong enough to handle anything.

With a still-shaking hand, she plucked the note off the wet floor before the ink could run. It bore the handwriting of the person she'd expected. There was only one amongst them who knew her secret, and knew it would divide Ouyang from her without repair.

She said to Yuchun, "Forget about him. Find Jiao Yu."

Jiao always picked the winning side. It was the reason he'd been with her from the beginning. She thought with violent incomprehension: *What changed?* Jiao had doubted her before they'd come to Qingyuan, but she'd proved him wrong. She'd secured the navy she needed. How could she and Ouyang not be the winning side?

All at once, Zhu remembered the invisible hand. She lunged to her belongings and tore out the spy's note, staring at its nonsensical words with a falling heart. Jiao had told her he couldn't crack the cipher.

Yuchun had come back. He sounded very young as he said, "Jiao Yu is gone."

"So is General Ouyang," she said numbly. "He's gone back to Yingtian to take his army back. I don't have any safeguards in place to stop him from doing it. He'll march to Dadu without us. We face Chen Youliang alone."

She barely heard his appalled sound. She still had Fang's ships, but Yuchun knew as well as she did what Ouyang's abandonment implied for their chances of winning against Chen.

Jiao had cracked the cipher, and within it he'd found the invisible hand: the person Zhu didn't know, and couldn't see; the person Jiao had placed all his bets upon as the one who would beat her to the throne.

16

KHANBALIQ

New white lanterns, installed especially for the night of the Winter Festival, shone brightly against the clouded ice texture of the window-paper in the Great Khan's banqueting hall. The ministers were arrayed at individual low tables around the perimeter of the room, cups of warmed wine set before them. Baoxiang, sitting amongst them, felt a powerful sense of unreality.

After the dry start to the season, snow had come all of a sudden upon Khanbaliq. The capital had been transformed, though not all changes had been by nature's hand. Lady Ki's efforts to weed out the Grand Councilor's supporters from the central army had left it drastically reduced, and a shortage of grain and salt had prompted an exodus of ordinary residents. Every day as Baoxiang rode to the Ministry, he saw further evidence of diminishment. His pulled threads were racing through the shriveling garment, eating it row by row. But inside the Great Khan's sheltered world of the Palace City was like the interior of a lantern: light so endlessly refracted from its own surfaces that it was impossible to see what was happening outside. The court of the Great Yuan sat feasting, without any idea of their own coming destruction.

"Ministers!" The dry winter air had deepened the color of the Great Khan's permanently flushed cheeks. The Great Khan, Baoxiang mused, was the strongest possible contradiction of the presumption that pink cheeks indicated a naturally joyful nature. "In reward for your continuously loyal service to ourself, the Great Khan, and the empire of the Great Yuan: I bestow upon you a cup of wine. Drink!"

How many of the ministers were actually loyal to this dullard? Surely not more than a handful. Baoxiang raised his cup in unison with the others. "Ten thousand years to the Great Khan!"

At the table closest to the dais, the Third Prince downed his wine with arrogant disinterest. But he didn't place his cup down. Baoxiang was curiously aware of knowing the Third Prince so intimately that he could tell, from nothing more than the nuance of a tilted hand, that the Third Prince was considering letting the cup roll onto the floor. If gaining his father's favor was impossible, he would choose censure instead.

The Third Prince put the cup down. Even reaching for that least form of acknowledgment had been too much for him. But for some reason Baoxiang was unable to find his usual scorn for the Third Prince's fear.

"Be rewarded, and eat," Lady Ki pronounced from the Great Khan's side, as servants bore in bowls of soft white filled dumplings in a sweet ginger soup. It was obvious the Grand Councilor's passing had made Lady Ki empress in all but name. It would only be a matter of time before she persuaded the Great Khan to make it official. Lady Ki's new elevation clearly agreed with her: she sparkled in the lantern-light like an icicle in the thaw.

For once the Empress wasn't wearing her customary lipstick. She looked pale and faceless without it. It must have been an agony for her to feel her power—her title—slipping away like egg whites between her fingers. She didn't touch her dumplings. At least she had the choice not to eat. Baoxiang, who had no appetite either, had to force himself to make the requisite show of gratitude. Even before he bit into the dumpling, it oozed filling into his mouth: grainy black sesame, released from its too-tender casing like an inevitability.

As soon as the ministers finished, the Empress stood impatiently to leave—then paused, looked bewildered, and crumpled.

A murmur flew through the room. Interest, more than alarm. Even Baoxiang, who preferred to let others handle the bodies, could tell they weren't looking at a corpse. It would have been a surprise if they had been. With time being on Lady Ki's side, there was nothing to be gained by a rash assassination. A glance at Lady Ki confirmed her surprise, followed by swiftly veiled calculation. Baoxiang allowed himself a flicker of grim amusement. So Lady Ki wasn't the only one who could play for the Great Khan's attention.

The palace physician hurried in a little too soon for plausibility. But he put on a good show, nonetheless: miming concern as he took the crumpled Empress's pulse, then the shock of realization. He dashed over to whisper to the Great Khan. The Empress's maids flocked around her and assisted her to her feet. She stood there, pale and swaying. Smiling.

The ministers gasped as the Great Khan sprang to his feet and cried, "Heaven has blessed the Empress!"

Baoxiang didn't bother to join the congratulatory rush to the dais. He watched the Third Prince from across the room. He hadn't risen, either. Baoxiang felt a pang at his stricken expression. He knew how it felt to have one's worst and most long-standing fears come true. For a moment he was on that cliff-top again: his father lying below; Esen staring at him with naked hate and blame. Baoxiang hadn't been able to believe it, at first. Despite everything that had passed between them, it had still seemed impossible: that Esen could have thought he'd *meant* it.

But Esen did think that. Baoxiang's realization had felt like the color running out of the world. It had felt, he thought, like what it must be to die.

On the other side of the room, the Third Prince shot a helpless glance to his mother. But Lady Ki neither noticed nor returned comfort. Her face was as stiff as ice.

Seyhan was outside when Baoxiang extricated himself from the crush. His pale eyes snapped with interest as he said, "It could be a girl."

"You'd bet your head on that?" They walked deeper into the privacy of the Great Khan's pomegranate grove. Snow capped the browned, twisted husks of the old fruit that hung splayed open like corpses, seeds long gone. How lucky the Empress had been, to have happen the only thing that could save her! The taste of black sesame persisted in Baoxiang's mouth. It should have been sweet, but instead left him fighting nausea. "I wouldn't. Neither will Lady Ki. She won't stand by."

As they looked back at the banqueting hall, a figure emerged. The spill of lantern-light flashed the dragons on his gown with silver fire against the darkness of the garden. When the Third Prince passed them under the pomegranates, he regarded them without seeming to register who they were, then strode away.

There was something heavy in Baoxiang's chest. He traced the dimming flashes of the Third Prince's gown as he passed out of reach of the lantern-light. He said to Seyhan, "Wait here."

The Third Prince hadn't gone much farther. Baoxiang found him in one of the open-sided garden pagodas. Away from the lights and clamor of the hall, it was cold and still. Baoxiang shivered. His ministerial over-robe was a paltry substitute for furs. The waxing moon shone on the snow-laden palace roofs. On the far side of the Imperial City's walls, silvered treetops made a bright distant ripple, like breaking surf on a dark shore.

The Third Prince wasn't looking at the view. He was staring down at his right fist. It would have been reddened with cold, but the moonlight had stolen the quick of life from his skin and rendered it as bloodless as their surroundings. "Do you know I still believed it could have been me?"

But he didn't believe, Baoxiang thought, with an ache that felt like being crushed by the ocean. If the Third Prince *had* believed, then he would have the Mandate. But he only hoped. How many times had he stood like this, alone in the garden or his room, and opened his hand with the hope of finding a flame there? He would have told himself each time that it wouldn't happen, and yet still hoped, despite himself, that one day it would.

Long after Baoxiang had ceased to believe things could be different between him and Esen, he'd still hoped for it. He knew how hard it was to let go of a future that seemed real because of how much you wanted it. Sometimes letting go was so hard that it only happened when what you held was crushed, so the fragments fell from between your still-grasping fingers.

"Did you see how happy he was?" The Third Prince's voice cracked. "Everyone saw it. He can't wait to replace me."

Baoxiang caught his fist before he smashed it into the pagoda railing. The Third Prince spooked, then stared at him with his hand trembling in Baoxiang's grasp, as if he were only just then realizing Baoxiang was there.

Baoxiang said gently, "Your mother will deal with this. Trust that she can fix it."

"Fix it. Yes. Fix it. That's what she does, isn't it? She fixed my brothers and their mother, and the Grand Councilor, and she'll surely fix the Empress. But you know what she can't fix? Me." The Third Prince's tone of deadened detachment was familiar. It was the sound of someone drowning inside himself, already too far away for anyone to reach. "Of all the sons Heaven could have given her, I had to be the one she ended up with! She hates me. She hates me as much as he does. The only difference is that she needs me. If not for that, better I had just killed myself already."

Baoxiang remembered the care beneath Lady Ki's polished stone facade. In an environment like the palace, where lives were lost by a moment's mistake, he could understand why she might have thought it safer to hide her attachment from a jealous husband, or grasping rival. But she had even hidden it from the one person who truly needed it. Perhaps, in her own mind, it was love. But how could it be so for the Third Prince, who had no idea it existed?

His heart ached. He didn't know whether it was for himself or the Third Prince. "Ayushiridara." He'd never said the Third Prince's name before. He wondered how many people ever had. He saw the surprise of it pierce the Third Prince's detachment—saw it call him back from that dark drowning place—as Baoxiang turned his face towards him with his fingertips. The Third Prince, born into the palace, born into his role, had never lived outside either of those strictures. Baoxiang had the feeling that by saying his name, he was summoning him into existence as a person for the first time. He let his touch linger a moment longer, then kissed him.

Their lips were cool from the garden air. Warmth sprang into being at their point of contact. There was an unfamiliar whisper of beard beneath Baoxiang's lips. He felt breached by his own impulse. It belonged to another person: to the person he'd been before the blackness swallowed him. To the kind of person who, upon seeing another's pain, didn't instinctively use it to cause more pain, but said instead: *I understand*.

Baoxiang cupped his hand around the back of the Third

Prince's neck, and opened that hurt surprised mouth with his own. Kissing was always different for him than fucking. It was too easy, when fucking, to accidentally slip away inside himself—to make his lover, if not quite into an object, then remote enough that her personhood became irrelevant to his pleasure. But someone's face against his—the insistence of another's lips and mouth upon his own—was an assertion of self he'd never been able to deny. Baoxiang kissed the Third Prince, and knew why his impulse had taken this particular form. It was the antithesis of rejection. It was the reciprocal creation of themselves as two people alive to each other, present to each other, each made real by the brush of another's personhood against his own.

The Third Prince responded clumsily but willingly as Baoxiang coaxed his mouth wider. Their focused concentration gained its own gravity, thickening the movements of their mouths into a slow, deep intimacy of mutual consuming. Baoxiang had a brimming feeling of excess: that they could continue taking from each other without ever running out. He was gripping the back of the Third Prince's neck as if it were the only thing keeping them together. His mouth burned from pressure, from the intensity of his silent witness: *I see you.*

It didn't feel like calculation, or a performance, to comfort and reassure the Third Prince. It felt true. A truth arisen not out of desire, but connection. And yet even as Baoxiang kissed the Third Prince, and held him, and pretended he couldn't taste his tears, he knew the reassurance was a lie.

The sweep of the River of Heaven was just coming into view above the treetops. But there was no brightness in the future. No cause for reassurance. The Empress would never have a child with the Mandate; but by the same token, neither would the Third Prince ever gain it. As Baoxiang let go of the Third Prince and stepped back, he saw a vision of himself with his hand outstretched: black flame roiling out to erase the moon and stars, the city with its silvered walls, and every trace of light, until there was nothing but void.

There was no longer any separation between himself and that blackness that had once been a refuge, but was now the singularly most awful feeling Baoxiang had ever had. It was like the dark inverse of the sun. Whenever he tried to look at it he had the feeling of turning uncontrollably away from it, as in his unremembered dreams. All he knew was that once he let it out, it wouldn't be just the world that was drowned, but himself.

"So you're here with us on this beautiful adventure, Minister!" Lady Ki said with a fury that Baoxiang understood was directed at another target entirely, as they crossed paths between the men's and women's hot springs. "I hope you find it more enjoyable than the rest of us are likely to."

The imperial family's excursion to the hot springs, located in the hills twenty li outside Khanbaliq, had been the Empress's idea—ostensibly for the good of her pregnancy. Now that she had the Great Khan's ear and favor, she hadn't hesitated to use her power to force the other imperial households to join the excursion as witnesses to her special treatment. No wonder Lady Ki was furious.

Half a month of humiliation at the Empress's hands had taken its toll on Lady Ki. Despite the rosy light filtering through the silk parasol her maid held overhead, her polished white-stone complexion had been replaced by a gray drawn appearance. All at once she looked as old as someone who had birthed a single defective issue and failed to produce another one in the eighteen long years since. It was the look, Baoxiang thought, of desperation.

"Enjoyable or not, when Lady Ki's son the Third Prince was so gracious as to extend an invitation to this humble official, how could he refuse?" Baoxiang gave her his blandest smile. "Perhaps the Third Prince has a mind to learn the techniques of landscape painting for which I have some small talent. Whatever his needs, I'm sure I can be of service."

As Lady Ki regarded him, Baoxiang found himself inexplicably wishing, counter to what he had expressly come here to achieve, that she not say anything. But at length Lady Ki turned to her retinue. "The odor of these springs is most disagreeable. Fetch some tea, and a bag of fragrant herbs I can hold to my nose as I bathe. Bring them to the bathing pool directly." When all except the parasol maid had left, she said, "Do you wish to offer a specific service, Minister?"

"Perhaps one suited to a specific problem," Baoxiang said, glancing at the parasol maid.

"She can be trusted. Speak openly, but be brief. It doesn't do for a consort to be seen giving audience to a man. Even a man such as yourself."

Baoxiang's strange wish had passed. Though it was midwinter, the Great Khan's gardeners had brought swaths of severed plum branches that had been forced to blossom indoors in front of braziers, and placed them in natural-seeming arrangements throughout the site to give the illusion of a spring grove. It seemed not even the dead could rest when in service to the Great Yuan. "If not forestalled, the Empress will have an heir to displace the Third Prince. Neither you nor I desire that to happen. Let me offer my assistance. I have readier access to the outer city than you do, and less eyes upon me."

It was a gamble on the trust he'd earned. At length, Lady Ki said with composure, "Should the Empress fail to carry to term, it would have to appear to be of natural causes. Were there to be any suspicion otherwise, I would be the suspect."

The letter he'd been waiting for had arrived that morning. Baoxiang said coolly, "I have the resources. Nobody will know."

"Not even the Third Prince," Lady Ki warned. As she turned away, he saw her ripple of concern: stone made tender with true feeling, for just an instant. "Keep him safe, Minister."

Something was wrong. Something awful was happening, but equally something was wrong with his eyes, because he couldn't see—

With a lurch of disorientation, Baoxiang realized he was awake. A gasp was stuck in his throat. It was dark in the Third Prince's bedroom; that was why he couldn't see. He was facing the Third Prince's sleeping back. But all his attention was on what was behind. Esen was there.

There were no external indications as to who the spectral presence was. But Baoxiang was all too familiar with this feeling inside his body. It had always been unique to Esen, as if a lifetime's emotions and interactions had been distilled into this single autonomous response. It was recognition that sprang from a part of himself that lay beneath thought. He simply knew.

Esen's presence was so strong that he had to be very close. Perhaps even standing at the edge of the bed. Close enough to touch Baoxiang's uncovered shoulder where it lay outside the covers. Cold rolled over Baoxiang like waves of dread. The bedroom was quiet enough that he could hear the rustle as his body hair slowly prickled against the bedclothes.

He could just make out the line of the Third Prince's body under the covers. He was aware of a bruisy internal ache, less than last time. It had been a surprisingly tender coupling, when they'd returned together from the hot springs. Baoxiang had intended to leave directly afterwards to his next appointment. He hadn't expected to fall asleep—hadn't even considered it as a possibility. Now it was late, and so was he.

He needed to leave. His appointment was waiting. But he found himself reluctant to tear himself from the warmth of the bed. Only an arm's length away in the darkness was that other person, someone he had held in his arms and inside himself. He felt a sudden ache of aloneness. It wasn't just an arm's length that separated them. The Third Prince's mind was far away, in a distant place Baoxiang could never reach. He was alone in the dark, except for a ghost.

And yet—he could call the Third Prince back from that far place. He could say his name and return him. The Third Prince would open his eyes, and be here again. It would be as simple as that. And Baoxiang could do it. He had the capability. He could still choose another path. He could still, he thought, stop.

But as the ghost's familiar disapproval and condemnation crushed down upon him, Baoxiang felt his own blackness come sloshing up, like a call and response they could never break out of. It was the same vicious tide that had brought him this far—that would carry him to the end—but as he let it sweep him away, he was simultaneously overcome by a horrific sense of alienation: that not only did he recognize the blackness, but that he had never properly known what it was.

He wrenched himself out of bed, trembling with fury at the

ghost. It didn't matter that the euphoria of his anger had gone. The blackness was inside him; he had already let himself be consumed. He couldn't imagine being without it. Without it, he would be nothing at all.

In his dreams he turned away, but in this waking nightmare that was his life he was always turning towards this ghost he couldn't see.

It was waiting for him when he emerged from the Third Prince's residence. Baoxiang could feel it skimming beside him as he rode. It was so close behind the curtain of falling snow that, had it wanted, it could have taken a single step through that thin barrier to let itself be seen. Baoxiang's need for it, to *see* Esen, was so deep as to be almost erotic. He would call Esen back from that unreachable place, he thought furiously, when he had the power. With all the power invested in him under Heaven, he would force Esen to show himself, and to bear witness, for what Baoxiang would do.

His minister's gate pass took him through the Imperial City wall, then Khanbaliq's outer wall, and into the suburbs beyond. The luxury residences spread farther apart as he rode, each one a lighted island in the blackness. When he found the anonymous residence he was looking for, the door opened to his knock.

She had been waiting for him. Her welcoming smile had the same ceramic perfection he remembered from their last meeting.

He said, in her own southern language, "Greetings, wife."

Madam Zhang's beauty had always existed independently from her physical features. It was her control—her performance of what beauty was—that spun the illusion of perfection. So despite the years since Baoxiang had last seen her, she was still beautiful. Her cheeks were heavier, and her complexion owed more to powder than nature. But her wrists flashed inside her fluttering gold-embroidered sleeves, and her neck was a bending flower stem. Even as she stood still, the lamplight struck her into motion as it shimmered from the hanging jewels in her hair, and her pearl-dusted skin. A single lock of hair lay along the line of her neck like a lover's caress.

It was a performance for a man who liked women. Ordinarily, Baoxiang would have felt a flicker of heat in response—an involuntary awareness of potential, even if he had no intention of acting upon it. But instead he experienced a disjointedness that verged on repulsion. Her performance addressed a past version of himself: someone without the Mandate, who hadn't been fucked by a man, who was capable of emotions other than this black torment. It felt like being tied face-to-face with his own corpse. It was grotesque.

She purred, "Should this woman be concerned about her husband's health? He looks too thin."

He caught her hand as she reached for him, hard enough to border on cruelty. "Don't."

Her face didn't change, either from pain or acknowledgment. It was as if she couldn't feel him. "No? I've heard that you let the world believe otherwise these days, but I remember you as a young man with a man's usual interests. Why not let yourself enjoy me, now that we're married?"

By all appearances, it was as if she wanted nothing so much as for him to fuck her on the utilitarian furniture of this rented house, in front of her mindlessly watching servants. But there was something dreadful about the way she held herself in his grasp—an absence of pliancy or responsiveness or ordinary human warmth—that suggested otherwise. His skin crawled. He had done this to her. He had seeded her husband's jealousy and caused her lover's death. He'd stripped her of all hope and power, so that even as she thought it was her choice to turn to him, it was no more of a choice than water had when it took the downhill path.

All at once her veneer repelled him. He needed to see the truth; needed to dig out of her the evidence of what he'd done. He dropped her hand and said sharply, "You don't need to perform, not for me. I know you loved General Zhang."

For an instant, he saw her grief. But it was as if he were glimpsing a great undersea storm bending the weeds and ripping the sand from the seabed as it moved through the body of the water, all without disturbing the surface.

"Love!" she said, and her self that laughed lightly with fury seemed to exist entirely apart from her body with its briny saturation of grief and despair. "How could that have been love, if only one of us felt it?"

She raised her hand again, and touched his face with her fingernails. Hers was a leopard's disemboweling anger that took pleasure in another's pain, because it couldn't feel its own. "But perhaps my husband is right, and a new couple should enhance their harmoniousness by seeking to understand each other. So tell me, Wang Baoxiang. I can feel when a man has power. I know you didn't have it when you visited me all those times as a provincial administrator with no higher ambitions than to do your job well." The lacquered tips of her nails dug in, and her desire to hurt him seemed performance and truth both at once. "What decision was it you made, that gained you the Mandate of Heaven?"

Had it even been a decision? Remembering it shot him back into the reality of that pain: the kind of pain that only knew how to return hurt for hurt; when instinct stood in for thought. He'd been standing alone in Esen's ger, watching his books burning in the fire. The horse screamed in the background. He remembered the terrible, singular purity of what he'd been wishing for, the moment the ghosts appeared. The wish that had been lodged in his heart like a shard of ice, cutting it open even as it continued to beat.

That Esen should die.

When Ouyang's traitor had walked in, there had been no feeling that he could stop. That first time the blackness had swept him away—long before it had become this inescapable pit of wretchedness and despair—had been the purest feeling of relief he'd ever had in his life.

"You told me you want to destroy the Great Yuan," she said. "To take the throne; to rule. But is that really what you want?"

Something had punched through his chest. He didn't know what it was, only that it was an agony. It was so painful that it temporarily rendered thought impossible.

Whatever his face showed, she smiled at it. Her smile was as sharp as her nails. "I'm glad we have an understanding. But let's not ask for the truth of each other, my husband. I don't think either of us could bear it."

She signaled to a servant, who left the room. "I should offer my compliments. Your use of Chen Youliang to break Zhu Yuanzhang's siege worked perfectly. My army is ready and waiting to join us here as soon as you give the word."

The servant returned with a single packet upon a tray. Madam Zhang picked it up, not quite offering it to him. "As for the rest of your plan—this is what you requested. But are you sure it's the formulation you want? It can be dangerous if not administered correctly."

Baoxiang plucked the packet from her fingers. Though the agony had subsided, he felt like a husk of a person. "Don't worry," he said. "I know."

⁂

"You're a useful one, aren't you, Minister." The top-level balcony of the temple pagoda provided a view over the flat expanse of the lake, with its stiff ruff of frozen reeds. The marble bridges inscribed white rainbows between the snow-covered islets. An unfamiliar bird called. It was high enough from here that Baoxiang could make out the roofs of the Third Prince's residence near the western wall of the Imperial City, and beyond it the sweep of Khanbaliq itself. With its trees and houses alike mounded under snow, it resembled less a plaything miniature than a ruin.

"I tested the medicine," Lady Ki continued. When she glanced at him, it was assessing, and he saw she was also testing him: whether or not he'd take offense at her refusal to take his help at face value. Baoxiang held steady, letting her see his lack of offense. He'd already known she wasn't one to take things on faith. He could still taste her man's fingers in his mouth.

At length, Lady Ki smiled. He'd passed. "Indeed, it worked very well. In taste and appearance my tester found it indistinguishable from normal tea. What was your source?"

"A courtesan of my acquaintance." As Baoxiang gazed out at Khanbaliq, he had a vision not of ruins sinking into the earth, but the earth rising in a chthonic embrace: up the trunks of the trees, up the Bell and Drum Towers and the compound walls, until even the tiles of their roofs lay entombed. "A friend."

"People do praise the Khanbaliq courtesans! Though from what I hear, they lack the true refinement of those from Lin'an." She added in a musing tone, "I've never met such a woman. But from the efficacy of the medicine, it seems your friend knows her business well." Her naïve curiosity on the topic surprised Baoxiang, until it occurred to him that a consort spent her entire adult life within the Imperial City's walls. Save for excursions in the Great Khan's company, Lady Ki had no more freedom to travel into outer Khanbaliq, or the world beyond it, than a prisoner.

"Now that I have the tools, I'll deal with the Empress. Better soon rather than later; it will look more natural that way." Lady Ki left the balcony and swept down the internal stairs to the shrine on the ground floor. Her brisk, sure-footed stride struck Baoxiang as jarringly masculine. His mind had already reaccustomed itself to Madam Zhang's tiny, swaying steps—graceful, but with that edge of hesitation that allowed the onlooker a pleasurable awareness of her fragility. Lady Ki knelt cursorily before the shrine, and as Baoxiang followed suit beside her, said, "But before that, Minister, I must presume upon you for one further act of assistance."

Through the open door Baoxiang saw Lady Ki's eunuchs coming up to the temple with a sagging burden between them. They didn't bring her in, of course: even Lady Ki scrupled to violate a temple's sanctity with the presence of eunuchs or a bleeding woman.

"As you can see, the medicine caused some small mess." Lady Ki rose. "I'll leave first. I trust you can take care of it."

Lady Ki's lady-in-waiting wasn't dead, which Baoxiang supposed had been the whole point of the test. A cloth gag had been inserted into her tear-swollen face. It hadn't been a bird he'd heard from the top of the temple, but her muffled cries of distress. Her pale pink uniform skirt showed the blood well.

The poor fool girl. He could imagine the girl's innocent happiness as she confessed her pregnancy to a warm, sympathetic Lady Ki. She would have told her about her plan to marry her guard lover after they both left the palace; about her hopes for more children, for prosperity, and to live happily ever after. Baoxiang's insides curdled at the thought. Who dared imagine a happy ending? Only someone who'd been treated too tenderly their whole lives, so they'd never had to learn how the world worked.

The curdled feeling in his stomach wasn't contempt, but pain. He'd assumed Lady Ki would test the medicine. But he hadn't imagined the test would have this face: of grief, and loss, and suffering. He didn't know why it hurt so much now, when he'd put that same misery into so many other faces before.

He was still kneeling when Seyhan stepped over the crumpled girl on the doorstep and came in. He looked around curiously, without any of the normal transformation that happened when people entered a temple and their bodies became weighted by reverence and respect. For a moment Seyhan was once again a stranger, a foreigner: someone who worshipped differently, and existed outside the normal order of the world as Baoxiang knew it.

But that, of course, was why he was so useful. "Take that girl to my wife. Make sure she's looked after."

Seyhan glanced at the weeping girl in her bloodstained dress. "Somehow I'm guessing that isn't what Lady Ki asked of you."

"If she finds out I didn't carry out her order, she'll have us both killed." Baoxiang dusted off his gown as he rose. "So be careful."

"I always am." In his secretary's pale eyes there was a flash of that ruthlessness that had silently and efficiently erased so many human beings on Baoxiang's say-so. "I assume you have your reasons."

Baoxiang saw a parade of faces: the lively girl, Madam Zhang's twin maids, the Minister. He hadn't personally killed any of them. He hadn't even touched them. And yet—he was responsible. It was what he had done, and regardless of how he felt about any of it: it could never be undone.

He said bitterly, "Perhaps I'm just being kind."

Esen was walking away from him down a long corridor, but it was one of the corridors in the Third Prince's residence, so Baoxiang knew he was dreaming. Without being conscious of his body he had the awareness of being small, as if it was long ago.

And yet at the same time he knew it wasn't Esen's flesh and blood he was seeing, but his ghost.

Esen was receding into the shadows. Baoxiang knew that if he turned the corner he would be gone. He hurried after him, calling with what he already knew was futility, "Brother, wait!" His desperation rose. He couldn't catch up; his legs weren't long enough, he wasn't strong enough. He had the terrible feeling in his stomach that he'd disappointed Esen somehow. "I'm sorry. I didn't mean to do it! I didn't mean to be bad. I'll try harder next time. I won't let you down. Please don't leave me behind."

Esen turned. He was his bearded adult self, in his ceremonial armor with a fur-edged black cape pinned to his shoulders. It was his perfectly normal appearance, and yet Baoxiang was overwhelmed by a recoiling horror. What had once been so familiar had been invisibly transformed into a different substance, something unknown and unknowable, and he knew there was no way of returning it to what it had been.

Though Esen's beard and braids were black, his eyes had crinkles at the corners even when he wasn't smiling. Marks of ordinary human vulnerability, placed there by the sun. He was looking over Baoxiang's head, as if there was something in the distance he needed to get to, something that was more important than Baoxiang.

Baoxiang was overcome by an unbearable feeling of self-hatred. He knew what he deserved for having been bad. Even to himself, his desperate attempts to cling to Esen felt sticky, needy, unworthy and unwanted. He needed to explain why he'd done what he'd done, and see Esen's face soften in understanding, even though he knew it was impossible. The worst thing would be to cry. Esen hated that, as he hated everything about Baoxiang. He would have preferred to have had no brother rather than the one he had, and no matter how hard Baoxiang tried, everything he felt or did made Esen hate him more.

Esen looked down at him, then. He said, gravely, "I don't hate you, Baoxiang."

Baoxiang woke, clenched in a paroxysm of weeping. He was in some vast unfamiliar place in which there was nothing but blackness. Though it had been a dream, he somehow knew it had been completely real. He'd summoned Esen's ghost into his dream. It hadn't been memory or dream-imagining, but Esen himself who'd spoken to him. He was crying so hard he couldn't breathe. There was an unbearable ache in his chest, and he had the sense that in this black place the pain would last forever.

Baoxiang gasped himself awake. His face was dry. He was lying beside the Third Prince, in the shadow-shuttered bedroom. He knew instantly it had been a dream within a dream. As if a curtain had been ripped from his consciousness, he suddenly saw the thinness and illogic of what his dream-self had so ardently believed. Esen hadn't been there. There had been nothing real about any of it.

He still felt like he couldn't breathe. It hadn't been real, and yet the false emotions of the dream had followed him back into the world like a haunting. His urge to cry nearly made him choke with rage at the sheer irrationality of it. Why couldn't he control himself? He knew what the reality was. Esen had hated him. Why should his mind conjure the sick fantasy of the opposite, and then make it so he not only believed it, but *wanted* it? He hurled himself upright, panting.

The Third Prince stirred without waking, and flung a questing arm into the space where Baoxiang had been. Would that have been enough to stop him, Baoxiang wondered dully, if it had happened the night he'd gone to Madam Zhang? Not that it mattered now. He shuddered in dry spasms with his arms around his drawn-up knees. What was done could never be undone.

Outside there was the faint clatter of approaching hooves. That had probably been the real cause of his awakening. It seemed fitting that it should happen now, in the cold ebb between third and fourth watches. It was the time of night that babies were born and people died, when the dark seemed endless and the idea of morning a cruel fantasy that not even a child could believe.

At length he managed to dress, and slipped into the long, cold corridor. Perhaps it was even the same corridor as his dream. The ghost followed him, but he didn't look behind.

He went to the guest room and waited for the messenger to wake the household, and to tell them: that the Empress was dead.

Lady Ki was already kneeling in the snow at the steps of the Hall of Great Brilliance when Baoxiang and the Third Prince arrived. She had been stripped to her white underdress, and her hair lay loose over her shoulders. Though the snow had stopped some time before, there was still a sense of an unfalling whiteness; of a residue, suspended in the stillness. The opaque air made it seem as if there were no buildings in existence other than this one building; there were no walls; there was no city beyond, because the entire world had been erased except for this blankness that had been its heart. The hall's red columns made long bloody smears high above.

Despite the shock of her situation, Lady Ki had kept her composure. Rendered small by the scale of her surroundings, she gave the impression of a jade-pale fragility that was moments from swooning into the snow. Every anguished line of her body flowed towards the Great Khan, where he stood glowering at the top of the steps, in a silent plea for him to remember his affection and understand: that she was innocent.

The Third Prince shoved through the crowd of officials and ran across the snowy forecourt to hurl himself down beside his mother. Lady Ki didn't so much as glance at him, but Baoxiang saw the sudden rigidity in her shoulders. She didn't want the Third Prince there. She didn't trust him not to make a bad situation worse.

"Stand back, Third Prince!" the Great Khan shouted, making an enraged brushing gesture as if he were physically clearing him away. After an uncertain pause, as if awaiting any acknowledgment of his presence from Lady Ki, the Third Prince rose and fell back a few steps. Everything about him radiated hurt. The Empress's death might have reaffirmed him as the Great Khan's sole male issue, yet his unwantedness hadn't changed. As he stood alone in the vast whiteness between his supplicant mother and the crimson-clad crowd, he seemed adrift.

A distant ripple knocked at Baoxiang's attention. Everything in him swiveled towards it like a horse's ear. It was a sound at the outer limits of his hearing, a haunting irregularity too faint to identify. But whatever it was, it wasn't an ordinary sound, like a passing vendor's clacking bamboo, that reminded him of the dream sound. Something in his shuddering flesh and bones knew: it *was* the sound. And in that same flood of certainty, he knew that if he were to hear the sound properly—if he were to know what it was—something unbearably terrible would happen.

"Everything's ready." Seyhan had wormed his way through the officials to Baoxiang's side. "Why did she kill the Empress, though? I thought she was going to cause a discreet miscarriage."

Distracted, Baoxiang answered, "She thought that's what she was doing."

"The medicine didn't work? It worked well enough on that maid."

Above, the Great Khan bellowed, "This consort has presumed too much upon my beneficence and favor, that she dared conduct this grave disservice upon our royal self and the Great Yuan!"

"The Empress was never pregnant," Baoxiang said. "She lied. It was the only thing she could do to prevent the Great Khan from stripping her of her position as Empress, and awarding it to Lady Ki. As for the medicine: it works well enough in its intended use. But the women who routinely use it know of its dangers. If the medicine can't find a fetus to act upon, it turns to the body instead."

He couldn't keep the sound out. He had the distant sense it was music, but at the same time it was empty: it was music made without human hands; music that had never been played by anyone who breathed. For the first time since childhood he wanted to crouch and clap his hands over his ears, and scream until he drove out the horror that had him in its grip. Waves of fear rolled through him. He was clammy with sweat, as if he were the one who'd been poisoned. Something inside him felt on the verge of breaking. He burst out, "That fucking sound! It's driving me mad."

Lady Ki was tearing her hair, weeping. Perhaps no woman in the history of the Great Yuan had ever wept so beautifully. The cold only enhanced her charm, giving her the entrancing fragility of an icicle. It wasn't just an exquisite performance. It was the performance of a lifetime by the one woman who, out of all women between the four oceans, had been able to catch and keep the attention of the Son of Heaven. With delicate, heart-breaking pride, she said, "This unworthy woman will be loyal to the Great Khan until her death. She has never wished a moment's displeasure upon him! If it is truly this woman's fate to fall to these false accusations, then she will gladly accept her punishment as the last way she can serve her beloved husband the Great Khan in this life."

Seyhan frowned. "What sound?"

"False accusations?" the Great Khan demanded. "Were you not burning with jealousy at the Empress's condition, Lady Ki?"

"How could this woman feel anything other than joy to know that her sister the Empress carried within her womb the flesh and blood of the Great Khan himself?" Lady Ki cried. "I prayed for the health of the Empress and her unborn child, and I prayed it would be a son so that the Great Khan might have his pick of successors. My greatest wish has never been for the success of the fruit of my own loins, but always for whatever will ensure our Great Yuan's prosperity and reign without end!"

"That clacking sound," Baoxiang insisted. "Can't you hear it? It's far away. *Listen.*" The wrongness was unbearable. That sound belonged in his dreams, where he could keep himself safe from it. The fact that he was hearing it *here,* out in the world, gave him the catastrophic sense of having been turned inside out. Everything that had been contained was spilling, and in the resulting mess there was no separation of dream from reality; his insides from the outside; the blackness from himself. His breath rasped in panic.

The Third Prince flinched at Lady Ki's speech. Despite what he had known in his heart, it meant more to hear it said out loud by the person he loved most in the world. Before, the Third Prince had hoped without belief. Now anyone who cared to look would have seen the moment even that hope was extinguished.

But the Great Khan's face had softened. Such was the power of Lady Ki's performance. And perhaps, another day, it would have saved her.

A ripple went through the black-hatted officials as a slight female figure made her way between them. Not so much parting, as shrinking back in horror and disgust. Like Lady Ki, the lady-in-waiting was in her underdress. But it was no longer white. The huge brown stains of dried blood had stiffened her skirt so that the hem rasped across the snow like Baoxiang's labored breathing.

"What's wrong?" Seyhan steadied him by the arm, concerned but confused. "It's all going to plan. Are you sick?"

Lady Ki's lady-in-waiting crossed the plaza and knelt at arm's length away from Lady Ki. She didn't look at her former mistress. "This lowly servant dares appear in the Great Khan's presence to give testimony against the imperial consort Lady Ki. Without telling me of her intention, and against my wishes, she secretly gave me a medicine, disguised as ordinary tea, that caused my unborn child to be dissolved into this blood that the Great Khan sees before him!"

The Great Khan recoiled as she spread her skirt with its horrible stain. His instant of softening had been cut off at the quick. He addressed Lady Ki furiously. "Is this true? This was the medicine you gave to the Empress, that killed her?"

A rising wind scuttled loose snow across the plaza. Baoxiang was spinning off into that blank whiteness, like a stumbling traveler who had lost the horizon and, with it, all sense of up and down. He was suddenly desperate for Lady Ki to look at him. If only she were to look at him with all the accusation and hatred he deserved, then that would be something to orient himself against. It would be a signpost leading him back to the self that, long ago, had burned with black fire at the idea of watching the world unravel.

But Lady Ki had no time for him. Her concern was solely, urgently, upon her own survival. "Great Khan, disregard that maid's reckless words! So many unborn children are lost in early pregnancy as a matter of nature. Women know this. The Great Khan's physicians likewise know it! This maid's grieving heart seeks a cause for the loss of her child, even if there wasn't one. Having failed to find anything else to blame, she simply points her finger at me out of spite." Lady Ki's performance of delicacy was giving way; she was a white stone bleeding pure will to survive. "Even the evidence fails to support her claims! If I had given the same medicine to both this maid and the Empress, why should one lose her child but the other—"

She covered her realization quickly, but not quickly enough. A look of sardonic bitterness flitted over the Great Khan's face. For the first time, he resembled the Third Prince. "Search the consort's quarters."

It didn't take the eunuch searchers long to return. If only Lady Ki had thrown away the evidence—but then again, who would have, when the weapon was so useful? When the eunuchs fanned an array of paper packets in front of the lady-in-waiting, she said unerringly, "That one."

Other eunuchs had brought out a tray with a teapot and a single cup. "If it's just tea," the Great Khan said, "then there should be no danger to anyone who consumes it. Isn't that right, Lady Ki?"

Lady Ki raised her head, proud to the last, as the Great Khan's head eunuch brewed the tea and brought her the steaming cup. She knew that though she had lost, she had played her hand as well as any woman could have.

But as she reached for the cup, the Great Khan said coldly, "Not you." His eyes stayed on Lady Ki, sullen with hatred, as he instructed the head eunuch, "Give it to the Third Prince."

It was shocking to see Lady Ki break. Her lifelong performance shattered in an instant, and the truth beneath it was the only betrayal of hers that the Great Khan could never forgive: that she loved her son more than him. She cried, "No!"

The head eunuch ran to the Third Prince and offered him the cup. The Third Prince hesitated, eyes flicking between his parents.

Even with his breath rasping in his ears, Baoxiang could still hear the sound. It came from every direction; it pressed in on him like the ocean, and he knew he was drowning.

From the moment at the Great Khan's Spring Hunt when he'd first seen that unhappy, desperate boy watching him across the banquet tables with fascination and disgust, Baoxiang had known what he would do, and what the outcome would be.

He saw it now, as clearly as if it were another power of the Mandate: the Third Prince turning his back on his mother as he snatched the cup from the tray. Lady Ki's protest had come too late. She had seen to it herself that the Third Prince could no longer imagine, let alone believe, how she might have risked herself for him; that everything she had done had been for him.

In Baoxiang's mind's eye, the Third Prince raised the cup in sardonic salute to the Great Khan, and drank.

The world had gone blurry, as if Baoxiang's blackness were forcing itself out through his eyes. Somehow his body was moving without his control. He lurched and staggered through the snow like a broken-limbed puppet, propelled by the single, mindless instinct: to get away from the Third Prince's death.

Away from what he had done, that could never be undone.

Baoxiang lurched to a halt in the corridor outside. The high stone walls cast the passage entirely into frigid shadow. Passing feet and hooves had churned through the top layer of snow, but beneath was only white sand that was as indistinguishable from the snow as bleached bones. From the plaza behind came a thin, high screaming: the wail of a mother's grief that seemed like one of the ribbons flung into the sky by Goryeo ribbon dancers, unfurling all the way to Heaven.

The world was spinning. Baoxiang had the terrible feeling of not knowing whether he was awake or asleep. He was in the clutch of a nightmare; he had been swallowed by the dream he refused to dream. Everything that had happened before was happening again, and there was no way to turn from it. He was dreaming, but the dream was a memory: because he had left before.

He remembered the tide of victorious feeling that had swept him from Esen and Ouyang, back along the white marble bridge and into Bianliang's crumbled hall of emperors. *Goodbye, brother.* With the unfamiliar weight of armor around him, he felt like he'd transformed into the strongest, most flawlessly cruel version of himself: an obsidian knife that parted flesh almost before it made contact. His entire body thrummed with savage thrill. He couldn't get enough of the look on Esen's face as he'd revealed his invisible collaboration in Ouyang's betrayal. Esen had *hurt*. It had struck Baoxiang with a jolt of pure pleasure: that he had done that; made Esen feel that. He'd known, even as it was happening, that it had been everything he wanted; that it was a moment to savor forever.

He'd made it almost through the hall when it hit him. A purely bodily awareness: a dreadful gulping sensation of knowing he'd overlooked something terrible and crucial—something so important that the realization of it stopped the world with horror. *Esen was going to die.*

The impact of it made him stagger. Killing Esen had been the entire purpose of everything he'd done. It had been the goal his anger had driven him towards. He'd envisaged the satisfaction of his death over and over, with the savagely joyful taste of blood in his mouth. And yet somehow, having done all of that, he had never truly comprehended what it would *mean*.

A fist of urgency pulled him back the way he'd come. There was nothing else in the world except for the desperate need that drove him. Every fiber of his body strained against a nightmare slowness as he stumbled towards the only thing that still existed: those great double doors opening wide onto the white staring sky, and the bleeding red wilderness beneath it. He had to get through those doors. He had to reach Esen. For what, he didn't know.

But he didn't go through.

As he stood there in the doorway, an eerie, melodious tocking came from above. Bamboo chimes stirred in the roof vault of the ruined hall. The chimes were so old that their sound was dry, hollow, splintered. Swelling and fading, the notes came in random clusters like the ruffles on a lake on a blustery spring day. The chimes went on and on, played by the invisible air, as Baoxiang looked down upon the motionless landscape of what he had wrought.

Esen had died once before. He had died in that summer thunderstorm of their childhood, when their father had held Baoxiang out in the courtyard while he wept in fear and grief. Baoxiang could still feel how absolute and overwhelming those emotions had been. He hadn't just believed it, but experienced the reality of it in every aspect of himself: that it had been the end of the world.

The next day he had crept into Esen's rooms and found him

there, sleeping. He must have come in after the storm. Even asleep, he radiated energy—a pure aliveness, pulsing within the safety of his whole and unharmed body. Baoxiang climbed onto the bed and sat next to him, watching him sleep with a tearful astonishment that verged on worship.

"Baoxiang." Esen smiled drowsily up at him as he woke. "What's the matter?"

Esen hadn't known that he had died and been resurrected; that it had been a miracle.

But there would be no miracle this time.

Baoxiang looked down at Ouyang cradling Esen's body, the crimson flag spreading across the marble. The chimes played, and their ghostly sound made everything unreal. The world had always had Esen in it. Whatever Baoxiang had felt about him in any given moment, he'd always been *there.* He couldn't conceive of how it could be otherwise. And yet somehow this outcome he'd wished for, with all the power of his rage and pain, had come true even though it should have been impossible.

The chimes merged with Lady Ki's wailing, the sound pressing into him in throbbing waves. Baoxiang was a spot on the surface of a black sun, a scrim on the surface of an emotion so immense he knew he would never be able to keep it contained. He remembered lying in the dark with the Third Prince, feeling the warm aliveness of his sleeping body, and how he had thought about stopping. But he hadn't. And now the Third Prince was dead, and what was done could never be undone.

He was trembling uncontrollably. It was the ghost that had spurred him on, when he could have stopped. The ghost that, he knew suddenly, was watching him now. The black emotion inside him ballooned dangerously, and then he was coming apart from the force of it. He was bursting, dissolving, being torn apart by the immensity of his anger. It was the most agonizing thing he'd ever felt, and it was *all because of the ghost.* Everything he had done, the torrent of misery and pain he had poured into the world: all of it was what the ghost had made him do. He was only anger; there was nothing else in the world apart from that anger; and he heard himself screaming, "I hate you. I hate you, I hate you, *I hate you.*"

But it wasn't true. It had never been true.

That outrushing blackness was the apocalypse of himself—it was the worst feeling in the world—but it wasn't anger. It wasn't vengeance, and it wasn't loathing. It had never been any of those. What he'd thought was anger was only a sharp point pushed up from below by the hidden enormity of the real feeling: something as pulpy and unbearably painful as the interior of a tooth.

He hadn't hated Esen. He'd loved him, even when Esen hurt him. He'd loved Esen, even while Esen hated him. It was because of that love that his hurt was the size of the world: inconceivable except from the inside.

He was collapsed in the snow against the wall. He turned his head to the icy stone and wept convulsively, and the blackness that was swallowing his vision seemed to be streaming out of that pulpy part of himself that was bleeding without end: black blood, bad blood, darkness and ruin.

He had the sense of the ghost settling in the same position on the other side of the wall, pressing through the stone until its cheek was against his own. The death-coldness of its touch was a burning agony, and somehow he knew it was the kind of pain that would never numb, but continue without end.

He would never have done any of this, if not for the ghost. He wouldn't have betrayed and killed people he cared about; he wouldn't even have the Mandate. But what other choice did he have, when this was the only way to make Esen understand the scale of his pain?

When you feel it, you'll know.

17

LAKE POYANG, NEAR NANCHANG

The banks of the narrow river bore a thick ruff of white reeds that blended with the mist until it seemed they were sailing through pure whiteness. Zhu's fleet traveled in single file. There was just enough breeze for the ships to keep moving without needing to resort to oars. The lantern-creased sails creaked as the ships' crews—Fang's women pirates—made minute adjustments. Zhu's own men and artillery crowded the middle and lower decks. Her white-masted flagship, the fleet's largest vessel, ran at the head of the line behind a small pilot ship that beckoned it onwards by the lantern on its stern.

It had taken Zhu nine days to bring her fleet along the Yangzi River from Yingtian. From her scouts she knew Chen's fleet was already positioned inside Lake Poyang—the connector between fallen Nanchang and the main thoroughfare of the Yangzi—where he was waiting for her. He clearly wanted Zhu to enter the lake from the Yangzi, which would force her to meet him head-on. But now that Zhu's forces were so reduced from Ouyang's abandonment, she knew that facing Chen head-on would be nothing less than suicide.

No, her only chance against Chen was to approach him from a direction he wasn't expecting. That was the reason Zhu was currently squeezing her fleet through one of the lake's tiny, obscure tributaries. Too tiny, really. For vessels any larger than Zhu's pirate ships, it would have been unnavigable. Even for the pirate ships, it was a risk. Sandbars skimmed perilously beneath the green surface. Zhu's ships were small, but they weren't flat-bottomed river ships. If a seagoing keel stuck into a sandbar, all the ships behind it would be trapped. But *if* they could make it through, they would gain that critical element of surprise by coming out into the lake on Chen's flank.

But now, as they glided through the mist, Zhu couldn't help feeling uneasy. For the time being she was wearing a hook rather than an imitation hand—it was more useful in a shipboard environment—and she idly fingered the sharp point as she thought. Chen was a planner. Back in Anfeng, when she'd professed to be on his side for his move against his rival Right Minister Guo, he hadn't disbelieved her—and yet he'd still taken Xu Da hostage to ensure her compliance. He hadn't left anything to chance. So if he *was* aware of this tributary's existence . . . even if it didn't seem like it was large enough to be used as a passage into the lake, he wouldn't have taken the assumption as fact. He would have done something to make sure.

Over the preceding weeks, Zhu's raw anger towards Ouyang for his betrayal had turned into a dull throb. But now as she considered the situation, her frustration rose. Ouyang had put her in this difficult position, when instead they could have stayed together and had the strength to defeat Chen head-on. But it was what it was. With a moment's concentration she released the past and its unpleasant emotions, and focused ahead. Perhaps it would be hard, but she'd never met a problem that didn't have a solution. She had never failed, and she wasn't going to fail now. Not because of Ouyang. Not because of Chen. Not because of anyone.

She called down to Yuchun on the middle deck, "Ready the artillery and keep an eye on those banks. We'll need to respond quickly if there's an attack."

The riverbanks were still close, but the breeze had changed: it gave the sense that somewhere ahead lay a vast open space. A muffled drumbeat from the pilot vessel warned them around a series of shallow shoals. The mist was growing denser, until Zhu standing at the forward rail could barely make out the pilot vessel's stern lantern. The temperature plunged.

Xu Da, shivering at the rail beside her, said, "The lake has its own weather."

Just as Zhu opened her mouth to reply, a sharp retort rang out ahead.

Zhu's body contracted with readiness. This was the attack she'd been waiting for—but even as she turned to command the response, she realized it wasn't. There were no more explosions; no clash of steel, or men's shouts. There was only eerie silence.

Then, high up in the mist: a dim blooming flower of red light. That was what the retort had been: the ignition of the emergency signal.

"Stop the ships!" Zhu shouted. Her mind was racing. Had the pilot vessel run aground? That was bad news for sure, but perhaps they were close enough to the lake that they could refloat it on the next tide. "Send the message down the line. Stop!"

As Zhu called, she was surprised to feel her gut clench in warning. She wasn't afraid, as far as she could tell. But there was something about this clinging cold that raised the hair on her arms, and stole the warmth from the pit of her stomach, that seemed to be making her body believe that it was.

Lanterns flashed and women shouted. The fleet's sails creaked and swung, and each ship bled momentum and eased to a halt in the middle of the river. They waited there, rocking gently. There was nothing ahead but blankness.

"There's something strange about this cold," Xu Da said uneasily. "Isn't there?"

The cold rushed over them in breaking waves of fear, as they stared into the blankness. And then, suddenly, there was a shape there.

Without any surroundings for scale, it took Zhu a disoriented moment to realize that the shape wasn't a ship, but one of the pole skiffs they used for putting ashore.

The skiff seemed to be flying through the whiteness like a bird. A single dark figure stood within it. The eeriness of the image was such that for a moment Zhu could have believed her fleet had accidentally crossed out of human lands and into the first realm of Hell.

"He's one of ours, isn't he?" Xu Da said, squinting at the figure. As the skiff neared, they could see that the bottom was laden with dark bales. "But why does he have cargo?"

"Not cargo," Zhu answered grimly.

The lone poleman's muffled voice reached them through the mist. With each stroke of the pole, his panicked hails became clearer and clearer. "Don't come any farther! Don't pass the line! They all died when we passed the line!"

☼

"There was nothing," the poleman said, after they brought him aboard. "*Nothing.* No sign, no warning. They fell where they stood, without a sound. Dead. Nine out of ten of us aboard. As soon as we regained control of the ship, the commander sent us back to warn you." He spoke in a tight tremble of fear and shock. "We were four who set out. Then it happened again, as we crossed that same line in the water. It was like their spirits flew out of their bodies. They fell down, and it was only me who was left . . ." His horror-stricken appearance reminded Zhu of a featureless face pressing itself through a veil of white cloth.

"Contain this information for the time being," Zhu said sharply to Yuchun. The presence of danger, its shape unknown, ran over her skin with cold foreboding as she and Xu Da went to the prow. The ship rolled lightly under their feet, stationary against the current.

"There *isn't* anything—" Xu Da said, then cut off and drew his sword as a flicker of color appeared low down in the mist.

It was there for only an instant. It disappeared as soon as the mist swirled again, but Zhu had already seen the spear standing upright in the shoal ahead: red banner around its shaft, and a single, blackened hand impaled on the tip as if it were waving. Beside her, Xu Da cursed. "*Chen Youliang.*"

Zhu's foreboding deepened. That was Chen's signature, but what was the message?

It was so cold. Deathly cold, like sharpened picks to the bone. And all at once Zhu knew. What they'd thought was the cold of the open lake wasn't that at all. She'd encountered this particular, dreadful cold before. On instinct she raised her hand and let her Mandate spill out. Instead of bouncing back from the mist as normal light would have, it reached deep within and found what was inside.

Perhaps half a li ahead, ghosts hovered above the water. Their pale forms spanned from bank to bank like the front line of a supernatural army. Zhu stared at them with mute aversion. These ghosts were the same as the one in the underground prison in Bianliang that had looked at her with such hatred and intent. These ghosts weren't ordinary ghosts, but hungry ghosts.

Ghosts that killed. Ghosts that *ate.*

Zhu's pilot ship had passed through this spectral line, and in that single instant of contact the ghosts had consumed her men's qi and killed them. Had those men even known they were dying, as their life force rushed into the mouths of monsters they couldn't see?

The water underneath the ghosts was too opaque to see what Chen had anchored to the riverbed, but a few scraps of familiar red fabric swayed just under the surface.

"What is it?" Xu Da said, casting around blindly in the various directions of Zhu's gaze.

"Do you remember what they say about someone buried without an intact corpse, whose body has been desecrated?" *Desecrated.* That was her own body; it was Ouyang's body; it was all those mutilated bodies that people recoiled from, for fear of what they would become in death. For a life worth living, though, Zhu had always been willing to give up her rest in death. "Their spirit can't go to Diyu. It becomes a hungry ghost that roams the earth until its reincarnation, seeking vengeance on the living."

"That's what you see out there? Hungry ghosts?" Xu Da was one of the few Zhu had told about the Mandate's powers. "People talk about such things, but I never thought—and it was *Chen Youliang* who did it?"

"He has the Mandate too." She'd put what Fang had told her out of mind after Ouyang's betrayal—it hadn't seemed helpful to dwell on how Heaven had deemed her opponent equally worthy of the throne—but now it came rushing back. "He can see what I can see, and he's worked out how to use it against us." Despite everything, she could appreciate the cleverness of it. "He's sunk desecrated bodies here to form a barricade of vengeful ghosts. Anyone who comes into contact with one of them has his life force drained, and dies instantly. The men who survived had the good luck to pass through the gaps between the ghosts."

"Desecrated bodies? Of our people in Nanchang?" His horrified assumption was written on his face: that gush of pickled hands, and the women and children they had been taken from.

But those submerged scraps of red fabric told the true story. Zhu had so often seen that same headscarf strewn around the battlefield; that flash of brightness amongst the carnage.

"Why drag around the bodies of murdered civilians when there was an easier way?" She wasn't sure if she wouldn't have done the same. "He killed his own men."

Xu Da blanched. He'd ordered enough men to their deaths on the battlefield, but even Zhu could appreciate how it was another matter entirely to refuse them honor once dead. She went on, "He knows I can see the barricade. He wants us to go back and enter the lake via the main entrance, so we'll be forced to go against him head-on."

Xu Da gave her a speaking look.

"I know. That's what he *wants* me to do." Her determination felt like a clenched fist inside her. Ouyang had lost faith in her; betrayed her; abandoned her. But without realizing it, he had left her with something that would let her win—if she was strong enough to use it. "I won't. We're going through."

"*Through*? But if it's nine out of ten men who fall—then what are our odds to win, afterwards?"

"Only nine out of ten if they could be killed. But there's one kind of person who *can't* be killed." When Xu Da gave her an puzzled look, Zhu told him, "Someone who's dead already."

Ouyang had shown not just that it was possible to bring drowned men back, but how. If they drowned their men so they were dead when they crossed the ghost barricade, they could use his technique to revive them on the other side. And if they could bring through their entire fleet against Chen's expectations, they would enter the lake with their surprise intact. Zhu added, "We'll need a skeleton crew awake on each ship to steer and perform the resuscitations. Since I can see the ghosts, I'll go with each crew, and guide them through the gaps in the line as best I can to minimize casualties."

Xu Da had gone even paler than usual. He was often pale these days. He needed rest, like they all did. Some days even Zhu herself felt tired enough to turn into a dried vegetable. But they were young. After her success, they'd have their whole lives ahead of them to rest.

"Little brother," Xu Da said, at length. "I'll follow you through anything, you know that. But to be drowned . . . Those men are just ordinary men. They'll be terrified to face such a thing. And they'd be right to be terrified. I know what it's like to drown. It feels like death." He gripped the railing as he stared out at the invisible barricade. "It *is* death."

"Not permanent death!" Zhu said indignantly. "So they'll be afraid and miserable, but don't they face fear and suffering every time they follow you into battle anyway? When the alternative is going head-on into a guaranteed slaughter, they should be grateful for a better option."

A visceral shudder ran through him, as if he were remembering what that better option had felt like. But all he said was, "If you're sure this is the way, then I'll do what has to be done to support you."

He strode out onto deck, saying to Zhu, "Explain it."

When Zhu did, there was a murmur of dissent. She said calmly, "I understand your fear. You don't believe it's possible. But it is. Watch."

With his hands behind his back, Xu Da made a picture of commanding ease in front of the crowd as a filled bucket was brought out. Zhu thought only she could see the fear and dread under that relaxed facade. It would be even more intense for him than the men he'd said would be so terrified. They would imagine the horror, but he *knew* it. And he was doing it again, voluntarily, for her. She considered calling the whole demonstration off to spare him. But this was the right approach, which made her loath to give it up. An army that would undergo fear and discomfort willingly, because they trusted her, was better than one that had been forced at swordpoint.

"Do it right, little brother. You're not as pretty as the eunuch was, but I don't think I'll be in a position to be picky," Xu Da said in an undertone, so the men couldn't hear. He gave her a faint smile, and she remembered him telling her before they went against Ouyang that time in Jining, so long ago: *Ten thousand years of past lives brought me to your side to support you. Trust that I'm strong enough.*

Zhu clamped down on her squirmy feeling. If he could be strong for her, she was strong enough to let him do it.

He knelt, saying, "This general follows the orders of the Radiant King, even into death."

Nobody had to hold his head under. A ripple of horrified awe went through the men, as they grasped how much will and courage it must have taken their general to force his body to breathe in, against all its natural instincts. Zhu felt her own lungs tighten in awful sympathy, as if she were the one breathing in water instead of air. *It feels like death.* He was suffering, she had no doubt about that, but at least it was only for a few moments.

She could see how Xu Da's performance had captivated the men. It was her turn, now. She was sharply aware that it would ruin everything if she faltered for even a moment. She said coolly to Yuchun, who despite her instructions hadn't managed to keep a stricken look off his face, "Pull him out."

For a moment she almost couldn't bear to look: to see him dead again. But he *hadn't* been dead then, she thought fiercely, as he wasn't now.

She pressed her lips to his and breathed her qi into him. She had the mental image of their energies circulating together in his body. It seemed a fitting entanglement for their brotherhood that hadn't come from blood, but a shared life. She could feel how he wasn't dead, even though his face was cold and blue from the immersion. His spirit seemed just beneath the surface, as if he were straining to reach her hand from some distant place. But to her mounting concern, his body remained still. She breathed until her lungs ached. How long had it taken for Ouyang's breath to restore him to life? Surely not this long. Beneath her lips Xu Da's mouth was warming, but she had the awful feeling that it was only because she was pumping her own body heat into him. His own qi was fading, slipping. Everyone was watching, and it wasn't working. She breathed until her head was spinning from effort, and all she could think was: *It will work, because it has to. Because I know I won't ever lose.*

And then, beneath her hands and mouth: a stir that was even less than a shiver. It was a spirit returning to the body, a fusing of energy and flesh, and Zhu had just enough presence of mind to let herself glow as Xu Da gasped and came back to life. Around them the men's voices rose into incredulous cheering: they had witnessed a miracle.

Xu Da coughed wretchedly, curling around himself where he lay on the deck. She wanted to let him rest, but she had to continue with the performance: *See, he's fine.* Under the eyes of an audience, she couldn't help hold his terror and his pain. All she could do was raise him to his feet, and feel his shivering weight against her. It was hard to reconcile how unnaturally dry he was, for someone who had drowned.

Xu Da knew what she needed from him. It was only because she was touching him that she could tell the effort it took for him to call to the crowd, "Do you have the courage to show the Radiant King your loyalty?"

They cried out their assent. It was only after they'd dispersed that he finally let himself collapse against her. She staggered under his weight, and they both sank to the deck. After a while, Xu Da suppressed his coughing long enough to manage, "Far be it for me to criticize, but your technique could do with some refinement. That was even worse than the last time."

Zhu gripped his hand. It was trembling violently, but he was there: he was alive, and returned to her. He had traversed that unknown place of death for her, and she would make it all worth it.

She said, "And do it once more, General, for me."

Zhu's flagship glided towards the ghost barricade. Zhu stood on the foredeck, the pirates lined up behind her as though she were Guan Yin casting a many-armed shadow. Those women's lives depended on her steering them between the gaps in the ghosts. More than that: her own victory depended on it. If she made a mistake and lost too many of these women, she'd lose the capacity to sail her ships. She'd lose the capacity to bring her men back to life. And that would truly be the end.

In the hold beneath her feet, dead men floated in their cold-water preservative. The ship rode low, heavy in the water, weighed down by the lives suspended within it. Xu Da had led the men into one of the several sealed compartments beneath the waterline that ensured the ship wouldn't sink even if breached. The women had hammered the hatch shut. Then they'd pumped the compartment full of water. If Xu Da hadn't been there . . . perhaps in the other ships, the men had screamed and scrabbled as the water rose in that dark space. But in her own ship, Xu Da's presence had kept them calm. They had simply fallen into a continuing silence. But Zhu knew it wasn't a silence in which nothing was happening. It was a silence in which lives were running out. What was it Ouyang had said? *Any longer than it takes to boil a pot of tea, and it won't work.*

The ghosts' chill enclosed them as the ship approached the line. As the outer envelope of Zhu's light breached the mist, she saw them waiting: dead eyes and ravenous mouths. It occurred to her that although she'd previously seemed immune to supernatural maladies, she didn't know if she was immune to *this*. If she accidentally brushed one of these ghosts, would she fall dead on the spot? The ship sailed so smoothly and silently through the mist that it felt as though it were being drawn by an invisible reel. There were no external landmarks by which to measure their speed, so it seemed slow even though Zhu knew they were traveling faster than a man could run. The ghosts loomed; they were *reaching* for her as the dead ship rushed towards its fate, and all Zhu could do was make herself small as she plunged into the gap between those clutching horrors.

And then she was through. From behind her came the rustle of bodies as the women shifted to stay exactly behind her, and then—alarmingly—a cascade of thuds. Zhu's heart sank. The ship had been moving too fast, and human reaction times were too slow. The women at the back of the line hadn't had time to make it into the correct position.

She spun around. At first all she could see was dead women sprawled to the left and right of where they'd stood just moments before. But in the next breath she saw perhaps half were still standing. That was enough—it had to be enough. And now every beat of Zhu's heart was another beat missed by the men floating beneath the decks, dead but still attached to the world.

She shouted, "Start pumping!"

Hauled out and laid on deck, the men made a horrific sight. The grayness of their faces, frozen in terror, reminded her of Chen's barrel of pickled parts. Zhu threw herself at the nearest corpse, and around her the women knelt and blew into each man's mouth. Zhu had never been so pleased in her life to hear coughing and vomiting. As soon as a man could sit up, he was moved aside so more bodies could be brought up and laid out.

"This one's not coming back," someone cried, and Zhu called back with cold dread, "Move on to the next." The bodies parading beneath her were no longer individuals she'd known, but tasks waiting to be completed. Her lungs ached from the effort; her clothes were saturated from the men's sodden bodies. How long could they afford to waste on one man who for whatever reason might not come back, when there were so many waiting their turn and time was running out?

So many men; so many fewer women than she'd started with. Zhu didn't want to dwell on what she'd known even before they'd started: that they would never be able to bring all of them back.

Dead body after dead body passed under her lips. All of them men who might well be dead again, in the battle to come. And then she reached for the next body, and there wasn't one. Through a haze of exhaustion Zhu looked up and saw men hunched over on every inch of the deck, their heads between their knees as they coughed and retched and groaned. She saw, too, the bodies still laid out in their midst. So many bodies. And her eye was roving, searching without intent, and she didn't know what it was looking for until, in a powerful burst of relief, it found him.

Zhu hurried to where Xu Da was sitting under the forward sail. His head was tilted back against the mast as he heaved for breath. With an amorphous unease she noticed a trace of blood by his mouth. "You're bleeding."

Xu Da wiped his mouth with a trembling hand. "Bit my tongue when I went under. I have to say, it doesn't get easier each time."

"That was the last time," Zhu said vehemently. "You did it. You died three times for me, that's enough for anyone to demand. You don't have to do it again."

Xu Da laughed breathlessly and got up with only a slight wobble. He glanced around at the men gradually regaining their feet, and shook his head in disbelief. "It worked. Nobody else would have thought to try this, let alone dared ask so much of his men. But they were strong enough. I guess you knew they would be."

In front of them the open lake beckoned. A line of snow-capped mountains lay on the horizon: Chen's fleet, oriented towards the main entrance of the lake. Zhu had nothing on her side but surprise, speed, and maneuverability. *Small and fast,* she thought of Yuchun saying. It had to be enough.

Xu Da, knowing her thoughts as he always did, said with determination, "It will be. We have a chance now. And we'll fight with everything we've got."

❋

The drum on Zhu's white-masted flagship had become the fleet's pulse, steadying the men's hearts into its own rhythm and urging on the nimble pirate ships under oars and sail for this sprint that would make them appear on Chen's flank as if out of nowhere. There was just enough wind in the sails that each beat of the oars propelled them with an ease that made it feel as if they weren't just skimming across the surface of the water, but flying above it. Zhu had never experienced this kind of wild speed before. The lantern-creased paper sails crackled deafeningly overhead, and the timbers beneath her feet groaned like a straining buffalo. The bitterness of Ouyang's abandonment and Jiao's betrayal were licked out of her by the pure fresh coldness of the waves spraying into the prow. Despite the challenge they were facing, her sense of exhilaration grew. If people doubted her capacities; if they refused to believe—she would prove them wrong, as she had proved them wrong time and again. She would prove them wrong, and win.

Chen's fleet loomed ever larger ahead. It was one thing to know the size of his ships; it was another thing altogether to see them. Red-lacquered hulls, lined with portholes like the breathing holes on a beetle's carapace, rose the height of a city's walls above the water. Decks stepped upwards towards a cap of iron-armored archers' towers. Higher yet, red banners rippled amongst ivory sails like scraps of flesh hanging from skeletons.

As they drew near, Zhu shouted to the drummer, "Prepare to engage!" and thrilled as she heard his rhythm change into the heavy staccato of her command. In response her ships drew their oars in. They were eagles folding their wings back for the dive. They hurtled forwards under nothing more than the power of the air, the water cutting away beneath their fierce-eyed prows. Zhu had become one with the ship: the strain of its sails was the heave of her lungs, and the galloping slap of waves against the hull her heart, as they arrowed towards the target. Her formation spread as each of her ships found and narrowed in on its individual target within Chen's fleet.

Her flagship's own target loomed in front, and Zhu braced herself against the sharp tilt of the deck as the ship sliced around to present its broadside. The moment it came level, she shouted to the men poised on deck, "Fire!"

The deck planks groaned as the trebuchets released their flaming missiles. The straight-sided hull and outspread wings of Chen's ship were so massive that it would've been impossible to miss. Zhu could only imagine how much Chen's men must be panicking as they were bombarded without warning. She couldn't see their individual shapes, but she could see their buzz of activity as they scrambled to muster a defense. The great sails of Chen's ship were changing configuration as its crew labored to turn the lumbering behemoth to face the attack, but it was too late. Zhu's comet-tailed projectiles crashed through masts and sawed through lines. The sail on the mainmast caught fire like a pine hit by summer lightning. Even if the lake spray meant Zhu couldn't smell anything other than water, she thrilled at the thought of its great tarry stench. Her men howled victoriously. Let Chen hear them yell, she thought with satisfaction. Let him marinate in her triumph, as his fleet burned.

So intent was Zhu on waiting for the conflagration, that it

took her longer than it should have to notice that it wasn't happening. Her men started to notice, too. Their howls dwindled as they registered what should have been impossible: Chen's ship wasn't burning. They could see the tiny figures of his men in a frenzy of smothering and controlling. They were releasing burning sails from the masts; cutting tangles of lines. Zhu saw now—desperately, disbelievingly, too late—that the upper deck had been laid with some kind of thick matting. Chen had predicted Zhu would deploy fire, and warded against it. When her pitch-soaked missiles had smashed onto the upper deck, his men had bundled them into that matting and smothered them before they ever touched wood. All Zhu had managed to do with her attack was burn some replaceable sails and lines.

With a heavy-hearted glance, Zhu saw the same series of events had transpired elsewhere. Under a cloud of wafting smoke, Chen's fleet stood intact. But there wasn't time for disappointment. She hadn't won outright, but her attack had made an opening—and if she didn't take it, Chen would recover enough to launch a counterattack. If he did, Zhu thought grimly, she would be crushed for sure. "Grab the short-range weapons!" she called down to the main deck. "Put the fire-powder weapons in front, with a line of men with tinder pots behind, then the archers at the back. Get us closer, and engage!"

Xu Da's tall shape plowed through the mad scramble on the main deck, marshaling lines of men. On the upper rear deck, Yuchun was readying the cannons: larger versions of the handheld fire-powder weapons Jiao had developed. Zhu's flagship nudged forwards, and Zhu yelled, "Now!"

The roar of fire-powder weapons was deafening. Zhu's men fired directly into Chen's ship, and she saw the crew on his exposed upper deck staggering and falling. Great holes appeared in its hull as she screamed hoarsely, "Again!"

Another barrage rang out, enveloping both ships in a cloud of flying splinters and rancid black smoke. Zhu could barely see past her own prow. Her ears were ringing so loudly that the world seemed to have been stuffed full of wool.

Then something loomed out of the smoke. Zhu had a bare instant to glance up—and up and up—before a bloodred, porthole-filled wall smashed into them. Her men who had been braced at her flagship's rail were instantly impaled on the bristle of lances that thrust forth from the portholes. From higher up, a projectile hurtled down and hit Zhu's top deck with an impact that sent her flying. When she picked herself up, coughing and covered in wood dust, she saw with horror that the projectile was a harpoon. It had completely penetrated the deck and held it fast with a taut rope leading back to Chen's ship. Even as she half staggered and half crawled towards the rope to slash it with her saber, more harpoons plunged down. A man screamed as he was pinned to the deck. She saw Xu Da run to him—not to save him, because he was already gone, but to cut the rope. But there were too many harpoons, and they sank into her flagship like a tiger's claws into its prey. All that Zhu's assault had done was anger the beast. It had shrugged off its wounds, and come for them.

Now it wasn't only harpoons flashing from the sky, but sheets of splattering liquid. The smell of sulfur cut through the meaty fire-powder stench of her own weapons. Some kind of flammable liquid, Zhu realized awfully. Chen's men were filling her ship with it, and when it was sufficiently saturated, they would drop fire on it and watch them burn.

Another harpoon whistled through the air and landed with a thunk high up in Zhu's mainmast. As Zhu's eye traveled to the mast, she noticed the long yardarm that held one of the ship's unused weapons: a giant firecracker. The firecracker, which under ordinary circumstances dangled well over the water, was less a single explosive than a cluster of hundreds of small ones, strung together like a bunch of bananas. The idea was that it could be lit to spray fire directly into the sails of nearby ships as they came alongside.

Chen's ship was so tall that instead of being anywhere near its sails, the firecracker pressed against the side rail of its upper deck. But perhaps that was enough. Without wasting another moment on consideration, Zhu grabbed the handle of a nearby tinder pot with her teeth, sprinted to the mast and with the combined action of hook and hand struggled up the rigging to where she could reach the long fuse of the firecracker.

For such a long fuse, it burned quickly. Zhu's spark raced into the base of the firecracker and disappeared inside. For a moment, nothing happened.

Then the firecracker started exploding, and once it started: it didn't stop. It made an endless ripping sound so loud that Zhu could have believed it was Heaven itself being torn apart. With each burst of explosions the firecracker sent jets of burning shrapnel through the upper deck rail and into Chen's men where they stood with the buckets of liquid they'd been pouring into Zhu's ship. As the men screamed, the buckets fell and drenched the thick matting that covered the decks. Then, as the firecracker sent forth another burst, the soaked matting went up in flame. A nearby mast followed suit almost immediately, as if the heat radiating from the burning matting had been so intense as to cause contactless ignition. This was what Zhu had wanted in the first place. Chen's ship was truly burning now.

Then, in a burst of horror, she realized: unless she managed to free her flagship, she would burn too.

She half climbed, half tumbled from the mast and fell upon the nearest harpoon, frantically slashing at the rope. When she spared a panicked glance across the deck, she saw Xu Da doing the same. Chen's ship shuddered like a dying animal as the inferno built inside it. Zhu's ship still wasn't free of its bindings when Chen's ship started listing outwards. As it rolled, it slowly heaved Zhu's ship out of the water. Zhu, clinging for dear life to a capstan as the angle of the deck headed towards vertical, realized she was looking straight down into the ripped-open guts of Chen's ship. Flames pillared outwards from the breached red hull, licking into Zhu's ship. In another moment those flames would find the residue of the liquid Chen had been pouring over them—

With a series of whip cracks the remaining bindings burst, and Zhu's ship fell. It smashed onto the surface of the lake, trailing an intestinal tangle of ropes, as Zhu screamed, "Get below to the oars! We need to get away before it goes down!"

They pulled away just as Chen's ship started sinking in earnest. Zhu draped over the rail, panting. Throughout the battle she'd been so caught up with her own ship's problems that she hadn't had the opportunity to keep track of what was happening with the rest of her fleet. Now, as she finally glanced around to take its measure, she was struck by despair.

In addition to her flagship's opponent, a handful of Chen's

ships were sinking. But a worryingly large number of them had successfully harpooned their smaller attackers, poured death into them, and then cut them free while they burned. And now those monsters were already forming up again. With deadly, ponderous gravity, Chen's reunited fleet rotated to face Zhu's scattered ships. Its livid banners streaked the blackened sky like a storm warning.

Xu Da threw himself against the rail next to her. He was gasping even harder than she was. "We need to get past that line and out of this accursed lake—"

Zhu's drummer crawled past them back to his station in the prow. Something was rolling against Zhu's feet: one of his drumsticks. She tossed it back to him as she said to Xu Da, "Trying to get past that line *will* be our defeat."

Xu Da gave her a haggard look. "We've already been defeated!"

"No. Not until I say we've lost. As long as we don't admit defeat, *there's always a way.*"

He said, "There's a fine line between determination and denial."

But there was pale water, in the distance. Pale meant shallow, and shallow meant Chen's ships couldn't follow. If she could manage to gather her fleet there, at least they'd live to fight another day. She instructed the drummer, "Tell the others to retreat to that shallow water, and regroup."

She turned back to Xu Da. "We haven't lost until I say we have. And that," she told him, "is the one thing I'll never say."

Zhu's regrouped fleet bobbed uneasily in the shallows. In the darker water beyond stood the blockade of Chen's enormous ships. Zhu didn't doubt that Chen had the patience to wait there until she broke—or, if not her, then her men. Their morale had already been damaged by Ouyang's departure, and the hardest of all options was always to do nothing. It would probably be easier to convince them to rush into an engagement with Chen—suicidal though that would be—than to keep them here stewing in doubt and fear.

It was such a solid line. As the sun set behind Chen's ships, it turned them into a brooding unbroken mass. Zhu, looking at it, had the sudden thought: Not just solid, but *too* solid. By forming his ships up that closely, Chen was ensuring Zhu had no chance of breaking through. But at the same time, wasn't he also making himself vulnerable? Except for his ships at the ends of the line, none of the others had any room to move. If a threat were posed to them, they'd have no choice but to stand still and take it.

In the scum of floating debris knocking against her flagship's hull, Zhu saw the broken neck of an oil jar, and a rainbow smear.

Fire from above hadn't worked to destroy Chen's ships. But perhaps fire from below . . .

Xu Da answered Zhu's request with a look of extreme dubiousness. "You want what?"

"Show the others how to make them." Zhu shoved the roll of paper at him. They'd already used most of the spare sail-paper for patching a huge harpoon hole in the main deck, but there was enough left for what she had in mind. "The lotus-flower lanterns we used to make in the monastery for Ghost Month. I know you always tried to get me to make yours, but since that isn't an option anymore, I have to hope you've retained *some* knowledge."

"As if we don't have enough ghosts . . ." Xu Da muttered. "Also, it's been years!"

"Muscle memory comes back," Zhu said unsympathetically. "If you bothered to develop it in the first place. If not, I guess you'll have to figure it out from first principles."

When the moon set, Zhu's team slipped into the water. Each man, held aloft by inflated water bladders around his waist, hauled two jugs of cooking oil. Their black heads and low profiles in the water would make them all but invisible to Chen's lookouts. They'd kick out to the blockade, release the oil to form a slick around the middle-most ships, then kick back without being seen.

Xu Da, standing next to Zhu at the rail of the forward upper deck, counted under his breath; at long last the team members returned and were hauled up the side, shivering with cold. Zhu called, "The lanterns," and the men with the lit lanterns stepped to the rail and dropped them into the water.

Unlike the swimmers, Chen would be able to see these coming. Hopefully, though, he'd think he was being approached by a flotilla of lantern-bearing skiffs, and ready himself for an attack. He wouldn't realize that what was coming towards him were a hundred fuses, all burning down towards paper bases, that would soon meet the oil slick that now encircled his ships. He wouldn't realize, and even once he *did* he wouldn't be able to move, and then it would be too late.

The swarm of small lights progressed into the darkness as the tide sucked them out of the shallows and into the deeper water where Chen's fleet lay. Listening carefully, they heard the distant shouts of Chen's lookouts as they spotted the lanterns. The wicks would have burned low by now; it would only be a matter of time before the oil went up. Zhu was so intensely focused on that tiny line of lights that her vision started wavering.

"What's happening?" Xu Da murmured.

It wasn't her vision wavering, Zhu realized with a nasty lurch. The *lights* were wavering. The lanterns were going out. But why? There was a moistness in the air that heralded a storm, but it wasn't raining yet. There was no wind to put out the flames. In her monastery years Zhu had seen countless floating lotus lanterns catch fire on the water when their candles burned low. Fire on paper was a simple equation; burning paper on oil even more so. Unless—

"We didn't make the lanterns from ordinary paper," Zhu said, her heart sinking. "We made them from sail-paper. Fang Guozhen must have had it treated against fire."

Xu Da cursed as the last lights dimmed in the distance. A sigh blew through the ship, like the exhalation of an extinguished candle. "So we're done."

"No," Zhu said instinctively, and even as she said it she had already solved the problem. "We need to get a skiff out there so someone can light it manually with a tinder bucket and torch. But we have to do it quickly. Chen is already figuring out that those lights weren't an attack. As soon as he fishes one of those lanterns out of the water he'll know what we were trying to do, and he'll move his fleet out of the oil slick."

"The person in the skiff will have to be *in* the oil slick if he's to light it," Xu Da said. "But the skiffs are even more flammable than those ships. He'll go up like a candle."

"The skiff will go up, but he doesn't have to. Not if he dives under the burning layer and swims out past the edge of the slick, where he'll be safe. Then he can swim back here like those others did. There must be a man around who was raised in a fishing family or something, who can swim. Find him and get him out there, *now*. But if you can't find a swimmer—"

They would have to force someone to go on a suicide mission, Zhu thought grimly.

"Don't worry! I know most of us Nanren grew up landlocked, but there were plenty of lakes and fishing villages. It can't be only the barbarians who can swim." Xu Da squeezed her shoulder and hurried amidships. "Leave it with me."

To Zhu's relief, Xu Da apparently had no trouble finding someone: in barely half the time it would have taken to boil a pot of tea, a skiff was being lowered from the midsection of the ship. Even when it was only a few zhang away Zhu could barely make it out against the dark water, and she couldn't see anything at all of the man crouched within it as he poled towards Chen's fleet. In another moment the skiff's profile had merged with the darkness entirely. She could only hold her breath in hope and trace along its heading. She could feel everyone around her doing the same, their eyes straining in the darkness.

Then, out where the horizon would have been had it not been blocked by the pitch-blackness of Chen's massive fleet: the arcing flash of a thrown torch.

Soundlessly, not yellow but blue fire sprang from the surface of the lake. It ran darkly across the surface and found the ships and surrounded them. For a moment the fire was so dark and transparent that it didn't seem dangerous at all. And then, gradually, it brightened. It became red, then orange, then yellow, as it climbed the hulls of Chen's ships and started feeding from them. It found its way into the portholes and onto the decks, and from there into the sails. And Chen, unlike that experienced pirate Fang, hadn't treated *his* sail-paper against fire. His mountain range of ships was a mountain range aflame. Ships from the sides of the flotilla were breaking off in a panic, perhaps hoping that if they gained distance from the worst of the conflagration they could at least spare themselves.

Chen's fleet had been cast into chaos. It had worked perfectly. Zhu glanced around for Xu Da, so she could get him to lead the next action. Then, when he didn't seem to be nearby, she squinted fruitlessly at the midsection of the ship where she'd last seen him. She grabbed a man dashing from that direction. "Where's the General?"

But even as she said it, she knew.

Instead of wasting time to find someone who could swim—instead of forcing the nearest man into the skiff at the point of his sword—Xu Da had launched himself into the dark water to light that roaring, geysering inferno that now reached halfway up to Heaven and was reflected in the water as if simultaneously reaching down into Hell.

He couldn't swim, but Zhu felt oddly calm. He was somewhere out there beneath the flame, in the safe and receiving darkness. She knew she'd be able to find him, because out of all the times she'd lost him before: he had always come back to her. He would be fine, and she would have her victory.

The crashing and groaning of Chen's dying ships made a low counterpoint to the roar of the fire that traveled clearly over the water. Zhu shouted over the pandemonium, "Send the message to all ships! Leave the shallow water, and engage!"

Flotsam knocked against the hull of Zhu's flagship as the crew maneuvered it through the field of destruction. Apart from a handful of ships that had limped away, all that was left of Chen's fleet were wrecks and smoldering hulks. Rain pattered on banners and drums, planks and baskets, charred bodies. For as far as the colorless light of Zhu's Mandate penetrated into the darkness, the water was a slickly churning sheet of barely distinguishable shapes, as if it were a frozen surface newly broken by a springtime thaw.

Earlier, they had seen Chen's flagship going down at the center of the conflagration, sandwiched between two other flaming wrecks. It was an unfittingly abstract end for a longstanding enemy like Chen. Zhu wished she could have seen his face as his ship foundered and he grasped that she'd won. He had been a powerful force in her life—though mostly unseen, like fate or gravity—but he'd been swallowed by nature without so much as a last word. Instead of triumph she felt a strange vacancy. She wondered if she would see his ghost floating somewhere over the water, as lonely and hungry as those of his desecrated men.

"Board and search for prisoners," she ordered, as her ship drew alongside one of Chen's wrecks. The rain was coming more heavily now as the storm arrived in earnest. Her flagship's hull thudded against the wreck as the two lashed-together ships rolled under the increasing waves. To the crew that hadn't boarded, she instructed, "Take the skiffs and search for General Xu."

The fact that there was so much debris was reassuring. It wouldn't have mattered that Xu Da couldn't swim after he'd surfaced from his dive beneath the flaming surface. In her mind's eye Zhu saw him clinging to a floating spar; a snapped mast. She could tell from her men's faces that they thought he was dead. But he wasn't, she thought ferociously. He wasn't, because if he was: she would have known.

Her ship emptied. It was normally such a crowded environment that it felt strange to be alone. The rain was an endless silver pounding that gave her the odd sense of achievement that came from being as wet as she could possibly be. She swayed to keep her balance as the deck's rocking intensified. There was never any stillness on ships. It was an environment of constant noise, vibration, and movement that the pirates seemed to read less by eye or ear than by feel. Perhaps Zhu was already beginning to gain that skill, because although she couldn't have said precisely what had alerted her: suddenly she knew something in that creaking, raining, shifting landscape had changed.

She whipped around.

Someone was approaching from the ship's midsection. A monstrous armored figure in a dark-winged helmet, dripping wet as though he'd risen whole out of a flooded underworld.

Because he had, Zhu thought with terrible recognition. He had clawed his way out of a sinking ship—out of the water that had saved him from the annihilation of Zhu's inferno.

For as long as she had known him, Chen had worn a scholar's robe. But he had been a warlord, once. When Zhu was still a child at the monastery, Chen was already an adult, already leading men into battle and burning cities to the ground. Somehow she'd forgotten. Everyone had forgotten. They had been lulled by his ministerial glide around Anfeng, and his monumental stillness. They had failed to recognize how physically powerful he would have to be to move that enormous bulk such that he *did* glide. Chen hadn't put his past behind him. It had always been within him. And now it had resurfaced. This was Chen, the battlefield butcher, shrouded in the faint bloody glow of his Mandate of Heaven.

And over his shoulder—

Chen carried his dripping burden as easily as if it had never been a person at all.

It was the first time Zhu had seen Chen truly furious. Fury made him even more controlled: it burned inside him with the same banked power as the red-coal glow that emanated from him. "It's been a long time, Zhu Chongba."

In Anfeng, Zhu had survived by skating beneath Chen's attention. But now that attention was on her, and there could be no more obfuscation. No more hiding. She was the Radiant King, and now she was facing the person she should have hunted down and killed while she'd had the chance.

Chen let Xu Da's body slap onto the deck like a bag of clay. Something seized awfully in Zhu's chest when she saw how blue and still he was. But then Chen put a huge booted foot on top of him and bore down until he stirred and gave a hoarse scream. And against her will—because the instant Zhu had seen Chen's burden and grasped his intention, she had warned herself not to be moved—something in her screamed too.

"There we go! Good boy," Chen said. "Still alive enough to be useful."

Chen spoke loudly to be heard over the driving rain. "You've caused me enough trouble, Zhu Chongba. But this is where it stops. If you don't want your brother to die."

The ship's lanterns had gone out. They were now lit only by

themselves: Chen's bloody glow that made his face as warmongeringly red as a statue of Guan Yu, and Zhu's own pale radiance that turned the rain silvery and flashing. Her light wasn't strong enough to find any color in Xu Da's face as he moved brokenly on the deck. She forced herself to put her heart aside as she called back to Chen, "What price do you set on my brother's life?"

"Do you think this a wet market, where you can haggle?" Chen asked coldly. "The price is everything you have. That should be sufficient to make up for the losses you've so generously inflicted upon me here, and to assure my future victory against Madam Zhang."

"To think Madam Zhang thought she could purchase your loyalty with her patronage!" Even as she spoke, Zhu was urgently scanning their surroundings for anything she could turn to her advantage. "You were nothing; would have remained nothing, had she not bought this fleet for you." She had her saber, though what good would that short blade be against someone as massive as Chen? But if she didn't fight, and ran—then what of Xu Da? The muzzy, frantic feeling that had swallowed her insides was wholly new. Was this what General Zhang had felt, when she'd taken his son and treated him callously? She could barely think through the internal churning. *Every problem has a solution.* But whatever that solution was, she couldn't find it. "Is there no one you wouldn't betray, Chen Youliang?"

Chen gave a knowing, humorless smile. "Madam Zhang, my patron? Do you think she's the only wealthy person who had their eye on you? That's the problem with giving yourself grandiose titles. There are more people who've heard of the Radiant King and his audacious desires than those you've heard of. My patron was happy to fund me to put an end to your run for greatness." The pounding rain kicked up a white spray from the deck as Chen said, "I was more than happy to accept."

But if his patron wasn't Madam Zhang—

Before Zhu could finish the thought, Chen pulled Xu Da to his knees by his bedraggled topknot. Xu Da had always been the most robust man Zhu knew. Now her heart knotted in desperation to see him hanging from Chen's grip in twitching helplessness. "Your run is over, Zhu Chongba. Surrender."

She *couldn't think.* In the pitching, waterlogged darkness, she felt as if she'd been plunged into a nightmare world—an older world from a time before civilization, full of char and bodies, that perpetuated itself through violence and brutality without any possibility of change. Or perhaps it wasn't the past, but the future.

"Such hesitation! Do you need me to make it clearer?" Chen released Xu Da's topknot and drew a knife. As he swayed there on his knees, Chen took his limp hand and sliced. Xu Da didn't scream, as though even that effort was already too much for him, but his desperate groan pierced Zhu through. The finger fell, a stab of white on the dark planks. It was cleaned instantly by the rain. "How many of his fingers will you give before you surrender? I know you've made do with five, but there must be some minimum number for a comfortable life.

"Decide," Chen said, and his knife flashed again in punctuation.

The sight of Xu Da's suffering sent waves of misery through Zhu. She could stop his suffering, if she surrendered. But if she surrendered, could she still win?

She thought of Ouyang, running on bloodied feet towards the army she had stolen from him. He had exceeded all ordinary human thresholds of pain and endurance, but in the end: even he had collapsed. There was the kind of impossible that could be overcome with determination. And then there was the truly impossible. Zhu knew which kind of impossible she'd be facing if she surrendered to Chen. If Xu Da had meant nothing to her, she wouldn't have thought twice about what to do.

Zhu had always known that she could lose Xu Da. Every time he'd led her forces out to battle, she'd faced the possibility. She'd thought of it as a consciously made choice. She'd thought of herself as ready. It was only now, faced with the reality of it, that she realized she'd never truly believed it could happen.

Someone she loved was being undone, and the sight of it was undoing her. He was slipping away, being eaten by the pain, and she couldn't bear it. She was holding him in one hand, and her fate in the other, and even as they pulled in different directions—even as they pulled her in half—she couldn't let either of them go. She heard herself make a noise almost as awful as Xu Da's own.

"Such an interesting experiment! Monk versus monk. Who's going to break first?" As much as Chen wanted her surrender, his anger relished the opportunity for cruelty. "Perhaps we'll run out of fingers before then, but there's always other parts to go on with. I know you can be ruthless, Zhu Chongba. We all know what you did to our Prime Minister, not to mention to that poor little boy. But this feels different, doesn't it? Look at your brother's face. His eyes are begging you to save him, aren't they? Are you really going to—"

The deck pitched violently. Zhu was thrown to her knees. Even Chen staggered. And the moment his grip slackened, Zhu saw Xu Da gather himself.

Splinter was the wrong word for the debris that littered the deck of her flagship. If those jagged wooden shards were splinters, they were the property of giants: arm's length or more, ripped from the hardwood decks by Chen's harpoons. Xu Da's eyes found Zhu. Under his plastered hair, they were lucid. She couldn't imagine the effort it must have taken to summon himself back through the pain.

He didn't hesitate. He knew he had only a moment. With his good hand he found a splinter, and Zhu's eyes were caught by the white-knuckled determination of his grip. He had to use all his force to overcome his body's instincts to keep on living, the same way he'd once forced himself to breathe water for her, as he plunged the splinter into his chest.

He was still looking at her. But when he opened his mouth as if to call her, the rain sluicing from his chin was suddenly azalea red, camellia red; the clearest, brightest red Zhu had ever seen.

Something was happening in her throat, as if the redness were choking her too. Xu Da's hand dropped from the splinter. It was sticking out of his chest, a gross violation, and Zhu was overcome by the insensate urge to rip it out and hurl it into the sea. She couldn't bear it: this thing that was killing him, tearing his beloved body apart, pulling his life out of him like a red thread of fate being wound back onto its spindle.

Xu Da's head slumped, and he fell. But even as he landed and lay motionless, Zhu knew he wasn't dead. She *knew*. She'd been run through before, and Xu Da had saved her, so she'd be able to save him in turn. That was how it worked. She was already stumbling across the deck towards him when Chen roared in fury, wrestled his sword from its sheath, and charged her.

Chen was a mountain coming to crush an ant. Zhu wouldn't last longer than the clap of two hands if he caught her. But now that he didn't have Xu Da, she was free to do what she hadn't before: run.

The layout of the ship had become familiar in the days since they'd left Yingtian, but now the shattered deck, with its tangled lines and downed sails, was freshly alien. Zhu dived into the chaos. The terrible image of the splinter in Xu Da's chest wouldn't leave her. Whichever way she'd find to beat Chen, she had to find it quickly. As she ran, she could feel Xu Da's tortured gasps in her own body. She had so little time. But however little it was, it would be enough. It had to be.

She was halfway down the deck, Chen on her heels, when one of the waves smashing over the rail caught them both and tossed them in opposite directions. It was the opportunity Zhu needed. Instead of leaping to her feet to be seen, she stayed low, slithering through the debris. A dim expanse of sails beat deafeningly overhead. The noise and visual clutter would make it hard for Chen to find her, but the key problem remained: Zhu could run, but she couldn't escape. Where was there to go on a ship? Zhu knew it, and Chen knew it.

"Zhu Chongba!" Chen shouted over the din. From her temporary hiding position behind a capstan, she could see him by the rail. His crimson glow picked out his edges while leaving the mass of him as featureless darkness. His winged helmet turned as he hunted for her. "Why are you running? I never wanted to destroy you. It was my patron who set us against each other. But there's no reason for it to stay that way. Instead of opposing me, come across to my side! If we join hands, as strong as we both are: Do you think there's anybody who could stand against us?"

Zhu recognized the old familiar pull of Chen's charisma. He hadn't been the leader of their Red Turban rebellion, and yet it had always seemed to revolve around him. He was someone who occupied his place in the world with such monumental solidity that it was everyone else who was forced to make way. At the beginning, it was what she'd admired about him.

"Your brother sacrificed himself for you, but he didn't have to, did he? You would have let him die. I know you! When you showed that harmless monk face to the world, wasn't I the one who saw your potential? I could see your willingness to do anything for what you wanted. Like recognizes like, and we're alike, you and I. *We're* the ones who should be family. Join me, Zhu Chongba! Let me be the family not of your blood, but of your nature. Raise me to the throne, and I'll name you my son and heir. My world will be your world. And when I go, I'll pass it to you. That's what you want, isn't it? Join me, and you can have it."

For an awful moment, it made sense. Zhu had always recognized in Chen some possible future of herself: someone of such ruthless cruelty that they were willing to do anything, sacrifice anyone, for their desire that was as large as the world.

Chen was closer, now. Zhu could see his boots advancing in her direction. The force of the rain against the deck sent up a knee-height spray, and where he stepped the spray gained a ruby glow, as if he were cloaked in the mist of a thousand disintegrated bodies.

"Come out, Zhu Chongba. I'm the one who's like you. I'm your fate. I'm your future. Stand up and accept me!"

And yet—Zhu's desire wasn't Chen's desire. He thought he understood her, but he didn't. How could he, when he had no idea who she was? All he could understand of her desire was what it looked like from the outside: a man's desire. He was offering her the same as what he wanted for himself, which was all he could imagine any man wanting: a world handed down, readymade for his satisfaction, from others who were just like him.

But even if Zhu had trusted Chen to keep his promises: that world wasn't what she wanted.

A clutch of loose metal tubes bashed her feet with each roll of the deck. Jiao's fire tubes. Zhu grabbed one on its down-roll. The ship's cacophony drowned out the sound of her rasping breath. She could feel herself breathing, but she was simultaneously suffocating: suffocating along with Xu Da, who lay dying where they'd abandoned him.

Zhu hadn't come to a decision by the time Xu Da had taken matters into his own hands. The awful truth was that she didn't know what she would have decided.

But whatever that decision would have been, Chen couldn't claim to know, *because she wasn't like him.*

She leveled the tube in the crook of her right arm. It had already been fired, so it wasn't even a weapon. It was just an empty tube. She placed her left hand over the nearer open end.

The only thing faster than thought was lightning. The instant Zhu's desire formed, her light had already shot through the tube and painted a bright circle on a tangle of sail behind Chen. As Chen whipped around, Zhu rose from her crouch and with all her strength brought the iron tube against his head.

Even over the rain she heard the clang. The impact was as hard as if she'd sunk an axe into wood. Chen reeled. If he hadn't had the helmet, it would have crushed his skull. But Zhu had already known one hit wouldn't be enough. Without pausing she flung the tube aside and drew her saber, and swung at the bared strip of his neck between helmet and metal collar—

—just as Chen whirled with his armored forearm raised to catch her blade, his teeth bared in a grimace of fury and pain. He batted the sword aside as if Zhu's entire weight behind it had been no more than a mosquito's, shouldered into the space created by her outflung arm, and backhanded her.

It might as well have been a cannonball. Zhu's perspective shifted without notice. She was on her back, gasping. Something was ringing inside her: not so much pain as an assault of sensation too intense for her body to process. Chen loomed over her. She couldn't roll away as he stamped on her left hand where it grasped her saber. This time her body *did* recognize pain. Zhu screamed as her hand crunched. Chen kicked the saber away. Then, with the same vicious, economical motion, he kicked her.

Zhu had seen her father kicked to death, and with horror she realized she was going to go the same way. Her ribs were breaking. In another moment it would be her organs being split and crushed. She was being eaten by the pain, spinning away into that nothingness that Ouyang had always sought, and there was nothing she could do.

Abruptly, there was no longer a solid surface beneath her. With mindless reflex, Zhu lashed out with her hook as she fell. The tip sank into the deck and stopped her from plunging down its sharply tilted surface. As she hung there, the wind stretched and twisted a woman's distant cries of pain. It took her a long time to realize they were her own.

Chen had fallen along with the deck. When it heaved back the other way, he came sliding back in a gush of water. He landed a short distance from her and struggled to his feet. But he was slower now; his bulk ponderous rather than nimble.

Zhu thrust herself to her knees, then her feet. Her body shook so uncontrollably that she could barely stay vertical. She wrapped her left arm with its crushed hand around her broken ribs and staggered away as Chen came in pursuit. They lurched and fell as the deck tipped them one way and then the other, like two ships tacking upwind.

A patch of deck near the foremast was a lighter shade than the rest of the dark planking. Zhu's hazy first thought was that it was a downed sail, until she remembered the sail-paper they'd tacked down over the hole in the deck. Although the sail seemed to be on a solid surface, underneath it was a hastily woven lattice of lightweight bamboo battens. The lattice was probably strong enough to hold her weight, Zhu thought fuzzily. If she could draw Chen onto it after her—

She staggered onto the sail-covered lattice. It shivered under her feet, but held. She didn't dare look behind. She could feel Chen's approaching presence, as if his Mandate were an ominous thrum beneath the rain. The thrum grew stronger and stronger, until Zhu could barely believe he wasn't close enough to grab her.

The next moment the lattice bucked so wildly that Zhu was flung off her feet. Chen's startled shout rang in her ears. Her body was screaming. But she didn't have time to waste on pain. She flung herself, half crawling, to where Chen was struggling to extricate his legs from a thicket of splintered bamboo and torn paper, and with the last of her strength sank her hook into the unarmored crease at his waist.

Chen roared as Zhu dragged the point of the hook through him. She could *feel* his flesh giving; it was the drag of a blunt knife through meat—

The hook jolted to a stop as Chen clamped his hand around it. Zhu yanked. The hook didn't move. Chen's grip was iron. She gathered herself and yanked again, and this time the desperate force of it separated her stump from the socket of the hook and sent her hurtling onto the solid deck on the other side of the lattice. She landed in a crumpled, panting heap. All she could hope was that she'd wounded Chen enough to stop him. Blood was pouring out of his side. As she watched, Chen pulled the hook out and cast it aside with a growl. Through the rent fabric, the edges of his wound gaped yellow. But there were no spilling coils of intestine. With exhausted horror, Zhu realized she hadn't managed to get deep enough. Chen, even more so than Fang Guozhen, had the fat that served men so well in battle by making them heavy, and powerful—and, crucially in this particular moment: protected.

Zhu's failed gambit had cost her the last of her energy. She was too spent to stand, let alone run. She couldn't even crawl properly, with her one crushed hand and one useless stump. All she could do was pull herself slowly along the deck by her elbows, gasping. She could feel from the vibrations through the deck that Chen had managed to haul himself out of the hole. And then he was on her.

As easily as a tiger scooping a fish from a river, Chen caught Zhu by the ankle and flipped her over. When he straddled her chest, her air came out in a whoosh. His weight was flailing her ribs; she was being crushed to death. There was no real need for him to take her by the throat, but he did. She had the dim memory of feeling stymied by the idea of his abstract death. She'd wanted the satisfaction of seeing his last moments. Now it seemed he didn't just want to see her own last moments; he wanted to feel them. Inside his winged helmet, his face was that of a demon in Hell: smiling with the bloody, vicious entitlement of someone who'd always known he would win. "Good riddance, Zhu Chongba."

Zhu choked and gasped. Her crushed left hand pattered against the hard shell of his armor. The stump of her abbreviated right arm, waving helplessly under his face, couldn't even do that much. What happened next wasn't intentional. It wasn't even fully conscious. But as if the desperation that preceded death had made her body call upon every memory of itself, her right hand burst forth. Her hand, made of light. Zhu's Mandate of Heaven had always been a faint white flame that was barely visible during the day. But now the phantom hand she reached to Chen's face was *bright.* Within an instant its brightness had already grown tenfold. At a hundredfold, it was incandescent. It was the sun itself.

Chen screamed and reared away, clutching his face. His blistered skin was already sloughing away from the fascia beneath. The gaping blackness where his eyes had been made Zhu think of how, long ago, Chen had removed a man's tongue before he'd made her watch him die.

She croaked at him, *"Zhu Chongba isn't my name."*

Chen wasn't her fate. He wasn't her future. She was Zhu Yuanzhang, and it was the name she'd chosen for herself that signified her future: the end of the Yuan, and her creation of a world made in *her* image, rather than anything handed down from before.

In the next instant the horizontal deck had become a sheer cliff, and they were tumbling down it. Zhu flung out both arms and managed to arrest her fall by catching her elbows over a protruding spar. Chen's blindly flailing hands found only empty air. Zhu looked down, tracking his huge armored form as it smashed down through spars and loose rigging. He landed heavily far below, checked by the side rail.

Then the ship tipped a fraction further. Chen went over the side rail with the cartwheeling force of being thrown from a horse. Zhu saw him hit the black water. And then he was gone.

Zhu lurched and slipped down the deck towards where she'd left Xu Da. She was a shadow puppet in which the sticks had been broken: the parts of her body either too rigid or flapping uncontrollably. While she'd been fighting Chen, every other thing in the world had fallen away apart from the clean, clear urgency of survival. But now her returned desperation felt as if one of Jiao's blood clocks had been installed inside her. Every moment that passed was a drop of blood into a bowl of unknown size. But even as the blood rose, a deeper part of her refused the dread that tried to rise with it. Xu Da would be fine. How could he not be, when he had survived bandits, and the battlefield, and come back three times from drowning for her? Finally she saw his crumpled, sodden shape, and threw herself to him.

When she saw that he was alive, she could believe it was her will that had made it so. His face was paler than a boiled chicken, but she knew that was just the way her light made everything look. The splinter in his chest was more horrific than she remembered, but at least the saturation of his gown around it was from water rather than blood. She must have looked worse herself after being impaled by Ouyang. Half the blood in her body had run out of that wound, and she'd survived.

"Why," she rasped at him. "Why did you go in the first place, you brainless melon? Anyone could have gone! It didn't have to be you."

Her left hand that Chen had crushed was already grossly swollen and all but useless, so she stroked his face with her phantom hand instead. It was a touch that wasn't a touch, but what did that matter when her will was strong enough to turn the universe to her desires? It was her will that had defeated Chen; it was her will that had kept Xu Da alive until she could reach his side; it was her will that would now bring death itself into abeyance, because that was what she wanted.

Perhaps he could feel her touch after all, because he roused and whispered, "You're back. Knew you would—win."

"I did win," she told him fiercely, trying not to notice the blood that was instantly washed away by the rain the moment it rose in his mouth. "It's over. Chen Youliang is dead. There are physicians on the other ships, so just rest until I can get them here! We'll get you fixed up in no time."

She had the sense of him laughing, even though there was nothing that would have indicated it from his awful rictus expression. "Pity that bastard Jiao Yu isn't here." He spoke slowly, between gasps, and she had to almost touch her ear to his cheek to make out the words. But even from that close, she couldn't feel any warmth radiating from his body. "Even he couldn't have fixed this one."

"What nonsense!" Zhu had no idea why her voice sounded as strange as it did. There was no reason to worry, because this wasn't their ending. "Don't be dramatic. I'm sure it feels that way, but you're not going to die. How could that happen? Those bad girls in Yingtian are waiting for you. You have to marry at least one of them, and have a dozen children, and give a couple of them to me. Who else is going to give me an heir?"

"I went on the skiff," he whispered, "because I knew it was better that I go, rather than someone with a whole life ahead of them."

For a moment she couldn't grasp what he was saying, because there was no sense in it.

"I was—already—" He labored for a moment, then gasped, "Dying. I knew I was, ever since Fortress Island. Since the first time the eunuch brought me back."

There was a terrible stillness inside Zhu, as if her heart had forgotten how to beat. *Fortress Island.* But if he'd been dying since then—

She'd been so pleased with her success on Fortress Island. She'd congratulated herself for having paid so little for it: just two lives that she didn't care about. She'd even told herself that she'd have been happy to pay more. In a rush she remembered all those times Xu Da had coughed blood, and reassured her, and pretended he was fine, so she would never have to know how much more she'd paid.

If he'd been dying ever since Fortress Island, then none of this was because of Chen.

She thought with cold, crystalline horror: *It was me.*

She managed to get her crushed hand underneath him, so she could cradle his head on her wrist. With her phantom hand she touched his cold white cheeks, and the wrinkles of agony under his eyes and across his brow, as she told him with a ferocity that seemed to warp the world around the pure strength of her will, "I forbid you to die. *I won't allow it.*"

This time he managed an actual smile, and it was the worst thing Zhu had ever seen. "Sometimes even an emperor's commands can't be obeyed. What's all this fuss, little brother? This is my fate. I knew from the beginning that I was going to give my life for you—for the one who defied fate. The one who can change the world. I thought you always knew that." He gasped, and she saw his eyes become glassy with an inwards-focused terror. "I just—wish—it didn't hurt quite so—" His strength seemed to fail him, and he fell into labored panting, as if it were both the hardest and only thing he could do.

"No," Zhu cried. The new vagueness in him was terrifying. It was as if his spirit, the part of him that bore the connection to her, was already leaving. She had the desperate urge to reach inside him—to grab his spirit, and force it to stay where it belonged. For a wild moment, she believed she could do it. If she could see spirits, why couldn't she hold one? Perhaps this was a power reserved for her alone, out of everyone who had ever lived: to defy Heaven and prevent death itself, with the sheer power of her will.

Something terrible was shaking her apart. She pressed her forehead to Xu Da's, as if by that pressure she could keep him there. Even from the beginning, when she hadn't yet been herself, he'd been beside her. She couldn't imagine a world without him. To witness him being undone beneath her touch was like feeling the shore eaten away beneath her feet by a tide that was stronger and greater than herself. Even as she screamed and struggled against it, she knew: the force that was wrenching him away from her was the cold implacability of fate. But Zhu had defied fate before. "Heaven can't take you from me. I refuse. *I refuse.*"

It had always been so easy to separate herself from the misery of others. Zhu had seen Chen Youliang flay a man alive, and sent her own men to die screaming on the battlefield. Even a child's innocence hadn't stopped her from ending him when he got in her way. Their pain had always been something she *watched.* She had never believed that to witness someone else's pain might be more unbearable than anything produced within her own body. But what she was feeling now was the pain of the person who had been beside her the longest; who had accepted and protected her from the beginning. It was the pain of someone she loved. It was drilling into her indefensible heart, destroying her even as it was destroying him. But if she held Xu Da's pain in her own body—if she felt it as he did—didn't that mean they were both fighting against it? Wasn't he sharing in her strength of will to live, when she was strong enough for two people; strong enough for a thousand; strong enough to defy the world?

She cradled him against the rocking of the ship as wave after wave crashed over them. Her tiny bubble of light in the darkness was penetrated from above by the endless falling sheets of water, and all she could do was shield him from it with her own shuddering, hunched body. She didn't know when it finally happened—when her will simply wasn't enough. His eyes were still open, but now when the blood that welled in his mouth was washed away, it didn't rise again. The body she held was no longer one that saw, or labored for breath, or had a spirit within it.

This was what she had given for what she wanted. Zhu knew if she looked up, Xu Da would be there: standing apart from her on the other side of a curtain of rain. In a voice so hoarsened that it was unrecognizable even to herself, she promised him, *"I'll make it worth it."*

18

OUTSIDE DADU

Ouyang's army was camped on the edge of the bald brown winter farmlands that fringed the wide corona of the city. It was the furthest north Ouyang had ever been. Dadu was drier than he'd imagined: the snow was no deeper than the ankle. Ideal for waging war. It was a thought that came without inflection: there was neither pleasure nor anticipation in it, only observation. Behind the front line of the defending central army were Dadu's suburbs with their many mansions and pleasure houses. The outer city wall placed all of those within its massive shadow. Within that wall lay the wall of the Imperial City, and within *that* wall, the wall of the palace itself. That was all that stood between Ouyang and his fate: an army and three walls. *Just a little longer.*

The wind gusting in the rolled-up flap of his ger was ferocious. At another point in his life, he would have minded the cold. Perhaps complained about it. But that all seemed distant. Was his body even here? He was in a world of his own, and it was a world of pain that permitted nothing else to enter. There was no longer any management possible. There was no separation between himself and memory; between himself and the pain. The worst of the pain came upon him in waves. His ascent to each crest was so excruciating that he couldn't imagine how he could possibly continue, but the numb respite of the trough afterwards was somehow even worse: a false extinguishment, when all he craved was the real thing.

His army was ragged and exhausted after the long fast march from Yingtian. Something—Ouyang wasn't even sure what, and he no longer cared to know—had happened to Chu in Qingyuan, but at least he still had square-headed, boringly dependable Geng to keep order. Ouyang had gained the distinct impression that his army hadn't been happy to see him return alone from Qingyuan, and even less happy at the news they'd be marching alone to Dadu, but he didn't care about the happiness of conscripts. His commanders obeyed Geng, and Geng obeyed him. The conscripts were whipped and forced to obey: a single organism driven by Ouyang's need.

And they were succeeding. His army had smashed through every layer of Dadu's central army that stood between them and the capital. Though they'd taken substantial losses, it hadn't even been as many as Ouyang had anticipated. He'd been surprised by the shambolic quality of the central army's defense, which seemed out of keeping with what he knew of the Grand Councilor's leadership. It was almost as if there *wasn't* a leader.

Ouyang distantly remembered Geng conjecturing about the Grand Councilor falling afoul of court politics. Perhaps that wild guess had been right, after all. But whatever the truth of the situation: what mattered was that he hadn't needed Zhu for this. He never had. He was succeeding, and now he was within arm's reach of his goal. Soon he would have his revenge upon the one who had written his and Esen's fates into the pattern of the world and stolen their choices in how they lived and died. And with the murder of the Great Khan, that one final act of Ouyang's life, every awful thing he had done—everything he had suffered, and all his pain—would be made worth it.

"You haven't had those looked at yet? I think you need a stitch or two." It was Geng, stepping blandly over the ger's threshold-board.

Ouyang followed Geng's glance down to his hands, and was surprised to see a number of cuts weeping thin striations of blood. He couldn't think of when during the last skirmish they might have happened. His hands—those small, fine-boned, hated hands—seemed even more foreign to his self than usual. He couldn't feel any pain in them at all. Were there other such cuts elsewhere on his body that he hadn't noticed and couldn't feel? He wondered if he were disintegrating in reality as well as within that private burning world. "It's nothing."

It didn't matter if his body was disintegrating, as long as it held together long enough to do what he needed to do. But its new painlessness made him long for a return of physical sensation, so that at least he might have an alternative to his emotional agony. He had the violent, almost lustful mental image of carving off his own flesh for the relief of it. But even as the image came to him, he knew it was past the time for relief. Now there was only the end.

"We'll probably only have a few more days of this, before they sound the retreat and withdraw back into Dadu," Geng said consideringly. "Then we'll have to start the siege. Given our reduced manpower, we may not be able to mount a strong enough assault to breach the walls. It could be a long one."

Ouyang had absolutely no desire for a siege, let alone a long one. Though he'd known there was a good likelihood of needing one, he could hardly bear the thought of all that waiting.

As if Geng had felt his aversion, he offered, "We might not have to siege. What if we pre-positioned a team inside to open the gates for us?"

While Ouyang couldn't imagine anything better than avoiding a siege—"The gate guards will be on high alert for exactly that. There's no way we'd be able to get a team in. It'd be a wasted effort."

"Not necessarily. I have a contact in Dadu. If I reward him handsomely enough, perhaps he could facilitate the passage of a team through the wall. It would have to be a small team, though. A handful of men. I'm not sure if it would be enough. But if you want to try—we'd have to do it soon. While Dadu is still open to the outside."

It struck Ouyang as strange that Geng, who was from Henan, would know anyone in Dadu. But at the same time, it seemed fitting: it was simply the universe bending him towards his success. He had a rising feeling of inevitability that brought no pleasure, only a sense of an end.

"Get in touch with your contact," he said. "Gather a team. We'll do it without delay."

☀

Ouyang and Geng approached the central gate of Dadu's south outer wall on foot. They had a pack donkey, whose saddlebags carried their swords and armor, and a string of goats that gave them a legitimate reason for entry. A city that was fighting off an invading army still needed to eat, after all. Their eight-man team had been divided into pairs. Using Geng's contact's gate passes that designated them as authorized merchants, each pair would enter Dadu via a separate gate—so that if one pair were detained, at least the rest could continue—then reconvene as a group on the inside.

The gate glowed in the flickering light of torches. The falling dusk turned the wall itself into a black silhouette so vast it swallowed the sky. The wall was sheer-sided rammed earth, solid as a mountain. It was the largest city wall Ouyang had ever seen, and seeing it up close made him freshly aware of how opportune Geng's intervention had been. During the founding of the Great Yuan, a Mongol army had laid siege to one particular Nanren city for three years before managing to take it. What if it had taken three years to starve Dadu into surrender? Ouyang could have done it, if that was what it took, but he was grimly sure he would have lost his mind in the process.

They'd left their entry for late in the day on the basis that tired guards would be more willing to wave them through without scrutiny. But now as Geng and Ouyang moved towards the head of the queue of merchants, couriers, and Yuan soldiers awaiting entry, Ouyang was unpleasantly surprised to see the gate guard rigorously checking passes against a list: presumably a manifest of passes. He and Geng wouldn't be able to get through with their stolen pass—and yet to withdraw now, within eyesight of the guards, would also be suspicious. With a dislocated feeling of dread, Ouyang sized up the dozen heavily armed guards in the vicinity. If he snatched his sword out of the saddlebag, could he cut down enough of them, fast enough, to dash into the city and disappear? He'd have no team, no equipment, and no armor. It would be just himself and his sword. But perhaps that was enough. All he'd have to do was gain access to the Great Khan, just once, for it to be enough.

At the front of the queue the guard took the pass Geng offered. He ran down the list, then looked sharply back up at Geng.

Ouyang drifted towards the donkey. The precise order of the guards he would kill floated through his mind like a dream he'd already lived.

"Don't you know the rules?" the guard asked, irritated. But to Ouyang's surprise, instead of denouncing their pass as fake or stolen, he handed it back. "I know some of the other gates aren't so meticulous. But the rules are clear: every merchant needs a pass of his own. Two people, two passes."

"Two—oh. But that one's not a merchant." Ouyang froze with his hand on the flap of the saddlebag as Geng lowered his voice and murmured, "That's a slave boy who helps me with the animals. I don't need a separate pass for him, do I? You can see how young he is. He'll stay by my side, inside the city."

The guard squinted at Ouyang in the dusk. Once upon a time a look like that would have roused Ouyang's fury. Now he just knew, with a dull uncaringness, exactly what the gate guard saw. "Long lonely roads need company, eh?"

Somehow, despite his terminal blandness, Geng mustered a smirk. "As obliging as he is pretty."

The gate guard waved them through with a matching smirk. Ouyang couldn't even find it in himself to be that relieved as they entered the city. It was convenient that the pass had been authentic—Geng's cousin, or whoever his contact was, was presumably an official of some kind. But even if they'd been stopped for having a stolen pass—well, it would have been too bad for Geng when Ouyang killed the guards and went in alone. But at least as far as his own fate was concerned, it would have worked out. How could it not?

He and Geng hurried through the gridded streets to the house in the city's western quarter that Geng's contact had nominated as a place for the team to gather until it was time to act. As Ouyang entered the house, something struck a familiar chord in his brain. It was a strange feeling: as if someone he knew had just stepped out of the room. He wasn't sure what caused the feeling. A lingering whiff of perfume, perhaps. But it must have been a coincidence, because he didn't have any connections in Dadu. And when he took another breath, whatever it was had already gone.

By nightfall, the rest of the team had gathered in the house and donned their armor. Ouyang was the only one whose armor wasn't the standard Yuan equipment that every other soldier in Dadu was wearing. But even had there been a set of plain armor in camp that fitted him, he would have refused. His unique mirror plate might be risky to wear in the street, especially when paired with his distinctive physical attributes, but at the end when it mattered: he wanted to be recognized.

On the street outside the house, they divided: the men tasked with the sabotage slipped away towards the nearby western gate, while Ouyang, Geng, and their team headed for the Imperial City.

Geng had been briefed well by his contact. They followed him along an ice-skinned canal that passed through several residential wards before it entered a forested swath of the city. It was so unnervingly dark in the forest that Ouyang had to glance up through the larches to check that the stars were still there. When he did, he realized the source of the darkness: the shadow of another immense wall. Geng led them into the canal itself—the fast-flowing water beneath the surface ice reached everyone else's thighs, but Ouyang's waist—and they waded towards the wall until they reached a tunnel mouth. Geng said in a low voice, "There's usually a grill here to prevent access, but my contact was able to get it removed. This tunnel will take us through into the Imperial City. After that, there'll only be one wall to go."

A pungent rooty aroma surrounded them as they ducked inside. It took Ouyang a moment to remember where he'd smelled it before: the tunnels beneath Pingjiang. His partnership with the person who'd called herself Zhu Yuanzhang already seemed like a series of events from a dream, featuring a person who'd never existed. He dimly recalled the stinging devastation of having been *deceived* when he had dared hope for a different ending. But now it no longer stung, or felt like anything at all. Whoever Zhu was, she was irrelevant to Ouyang's future.

The tunnel brought them into an ice-covered lake. Unlike

the canal, this ice was thick enough to stand upon. They quickly made their way across the frozen black surface and over an equally frozen moat, and scrambled up the slope at the base of the wall of the Palace City.

Wet and shivering, they huddled in a circle to preserve their body warmth as they waited. The dry Dadu air was so still that their collective exhalations made a mist that settled over their heads and caught the starlight. The outer city's Bell Tower sounded one night watch, and then another. Then, finally, what they'd been waiting for came: not bells, but emergency drums. Fire flower signals bloomed high above the western wall. A streamlike murmur in the outer city strengthened into a waterfall of panicked noise as the population awoke and realized what had happened: the gate had been breached.

A similar clamor was erupting inside the Palace City. As more and more torches were lit within its walls, the Palace City became a glowing island of such brightness that the stars above it disappeared under a wash of false dawn. At length its main gate burst open and a horseborne mass stormed out. The Great Khan's private troops, rushing to help stem the tide of Ouyang's army as they surged into Dadu.

"Now!" Ouyang commanded, as soon as the mass was out of sight, and the team threw their grappling hooks over the wall. After the darkness of the Imperial City, the dazzle of the Palace City almost blinded him as they dropped onto the cold white sand. Two remaining palace guards saw them in the long corridor and shouted alarm. But Ouyang was already cutting them down. His team pounded after him as he ran down one corridor, then another, always turning towards the heart of the city—towards increasing brightness—until he broke through a looming archway and into a broad plaza. An illuminated hall soared into the night. Ouyang had known, intellectually, of the magnificence that lay in the heart of the Great Yuan, but he could still barely wrap his mind around how big it was; how glittering with jewels, even in the nighttime.

In the plaza it was no longer pairs of palace guards they faced, but crowds of them. Ouyang plowed into them. He had the feeling of wading through a mass of flesh the same way he'd waded through the crackling ice of the canal. His sword found bodies to the left and to the right in a constant rhythm as they advanced, step by step.

When he reached the marble stairs leading up to the hall, a new wave of guards came running down towards him. He met them, running up. This was the dance he'd been made for: this press of bodies and blood. He was distantly aware of Geng on his left, holding steady. Something slammed against his leg, and even in his painless state he knew it had found flesh rather than armor, but he didn't care because it didn't slow him down. He could make out the massive open doors of the hall now, torches burning inside, as even more guards hurtled out onto the colonnade. To Ouyang they weren't so much people as fleeting obstructions. How could they have stopped him? That was his fate there, above.

The last guards fell away from his sword as Ouyang stepped inside the hall. The vast space had been filled with such a density of white-flowering cut branches that the Great Khan, in his glowing gown on the throne at the far end of the hall, seemed like a single gold tael shaken out of a purse onto the snow.

If the branches had a fragrance, Ouyang couldn't smell them over the blood.

He said to Geng behind him, "Bar the door."

As Ouyang limped towards the throne he felt an internal collapsing, as of his every deliberately erected partition falling. This was the future, and it was the now; this was the moment that he had come into existence for. Something was deeply wrong with his leg, but that hardly mattered. He was where he needed to be. He remembered how walking down that marble bridge towards Esen had felt like ten thousand years. His passage though the hall was that again. The Great Khan was staring at him in terror. Ouyang thought of what the Great Khan must be seeing: his past and his death in a single unstoppable figure, coming for him with a wake of ghosts.

It was so easy to bat away the Great Khan's insubstantial flailing, his meaningless begging. He was saying something about Ouyang's father, so at least he'd put together who Ouyang was and why he was doing this, but it was as inconsequential as the rest of it.

Ouyang pushed the Great Khan back onto the throne and leaned over him. Nothing could stop him now. He placed the tip of his sword on the Great Khan's chest and very slowly, very carefully, pressed in. The Great Khan wasn't dead yet, but he did abruptly stop talking. Ouyang wasn't interested in the Great Khan's pain, but he wanted to make sure he saw the exact moment the Great Khan died.

It was different, killing someone like this: both intimate and butchery. Flesh and fabric were surprisingly resistant at slow speed, and his sword was dull from hewing through so many bodies. The Great Khan's tortured, terrified eyes met his as the sword sank deeper and deeper. It couldn't hurt that much, Ouyang thought with contempt: this little wound; this short pain. How could it compare to everything he had endured?

He leaned harder; gave his weight to the sword. The Great Khan's hands rose in a flutter to clutch at him, then fell away. Ouyang kept driving, gripped by a sudden mania to expend every scrap of himself in the effort. *To finish it.* He punched through the Great Khan's body until his sword slammed into the back of the throne and he felt it break.

It was over.

But as Ouyang leaned panting atop the Great Khan's body, he realized that the moment had slipped away. There were only two states: alive and dead, and death itself was only a transition. He'd had his revenge, but it hadn't been his to keep.

Ouyang had seen men with their heads half-gone, skulls blown off and brains exposed, and although their bodies still breathed and their hearts still pumped, they no longer had consciousness or pain. That was the state he was in now, he understood. It wasn't a place of triumph, or even relief, but simply the cessation of all thought, hope, feeling. He wasn't disappointed. It was what he'd wanted.

His violent journey to the hall had loosened his braids, which made him think of Esen's ever-fraying hair. The strands fell around his face and made a tent for him and the corpse that was a mirror of all that remained of his future.

He couldn't see the ghosts, but he could imagine them standing around him and the Great Khan in a circle of white faces and black, expectant eyes. He told them, "It's done."

All of it, everything that had happened between his father's death and now: with the Great Khan's death, it had all been made worth it. He wrenched his broken sword out and stepped back from the slumped body. A dark pool was expanding under the throne. It was the Great Khan's blood, but mingled with no small proportion of Ouyang's own. With a sense of welcome, he felt a growing dizziness from wounds he hadn't noticed receiving. In another moment he would leave, and let it all end.

But as he stood there, he felt a sudden wrench of disorientation: as if without being conscious of having done so, he had already stepped outside to meet his death.

No, that wasn't it. He was still in front of the throne, and the breeze that was sweeping over him was because the door that had been barred behind him, when they first entered, was open.

Why had Geng opened the door? The plaza outside had been bright with torchlight, but all Ouyang could see now was shadow, as if an impenetrable blackness had swallowed the world outside. It was a wall of blackness, dense and swirling, that billowed into the hall around a thin black-hatted figure as he stepped inside.

"Congratulations, General," Wang Baoxiang said, in Mongolian. "After all these years, you finally did it. You killed the Great Khan. But, oh! You've lost your looks. I barely recognize you."

Ouyang laughed brokenly in surprise. "Lord Wang. I should have known." He had thought he would never speak Mongolian again, but as it came out in automatic response it felt right: the language of their past, the dead past. "Making the puppets dance, as always. Did I do as you wanted?"

He would have cared, before, to find himself a piece in one of Lord Wang's games. But now there was nothing. He was in a long version of that detached moment before violent death—the animal with its throat ripped out, or the person speared through—when, knowing it was beyond recovery, the body gave solace to the spirit inside it by ceasing to feel pain. Ouyang knew, in the abstract, that there must have been a time—before they castrated him; before his fate was fixed on this path—when his life had been the same as anyone's, with no more pain than the usual mundane discomforts of existence. But it seemed that this, now, was the first time in his life that he was truly without agony. It felt like floating.

"Lord Wang? No, not him," the other said, with familiar viciousness. "Call me by my real title, General, since it was you who was so kind as to bestow it upon me in the first place: Prince of Henan."

As terrible as Ouyang knew he looked, he thought it was Lord Wang—not the Prince of Henan, *never* the Prince of Henan—who had become the more unrecognizable. In Henan, Lord Wang's appearance had never been anything less than polished as he swished around in his ridiculous gowns. Now he wore a drab imperial uniform, and seemed a shell of his previous self. His face, gaunt as a skull, had the bruised look of someone whose only remaining capacity was to feel torment.

Lord Wang said, "You did so well for me, General. When I allied with Madam Zhang to take Dadu, I already knew her forces wouldn't be enough to overcome the central army. I needed someone else to smash the city's defenses. Someone who wouldn't stop to achieve it, even if it required sending his entire army to the slaughter. So I planned ahead to make sure I had that person. I'm sure you never bothered to wonder why your path was so much easier than it should have been. Why you didn't die in prison in Bianliang, or lose against General Zhang in battle, or why Dadu's gates opened so well for you."

"Senior Commander Geng," Ouyang said slowly. "He was your agent. You were sending him those ciphered messages." He realized that Geng had told him, over and over, exactly what he wanted. Geng cared about his farm and family in Henan, and all he wanted to do was return. The person he wanted on the throne was the one he knew could restore stability and functioning to the Great Yuan, the same way he'd managed the entire province of Henan. Geng had told him. But Ouyang hadn't listened.

It all slotted into place, but he no longer cared. Now that it was over, his only yearning was for what would come. With effort he tipped the Great Khan's body onto the floor so the blood-smeared throne stood empty. "Is this what you came for? I don't want it. Take it."

He saw some immense feeling run through Lord Wang, as of mingled pain and anticipation. He didn't move to take the throne. For some reason his attention was fully on Ouyang. Despite his detachment, Ouyang felt a flash of unease.

After a long moment of disturbing scrutiny, Lord Wang said, "Esen hated me. I tried to hate him back, but no matter how I tried I never could. It was like something in my blood, my bones: that he was my brother, and I should love him. Worship him. You have no idea how much it hurts to love someone and receive not even indifference in return, but hate.

"He hurt you too, didn't he? He hurt you, and never saw how it was hurting you. That's the thing about my brother, General: he never understood people. So don't die quite yet. You're the last thing in the world that mattered to him, save the Great Yuan itself, and with your help: I'm going to make him understand what it means to hurt."

Deadened as he was, Ouyang's hackles rose. Lord Wang was going to make Esen understand? Ouyang had never heard such irrational intensity in a person's voice before. *Except in my own.* He said uneasily, "Esen's dead."

"He is, isn't he? You made sure of that, when you killed him. He's dead," Lord Wang said softly, "but not gone. You've known many people with the Mandate, haven't you, General Ouyang? You must know by now what we can see. Ever since he died, Esen's been taking pleasure in torturing me. He's been watching me, following me, ruining my sleep. But if the dead can hurt the living, then the living can hurt the dead." As Lord Wang's voice rose into a shout that was naked in its agony, Ouyang had the sudden feeling of seeing madness. "You're there, aren't you, Esen? Watch well, brother! This is the show I arranged just for you."

Lord Wang was pouring his pain into the world in some desperate effort to make it resonate, but Ouyang wasn't interested. All he wanted was the end. He limped to Lord Wang, feeling a distant curiosity at how awkwardly his body moved, as if finally too many vital pieces had been damaged, and pressed his broken sword into his hand. "If you want to kill me, then do it."

Lord Wang looked down at the sword. His was a soft, thin scholar's hand, and yet the hilt was small in it. Ouyang thought it should have been violating to see him holding that mutilated, broken piece of himself. But what value did that piece have, now that it had performed its function? No more value than the rest of him.

"This is the sword that took my brother's life, isn't it? Perhaps you think it will bring our tangled fates to an end if I kill you with it, after you used it to kill him. But it would hardly hurt him," Lord Wang mused, "to give you what you want."

They were in the time after the end, when nothing more should have mattered, but somehow: something was going wrong. A shudder of premonitory unease ran through Ouyang as Lord Wang called, "Bring him in!"

To Ouyang he said, "Everything you did was because you had to avenge your noble father, who died a hero's death at the hands of the Great Khan. You went on your knees, you let yourself be shamed and disgraced before the world's eyes, you even killed the person you loved, all so you could do what was required to honor his memory: kill the one who killed him."

The soldiers who came through the door ushered between them the halting, stumbling figure of a ruined old man with gray hair and a long beard.

Lord Wang said pleasantly, "General Ouyang."

With rising confusion, Ouyang realized Lord Wang wasn't talking to him.

Lord Wang went on, "Rumors of your need to be avenged were much exaggerated, it seems. Rather than accepting a hero's death, I hear that you fell to your knees and begged the Great Khan for mercy. He spared you, and cast you into the dungeons instead. Isn't it ironic? Your son came all this way to avenge you. He committed such unspeakable acts of betrayal for it. He even killed the Great Khan. But you were alive the whole time!" Every word was a performance: not for the old man he was addressing, or for Ouyang, but for the audience that neither of them could see. "Well, your suffering wasn't in vain. You're not too old to start a new family. Don't let your name end. Go free."

Ouyang could barely grasp what was happening—what *couldn't* be happening—but all the pain had already rushed back into the world. He heard himself utter, terribly, "Father."

The old man raised his head with a broken remnant of a general's haughtiness and looked at him without recognition. It was a look of confused disgust: the crushing look someone might direct at a slave, a thing. "You—" He struggled for a moment, as if he couldn't quite remember how to speak. Then he said distantly, already stumbling away, "You're not my son."

Ouyang stared after him. He was so cold that his teeth clacked. *I did it all for you.* All his previous pain had become nothing compared to what he felt in this moment. He was cold, but he was being burned alive. *I did it for nothing. I avenged nothing. I killed—*

I killed—

The world spun and spun, and he couldn't get his balance; he couldn't find his bearings. Everything was being undone.

As if from a great distance, Lord Wang said, "So, General. Was it worth it? Was it worth my brother's life?"

Ouyang couldn't breathe; he was gasping.

"You had everything that mattered, but you could never believe it. He loved you, and you loved him. But you had to cling to this path that you thought was your fate. You killed him, even though it didn't mean anything at all. It wasn't fate that cursed you, General. It was *you.* How you scorned me for being so afraid! And yet you were the one who was too afraid to be yourself, and to claim what was given to you." Lord Wang had a hectic, transported look, as if Ouyang's torment was the best thing he'd ever tasted. He'd found the core of Ouyang's pain and was drinking him dry. "Well, General. Perhaps in your next lives, or the ones after those, or in a thousand years, you'll find each other again, and the world will be different. Perhaps next time, you can have the courage."

There was an impact from behind, and Ouyang knew what it was and what it meant: that this was his end. There would be no change, no undoing, no justifications. There was only what he had done, that had never meant anything at all.

He was burning, and it was the kind of infinite directionless pain that he knew would continue forever, even after death, through a thousand more years of suffering.

Esen, he thought. *Wait for me.*

It must have taken all of Geng's strength to punch through both sides of Ouyang's armor. The signature gleaming mirror plate in the middle of his chest had flowered outwards around the protruding blade, its dozen twisted edges flecked with crimson. Ouyang grunted in agony.

The sound filled Baoxiang with a transcendent sense of accomplishment. Ouyang was the last thing in the world Esen had loved outside of the Great Yuan itself, and this was his moment of annihilation. It was more than just his death, which in any case Ouyang had wanted. By producing Ouyang's father, Baoxiang had ripped away every justification for Ouyang's actions and rendered his entire pathetic life meaningless, and with that, destroyed him.

Ouyang didn't look down at the blade coming out of his chest. He had dealt death often enough; he knew what it looked like. His face was naked in devastation. Baoxiang was suddenly furious. Ouyang dared feel like that? He'd had everything in the world that mattered, everything Baoxiang had never had, and he'd never treasured it. He'd thrown it away for the lie of honor. Baoxiang was overcome by a savagery that made him pant like a raptor about to tear into a meal. So Ouyang was hurting as he died? *Good.* He wanted Ouyang to hurt as much as he did.

I want you to see it.

Ouyang's eyes were fixed on Baoxiang's face. His expression of devastation gradually shifted to something deeper, stranger, that made Baoxiang's skin crawl. In his eyes there was something of an animal's gaze, alien and unknowable, as death's process smoothly and irreversibly rendered him inhuman. His hateful face with its haughtily delicate brow and jaw, its woman's feather-fine eyebrows, twisted into a rictus of silent agony.

Baoxiang's internal howl sharpened until it seemed one with the shining, bloodied blade coming out of Ouyang's chest. *Watch, brother!*

He wasn't even aware of having closed the few steps of distance between them. Only the point of the sword against his breastbone stopped him. He had a momentary urge to press harder, to gain a physical acknowledgment of the monstrous enormity of his own pain. Pain that he was finally able to repay to the one who had put it there.

Does it hurt to watch him suffer? Does it hurt enough?

The accusation sprang out of him, uncontrolled. *"He loved you."*

For a moment he heard the echo of a child scrambling after his object of worship. *I'll try harder next time. Please don't leave me behind.* He recoiled from the memory. His self-hate was as intense as pain; it swallowed him whole.

A flicker of humanness returned to Ouyang's eyes, a consciousness pressing back against the dark. Not sympathy, but an understanding. It was the last weak vibration of the kinship they'd shared, amidst their hate and resentment and jealousy, that had come from loving Esen. As Baoxiang gasped, breathing for Ouyang, who no longer could, he became aware of the terrible finality of the moment. Ouyang was the only person in the world who knew what it felt like to be loved by Esen. When Ouyang died, that knowledge would go with him. It would be destroyed, and it could never be undone.

Geng wrenched his sword out with a metal shriek. Baoxiang startled violently. For a while there had only been himself and Ouyang. Geng's interjection felt like someone had reached between them and snapped that fragile understanding before Baoxiang had been ready to let go.

Ouyang stood there, swaying. He was small, smaller than he had ever seemed; even with the weight of his armor, Baoxiang could have carried him. But the connection between them had gone, and Ouyang was just another part of the unraveling world as it came apart under the pull of Baoxiang's desires.

Ouyang fell, and Baoxiang didn't catch him.

He landed splayed, a broken doll. His bloody, grimy, beautiful face stared past Baoxiang at the distant ceiling. For an instant the wetness in his eyes shone as if he were still alive. His awful grimace of pain had gone. The last imprint of feeling etched on his face, the footprint in the dust before the wind swept it away, was that of the worst grief in the world.

Baoxiang realized he was still clenching Ouyang's broken sword. The finger impressions in the hilt leather fit wrongly against Baoxiang's bigger hands. Ever since childhood, Ouyang had loomed in Baoxiang's life. It had always been him at Esen's side, effortlessly superior, his face a mirror of Esen's disapproval. Even when they'd met as adults, Baoxiang's impression had been of someone who was everything he wasn't. But now in death, with Ouyang's rage-filled warrior spirit and his machinelike capacity for violence gone, there was no longer anything to contradict the fact of that small, crumpled, incomplete body slowly being swallowed by the expanding pool of darkness around it.

"Leave me."

The closing door sank the hall and its fallen bodies into shadow. White petals ghosted from the cut branches in the settling wake of air. Their descent was reflected in the beaten-silver walls. Far above, the silver roof glimmered like the stars seen darkly through an oncoming storm.

This was the moment Baoxiang had been waiting for, and he felt the anticipation of the coming release. This was what he had done everything for: when all his hurt would be repaid.

The hall with its immense dragon-carved pillars was empty, but it was full of the flickering dead. As Baoxiang made his way up the steps to the throne, he knew one of those dead was watching him. Esen was there in the hall, separated from him by nothing more than a shadow—a filament of membrane between their two worlds—ready to be called forth. To be forced to show himself.

This power was what it must feel like to kill someone with your own hands. It was savage; intimate. When Baoxiang was just a man, he'd been unable to bend the universe to his will. He hadn't been able to make Esen show himself. But now he had the power. It was a voluptuous darkness: the power of destruction, mounting inside him as he stood trembling before the throne. Its golden twisting dragons were no longer bright. Blood-smeared, they struggled against the darkness.

Baoxiang sat. His skin felt too small to contain the savage

ballooning hurt of his success. He was shaking with a febrile violence.

He had made himself into what they all thought he was: everything they feared and hated and shunned and fought against. He shamed his ancestors with every breath he took and everything he did. And now he was the center of the world. He was the Son of Heaven—but not the life-bringing sun in the sky. He was the eclipse that sucked the light and life out of the world. He was the moon eating the sun, and it was his racing shadow that stole the life from the world below. He was the Great Khan of tainted blood, the Great Khan who went on his knees and was fucked and beaten and shamed, the Great Khan of weakness and cowardice and treachery and cruelty and shame and fear. And in him, everything good and noble and honorable found its end.

The blackness was consuming him. It sucked the light from the hall until shadow fell over the bloody carnage at his feet. It swallowed the body of the Great Khan, the bodies of the guards, Ouyang's body. A darkness that was empty, except for himself.

His anticipation reached a peak that was sweeter and more painful than he could have imagined. It was a dizzying feeling; a stretching tunneling feeling of seeing himself at a distance. "Esen! I know you're there. Come now and witness how worthy I am of your hate! Did I surpass your expectations?"

His joy was pure thirst for what was to come: his own hurt meeting Esen's in some great karmic rebalancing that would free him.

"Esen!" he called again.

A gust of wind, thick with the smell of foreign snow, pushed through the crack in the great doors and made the white flowers flicker and dance.

"Esen! I know you've been watching me all this time!"

Suddenly the emptiness, the echoes of his own voice, produced a squeezing feeling in his chest. It squeezed until the world spun, and he all but fell as he lurched to his feet in a desperate attempt to orient himself.

Where was Esen? He had felt him for months, had seen him so many times out of the corner of his eye, so why was he absent now? He couldn't understand what was happening. How could he not be here to witness Baoxiang's triumph?

He strained all his senses. He was in an agony of awareness, waiting for the *feeling* of Esen's presence that was more familiar than anything Baoxiang knew. But all he felt was the ache of emptiness. He was straining, yearning; yet nothing was happening.

"Come see what you made me do, Esen! Come! You dare disobey, when I command everything under Heaven?"

But still there was nothing.

He stood there, gasping. He was unlocking, dissolving. "I did this for you." He was the Great Khan, yet now when he spoke it was without command; it was nothing more than a helpless, disconsolate plea. "Where are you?"

But even as he said it, he knew.

Esen had never been there.

If what he'd really seen had been Esen's ghost, why had he been wearing armor—why had he looked as he'd looked in life? He would have been a specter in dreadful white rags, like the rest of them.

Baoxiang had always known, but he hadn't wanted to know.

Esen had never been there, but Baoxiang had kept seeing him because Esen was an ineradicable part of the fabric of his world. He'd been seeing the imprints of someone who persisted because he was remembered, and sought after, and yearned for, by a person who couldn't imagine life without him.

It had all been in his mind, he thought, shuddering. He'd been talking to a void. He'd done everything he had done for someone who wasn't there.

From a dream within a dream, he heard Esen say, "I don't hate you."

He remembered now, as if from a lifetime ago. It had been that winter of Esen and Ouyang's defeat by the Red Turbans, but before the Spring Hunt that had changed everything between them forever. Baoxiang had been in his office working on flood relief for the peasants when Esen had wandered in. His curiosity as he looked around made Baoxiang think, uncharitably, that it was quite likely the first time he'd ever set foot inside an apparatus of the bureaucracy. "Brother! Here you are."

"Where else," Baoxiang said acidly, "would I be."

"Well," Esen said, "I don't know. But it can't be good for you to spend every waking hour of your life in here. The peasants can wait for—for—" He broke off, looking stymied.

"For?" Baoxiang asked with fascination, wondering if Esen had the faintest clue what he spent his days doing.

"For whatever it is you do with your peasants," Esen said, brushing it off. "How urgent can it be? You can take a break." And against Baoxiang's protests, he wrestled him out of the office and onto a horse.

They rode west, into the marshlands where Esen liked to hunt. Although Baoxiang had been perfectly happy at his desk, and he disdained the concept of chasing animals for entertainment, he found himself content to pander to Esen this once. Slushy, mephitic water winged up from their horses' racing hooves; swans launched themselves from the reeds in explosion after explosion as they passed. All around them was the vastness of the Prince of Henan's estate. Baoxiang had the sudden urge to capture the melancholic freedom of that landscape in ink: the steel gray sky; the white egrets arrowing over the dark mountains on the far western horizon. He knew down to the last tael how much destruction the excessive rains had wrought upon the estate. And yet: this inundation of the world was beautiful.

Esen raced ahead, his kingfisher-blue riding gown already streaked with mud and water. When it was just him and Esen together, they could be free like this. There was no pressure of needing to be who they weren't; there were no expectations. Their father wasn't here to judge. As Baoxiang watched, Esen drew his bow from its leather case slung at his side and shot haphazardly at a rising swan. When he missed, Baoxiang felt a flush of fondness: it was like watching a hunting dog falling over itself in its own excitement. From his position farther back he had more time to draw, sight, and loose.

Esen whooped as the swan fell, and leaned effortlessly from his saddle to scoop it from the knee-deep water. He was flushed and bright-eyed, his hair coming undone, as he wheeled his horse around and came galloping back: dripping, laughing.

They paused to rest on firmer ground. "You could be a talented archer, if you applied yourself," Esen mused, when they'd both caught their breath. "Our father wants to be proud of you. I don't understand why you don't try, when it wouldn't even be that hard for you."

Baoxiang had just wanted to be together with his brother, without getting into a fight. He regretted Esen bringing the outside world to them. "Perhaps so." The bulge of darker gray sky over the mountains promised more rain, more floods. Baoxiang thought of the desperation of the peasants who lived on and enriched the estate. He was the only one who bothered to address that desperation. He was the only one who built ditches and roads and villages, and brought order to the world of the estate, and made it run well. He enjoyed what he did, even if nobody else appreciated that it was important. "But it's not what I want to do."

"You always did do what you wanted, regardless of what the rest of us thought." In profile, mounted on his handsome horse, Esen was the perfect lord.

Baoxiang said bitterly, "No need to stop yourself from saying it. I'm selfish. Disgraceful."

"I just think it would be easier not to be the way you are. Not just for you, but for all of us. I think you're wasting your potential." But just as Baoxiang was feeling a combative defensiveness, Esen went on, "But I see how much you want it: to be the way you are. To see you fight so hard—I know it matters to you. So what if I don't understand it? Perhaps I don't need to."

After he was dead, that was the image of Esen that Baoxiang remembered. The wind drawing the loose strands of his braids across his face; the fur ruffling at the collar of that blue gown; the wrinkles at the corners of his eyes as he smiled. "We're different people. We've chosen different paths and want different things. But you'll always be my brother."

The weeping feeling from Baoxiang's dream overcame him. He fell to his knees in the throne room, and this time he was crying for real in the black world of his own creation. Even back then, when the cascade of events that led to Esen's death had already begun, he had loved Esen. And in his own fractured, frustrated way—Esen had loved him. Even when they had wanted to only hate, they had been incapable of it. Because of their history; because they were brothers.

Baoxiang hurt more than he could have believed possible. His protective anger had gone. The pain inside him was constantly changing, so he could never become accustomed to it. It was physical; it was in his body; it was a part of him. It was unbearable. His grief was as large as the world.

He could feel the blackness leaching out of him as he lost control. It was drowning the world, and himself along with it. He had gained the throne and his revenge upon the dead, but none of it mattered because Esen was gone, and there was nothing he could do to bring him back.

PART THREE

19

YINGTIAN

Zhu wasn't wearing white mourning, as she stood with her commanders in the throne room in Yingtian. She didn't need to. Her mourning was written all over her, as it was on her commanders: their faces haggard with grief and loss. Xu Da had been beloved, and not just by her. The room of familiar faces was wrong without him. Every time she noticed his absence, she found herself thinking that he'd simply stepped out. He was over in one of his usual haunts, and when she went to find him, he'd turn to her with that easy smile—

Then she remembered, and he died all over again. She couldn't stop seeing him wipe blood from his mouth with yet another excuse she'd let herself believe. A cut lip; a bitten tongue. If she'd considered it properly, she would have known. But she hadn't wanted to know.

Xu Da had followed her into that drowned tunnel knowing it could be his death. And it *had* been his death, even if the fact of it had been delayed by months. *I killed him,* Zhu thought wretchedly. For the sake of what she wanted, she'd destroyed his future. She'd robbed him of his joys and pleasures. She could still feel his pain within her, as if witnessing his last suffering had burned it into the very fabric of her being. Each pulse was as raw as it had been in the moment, a category of agony wholly different from the sick ache in her ribs and hand. It was so awful it made her tremble and sweat. Her heart raced in random bursts of terror.

This was what Ouyang had been feeling, the whole time she'd

known him. This was his pain; his desperation. She'd thought she'd understood, but how could she understand the unimaginable? She thought of the first time she'd seen ghosts. It had been a moment like this one: a new, terrible knowledge revealed to her alone, while everyone else continued in ignorance. It had been a step into a dark, sideways world that always shadowed the real one, and from which there was no return. Zhu had dared to desire the world. But how could a human body—a human skin, a human soul—hold this agony that was the price of that desire, and survive?

This was the true test of her strength. It had never been whether she was strong enough to be ruthless. It was whether she could endure *this.* She had never imagined she had the capacity to feel this much. To hurt this much. She'd never imagined how she would have to hold it inside her, and keep holding it, even though a single moment was unbearable.

But she had to, to make it worth it.

Yuchun was saying, "According to the latest reports we have from the north: as of ten days ago, that beast in human skin"—he meant Ouyang, whom he seemed unlikely to forgive for the betrayal even in his next life—"was within a hundred li of Dadu. The observers said he was making strong headway against the Yuan's central army, albeit with substantial losses."

Ouyang's better-than-expected progress was surprising, given what everyone had said about the Grand Councilor's capabilities as a general. When Zhu said as much, Yuchun said, "Apparently there's been no sighting of the Grand Councilor on the Yuan's side, but our sources couldn't confirm whether he was still in charge."

That was strange. Had something happened to the Grand Councilor? Zhu couldn't help thinking of the other news she'd received upon returning to Yingtian: against expectations, the Grand Councilor had failed to launch his campaign against Madam Zhang. There could hardly have been a more well-timed stay of execution for the Zhangs.

And then there was what Chen had told her during their encounter: Madam Zhang hadn't been his patron. Could it be that his patron was the invisible hand that seemed to be moving pieces in the shadows? Was it connected to the Grand Councilor's disappearance? Even thinking that, Zhu didn't like it. She had an uneasy, obscured sense that there was some bigger picture. But being in the south necessarily meant her information was old and incomplete. With frustration, she thought: *I can't see.*

Yuchun said, "Presuming that eunuch managed to maintain his momentum, by now he could have forced the Yuan to cede defeat in the field. There's a good chance they're already besieged inside Dadu."

"But the reports said he's had major losses. If that's the case, he won't have the numbers to make an overwhelming assault on the walls," Zhu observed. "If he's stuck outside trying to starve Dadu into defeat—the Yuan will call on their allies to come break the siege."

"Who do they have *to* call? There isn't anyone. Not with the Prince of Henan gone, and all their other loyalists fragmented."

"They don't have any allies left *inside* their borders," Zhu said. "But they do, outside them. The vassal states. The Yuan will call on Goryeo for assistance."

Ouyang had been lucky not to have to face the Grand Councilor, so he'd made it further than expected. But his luck would run out if Goryeo entered the fray. Yuchun, thinking along the same lines, said with a distinct lack of regret, "He'll be finished."

"No," Zhu said. "He won't. We'll help him."

There was a pause. "Help that rotten scum *who betrayed us and left us to die.*"

It wasn't as though the idea didn't hurt. Ouyang's vicious rejection had stung. But there was only one way to make that pain, and all the other pain, worth it. And it wasn't by letting Ouyang fail.

"He abandoned us at a critical moment, it's true. But regardless of what that cost us, it doesn't change what I want. Because of that, we're going to help him with the assault on Dadu. We'll do it whether he wants to acknowledge our existence or not. I don't care if he curses my ancestors or spits on me while we do it. All that matters is that he gets inside, gets rid of the remaining defenders without burning down *all* of Dadu, and kills the

Great Khan. And then," Zhu said, projecting her determination as fiercely as she ever had, "then: I'll have what I want."

She could see from their faces that they would follow her, even as Commander Lin said uncertainly, "There's still the matter of Goryeo. If the Yuan call them now, they'll reach Dadu at the same time as we do. Even *if* we coordinated well with General Ouyang, it would be a challenge to take them on when we've had our own losses against Chen Youliang."

"Goryeo won't be a problem." Zhu turned to Yuchun. "I'm going to have to bother you to organize the resupply and start leading our army north."

Yuchun looked grim, and abruptly older. They both knew what the request really was: for him to step into Xu Da's shoes. "Where will *you* be?"

With a burst of pain, Zhu remembered sitting on horseback next to Xu Da as they looked down at the golden land spreading beneath them towards the eastern sea. Somewhere across that sea had been the peninsular kingdom of Goryeo, and she'd thought: *One day, all of this will be mine.* She could barely comprehend how she could have taken such boisterous joy in her ambition. Her ambition still burned, but now it was a burn laced with desperation. She *needed* it to be fulfilled, even more than when she'd simply wanted it for herself. She had to win, because that was what Xu Da had died for. She had to make it worth it.

"It's time," she said, "for a king to meet a king."

When Ma went into the bedroom, she found Zhu sitting on the bed. It was disconcerting to see Zhu wholly absorbed in her thoughts, when in the past she'd never have been without some kind of work.

Ma settled next to her, the skirts of her white mourning robes overlapping Zhu's gold gown, and took her hand. Gently, because she knew the bruising between her bones still hurt. "Word just came. Your ship is ready. You'll be able to depart for Goryeo tomorrow morning."

Losing Xu Da had changed Zhu. She who had caused so much loss to others, and seemingly never dreamed it could happen to her, now carried her pain and grief openly. The skin above her eyes had fallen slightly, as if the gravity of devastation had finally conquered her endlessly resilient youthfulness. It gave her an older, hooded look. The sight of her like that was wrenching. Ma thought perhaps she should have been glad Zhu *could* feel such ordinary human emotions as grief. But for now it was only agony to see the person she loved in pain, knowing she was powerless to relieve it.

"Yingzi," Zhu greeted her. She couldn't squeeze Ma's hand as she normally would, but she rearranged their hands to cut their fingers between each other. Two small hands, kissing. "We're so close. Can you feel it? Imagine: after I deal with Goryeo, there'll only be one more march. One more assault. Then it will be over. No more sacrifices. No more of this pain and suffering. I'll finally have that new world of mine. Everything we've gone through will have been worth it."

Zhu had always talked about the future with joy, but now there was a desperate edge to her that Ma found uneasily familiar. It took her a moment to realize that it reminded her of General Ouyang.

"Will you come with me, Yingzi? This is what you suffered for, too. Once we're done in Goryeo, we'll go straight to Dadu and meet the army there. I'd like you to be with me as I ascend the throne." Zhu looked up from their hands to give her a shadow of her ordinary smile. "My empress."

Ma had never doubted that Zhu would succeed. And how could Zhu's future not be wonderful, if it was a world in which everyone could be themselves? She still remembered her trapped frustration of having been set on a path she'd never chosen for herself, until Zhu had taken her hand and drawn her forth. Now Ma could see the future as clearly as if it were already real: Zhu taking the hands of the entire world, as she'd done for Ma, and freeing them all.

But Ma couldn't put aside the thought of all that pain and suffering; all those people already sacrificed to Zhu's dream. Not just Xu Da, but those countless other lives whose endings hadn't affected Zhu in the same way. Men sent to their deaths in battle; ordinary men and women killed and tortured when their cities were taken; a child Ma had once held in her arms.

She found herself remembering Ouyang again. What he'd done for the sake of what he'd wanted had caused him seemingly infinite agony. And yet, she thought with a chill, he'd never regretted it.

She asked quietly, "Have you ever thought that it might not be worth it?"

Zhu glanced over. She seemed surprised, as if Ma were posing a paradoxical koan. "How could that be? If being the emperor means having the world, then its value must be infinite. It's worth anything."

Perhaps so. But if each death could also be considered the end of that person's unique world—

Then isn't pain infinite, too?

SONGDO, CAPITAL OF GORYEO

It was snowing in Songdo when the ship made port after the weeklong journey that had taken Zhu and Ma first to the mouth of the Yangzi River, then across the Eastern Sea. The snow came down more thickly than Zhu had ever experienced, mounding against the plain wooden buildings of the small town and masking the surrounding landscape from view. Goryeo belonged to the Mongols as much as Zhu's native lands had, but its foreignness was inescapable: present not just in the strangely shaped clothing that masked the bodies hurrying through the streets, but in the very taste of the cold, pine-filled air. She was filled with a terrible loneliness. She and Xu Da had seen so much of the world together. But now he had gone on without her, and Zhu's unmeritous desires had ruined her karma enough that even a thousand years of next lives might not be enough for her to see him again. All she could do now was continue towards her victory that was so close that she could have stuck out her tongue and licked it. She thought with fierce pain: *It'll be worth it.*

When Zhu reached the palace, she couldn't tell whether its simplicity was the Goryeo style, or because the Great Yuan funneled away all of Goryeo's riches for its own use. Perhaps both. Palace attendants scurried past her with armfuls of wood—in the rest of the Great Yuan, it would have been coal—and Zhu caught their curious sideways glances. It wasn't solely to them that Zhu's clothes announced her alienness, but even to herself. She was wearing one of Ma's queenly southern-brocade dresses with a fur cloak draped over her shoulders. Ma had braided and piled her hair high and added a hairpiece nearly as large again as her head, and her wooden hand was carefully hidden within her sleeve. Zhu had known she'd needed a disguise, given how Songdo crawled with loyalists to the Great Yuan. If any of them caught wind that Zhu Yuanzhang had made an agreement with the King, who knew what pressure they'd apply to get him to renege? If she didn't manage to keep her visit secret, her agreement would end up getting unpicked before she'd even left the country.

It was only last year that Bayan-Temur, as he'd been known then, had been living at the imperial court of the Great Yuan as a hostage prince. Now he was King Gongmin of Goryeo. As Zhu entered his throne room with a gaze not quite lowered enough to prevent her from observing the room, she saw a sturdy man in a robe the color of a roasted peppercorn. It bore extravagant gold embellishments upon chest and shoulders, and the skirt was pleated in the Mongol style. But rather than Mongol braids, the King's hair was clasped with gold in a topknot of much the same style as Zhu was accustomed to wear. His bulbous features were exquisitely made-up in a way that verged on effeminate. Zhu couldn't suppress her bitter amusement. For someone as disgusted by the feminine as Ouyang, it was ironic that it would be a pair of unmanly kings who would save him.

She knelt. It was probably one of the least pretty gestures Gongmin's court had ever seen, since it turned out that managing the enormous volume of Ma's skirts was harder than it looked. "Most respectful greetings to the King of Goryeo," Zhu murmured in heavily accented Mongolian. "If this lowly woman could beg a private audience—?"

She could feel how his initial impulse was to refuse—but then, apparently remembering the gold taels this foreign woman had sprinkled so liberally into the hands of his retainers, he made a brushing motion that emptied the room. When the last attendant shut the doors, Gongmin said with undisguised disdain, "Speak."

Zhu thought wryly that even had she been wearing male attire, she still wouldn't have been handsome enough to command his attention without that sense of resentment: that he was being forced to look upon something that bored and displeased him.

She rose. Shedding her demureness was as pleasing as casting aside armor after a long day's march; she could feel her shoulders squaring. "We hope the King of Goryeo might meet the Radiant King as equals. We traveled quite the distance to meet His Majesty."

Gongmin reeled satisfyingly. "*You're* the one who's been in rebellion against the Great Yuan?" Zhu watched him grappling with the two facts she had laid upon him: firstly, that Zhu Yuanzhang was in Goryeo, and secondly, that she wasn't what everyone thought she was. "But you're a—*are* you a woman?"

He seemed vexed by being unable to reconcile Zhu's ambiguity: her masculine carriage and boldness, her unattractive face, the beautiful dress—and, of course, everything he'd heard about the impressive accomplishments of Zhu Yuanzhang, the Radiant King. "Or are you a eunuch, like that other one? How many traitor eunuchs can one empire possibly produce? I met the other one once, at one of the Great Khan's hunts. He had a"—he waved a hand vaguely in the direction of Zhu's face—"similar thing happening. You'd think he was a woman, but there was always something wrong about him that you could never put your finger on."

"Few could claim such beauty as General Ouyang," Zhu said, enjoying how his discomfort deepened at her refusal to provide a clear answer. It was pleasing to force him to confront her, as she was.

"Well," Gongmin said, gathering himself. "This is all a surprise. Had we known who you were, we would hardly have acceded to your request for an audience. How can we be seen to receive one of the enemies of the Great Yuan?" He spoke Mongolian with the same Dadu accent as Ma did. "It would be more comfortable for all of us if you left." No doubt he was thinking about those Great Yuan spies.

He was about to cut her audience short. Zhu said hurriedly, "You mentioned General Ouyang. I assume Your Majesty has received a message from the Great Yuan about their present difficulties?"

He'd leaned forwards as if to call his attendants. She saw his posture change to thoughtfulness, although it was still unfriendly. But Zhu didn't need his friendship for what she wanted. She didn't even need his respect. "I intend to join my army with General Ouyang's outside Dadu. Against the two of us, the Great Yuan *will* fall. But that's as long as Goryeo doesn't come to its aid, which I'm sure it's already requested of you. I'm asking that instead of answering the Yuan's call, you ally with me. Don't mistake me: I'm not asking for military assistance from your forces. All I'm asking is that you fail to answer the call. And for the price of doing nothing: when Dadu falls and I sit on the throne, I'll reward you with what Goryeo wants most." She could tell he was listening carefully, even though his face was expressionless. "How your country must have suffered through all these years of being forced to pay tribute; of sending your princes to be held hostage; of the shame of being vassal to a foreign overlord! I'll put that to an end." She said in a triumphant rush, "I'll give Goryeo its freedom."

On the low table in front of the throne, pickled slices of lotus root dyed pink and yellow, and in its original white, had been shingled in a container made from a lacquered section of bamboo stalk. Gongmin took a slice with a pair of steel chopsticks, and ate it. There was a deliberateness to the gesture that Zhu couldn't interpret. When he finished he said slowly, "Who could turn down an offer of something for nothing? You came knowing I could hardly refuse. As indeed, I wouldn't have refused, had the situation been as you seem to think it is. But I suppose your center of operations is very far from Dadu, and it takes news time to travel."

Songdo's thick snow made it unnaturally quiet, as if the spaces between things grew vaster and emptier the further north one went. Zhu had an abrupt, vertiginous feeling of distance, as if she had come too far and lost all sense of direction back to home. Or perhaps the distance was inside her, because when Gongmin rose from his throne and paced down the steps to scrutinize her up close, his voice seemed to reach her from an immense remove. "Ah, now I see you. Not a eunuch after all. Just an ugly little girl with dreams of greatness. Hard to believe you could make it this far! But even if someone like you could rule—as far as the throne of the Great Yuan is concerned, you're too late.

"Dadu fell a week ago. The game is over." The King said, "Someone else has already won."

Dark was falling in the palace garden, and the snow along with it. The silence registered in Zhu's ears as a dull pressure. The heavy folds of her dress bled their color into the twilight. In that distant land she had once dreamed of ruling, she was a single grain of light kneeling on the snow as the night sky lowered around her. Its caress drank her in and swallowed her whole.

Ouyang was dead. The Great Khan was dead. Madam Zhang was the new empress. And he who had moved within the obscuring darkness—within that all-touching shadow—he had a name. A name that could no longer be uttered upon pain of death, when the one who had borne it was the Great Khan, but Zhu thought it anyway:

Wang Baoxiang.

The Prince of Henan. Not Ouyang's beloved, but his younger brother. Zhu only had a faint memory of that brother from that day she'd looked down at the Prince of Henan's retinue from the monastery roof. A scholar, amongst warriors. But back then he hadn't been darkness. Zhu remembered a gangling youth in a gown so flamboyant it had put her in mind of a flashing butterfly. He'd been the one held even lower in the world's esteem—the one loved even less by his own father and brother—than a disdained eunuch. Now, all these years later, he was the one who'd been in the capital for the entire duration of the struggle for the throne. He'd played everyone, Zhu included. None of them had seen him coming.

The Great Khan might have changed, but King Gongmin's commitment to the Great Yuan hadn't. He'd refused all Zhu's entreaties to join his forces with hers for an assault against Dadu. If what she'd been offering him had been something for nothing, she knew he'd have been happy to agree. But when it came to risking himself or his position—he would never accept it, even for the sake of his own people. Not that Zhu had expected any better of him. Had he been a man of strong character, the Yuan would never have allowed him upon the Goryeo throne in the first place.

Now her army, marching alone to Dadu, wouldn't be enough to take it. Wang Baoxiang controlled the Yuan's central army—or what remained of it, after Ouyang's efforts—as well as Madam Zhang's forces. With the proper leadership they'd lacked when Ouyang had encountered them, those combined forces would be capable enough of defending Dadu. And now Zhu had run out of options to tip the balance in her favor. There were no more allies to seek. No more leverage to gain.

But she couldn't give up. Gongmin had been wrong. Wang Baoxiang might sit upon the throne, but so long as Zhu had the will and desire to continue: he hadn't won. She knew, desperately, that she would continue towards greatness as long as she breathed. She would continue, even when she didn't have enough to win. Even though when she looked ahead, all she could see was her army throwing itself into the slaughter.

When Ouyang had marched to Dadu, he'd been in a similar situation. But he'd succeeded against the odds. He'd done everything he had set out to do. He'd found his fate and his end, and with it he'd made all his suffering—his pain, and betrayals, and sacrifices—worth it.

Zhu thought with shuddering determination: *And so will I.*

As she knelt there, her fist clenched on her skirted knee, she gradually became aware of a figure curtained by the falling snow. A ghost made a fitting accoutrement to this dead winter courtyard. Its ragged clothing wept down onto the snow, and its tangled hair was the same color as the soaked branches of the drooping willows. The figure was becoming clearer, as if the snow were thinning, and then Zhu realized with a start: not clearer because there was less snow, but because it was coming towards her.

In that darkening soundless garden there was no life except Zhu herself, and she had the feeling of the ghost standing over her and watching her sink, while the black water closed over her head.

Except—

The ghost's white-slippered feet were *in* the snow, not above it. Even as more snow came down to erase its tracks, for a moment those tracks had existed. It wasn't a ghost, but a woman. As the woman approached she brushed her hair aside to reveal an unfamiliar bony face. Perhaps the bold lines of those bones had once read as elegant or haughty, but now all Zhu could see was the skull beneath the skin.

"Zhu Yuanzhang," the woman said, looking down at her. "The one known as the Radiant King, who desires nothing less than the throne of the Great Yuan." The ravaged quality of her voice in a living person produced a dread worse than the horror of ghosts, because this was someone who felt as Zhu did; someone who felt as Ouyang had. It was someone who burned with the grief and pain and rage of loss; someone who had lost the world and continued in the darkness as an ashen husk. "If such a great desire is to be achieved, the suffering must be that great or more. So tell me, little sister: What are you prepared to do, for what you want?"

As Zhu knelt there in that ghost world of snow and darkness and pain, she felt a wild surge of hope. *Anything,* she promised. Whatever the solution was that would let her win, she knew it would be worth it, no matter how terrible it felt in the moment. *I can bear anything.*

The woman read her answer in her face. "Are you really that strong?" she murmured. An aura of ferocity, like the bloody veil over an eclipsed moon, fell across her ice-white countenance. Had her teeth been visible at that moment, Zhu could have believed they were as sharp as a liver-seeking ghost's. "I was that strong, once. I was the favored consort of the late Great Khan, and my son was the Third Prince of the Great Yuan. What I wouldn't have done for the one and only child of my flesh! For more than eighteen years, I kept him safe. But then I made a mistake. I trusted the last person I should have trusted.

"The King refused to help you, Zhu Yuanzhang. But for the sake of what Wang Baoxiang did to my son," Lady Ki said, "I will."

20

THE PALACE CITY, DADU

There was no whip, but the eunuch overseer's voice might as well have been one as he barked, "Move it, slaves!"

Zhu, in the line of ragged female slaves, emerged from the stone arch of the gateway into the Palace City. As she and the other slaves had been brought to Dadu, they'd been stunned by the destruction Ouyang had wrought on the surrounding countryside. Blackened spindles of tree trunks punctuated the ruins of hamlets and ravaged pleasure mansions, and in the fields bright spring weeds tangled with last season's uncleared crop straw. It was the violence of someone who hadn't cared about what he left behind, because all that mattered was that single moment, of twinned achievement and annihilation, that lay ahead. That moment that he had finally found, here in the Palace City.

Monks traveled more than most people, and many of those visiting or returning to Wuhuang Monastery had spoken of the shining Mongol capital. They had described a city whose golden walls and buildings had blazed with newness against the backdrop of sere hills. But what Zhu saw was a world that seemed to have lost all color and splendor; that grew ever dimmer as the eye traced down from the dark clouds boiling on the underside of Heaven. The churning flags atop the walls weren't the azure blue Zhu knew from battle, but had the tint of a forest-edged lake at dusk, as if night had finally come to the sky of the Great Yuan. The walls were indeed golden, and the buildings likewise gilded and the courtyards paved with the purest marble. And yet nothing shone. When Zhu rubbed her fingers over a once-white balustrade, they came away black. The grime of war, forming a patina over everything it had touched. Wang Baoxiang, who had emerged from the shadows to beat her to the throne, hadn't ended the Great Yuan. He had continued it: a world entombed in the ashes of its own destruction.

It hadn't had to be like this, Zhu thought with grief. If Ouyang had stayed with her—if only he'd been able to overcome his self-hatred to believe in her, trust her—he could have lived. Together, they could have brought a different world into being, instead of this one in which light had been transmuted into dark, and pain into eternal suffering.

The slaves trudged onwards, heads lowered. Zhu's hair was loose, her undyed dress stained and tattered, wooden hand hanging by her side. She knew what a familiar figure she made in this dark and despairing place. Just another broken woman from the fallen city of Nanchang. Another woman who had been raped by Chen Youliang's men, mutilated as an obscene mockery of his rival the one-handed Zhu Yuanzhang, then sold into slavery with her face a mask of loss and pain. Zhu didn't even have to pretend in order to sell the disguise. She simply showed her real pain. She bared the awfulness of it, and saw the other slaves recoil with even greater hostility than from her disfigurement. She could understand why. To be in contact with someone else's pain was to risk feeling it yourself, unless you severed the connection by hating them. When most people's greatest desire was to avoid pain, of course they would rather hate.

As the slaves followed the overseer through one after another of the tall blue-shadowed corridors of the Palace City, Zhu became aware of a distant yelling. All at once the overseer barked, "Get down!" The slaves milled uncertainly until the overseer grabbed the woman at the head of the line, kicked her leg so she fell with a scream to one knee, and bowed her head with a strong hand. "Do you want to die? If not, then *get down* when the Great Khan approaches!" His tone brooked no argument. The rest of them quickly sank down onto the cold white sand of the corridor. As the noise crescendoed, a high sedan chair rushed past; all Zhu saw was so many churning legs beneath it that it looked like a millipede.

By the time the slaves had risen and re-formed their line, the sedan chair had reached the great square through the archway at the end of the corridor. It halted at the foot of steps leading up to an immense jewel-roofed hall surrounded by columns. Zhu could just make out the figure descending from the sedan chair. Unlike his predecessors, he wore black. The gold dragons that proclaimed his rank swam across the surface like midnight constellations.

Zhu stared at Wang Baoxiang, the Great Khan, unbreathing. There was a huge sensation within her that wasn't anger or hate, but simple recognition. Here was the person who had what she wanted.

The person who stood between her and her desire.

He stepped down, and was momentarily lost in a crowd of eunuchs and retainers and guards.

"I can't give you an army," the white ghost that was Lady Ki had said. "But if, as you say, you're prepared to do anything, I can give you another way to win.

"Wang Baoxiang is currently the only one in Khanbaliq with the Mandate of Heaven. Although this was likewise the case for the previous Great Khan, it is not the norm, but rather a failure of the system. Usually even before ascending the throne, a Great Khan will have established his line of succession with a legitimate heir who also has the Mandate. But were a Great Khan to die without a recognized successor—the ministers and military would have little choice but to accept his replacement by another individual Heaven has deemed qualified. Especially one with an army standing outside."

Lady Ki regarded Zhu where she knelt. "The Son of Heaven has always been a man. To change that seems a violation of the order upon which our world rests. But perhaps it makes sense that the one to end the Great Yuan will also break the world in which it existed. A new world for a new ruler. And I find I have no attachment to the old, since it denied my son his place in it, and let him die at the hand of his own father who saw him as unfit to carry his legacy, simply for the fact of what he was."

A wind stirred the garden, sending the snow from the willow's branches to the ground in a cascade of soft, swallowed explosions.

"You're not a man, Zhu Yuanzhang. Are you nonetheless qualified?"

Zhu reached past her pain and her grief, and gripped that essential part of herself—the part that could never be extinguished. With the remembered fierceness of that moment in which she had become herself, and for the first time claimed her life and her fate as her own, she said, "I am."

"Then enter the palace with my help. Assassinate Wang Baoxiang, and stand and proclaim yourself, and take the throne from the inside."

From across that vast courtyard, Zhu watched the dark corona of attendants ascending the steps with the gold fleck cocooned in its midst. Despite the murders and betrayals that had produced the plentitude of ghosts lingering in the cold shadows of these corridors of power, there was a good reason why few of those ghosts would be those of reigning rulers.

The Great Khan might be the sole person at the center of the world, but he was never alone.

Slaves did the work in the Palace City that even the lowest maid wouldn't have touched. A female supervisor led them around the various residences, where they emptied chamber pots into the buckets on their shoulder poles, then they hauled the buckets outside the Palace City walls to where the night-soil carts waited. It wasn't that the work itself was so unbearable. Zhu had done worse in her time—shoveling out the monastery latrine was still a vivid memory, all these years later—and probably so too had all the other slaves in their previous lives. No, the true torment for a slave was knowing there was no longer anything else for them except the work. They would do it until they broke, and when they did, nobody would care: because they were worthless.

As Zhu had quickly gathered, slaves were all but invisible to the other workers in the palace. There were the lower maids, who scrubbed laundry and rushed around with baskets of coal. There were the kitchen maids and the skilled maids, who could be seen sitting in their dozens bent over embroidery. There were maid supervisors and ladies-in-waiting and household managers, and eunuchs who did everything from carrying palanquins to assisting the imperial physicians. There were people from seemingly every corner of the empire, speaking every language between the four oceans, although there was a preponderance of those from Goryeo and the other vassal states who had presumably been sent to the Great Yuan as tribute. The Palace City, Zhu reflected, was in truth a city. Currently the only member of the imperial harem was the Empress, but in the future when there would be dozens of consorts each with her own household: all these thousands of workers would be needed, and more.

Night-soil collecting had only been the first task of the day. After that, the slaves had disposed of buckets of coal ash from the residences' numerous braziers, and food scraps from the kitchens, and now they were queuing at the well to take their turn drawing up buckets of water to be distributed. Zhu was surprised at the intensity of her exhaustion. Too used to the soft life of a king, she thought wryly.

"Keep it moving!" the maid supervisor yelled, as the slave ahead of Zhu shuffled from the well with her load of two full buckets.

It wasn't easy doing with one hand what was meant for two, but it was manageable. The well had a simple pulley system for raising buckets. Zhu hooked her first bucket to the end of the rope and threw it into the well to fill, then hauled it to the top and stepped on the coiled end of the pulley rope to keep the bucket raised as she went to lift it from the hook with her left hand.

She had just grasped the bucket handle, but not lifted it free, when the call came, "The Great Khan comes! You slaves, get down!"

It happened all at once. As the slaves turned in unison towards the road, Zhu was struck on the back by the swinging shoulder pole of the woman behind her. As she jolted forwards with a yelp, her anchoring foot lifted off the pulley rope; the bucket plummeted from under her left hand with such force that it nearly drew her in with it; and her right arm, flung high for counterbalance, passed inside the rope's lashing coils as it was drawn violently upwards through the pulley.

There was a crunch, and the bucket came to halt, bouncing, halfway down the well.

Zhu looked up, panting, at where her wooden hand, entangled in a snarl of rope, was wedged between the pulley and its suspending bracket. Her arm felt as if it had been just about ripped from its socket. She tugged hard at the hand, then again with rising urgency as it was held fast. Zhu was used to being the one standing while everyone else around her bowed, but now it was the last thing she wanted. *If you don't want to die, get down.*

She yanked harder. Her back, facing the road, prickled as if it were against a bed of needles. She could *feel* the darkness coming, rushing towards her like a multi-legged devourer. What kind of irony would it be, to be beaten to death as a slave for refusing to bow before the one who'd taken the throne from her? She wrenched with all her might. She had to get *free*—

The force of the release catapulted her from the well, and she fell stumbling to one knee at the roadside with her head bowed just as the Great Khan's procession ran past without halting. It was already over. Zhu's heart continued to pound. Her stump rested across her bent right knee, throbbing painfully and trailing a partially unwound cushioning bandage. Rather than freeing the hand itself, in her desperation she had wrenched her stump out of the tight wooden cuff that held the two together.

She realized, belatedly, that a shadow had fallen over her. At first she had no idea why there might be ten pairs of eunuchs' sandaled feet in front of her lowered eyeline. Hadn't the Great Khan already passed?

A woman said from above, "*You.*"

Zhu knew that voice. She remembered seeing its owner through a gauze curtain in a carriage above a plain where two armies stood opposed. It felt like an age ago. She was filled with cold foreboding.

Madam Zhang said again, "You, slave."

A eunuch ran over and kicked Zhu in the shin, making her gasp. "*You,* worthless one."

What choice did she have? Zhu's feeling of foreboding sharpened until she had the sense of resting on a knife edge of disaster. She raised her head, keeping her eyes lowered deferentially. Madam Zhang, high above her, was only a sensed shape in front of the diffuse northern sun.

"Slave. What happened to your hand?"

The best story was the one that had the most truth. Zhu kept her eyes fixed on the road as she murmured, "This lowest slave dares answer the Empress: Before she was a slave, this woman was from Nanchang. The Empress, in her vast knowledge, has surely heard what befell that city and its people when Chen Youliang took it from Zhu Yuanzhang."

"Zhu Yuanzhang!" Madam Zhang said with sharp satisfaction, as if Zhu had confirmed what she'd already been thinking when she saw a kneeling woman without a hand.

Madam Zhang had never been suspicious of her identity, Zhu realized. A flood of relief went through her. She hadn't suspected, because who would ever see a king in a slave; a man in a woman? Madam Zhang's interest had been caught by nothing more than the specter of her old rival. She said now, "That foolish boy. He should have surrendered to me when he had the chance. How his greed and ambition betrayed those upon whose bodies he built his kingdom! Look at you, kneeling before me: a ruined slave."

"He never thought about us. For the sake of what he wanted, he let us suffer. My hand, my body. My older brother—" Zhu was shocked to hear her voice break. For a moment she was the person she pretended to be, that maimed and grieving woman whose family had been taken from her by Zhu Yuanzhang's desire that would give anything, do anything, to see itself fulfilled.

Zhu Yuanzhang killed him. I killed him.

I made him suffer for what I wanted.

A slave was supposed to be an unseen, voiceless object. But Zhu's pain, spilling into the world, proclaimed her a person. The eunuch stepped sharply towards her, saying, "Worthless filth, you dare speak freely in front of the Empress—!"

Madam Zhang held up a silencing hand. Her jeweled nail guards flashed. "How very much you feel!" She regarded Zhu with the appearance of lightly disgusted amusement, as if Zhu's pain were a polluting aura. But beneath her performance Zhu sensed something sharper: an interest that verged on hunger. *Envy,* Zhu realized with a start. But what kind of person envied another's pain?

"I'm sure you've dreamed of how it would feel if Zhu Yuanzhang could feel a fraction of your pain," Madam Zhang mused. "Dreamed of revenge, or justice, although perhaps those are one and the same. Did you know he's on his way here right now? A fool on a fool's errand, to dash himself against Dadu's walls, intent on his own destruction."

To hear her speak of Zhu Yuanzhang gave Zhu the eerie feeling of being in two places at once. It was as if she had been artificially separated into two selves, each flattened into something lesser than herself, but that the world could understand and had a place for. Male and female, king and slave. Worthy and worthless.

Madam Zhang made a negligent gesture to the lady-in-waiting nearest her sedan chair, saying to Zhu's surprise and disconcertment, "Bring her along. Clean her up, put her in a maid's uniform."

Her light smile suggested it was nothing more than a whim pursued for her own entertainment, but Zhu could still feel her desire for vicarious pain, as if being in proximity to Zhu's flesh-and-blood feelings might bring some life into a hollow porcelain doll. "Zhu Yuanzhang is coming. And since you were someone who suffered so much for his desires," she said, "it will please me to let you watch him receive his fate."

Zhu had never been inside an aviary, and even as a king it hadn't occurred to her that it was something one might seek to have. Madam Zhang's aviary was clearly a point of pride. It was less a cage than a contained garden, the finely drawn wires of the enclosing mesh barely visible where they soared high above the spring-flowering trees. Manicured pebble paths wound through the dense shrubbery. And everywhere, birds. Birds as small as teacups; birds that stalked on longer legs than Zhu's own; birds with crests and crowns; birds with jeweled plumage. They must have cost a fortune. The only birds Zhu recognized were the pheasants (delicious), and the pigeons (also delicious, but more useful if left alive to deliver messages). Not that Zhu thought Madam Zhang's painstakingly bred pigeons had carried a message in their lives. They were shimmering and fanciful, frilled and ruffed; it was a wonder they could fly at all.

Madam Zhang, as richly dyed and elaborately adorned as her birds, was at the wooden roosting boxes amidst a cluster of somber-hued maids. "Take it, quickly!" Madam Zhang was saying impatiently as a maid reached, cringing, into one of the boxes. There was a fluttery panic; the maid snatched her hand back; and a tiny chrysanthemum-colored bird shot to freedom like an arrow. The maids screamed and ducked as Madam Zhang shrieked, "You sheep-faced mules!"

Zhu, who had been raking a path nearby, threw up her hand in blind instinct.

"Don't let it go!" Madam Zhang hurried over.

Zhu stared at the bird. The bird stared back with peppercorn eyes. Its heart pattered like rain against her palm. She'd caught it with the same reflex she'd have used to parry a descending blade.

When Madam Zhang gave her an assessing look, Zhu felt a stab of concern. If anyone in the palace was capable of recognizing the traces of Zhu's manhood, it would be a courtesan: someone who read men's bodies for a living.

But all Madam Zhang said was, "How pleasing! A cricket with one limb wrenched off can still make itself useful." Only her lips moved as she smiled, as if she had learned not to crack her makeup with unnecessary expressions. "Useful as more than bird food, that is. Now, hold its wing out, like so—"

Gold scissors crunched through the splayed feathers. "Good," Madam Zhang murmured. Her porcelain face held an almost erotic intensity. "There we are. All tidy now." She took the newly flightless bird upon her finger. It scrabbled at the metal surface of her nail guard in an effort to stay upright. Its tiny beak panted in terror.

Madam Zhang stroked the bird's back with one fingernail. "Did you know every one of these birds was given to me by the Great Khan himself? He has unusually refined taste for a Mongol. All these beautiful things are the sign of his highest esteem." She said, musing, "Perhaps I'll give this one as a welcome present to the new consort from Goryeo, when she gets here. I hear she's a sweet, biddable girl. A sweet bird for a sweet girl. Yes, that would suit. She'll need to have something to keep her entertained, since the Great Khan won't have any interest in her."

Catching a flicker in Zhu's look, she laughed lightly. "Not for the reason you might imagine! Despite his manner, I can assure you: he can perform with women. But I wouldn't say his tastes run towards sweetness." Her smile curled like a satisfied cat. She went inside on her little flickering feet, where maids were artfully arranging a circular table for a party of two, saying, "Come now, little cricket. When I have such a lack of useful maids, there's no need for you to be wasted outdoors. The Great Khan is visiting tonight, so you can assist my ladies-in-waiting in preparing me as he likes."

Madam Zhang was readied and waiting, as pristine as the dining ware upon the table, when a short while after the sunset Rooster hour the Great Khan's head eunuch swept into the residence as if he owned it. "The Great Khan approaches!"

As Zhu and the other maids prostrated themselves, Madam Zhang rose and performed a gracious courtesy as the Great Khan entered the room within the protective ring of his black-clad guards.

It wasn't until she saw Wang Baoxiang up close that Zhu understood Madam Zhang's comment about his manner. That manner, upon an ordinary man, would have caused the world to look at him with contempt, and consider him nothing. Upon the Son of Heaven, gowned in power, it shocked. It was a disruption so profound that Zhu felt an unexpected thrill, as she had the first time she'd gazed upon Ouyang's in-betweenness.

Instead of striding, this Great Khan swished. His pale, long-fingered hands fluttered. His carriage and gestures were a woman's, but performed by what was an unremarkably male body except for its pronounced thinness. His effeminacy was perhaps genuine to his nature, Zhu thought, but at the same time it *was* a performance. It was a performance that had made everyone else in the court overlook him. He had been amongst them the whole time, with murder in his heart and an ambition that outstripped their own, but none of them had believed those qualities could exist in someone who looked like him, who acted like him. None of them had seen him coming.

Though the brightness of the room shouldn't have been sufficient for it, Zhu felt a shadow fall over her as the Great Khan passed. She thought suddenly of the flags flying above the once-shining city, a blue so dark it was nearly black.

Black for a ruler whose Mandate was a flame that cast shadow instead of light.

The shadow brushed the edges of the sphere of brightness inside Zhu. Two Mandates, alike yet opposite, sang together like struck glass. The Great Khan twitched and glanced frowning around the room. Nobody around him had ever recognized the threat he posed, because of who he was. But now as his gaze passed unseeing over the maids, with Zhu kneeling amongst them in her identical uniform, she thought, *Nobody saw you coming. But you don't see me coming, either.*

Zhu was only a few paces from him. It was perhaps the closest she would ever come. And yet his bodyguards, their sheathed swords in their hands ready to be drawn, were a wall around him. Even had Zhu stolen Madam Zhang's scissors, or a knife from the kitchen, and hidden it in her sleeve, the short distance between them could have been a thousand li.

The Great Khan sat down to the meal with Madam Zhang. There was nothing spontaneous about the interaction, from the poison taster who sampled the dishes, to the Great Khan's courteous phrases and Madam Zhang's feminine flattery and charm. Zhu wondered if this was how she had been with all her men. There was an impersonal quality to her performance, as if all that had changed were the actors. Neither did the Great Khan seem truly pleased to be in her company. It was only a performance of pleasure. It was as if they were both putting on a play: not for the servants and guards around them, who were so low as to barely exist, but for themselves.

Zhu felt a growing uneasiness as she watched them. She had given so much, she was bearing so much, for what she wanted. Now, here in front of her, were two people who had done the same, and achieved their greatest desires. They were as high as a man and a woman could each be.

And yet, though she scrutinized them in every detail, she couldn't find a trace of what had to be beneath those bloodless performances: the satisfaction of having made it all worth it.

☼

Zhu stood with Madam Zhang's other maids at the back of the crowded Hall of Great Brilliance as the procession from Goryeo filed up to the distant dais to present their tribute. The distance reduced Madam Zhang and the Great Khan to puppets against a screen. Their small figures were indistinct amidst shadow. Despite the doors cast open to the spring sunshine, and the numerous lanterns, the hall seemed mired in a persistent gloom.

The crowd's reflections moved on the beaten-silver walls. The reflections weren't the sharp images of carefully polished bronze mirrors, but blurred, shifting shapes of pale and dark. Zhu gained the disturbing impression that it wasn't a wall at all, but a transparent skin, and the blurry shapes weren't reflections but a view of a different place they would all one day visit: a world of spirits instead of people.

There was something deeply unsettling about the hall. Zhu wasn't sure what she had expected to feel when she finally came here. As she'd moved through the Palace City, she'd been aware of how Ouyang had moved through it before her. Her footsteps had settled over his ghostly ones; her body had fit through the invisible holes left by the passage of his body through space. Now she had reached his end. That golden throne where Wang Baoxiang sat was where Ouyang had killed the previous Great Khan. This was where he had achieved his revenge. He had taken countless lives, he had betrayed the one he loved, he had betrayed and hurt Zhu herself, but he had finally succeeded.

Somewhere beneath the feet of the crowd were the last traces of that body that he had so hated. His blood would have soaked the tiles, and been scrubbed away, but it would have left its stain: the faint but ineradicable imprint, here in the center of the world, of who he had been.

It should have been a relief to know that at least his pain was over. But as Zhu stood in that hall where Ouyang had died, the feeling that crept through her wasn't relief. It moistened the soles of her feet, and chilled her kidneys, and traced her skin with a light cold touch.

Fear.

The fear grew, as strong as it was inexplicable. Zhu's body wanted to run. It insisted that there was something awful in the hall, something that couldn't be faced and survived. Something that called like to like, but instead of the familiar clear, ringing resonance, it stimulated a sensation so grotesque that Zhu's every nerve flinched away in horror. She had never felt anything like it.

But even as she searched the crowd, shuddering, she couldn't find the source.

The tribute procession had concluded. All that remained of the Goryeo delegation was a lone woman in a voluminous bell-shaped dress, a stiffly pleated cloak of the same material clutched around her head like a shawl. The woman made an obeisance before the throne.

The Great Khan's voice traveled faintly down the hall. "Rise, loyal princess."

The princess from Goryeo rose and shucked her cloak. The rulers of Goryeo, by the Great Yuan's design, had more steppe blood in their veins than half-caste Wang Baoxiang did. The princess, who would have missed the standards of pure Nanren beauty, was beautiful to the Mongol eye. A ripple of appreciation went through the palace attendants. Her smooth features were the very essence of unspoiled loveliness. The tenderness of her glance was only enhanced by the shadows within it of bittersweet sorrow.

Lady Ki had known, of course. *The Great Khan is never alone.*

Then how?

In the garden the dusk had closed in upon Zhu and Lady Ki like a guttering lamp. *There is one exception. The only time the Great Khan is ever alone with another person, without his bodyguards, is when he summons one of his consorts to his private chambers for the night.*

"This is the last time," Zhu had said, returning to the ship docked in Songdo's harbor. "The last time, Yingzi, I promise. But I need your help."

Zhu remembered how Ma's face had drained of color when she told her the details. She was silent for so long that Zhu genuinely didn't know how she would respond.

When Ma finally spoke, it was in a tone of devastation Zhu had never heard before. "Don't ask me to help you, Zhu Yuanzhang."

Zhu's heart lurched. There was a strange pressure in her head that made it hard to think. But before she could react, Ma said again, quieter, "Don't ask me." Zhu was suddenly struck by a sense of distance: that they were so achingly far from where they had begun, that they had traversed too much ground for any two hearts to bear. The small dark cabin pressed around them with the smell of the sea. Ma's gaze was so open that it had always felt to Zhu that to look into her eyes was to press their hearts together. Now those dark eyes held grief and pain, but also understanding. Ma took Zhu's hand and intertwined their fingers: a warm, familiar gesture. "I'll help you. But don't ask me. Don't command me, don't force me." Zhu had no idea why the distinction mattered, but now her tender wife said with the most steel Zhu had ever heard from her, "Let me choose."

Now, in the Hall of Great Brilliance, there was no longer anything Zhu could do to change what she had set into motion. All she could do, she thought in anguish, was bear witness to pain. She had made Xu Da suffer, and she had destroyed him, and that had hurt more than she had ever dreamed possible. But this was a different kind of suffering and destruction. It wasn't a destruction of the body, but of the qualities of kindness, compassion, and tenderness that constituted the very spirit of the person Zhu held closest in her heart.

"This woman greets His Majesty the Great Khan of the Empire of the Great Yuan," said Ma Xiuying, the only one who would ever be able to get close enough to the Great Khan to kill him.

21

"Greetings to the Empress." Ma, bent in her courtesy, welcomed the strangeness of her Goryeo clothing as it pressed around her. It shaped her body and her thoughts, never letting a moment's absence where she might forget the person she was supposed to be. She was flush with dread. It was the feeling of walking through a forest, waiting for a single twig to crack beneath her feet to alert the hunters nearby. Being found out would lead to their deaths, but any other mistake might, too. One wrong look; one enemy made. Behind her, she heard the rustle as her small retinue of Goryeo maids bent in identical courtesy.

Ma was made to wait a beat longer than was comfortable, before Madam Zhang pronounced elegantly, "Our greetings to Lady Shin, the new consort from Goryeo. Rise."

Madam Zhang's spacious, wide-windowed apartments were rich and alien. Ma might have been a queen, but Zhu's new-made splendor could never have competed with wealth harvested from a whole empire. Each generation had layered these rooms with its own touches of luxury over the ones that came before, until as with mother-of-pearl, the eyes staggered to receive the entirety of its magnificence. Madam Zhang's own touch appeared to be the golden birdcages hung from every beam. Beneath the perfumed incense lay the faint acridity of bird droppings.

On her raised chair at the front of the room, Madam Zhang was as impeccable as a vase. But she was older than Ma had expected—at least a decade older than her husband—and less beautiful than her exquisitely calculated performance led the eye to believe.

Ma knew she should have paid all her attention to Madam Zhang, upon whom her future safety rested. But she could hardly tear her eyes from Zhu, at Madam Zhang's side.

Zhu in a maid's uniform, her hair in a clumsy braid: a shape-shifted fox. It gave Ma the curious feeling of being able to see an otherworldly truth beneath a seemingly ordinary surface that nobody else could penetrate.

But this wasn't part of the plan. Had Zhu placed herself near Madam Zhang deliberately, or been forced to improvise on the fly? Ma tried to reassure herself. If she could barely recognize Zhu in this female guise herself, there was no chance Madam Zhang could guess who she really was. And yet. Ma recognized the unpleasant feeling of certainty slipping out from under her feet. It was exactly what had happened in Bianliang.

Zhu had been exhilarated by adventure, Ma remembered, while she herself had been terrified. Zhu hadn't even seemed to understand Ma's fear and discomfort. She was clearly different now, after what had happened with Xu Da. She understood pain. But Ma couldn't help wondering, uneasily, whether that pain might only increase the blinkered relentlessness of her drive towards what she wanted, as it had with Ouyang. She had pleaded with Zhu, though to what effect she wasn't sure. *Don't be too like him.*

"Your Han'er is very good, for someone from Goryeo." Madam Zhang's assessment dug into Ma like a needle point. "I suppose you must be considered pretty, where you're from. How different the tastes of each people!" Her little laugh made Ma's skin crawl; it felt like the skim of claws against her throat. Madam Zhang reached into the cage Zhu offered and brought out a small yellow bird. Ma was captured by its tiny dark eye, its trembling smooth body in Madam Zhang's small white hands. "Do you like birds, Lady Shin? This one is a rare songbird from the region around Yangzhou where I used to live. A personal gift from the Great Khan. Look around. All of these are from his generosity." Ma understood what she was really being shown: how much the Great Khan valued Madam Zhang, for what she had done for him. "Let me bestow this one upon you as welcome."

Madam Zhang was smiling, but Ma felt the danger. *One wrong look; one enemy made.* At least it was realistic for a new consort to be shaking in fear. She said with eyes so lowered that all she could see was the luxuriously carpeted floor in front of her, "How could this lowly consort dare accept a gift that the Great Khan had granted to the Empress herself?"

"Lowly? Why should you speak so, Lady Shin, when you must be so accomplished to have won out over all the other Goryeo princesses who must have vied for the honor of becoming the Great Khan's consort? But perhaps," Madam Zhang said with slow consideration, "you don't even consider it an honor."

Ma didn't dare respond. She thought she might vomit from terror. Was there a punishment for being an unwilling concubine?

"Poor little sister!" Madam Zhang suddenly smiled. There was no true benevolence in it, but the threat of claws was gone. Ma nearly gasped in relief. "Of course you find it frightening! But rest assured: gaining a man's attention is an art that needs to be learned and practiced. It doesn't happen accidentally. You'll be able to pass your whole life quietly without him summoning you to his chambers more than once or twice, if that's how you want it."

A maid had brought a tray of tea and treats to the table. Madam Zhang descended from her chair with Zhu's assistance and indicated for Ma to join her.

As Ma took a sweetmeat, Madam Zhang said conversationally, "Since you're a foreigner, I wonder if you've heard of Bolud-Temur of Shanxi? The father of the previous Empress. What a reckless fool! As soon as he heard that it was my husband that had taken the throne, he tried to muster a rebellion amongst the western steppe tribes. A pitiful attempt! He was put down quickly. He'll be arriving soon for his public execution. You and I should certainly go watch together. And then the only remaining loose end to the Great Khan's reign will be that little mosquito Zhu Yuanzhang. For him, I'm sure my husband has an even more spectacular end planned."

The sweetmeat was suddenly so dry that Ma didn't think she'd be able to swallow it. Zhu, standing directly behind Madam Zhang's shoulder, was so calmly blank that it seemed in that moment that she and Zhu Yuanzhang had separated into two people. Ma knew it was just that Zhu couldn't react, but she felt pierced by abandonment, as if in that moment she were completely alone.

"Ambition for the sake of ambition must be punished. Only when everyone knows their place, can there be harmony. As there is order without, in the wider empire, so too should order be maintained in the palace that reflects Heaven's will. Yes," Madam Zhang said, biting delicately into the cake without marring her lipstick or revealing her teeth, "as long as we each know where we belong, I foresee both of us will be very happy here."

The Goryeo princess was waiting for him in her suite.

He had always taken pleasure in extending his presence beyond his body. The swish of his gowns, his perfume, the flutter of his fan: all of it forcing himself upon those whom he disgusted, no matter how they might recoil to protect themselves. And now that he was the Great Khan—how deliciously his presence was magnified! Oh, he still disgusted them. That was clear. But now when that presence touched them, it pressed their foreheads to the floor. The very sight of him filled them with horror. They looked into the center of the world, where the sun should have been, and instead found a dark, loathsome hole that drew everything good into itself until there was nothing left but despair.

The princess sank into a reverence as he entered.

"Rise."

He took a seat at the table. He no longer had to think about the ordinary human gesture of pulling out a chair, or even commanding someone to do it for him. He was the Yuan, and everything moved around him. He simply sat, and the world reordered itself to his will.

His visit to the new consort was nothing more than a courtesy, one he had no intention of repeating. The princess sat with her head lowered as the poison taster flitted over the dishes laid between them. She still wore her native dress: voluminous layers of skirting, and a short brocade jacket secured with a flat ribbon, in hues of peach and green that were suitably pastel for a lower-ranked member of the imperial harem. She was slightly older than he'd assumed during the tribute presentation. A young woman, rather than a girl. She was even pretty enough, in that broad-faced steppe way that any normal Mongol man would have found desirable. It was surprising she'd still been unmarried when the call had come.

Most of the table was taken up with a platter bearing a thick yellow fritter threaded with long green onion stems, pieces of crosshatched squid that had curled into flowers as they cooked, and tiny purple-headed whole octopuses. Presumably it was some Goryeo speciality. Once he might have been intrigued to try it. Now, though, he had the idea that he hadn't just forgotten how to be hungry, but what being hungry even felt like. When the princess rose to serve him, he flicked his fingers in dismissal. "We have no appetite."

Her head was lowered, but he still caught it: that familiar flash of attention to how he used his hands. He felt a corresponding pulse of hatred. It came so instinctually to them, as if it were a primal urge even stronger than fear: to catalogue how his every movement, every syllable, the precise heft and set of his body, all deviated from what they should be.

The princess's lowered head wasn't demureness, he realized with anger. It was avoidance. She was his, and yet she still dared think she might escape contamination? His cruelty quickened. He wanted to tear away her composure to reveal her revulsion. He wanted her laid open, so that when he forced her to see him, he could see the moment of her ruin.

He curled his fingers delicately around his wine cup, feeling how it drew her notice, knowing how it wouldn't fail to thicken her disgust. None of them could resist imagining what else he might have grasped—what *service* he might have rendered—with that same touch.

"Lady Shin, do tell me: What clan war did your family lose, for you to be the one who ended up here? It surely couldn't have been otherwise. Any family with the power to protect their innocent daughters from the depravities of the ruler of the Great Yuan would have done so. How you must have cried when you learned your fate! To be sent for the pleasure of *someone like me*."

He loved how an ordinary phrase could become perversion in his mouth. A normal person's pronoun, where a ruler's pronoun belonged. His very self as a wrongness in the heart of the world, turning an empire into a mockery of itself.

"I'm sure they must have told you what I did to get where I am. Who I lay beneath, and how shamelessly I did it. Perhaps they even speculated on whether I enjoyed it. Whether I bent over only for the Third Prince, or for anyone who asked, because what I truly wanted was abasement and not the throne."

She was controlling herself, but to his satisfaction he could feel how he was stirring a reaction. Her composure was no more than the thin skin that kept water in a cup.

"So now that you're finally here: Am I everything you expected?" He was filled with the savage urge to find her disgust and squeeze it from her like pus from a pimple. "Or perhaps it's the opposite, and my reputation is clearly nothing but slander. Perhaps you see before you a man worthy of desire. Perhaps you'll welcome my touch, and let me between your legs, and even beg me to use you for my satisfaction. Is that the case?"

He reached across the table and raised her chin with one finger. *"Look at me."*

Her eyes met his. Her gaze was luminous, as transparent and trembling as a pool of water. He felt a jolt. Not at what was there, but what wasn't. His first thought was that she must have been managing to conceal her revulsion. And yet—disgust was one of those emotions that always seeped to the surface, because those who held it never truly wanted to hide what they felt. It was too useful as a reassurance to each other—that they all knew what *they* should be, and it wasn't like him.

The princess said quietly, "I know the Great Khan's character. I came here willingly."

His rising fury mixed with incredulity. He didn't know why she'd proved immune to his effeminacy, but to dare think she *knew* him? He existed outside the imagination of any sheltered girl. Her face was so innocent. He could imagine the kind of life she'd led: pampered and cherished; never treated harshly in her life. No doubt she still assumed the inherent kindness of everyone she met, and believed the world was a good and fair place absent of cruelty and people like him. "Willing?" he spat. "What that tells me is that you *don't* know."

He stood abruptly, suppressing the impulse to lash out. "I'll take my leave."

What was a consort to him, after all? Nothing more than a living decoration for the palace, one he had no need to concern himself with if he didn't desire to. If he didn't summon her to spend a night with him, he would never see her again.

He could feel that impossible, undisgusted gaze burning between his shoulder blades as he left.

Ma had been a queen, so palaces weren't entirely foreign to her, but it was strange to be enclosed in one. To know that she could never step outside the walls even if she wanted to. Had she truly been a consort, this would have been her entire world.

It was, superficially at least, a beautiful world. The Palace City was more monumental than anywhere Ma had lived before, with edifices that loomed like cliff faces, and white-sand corridors with walls so high that the sky was reduced to a ravine's single strip overhead. But tucked behind the residences and plazas, gardens provided a comforting human scale. Pagodas overlooked frothing spring flowers; exquisite marble bridges made rainbows over lakes dense with pink lotus blooms. It was pleasure enough to satisfy an entire harem. But since the only members were currently the Empress and Ma, and the Empress preferred to be carried directly to her destinations rather than stroll, for the time being the gardens were Ma's alone. And it created a peaceful fantasy, that this was all there was. That the moment of crisis wasn't coming, when Yuchun would arrive to hurl Zhu's too-small army against the city's outer walls. When Ma would have to place her finger on the scale by doing what she'd been brought here to do.

She noticed a crumpled paper by her foot. When she picked it up, she saw it bore only a few words. Poetry, made senseless as a fragment. At the end of the fragment the author had pressed his brush so hard in frustration that the bristles had separated and rendered a visual screech. It was only then that she saw how the balls of paper were as numerous as the fallen fruit of a tree, hurled from an open garden pagoda that was surrounded by a motionless line of eunuchs and attendants. Within it, a man with a topknot clasped in gold slept with his head lowered upon black-clad arms.

She'd *thought* the Great Khan had been sleeping. But the instant her eyes fell upon him, he sat up. Ma saw a momentary flash of that thin face, even more haggard than when he'd visited her, as if whatever sleep he'd found had left him more drained than refreshed. His red-rimmed eyes found her, standing with the paper in her hand.

She dropped quickly into a reverence. When he'd come to her that past evening, he hadn't been at all what she'd expected. She'd imagined someone like Chen Youliang: someone fundamentally untouchable, whose power held people at a distance from which they could be crushed or controlled. But this Great Khan had wielded himself like a weapon. She remembered his thin fluttering fingers that were more suited to brush than bow; the swish of his hems; the silky insinuation of his speech. He was a man who was feminine, and it made her want to observe him from the corner of her eye so she could see how those qualities looked without his corrosive self-consciousness. She knew, instinctively, that what appealed to her must repulse others. During their meeting, he'd tried to provoke that repulsion from her. It was, for whatever reason, what he wanted.

He'd been confused as to why his provocation hadn't worked, she thought, because it must have worked on everyone else he'd known.

Now he glided down the steps and stood over her. When he didn't bid her rise, she felt a stir of danger.

"Lady Shin. Will you add your censure to that of my attendants, that poetry isn't a suitable pastime for a Great Khan? How those tiresome ones keep urging me to take up suitable pursuits! In springtime a Great Khan should be hunting swans, you see. Although had they dared collect my discarded papers—as you seem to have taken it upon yourself to do—at least they could reassure themselves that the output of my labors hardly merits the word 'poetry.'"

Ma opened her mouth—the bitterness of his self-castigation

demanded a response—but the Great Khan got in first, exclaiming with deep sarcasm, "Oh, but the noble consort would give me her knowledgeable assessment of my verses! I forgot that women are well educated in this field, if in no other. Surely I condemned my own talents too harshly. Perhaps there's been no finer composition by a ruler's hand since that poor humiliated wretch, the Huizong Emperor. Or did you seek to comment upon my exquisite calligraphy? They do say you can tell a man's heart from the energy he brings to the page. Does the way I *use my brush* confirm what you know about my character?"

She realized, unpleasantly, that he hadn't forgiven her their last meeting.

His thin, tense body had a febrile quality that seemed both poisoned and poisoning, ripe with the anticipation of its own spreading contamination. For the first time, Ma felt afraid of him as he said softly, "Perhaps you'd like to really see me."

He called his head eunuch, and spoke a few words that sent him scurrying. The Great Khan followed him at a more genteel pace, saying over his shoulder, "I was waiting for an auspicious moment to get started. Come, noble consort."

He brought her to the main plaza outside the Great Hall. Even before Ma registered what the strange new construction at the center of the plaza was, her feet stuck in the ground. She heard herself make a primal moan of protest.

The Great Khan glanced back at her. His amusement was entirely cruel. "Unless Goryeo is run more smoothly than I thought, I can't imagine there was a shortage of executions at your own royal palace. Do they do it privately, there? Here, we prefer to make it a message to those who would defy our rule." He continued into the plaza, giving no consideration to the possibility that Ma wouldn't follow—because what choice did she have?—adding, "Not that we think Zhu Yuanzhang will take it."

Palace attendants bustled around the construction. An iron cauldron, its circumference greater than the reach of Ma's two arms, rested atop a pile of wood and kindling. On top of the cauldron was an overgrown bamboo steamer. It was large enough to fit a man, if he were curled up on his side. The lid of the steamer was already lashed shut. They had, as the Great Khan had said, been waiting to get started.

The Great Khan didn't issue an instruction. The mere fact of his presence made it begin.

For a while the only activity was the attendants lighting and stoking the fire. The Great Khan said conversationally, "You can take some credit for this, Lady Shin. Your own king helped me put this man down. His name is Bolud-Temur, the former governor of Shanxi and father of the previous Empress. I think he could have borne anyone else on the throne other than me. His grudge against me has been exceptionally long-standing." He gave this some consideration. "Although no more long-standing than my grudge against him, I suppose. His son used to make my life a torment. I got him banished, which was about what he deserved. And no doubt you heard of the misfortune that befell his daughter. I confess, that was also my design." A sound was beginning to make itself known above the crackle of the flames. The Great Khan said, vicious now, "But for the father, who dared rise up against me, I reserved this special punishment."

The sound wasn't a scream, not yet. It was a fluctuating wail, a sob of existential terror at the knowledge that one's ancestor-given body was about to be undone.

Ma cried, "Stop. *Stop.*"

He gave her wet face a look of contempt. "Would you seek to command the Great Khan, consort? This is my will. *This is who I am.*" A ferocity was building in him, a force so dense with self-loathing that it seemed to overspill his thin body and make the air itself shiver into darkness. "Everyone who stood in my way, everyone I could use: I killed them all, and I didn't even stay to watch them die."

As he spoke the sound built, too. At last it became a true scream. A scream of pain that, though it was a stranger's pain, was still another human being's pain. It reached out for connection, and Ma was there for it to connect to. She couldn't deny it, she couldn't refuse it, even though she so desperately wanted to. Something in her seemed unalterably open to others, as if Heaven had selected her as the single person by whose helpless witness all the hurt and suffering in the world would be made real.

"Make sure to enjoy it until the very end," the Great Khan said, in parting.

Later, she wondered what had possessed her. Perhaps the scream had abraded her self-control, until she was nothing but raw nerves. But she found herself crying out to his retreating back, "You regret it, though, don't you?"

He stopped as if he'd been speared. Then he whirled and stalked back to her, holding up a quick hand to prevent his head eunuch from striking her for her impudence. His fury pressed her to the ground, but it wasn't fear that blazed through her but pain, *his* pain that she was as open to as she was to the dying man's. "Regret? What is there to regret? For what I did, *I rule the world.*"

As he stood over her, shaking, she wondered if he might order her to be executed on the spot. But after a moment he unclenched his fists without speaking further, and left.

Ma was still kneeling where he'd left her by the time Bolud's scream faded to an inhuman whistle. After a few more moments even that ceased. The Great Khan had sentenced Ma to stay, but there was some irony to the fact that Bolud's end had come quicker than that of many people she'd known. She wiped her eyes with a shaking hand, and stood.

I rule the world.

He'd spat it as though it was its own incontrovertible proof. But Ma knew what she had seen in his face before it had closed with anger: grief, as deep and jagged as a split in the heart of a tree.

You could only hurt that much—hurt enough to turn the whole world into a reflection of your pain and misery and despair—if you had, once, loved.

He ruled the world. But it wasn't what he had wanted.

It was probably a distinction, Zhu reflected, to have been identified as non-squeamish enough for this particular task. She knelt in front of the basin of asparagus-scented medicinal water and rubbed gingerly at Madam Zhang's naked feet. They smelled the same as if she'd worn her wooden hand for five days straight without changing the bandages around her stump.

"Harder, girl. Clean under each toe," Madam Zhang instructed, pouring herself a steaming cup of fertility tea. Zhu saw with interest that she had only three toes on each foot. The small toes had been folded over to rest under the sole, giving each foot the wrinkled, compact look of a wedge of sticky rice steamed inside a lotus leaf. Perhaps that was what they meant by lotus feet. Zhu didn't see the appeal. She cleaned the feet, rebandaged them with a judicious use of her teeth, and slipped them into shoes that had been embroidered with an abundance of pomegranates. Each shoe was less than the length of her hand.

Madam Zhang sipped her tea with a sucking sound of displeasure. "Why should it taste so much worse to begin pregnancies than end them?"

Zhu said curiously, "The Empress never—?" She hadn't thought about it before, but now that she did: it seemed unusual for a woman of Madam Zhang's age to not have had at least one child.

"Should every man who plants a seed be allowed to see it sprout?" Madam Zhang was scathing. "My previous husband didn't deserve the potential of my womb. And other men don't come to courtesans for sons. Not even—"

Her hand jerked and sent tea spilling across her lap. The delicate skin of her thighs was protected by nothing more than a thin layer of silk; the tea had been scalding. But when another person would have flinched, if not cried out, Madam Zhang only glanced down. It was as if the spasm, and the subsequent injury, both belonged to someone else. Zhu thought of how Madam Zhang's enchanting, swaying footsteps became uneven by the end of the day, and the obvious relief that entered her posture whenever she sat. But Madam Zhang's face had never once betrayed a flicker of discomfort. Zhu had assumed she was excellent at masking her pain. Now she had the strange idea that Madam Zhang didn't feel it at all. It was an eerie thought: that a woman's body might have become as numb to her own thoughts and feeling as that of a doll.

Madam Zhang had envied Zhu's pain. Zhu thought of the

dinner between Madam Zhang and the Great Khan, where she had wondered whether Madam Zhang found all her men interchangeable. But some man's name had been swallowed by that uncrossable crevasse between interior and exterior. *Other men don't come to courtesans for sons.*

General Zhang, Zhu realized with surprise. She had thought Madam Zhang was merely using him, as she had used Rice Bucket before him and the Great Khan afterwards. Had it been a true attachment, after all?

Madam Zhang had already moved on. She said restlessly, "Where is the Great Khan's invitation to spend the night? It should be here by now. You—!" The metal talons on her last three fingers singled out a hapless maid by the door. "Go to the Office of Administration of Domestic Affairs and get it for me."

As the maid bowed herself out, Madam Zhang put her teacup aside and opened her jewelry box. And then it was Zhu's turn to move on from thoughts of General Zhang, as she saw the simple bracelet of jade and gold beads lying alongside that multitude of necklaces and rings and hairpins.

Madam Zhang saw the direction of Zhu's interest, and scooped it out. "Beautiful, isn't it?" When she slipped it on, it fit her wrist as perfectly as if it had been sized for a woman rather than a man. "I took it from that sad fool, the eunuch general. A pity it doesn't please the Great Khan for me to wear it. He doesn't like to be reminded of his brother." She held her wrist this way and that, admiring the play of light on the gold.

The last time Zhu had seen that bracelet around Ouyang's wrist, he'd been trembling half-naked at her feet as she hurt him. Helped him. But her help hadn't been enough. It had been the analgesic applied to a battlefield casualty who had already lost too much blood to survive. She would change the world, but it would come too late for him. An unfamiliar feeling was lurking in her chest. She identified it, with difficulty, as sadness.

Something Madam Zhang had said was niggling at her. "Why was the eunuch general a fool? I thought he killed the Great Khan, and succeeded in his revenge. He died, but he got what he wanted."

"Ah, so you've heard of him! The famous eunuch general." As Madam Zhang gave her an arch look full of cruel, private amusement, Zhu suddenly felt uneasy. "I suppose it shouldn't surprise me that servants and peasants tell his tale amongst themselves. Revenge, death, honor: Isn't it delicious? But let me tell you the real version.

"Indeed, General Ouyang did storm Dadu, and he slaughtered the previous Great Khan where he sat on what is now my husband's throne. But revenge for an executed father—oh, it was hardly that. What execution? The Great Khan never killed the General's father. He was alive in the imperial prison the whole time! There was no filial duty; there was no honor to defend; there was no death to avenge. General Ouyang based his entire life upon the fiction of his father's noble death, when in reality his father was a coward. He had begged for mercy, preferring to spend the rest of his life rotting in ignominy rather than die with pride.

"My husband released him, afterwards. He wasn't even so old. He'll be able to start another family; have other descendants, real sons, to remember him. So it was quite the happy ending for the Ouyang clan." Madam Zhang smiled as she put the bracelet back in the box. "For everyone except General Ouyang, that is."

The floor had gone out from under Zhu. All she could think of was that scream of existential pain in the Hall of Great Brilliance—of that inexplicable dread and fear, as if something had clutched her, rung within her, with a terrible likeness. Ouyang had done everything he did, thinking that it would be worth it—that it *had* to be worth it. But in the end—

In the end—

As she stood in a paralysis of awful realization, the door opened and the maid slipped back in. She was carrying a gilded cage with a frilled white pigeon inside. Folded almost in half with supplication, she whispered, "The Great Khan is spending the night with the new consort. He sends this gift as a token of his continuing regard for the Empress."

Madam Zhang's nail guards closed together like claws. After a moment she smiled thinly. "I hadn't expected him to choose her so soon. Well! Let him have his one night with her. When he gets his curiosity out of the way, he'll realize she doesn't have what it takes to please him."

She snatched up Ouyang's bracelet, and with a flash of spite put it back on her wrist.

Madam Zhang was the Empress, the most powerful woman in the world. But now Zhu saw someone who had lost someone she loved, but wasn't even able to mourn. Someone who was forced to wait upon the Great Khan's convenience and, as long as she failed to conceive, could be cast aside whenever he wanted.

As for the Great Khan himself—he resided at the pinnacle of the world as the Son of Heaven. And yet he cast a shadow over everything around him, as if it were a physical emanation of his unhappiness and pain and despair.

Ouyang had killed the one he loved, for the sake of a blood debt that didn't exist.

All three of them had caused and endured untold suffering in pursuit of what they wanted. And in the end, they had all achieved what they had set out to do. Zhu thought with eclipsing horror:

But none of them had made it worth it.

Ma stepped naked out of the sunken bamboo soaking tub, her hair streaming water, and let her maids dry her. The fragrance of the bath lingered on her skin.

As soon as the Great Khan's eunuch had presented her with the wooden tag that had the name Lady Shin carved into it like a tombstone, she'd known that this was his revenge. She had dared see his private pain. She had wounded him by laying open to the air what he needed to keep to himself, and for that: she had to be punished.

She couldn't shake the memory of Bolud's awful punishment for daring to defy the Great Khan. The petals in the bathwater hadn't been enough to overpower the tub's smell of waterlogged bamboo. Only days ago, that particular smell would have evoked the comforting sight of food steamers stacked in a pan. Now it made her nauseous with horror.

She knew that as much as the Great Khan's driving hurt and pain was a truth of him, what he'd shown her—his cruelty, and his capacity for ruination—was equally a truth. He had ruined Bolud. Now he wanted to ruin her, too.

But to ruin the kind of woman who was given as a gift between men, there was no need for an execution. All one had to do was destroy the only thing the world valued about her.

The maids massaged Ma's dried body, then smoothed it with pumice stones. They trimmed her pubic hair, and removed the hair from her underarms and forearms with a caustic paste. They dusted her skin with luminous powder of crushed mother-of-pearl, stained her fingernails with the juice of crushed red petals, and polished her teeth with charcoal. They painted her lips and face, and combed her hair so that it hung in a silky sheet down her back like a girl's. But they didn't dress her.

Ma thought of how the palace ordered itself around the Great Khan's needs. Chairs appeared as he sat; doors opened at his approach; food was laid before he had even formed the thought of eating. And so when women were rolled naked in carpet and carried to his chambers, it wasn't only about protecting him against assassination. It was for his convenience. He was delivered an object he could make use of, without having to say a word.

But when Ma had made her choice, she'd already known what she would have to do.

She called to her eunuchs, "Take me to him."

22

Unwrapped, the consort stood quietly as her eunuchs withdrew and the doors closed behind them. To his surprise, she bore her nakedness without visible embarrassment. She was never as she should be, and he couldn't understand it. It provoked him into hate. She had an innocent girl's wide eyes and gentle demeanor, she had been anguished by a stranger's death—and yet now, when it was obvious she should have been afraid, she wasn't.

His anger renewed itself. How had she dared lay him open to his grief and regret, as if they mattered? The only thing that mattered now was what he was, and *this* was what he was: the darkness in the center of the world, a world that was pain and misery and spreading despair. And it could never be any other way, because with every action, every breath, he remade it in his image.

He said coldly, "Get on the bed. Lie on your back."

He let his gaze turn her into a thing. She was his to consume, use, throw away. Afterwards, she would be exactly the same as all those others who cowered from him in fear and horror. He was the Great Khan, and nothing in the world could withstand the ruination he brought.

The consort lay down. Her body against the pheasant-patterned coverlet of his bed was entirely unlike the Empress's manicured perfection. It was oddly reminiscent of the bodies of the girls he used to lie with before any of this happened—girls who had been laughingly unbothered by their stocky thighs and curved hips and sun-touched skin that fashion deemed unbeautiful. He had found their unruliness feminine. Desirable.

His body was already responding to that desirability. But it was nothing more than a mechanical response, devoid of any of the pleasure or emotion it had once brought. It made him feel dead within his own body. He knew that deadness was his own fault. He had taken some capacity of himself that was meant for joy and tenderness and used it as a weapon, and in so doing had broken it irreparably.

He'd been avoiding looking at her face. But he could feel her gaze on him as he knelt between her legs and undid the tie of the chrysanthemum-embroidered gown that was the only thing he wore. Her refusal to flinch stoked his anger. "Not afraid, Lady Shin? Did someone tell you, perhaps, how some of the other Great Khans wouldn't sleep with unwilling new consorts, and they would simply send them away if they cried? Unfortunately for you, my unique path to the throne has left me with little chivalry. I know what it's like to lie back and take it from a man. No matter how unpleasant it feels in the moment, I assure you: you'll survive." Whatever sheen of pretense he'd managed elsewhere had worn off; he could feel his savagery bared to her, like the teeth of a skull. "I won't show you mercy, no matter how much you cry."

There was a faint rustle in the corridor, and he realized with disgust that it was the eunuchs with their ears pressed to the latticed doors. Unable to hear the exact words that passed between them, but hoping for the vicarious thrill of hearing him take a woman's virginity.

"I don't expect mercy," she told him. To his surprise, there was no hint of self-pity or noble duty in her voice. Under the softness, he felt steel. "You took pains to make sure I know who you are. That you're someone who kills, tortures, betrays; who can't stop himself from perpetuating cruelty and pain. Someone who does the unforgivable, so he can make himself worthy of hate."

The dull clench he felt in response wasn't hurt, but simply recognition of the truth. He looked away, knowing she could still see his sneer. "How much more you'll hate me, after this."

She shocked him, then, by taking his hand and placing it upon her breast. The warmth of it rose and fell steadily as she pressed it there, as if she were the one not letting him escape. His anger flooded back. He didn't want *performance.* He wanted to rip the ugly truth out of her, the way she'd had the truth of him. He wanted her hate with a ferocity that seemed indistinguishable from desperation.

He pressed his body against her, hissing, "Don't pretend you want this." His body was a promise of ruination. His body was the tool that would yield him the moment she finally recoiled from him in fear and loathing.

"I don't want it," she agreed, and even as he absorbed that response she changed some interior angle and he fell. He sank into where she was soft and vulnerable, where she was penetrable and breakable. His body over her body, his body inside her body, and he was overcome by a cold and motionless despair, because this was all he had ever done, and all he was worthy to do: to break and ruin.

Her chest rose and fell beneath him as it had against his hand. Her face was as close to his as a kiss. He could tell she was looking at him. She'd never looked away. And as if he were helpless to witness the fact of his own monstrosity writ in her face, he looked back.

Her lashes were very thick, her eyes dark. She was wide open to him. She had never even tried to shield herself. What he saw in her now was the mercy he had refused to give her. She was beautiful with it: luminous and vulnerable, full of sorrow and pity, but without hatred. She didn't tremble, and she wasn't afraid.

She held him inside her, and whispered an impossible promise: "You can't ruin me."

She put her arms around him, and her softness was a strength beyond anything he could have imagined, and it contained him without breaking.

Instead he was the one who broke, who dissolved at the touch of another person against and around him, a person who didn't recoil from his touch even though he deserved it, even though he had made the world this way and poured all his pain and poison into it. Even though this was what he was.

The Great Khan slept.

He hadn't hurt her. But Ma couldn't help thinking of the pleasure Zhu had always given her, in an act that had never felt destructive, but creative. Ma had long ago lost what the world most valued in a woman. But losing it hadn't ruined her. Instead she had stepped into a new reality of Zhu's making, and found a different way of being. New paths, new choices. That reality, sized for the two of them, was no more than a seed. But that was why she was doing this, Ma thought with a fierceness that was love as well as sadness. If Zhu got what she wanted, then that seed would become the world.

The Great Khan woke. He looked momentarily shocked, as if waking hurt him. It was the same way he'd looked when Ma interrupted him at the pagoda. Not so much awoken as wrenched from sleep, the violence of it pressing bruises under his eyes and hollowing his cheeks. She remembered the febrile tension of his body over hers; his thinness that was of something scraped down to its limits.

"Lady Shin," he murmured. There was a new vulnerability in him. It made Ma think of a small child who raged with the murderous desire to hurt the parent who had frustrated it, then afterwards clung to that same parent with hysterical cries of guilt, because its desire had been genuine, and of relief, that it hadn't been strong enough to make its wish come true.

The Great Khan had called Lady Shin to his chamber. He had intended to break a sheltered virgin girl with that name, a girl who would never have strayed outside expectation. Instead he had found Ma: a woman who had already lived and lost, loved and been loved. Like a parent for a child, she had been safe from him, and safety for him.

He couldn't hurt her, because he had no idea who she was.

All at once she couldn't bear to stay beside him for any longer than necessary. "Does the Great Khan have any further requirements of this consort?"

She saw the moment he awoke fully, because his vulnerability slipped out of sight under a shell of control. "Before you leave, I understand it's traditional to give a gift to a consort for her first night with the Great Khan."

It came back to Ma in a terrible rush: what she had come here to do. She felt a strange premonition of sadness. *You can't hurt me, but I can hurt you.*

"Enter," he said, without raising his voice. It wasn't even as if he knew his head eunuch was waiting outside, but as if it hadn't occurred to him that he might not be there to serve.

He sat up, careless of his nakedness, and looked through the tray of jewelry the eunuch held out. He must have been observing her at the same time, because when her eye went to the hairpins he said with some irony, "As I wasn't always a Great Khan above reproach, I know how it behooves a man to consider a woman's preferences when picking a gift."

His thin fingers ran across the sharp-ended pins with their twinkling chains that ended in pearls, coral, lapis, tourmaline, then halted on a breathtaking golden pin. The shaft, rounded rather than sharp-ended like the others, was thicker than a writing brush. It was crowned with a single long strand of gold wire that had been bent around and upon itself to create a shimmering filigree sculpture of a phoenix. As the Great Khan looked at it, a shadow of self-recrimination crossed his face. "This one lately belonged to Lady Ki, your compatriot. Though she wasn't much like you. She was my predecessor's favorite. The mother of—" A spasm of pain went through him. With effort he shrugged away whatever the memory had been, and handed her the pin. "Wear it next time, to please me."

His voice cooled; became brisk. "Eunuchs, return your mistress to her residence."

As the eunuchs rolled the carpet around her, blocking out the room, Ma closed her fingers around the pin. With its rounded end, nobody would think it a weapon, but it fit her hand like a knife.

"Every night," Madam Zhang hissed. Her fingernail, dragging down the column of neat dated entries in the Register of Domestic Affairs, pressed so hard that the paper beneath it wrinkled and tore. "He's been saying he was *too busy* to visit and eat a meal with me. But he was spending every night with her? That flat-faced cow?" She hurled the register away.

Zhu was as taken aback by this turn of events as Madam Zhang. If she had remained an invisible slave, as had been the original plan, she would have been able to engineer chance encounters with Ma's maids to stay abreast of what was happening. But since becoming a member of Madam Zhang's closely observed household, she'd had no such opportunity.

The original plan had also been for Ma to sleep with the Great Khan just once, to obtain the weapon he would unknowingly gift to her. Ma would wait until Zhu's army had reached Dadu, and only then arrange to be called again, when she would use the weapon to end it. So what had happened in the Great Khan's private chamber that first night, that he would call Ma back again and again? Zhu's stomach burned with unfamiliar guilt. Every day that she had been continuing obliviously inside Madam Zhang's household, Ma had been enduring the Great Khan's touch. How bad was it? How much was she suffering?

It had been Ma who had tried to warn her, even before Zhu had learned of Ouyang's terrible ending, and Madam Zhang's numbness, and the Great Khan's black shadow that he cast across the world.

Have you ever thought it might not be worth it?

She had always been so certain, but now she didn't know. It filled her with a hollow horror.

"I haven't seen her since she arrived," Madam Zhang spat. "She's been avoiding me. Does she think she's too good to pay the Empress courtesy calls? Summon her to pay her respects!"

Ma arrived a short while later. To Zhu's relief, she looked sick with nerves but otherwise unharmed. Ma's eyes, modestly downturned as she entered the Empress's presence, slipped to Zhu. It was like the secret brush of two forbidden lovers' little fingers as they passed on the street. Zhu felt a renewed wave of pain when she realized her relief about Ma was because she had been expecting to see bruises in line with the Great Khan's reputation for cruelty. The whole palace had heard about how he'd had Bolud-Temur steamed alive. The one good thing was that Ma was wearing an elaborate gold hairpin that could only have been her first-night gift from the Great Khan. That, then, had worked.

Ma said, in passably Mongolian-accented Han'er, "The lowly consort Lady Shin offers her respectful greetings to the illustrious Empress."

She dipped into a placating one-knee reverence. But as the top of her head became visible, Madam Zhang sucked in a breath. "He gave you the phoenix pin?"

The uncomfortable rustling of the maids' uniforms was very loud in the sudden silence. At first glance Zhu hadn't realized *what* the gold pin Ma was wearing was. But she knew what the phoenix pin was. It signified the Great Khan's favorite. And he had given it to Ma, not Madam Zhang.

That was why Ma had looked so sick upon coming in, Zhu realized. That was why she had never visited Madam Zhang, though courtesy demanded it. She had known that wearing the pin would be construed as a challenge to the Empress. But neither would she have been able to leave it off, after having been given it by the Great Khan himself. To cast aside the token of the Great Khan's favor would be a grave insult that nobody, not even a favorite, would dare risk.

Madam Zhang rose abruptly, the decorations in her hair swinging threateningly like a bird raising its fighting plumage. The force of her movement must have sent agony stabbing through her feet. Zhu had the unpleasant idea that instead of feeling it as physical pain, Madam Zhang experienced it as an amplification of her rage.

Madam Zhang descended to where Ma knelt and, as neatly as a carnivorous fish taking a bite, snatched the pin from Ma's head. It came away trailing a clump of hair. Ma let out a pained cry that pierced Zhu to the core.

"How dare you!" Madam Zhang flung the pin down. For a moment she stood there panting, as if that might be the end of it. Then she attacked. Zhu watched in helpless horror as her nails caught Ma on the face, on the scalp: they drew long bloody streaks on her skin and tore into the beautiful smoothness of her hair. Madam Zhang lashed out without reprieve, an animal clawing and ripping at its prey. Ma screamed and flung her arms over her head in a futile effort to protect herself. Blood from the scored backs of her hands smeared the sleeves of her little ribboned satin jacket, and the white linen beneath.

Once upon a time, had it been necessary for what she wanted, Zhu thought she might have been able to watch unmoved while Ma cried in pain. She probably would have prided herself on her strength that allowed her to endure what needed to be done. But that had been before she had seen Xu Da dying in agony. It had worn new paths of grief and pain into her, and now, as she watched Ma suffer, her pain found those grooves and flowed smoothly. She'd been newly shaped by her pain, and as a result she felt pain so much more than she ever had before.

What if it already wasn't worth it? Could she have paid this much, only to now walk away from what she wanted rather than cause more pain?

Zhu thought of the original Zhu Chongba letting go of his fate. She had seized that abandoned destiny, and resisted every attempt of the world to wrench it from her, and as a result of her suffering had become the person who could rightfully claim it as her own. She felt a wrench of pure anguish. How could she give up her desire for that fate: her greatness, and her new world? That desire was the burning star inside her; the radiance that filled her; her self. Without it, what would be left of her?

Ma collapsed, crying, and plastered her forehead to the floor in abjection. "Mercy, Empress, mercy on this unworthy woman!"

Madam Zhang looked down at her, panting and swaying on her tiny feet, the gleam in her eye undiminished. "Unworthy? Yes, unworthy to speak to me, unworthy to be in my presence!" Seizing a long-handled fan, she beat Ma's back and cringing shoulders. "You don't deserve to cry!"

Madam Zhang's other servants watched impassively. They knew this was the natural order of things, as if life inside the palace were nothing but a simulacrum of cruel nature. But every blow upon Ma's sobbing body seemed to hit Zhu's heart.

Was there a future in which Zhu didn't become emperor?

Could I let go?

When Ma had gone, Madam Zhang said with satisfaction, "Let's see how well she pleases him with a face looking like that."

The birds, alarmed by the violence, were as silent as the servants. The golden phoenix pin lay on the floor in a clump of hair. That pin had brought Ma so much suffering. But, Zhu realized, she still needed Ma to have it.

"Empress, if the Great Khan found out you took the phoenix pin—"

She left the specter of the Great Khan's punishment hanging ominously. Apparently even an empress didn't dare test her power against the Great Khan, because at length Madam Zhang said in high dudgeon, "Fine! Return it to her." When she turned away, the sliver of her profile seemed like the interior whiteness of a porcelain shard that could slice a careless finger down to the bone. "Let's see if she's foolish enough to wear it in front of me again."

Zhu caught up with Ma's sedan chair within sight of the northwestern corner of the walls. This section of the Palace City, lacking the wide-open plazas that characterized the area around the Hall of Great Brilliance, more closely resembled an ordinary residential compound. Numerous consort residences interlocked densely with small flowering courtyards. Since Ma was currently the only consort in residence, the area had an abandoned air. The courtyards were too small to catch the sunshine, and drifts of decaying spring blossoms had fetched in the corners like forgotten snow.

Atop the sedan chair, Ma sat hunched over with her tangled hair across her face like a woman in mourning. Zhu trotted up to the sedan's comet tail of Goryeo maids and announced in Mongolian for the benefit of any onlookers, "The Empress sent me with an item to be returned to your mistress."

The head maid's mouth opened in surprise as she recognized Zhu. She tapped the lead eunuch on the shoulder in a signal to halt.

Ma looked up with a start as the chair lowered. One of her eyes sprang wide as she caught sight of Zhu. Zhu's heart wrenched as she saw that Ma's other eyelid was already badly swollen.

Ma's surprise was quickly overshadowed by concern. She gave a nervous glance around the courtyard, then whispered to her maids, "Maintain our privacy."

As the maids spread in a protective circle around the downed sedan chair, Ma grasped Zhu's one flesh hand and one wooden hand fiercely. She withdrew after a moment, pale and urgent, saying, "We shouldn't—"

Zhu showed Ma the pin. "We have a few moments." Even so, she knew Ma was right to be anxious. Palaces had more eyes than a scallop. Even though Zhu had permission for the meeting, she knew any reported friendliness between herself and the Goryeo consort could well be enough to undo Madam Zhang's trust in her.

In lieu of a kiss, Zhu pressed their shoulders together. The sight of Ma's swollen eye filled her with a terrible tenderness. The more she catalogued Ma's injuries, the worse the tenderness became. It grew inside her, until it was crushing her organs so badly that she thought she might not survive it. She realized she was gasping. "I'm sorry, Yingzi. All this pain, all this suffering—I believed it would be worth it. You warned me, but I wouldn't listen. I'm sorry."

Ma was very quiet. Then she said, "Zhu Yuanzhang. Do you know why I said to you back in Songdo, 'Don't ask'?"

Zhu remembered being confused by Ma's insistence, but her overwhelming emotion at the time had been one of guilt and relief: that Ma would help her, even if she didn't fully understand why.

Ma said, "You've been thinking of my pain and suffering, and Xu Da's, as a price you extracted from us for becoming emperor. That's why you feel that if you don't gain the throne, or if gaining the throne could never be worth our pain, then it would be a failure.

"But you didn't *make* us. That's why I didn't want you to ask me to help you. Didn't you wonder why Xu Da never asked you to stop, even when he had his doubts about your methods? He didn't want to risk you ordering him to continue. He wanted to continue of his own free will, even as he knew it would be his death.

"Our suffering wasn't a payment. It was a gift. We gave it to you so you can achieve your fate. And your fate isn't just the throne, or greatness. It's greatness enough to *change the world.* What incentive did any of the men who sat on that throne, or who would sit on it if not for you, have to change how things are? But you understand what it's like to be nothing. You understand what it is to feel, and to hurt. You understand what it's like to be someone who's judged as worthless because of their sex or the shape of their body or what they do or who they like."

They heard a snatch of laughter as palace servants entered the area. Their time was already up. Ma reached up from the sedan chair and touched Zhu's face with a terrible, sorrowing gentleness, and Zhu realized with a shock that there were tears there. "Can you really cry? This is the first time I've seen it." Zhu only remembered the existence of the pin when Ma took it from her. "Don't worry about me. Don't think about my pain. I chose my fate, just as Xu Da chose his. Let us have done this for you, so you can do something nobody else could or would do."

Ma summoned her maids back to her with a glance of her uninjured eye. As the eunuchs lifted the sedan chair, she said with that compassion that refused cowardice; that refused pity; that was the strongest force in the world: "Zhu Yuanzhang, my husband. Once you refused your fate. Now commit to it. Not from fear or obligation, but because you choose it."

The Great Khan's eyes widened as Ma was delivered to his private chambers that evening.

He wasn't actually a brilliant actor, Ma observed, as she noticed him scrutinizing her injuries. His feelings ran too deep; they showed as clearly as blood through gauze. He was able to hide what he felt from others only because they were too transfixed by the surface he presented to them. They assumed that because they could see his effeminacy—something any other man would have hidden for shame—he must be incapable of hiding anything at all.

Now she could see he was furious, perhaps more furious than she had ever seen him before, but she thought it might only be she who could see it.

"I *could* execute my own empress," he said, with unsettling mildness. "But I probably shouldn't. What would you consider an adequate punishment? Do you want her residence? I'll give it to you."

"I don't want her residence!" Ma exclaimed. "That would just make it worse. Besides, she's your empress. Who wouldn't be upset, if they felt they were losing favor? Sending for me every night is too much. If you paid her more attention, she wouldn't be jealous."

He gave her a crooked smile, and drew her to him. "But I wouldn't want to make *you* jealous."

After he had taken his pleasure, they lay together with his head upon her chest. "I'm serious," Ma said, picking up where they had left off. "About the Empress's jealousy. Given what she's done for you, don't you owe her respect? You still rely on her army." She forced herself to sound casual, and added, "After all, there's still the matter of Zhu Yuanzhang."

"Ah, but you forget," he said. "The Empress isn't a ruler any longer, but instead my woman. She doesn't control her army. I do. And if I give her respect, it will be because I choose to, not because I owe it to her. A Great Khan owes nothing to anyone." His hair was coming out of its topknot. Its texture was softer and more straying than Ma's own waterfall of hair. The ends tickled her. "And don't worry about Zhu Yuanzhang. I've been thinking about him out there, daring to march upon me." Ma realized, belatedly, that he thought Zhu was the one physically leading her army towards him. Of course he didn't know that Zhu had given command to Chang Yuchun. "I have a good idea how to take care of him."

He was silent for a while. When Ma craned her neck for a glimpse of his face, she saw he'd fallen asleep. He only ever seemed to sleep like this, in naps that seemed more like snatched gasps than true rest. Even asleep, his body was tense. But without his sardonic intelligence that raked at anyone who dared get within reach—without his defensive shield of performance—he was abruptly a young man. She was surprised by the idea that he might only be a few years older than Zhu.

Ma touched his frowning eyebrows. They were finer than many men's, but it seemed a matter of grooming rather than the natural femininity of Ouyang's delicate moon arches. Even when their bodies meshed, Ma was aware of how her lie was a veil between them, much as sleep was now. It was a lie that should have protected her. It should have let her keep her distance. But now she wondered if she'd ever had a chance of not feeling empathy for someone who had let his vulnerability press against her in an intimacy greater than anything their bodies could have done.

There was a twinkle of gold from the table beside the bed. The phoenix pin lay where he'd placed it after taking it from her hair. As she looked at it, Ma heard the echo of Bolud's agonized scream. That was what the Great Khan would do to Zhu, once he defeated her army and identified her, if Ma didn't stop him. And she knew he would do it without grief, or regret, or even a second thought.

It wasn't a competition, Ma thought with a sick feeling. She'd always known who she would choose. Who she had already chosen, long before she came here, long before she ever met this man who was the Great Khan. The only thing that was changing over time was how much that choice was going to hurt her, and how much of herself it would break.

She was conscious of what else she knew, that he hadn't yet realized. Though he'd summoned her to him every night for well over a month, in that entire time: she'd never bled.

She felt him wake even before he murmured, "All this time, and to think: the cure for my insomnia was a woman beside me."

Ma hid her pang of sadness. "Maybe only this particular woman."

"Maybe," he agreed, amused. He had summoned her early, so it was still evening. From the soft twilight outside came the deafening chorus of starlings where they had flocked into a single tree in the courtyard.

"Speaking of women, and Zhu Yuanzhang," the Great Khan said. "Here's a funny thing. What do you think about the idea that Zhu Yuanzhang isn't a man, but a woman dressed as a man?"

It was as if the world, and even her own body, had snapped out of existence around her.

He laughed at her expression. It was a surprisingly nice laugh. "Yes, it's too strange, isn't it. I wouldn't have put any stock in it, except that the information came from someone who proved himself quite useful to me in the past. He used to be one of Zhu Yuanzhang's inner circle." Ma's ears buzzed. She felt distant from herself as the Great Khan went on, "He's here in the palace now, as my Minister of Public Works. An engineer, by the name of Jiao Yu."

☼

The lids of the bowls and tureens on Madam Zhang's dining table made a good secret of their distastefully cooling contents. Absent being opened, their jewel-like array was as pretty as it had been an hour before. Madam Zhang faced the empty place setting, her composure as tightly lidded as the dishes. Her hair ornaments shimmered in the falling lamplight. She was managing to maintain face in front of her curious servants, but Zhu knew how furious and humiliated she must be: left waiting for the Great Khan, who had promised that evening to come.

"He'll be here soon," Madam Zhang snapped, when a maid finally ventured that perhaps the dishes would keep better in the kitchen. "The Great Khan has many demands upon his time. How could we begrudge waiting while he manages affairs of empire!"

Zhu was amazed Madam Zhang didn't choke on her own vinegar. She suggested in a discreet undertone, "Perhaps this maid could go check with Domestic Affairs—"

After a moment Madam Zhang gave a stiff nod, and Zhu shot out the door.

The Office of Administration of Domestic Affairs was a long trek to the other side of the Palace City. When Zhu arrived, the eunuch in charge of handling the Great Khan's domestic schedule frowned. "The Great Khan's office informed the Empress that he would dine with her tonight? But Lady Shin has been in his chambers since before sunset." He showed Zhu a flat box with the pegs that held the name tags of all the Great Khan's women; the only one there belonged to the Empress. "The noble consort received her invitation this morning. There must have been a mistake."

Not a mistake, Zhu realized. Madam Zhang had attacked Ma, the Great Khan's favorite, and this was the punishment he had devised: leaving her to discover her relegation to the status of an inferior woman. Zhu's memory of Ma's suffering was still painfully fresh. But the thought of Madam Zhang, waiting alone as she was made into the palace's fool, gave her a surprising pinch.

Despite the longer spring days, it was fully dark by the time Zhu trotted back towards the Empress's residence. The palace was mostly quiet, but as she entered a long thoroughfare she saw one of the palace's many maroon-clad officials heading in her direction.

There was something familiar about him. Zhu puzzled over it as they drew closer, still not quite at a distance where she could make out his face, until all at once familiarity flashed over into recognition.

Zhu's body went cold, then hot. She had never felt such fury.

Jiao Yu.

She'd all but forgotten about him. But of course he was here. Zhu could have kicked herself. When Jiao had betrayed her, he'd come straight to Dadu to offer his services to the person he'd known would beat Zhu to the throne. And when that person had become the Great Khan, he'd stayed to reap his reward.

Jiao knew Zhu, and he knew Ma. He was the one person who could bring everything down. But, Zhu thought quickly, he also had no idea that either of them was here. He was unlikely to come across Ma, since she spent most of her time secluded from the public eye. And now that Zhu knew he was here, she could stay alert and avoid him if she saw him from a distance. All she had to do now was let him pass.

She stepped to the edge of the path and fell to one knee, head lowered and hands folded in a maid's respectful genuflection to an official. It was bad luck that the thoroughfare was well lit, but she couldn't credit the idea that he might recognize her. Jiao was interested in things, not people, and he never lowered himself to look at someone he thought beneath him.

As she'd expected, Jiao's gaze passed over her. He was continuing—

—until, suddenly, he wasn't.

Jiao swung around, and as the torchlight caught his shadow-hooded face, Zhu saw what he was looking at. Not *her.* Her hand.

Her wooden hand, which Jiao had made.

He hadn't recognized her, Zhu thought bitterly, but himself in her. He recognized the part of her that had come out of his imagination, which bore the mark of his hands and tools, and that he claimed as his own. It felt as violating as the knowledge that he had seen and touched her unconscious naked body.

Zhu had never liked Jiao. Now, in a burst of insight, she discovered that she had always hated him.

He stood over her as she knelt there. Zhu was caught. There was no denying it, and there was nowhere to go. She raised her head, and looked him square in the eye.

Even suspecting—*knowing*—who he'd find, he recoiled. He'd found the familiar, but found it distorted by a new frame and transformed into a perversion of what he'd known. His lips peeled back from his teeth in disgust.

Zhu knew she couldn't fairly blame Jiao for Xu Da's death. He'd been dying even before Jiao split Ouyang from her. But what Jiao *had* done was refuse to believe in her. He had weaponized her self against her, and ensured that Ouyang's last memory of her was a false belief: that the body she was in was the entirety of who she was.

Because of who he thought she was, Jiao would dare deny her what she sought to achieve. He would dare try to keep her down, in what he thought was her place.

But Zhu would be the emperor: not despite who she was, but *because* of it.

Zhu looked at Jiao and knew, deep down in a way she'd never felt before, that she would feel satisfaction in his death—in his erasure from the histories of the world, that she would be the one to write.

"Jiao Yu," she said, looking up at him, "when you lost faith in me, when you betrayed me and tried to use my self as a weapon against me, you should have run."

23

Jiao Yu picked up his black skirts and ran. But he didn't run in fear. He ran as hard as he could towards the distant epicenter of the Palace City. Towards the Great Khan.

By the time Zhu was on her feet after him, he was already around a corner. It was the first time Zhu had run as a woman, and it rapidly occurred to her that her uniform wasn't made for running. Her slippers filled with sand; her billowing dress braked her like a sail. It was like running in a nightmare. As she labored along she wrenched her hand from its round wrist joint, baring the metal tang that protruded from the ball of the wrist. The end of the tang was a flat tongue rather than a point, but if she were to stab it with enough force—

Zhu rounded the corner in time to see Jiao sedately entering a cut-through between two buildings. She stopped short, panting. The cut-through fed into one of the Palace City's main thoroughfares. It was bright and heavily patrolled, and more importantly: it ran all the way to the Great Khan's residence at the rear of the Hall of Great Brilliance. Jiao knew she couldn't chase him on that street, lest she reveal herself. She had no way of intercepting or stopping him. He felt so secure that he'd even stopped running.

He thinks he's won.

The sheer arrogance of it filled Zhu with renewed anger. If she'd been able to manifest that feeling into the world, it would have smashed him like a bug on the pavement. Her desire to hurt Jiao felt new, like slipping into something dark and welcoming and savage. She wanted to rip Jiao's liver out with her teeth. She'd spared him for his arrogance before, but even then he had never bowed. He had never acknowledged the legitimacy of her leadership, preferring to maintain that he was only pursuing his own interests that coincidentally intersected with hers. Zhu had put up with it for years, and now she wanted to see his face change with the awareness of failure. For him to see, in his last moments, the mistake he'd made: that he wasn't the smartest one after all.

Zhu thought furiously as she wedged her hand back on. In less time than it would take to burn a stick of incense, Jiao Yu would be mounting the steps to the Great Khan's residence. He was an official on urgent business; the guards wouldn't deny him, even at this late hour. She had no way of stopping him.

But—someone else did.

Someone Jiao didn't know about; someone who was already in the Great Khan's residence. Someone who was Zhu's last layer of defense between the Great Khan and messages from the outside world.

Even as the idea formed, Zhu was sprinting in the opposite direction from the one Jiao had taken. Ma could stop Jiao from reaching the Great Khan, but only if Zhu could get her a warning in time.

It wasn't a long run back to the Empress's residence, but Zhu was preternaturally conscious of time. Time, time, time, beating away with each of her slippered footsteps.

The residence glowed like a lantern. In those front rooms Madam Zhang was still waiting for the Great Khan, who wouldn't come. But instead of going in, Zhu skirted around the outside and slipped into the garden.

In the garden was the aviary, and in the aviary were Madam Zhang's gifts: those exquisite birds, far different in appearance from their message-carrying ancestors, but still remembering that they had been born and raised in the residence of the Great Khan.

The light from the residence had kept the pigeons awake. They purred in their nesting boxes, and strutted restlessly in the undergrowth. There was no time to think further, and after this there would be nothing further to be done. All Zhu could do was send her warning, and trust Ma to decipher where it came from—*who* it came from—and act.

She flung the aviary door open, and the birds exploded into flight.

⁂

A muffled sound woke Ma from her light sleep beside the Great Khan. It seemed to be coming from outside the window. Rain, but not rain: a fringed, undulating hum that rose and fell like the sea. Men's voices rose over the sound. The courtyard guards.

Ma rose, disliking the now-familiar ripple of nausea that accompanied waking, and slipped out of the cocoon of the drawn bed-curtains. The circular window behind the Great Khan's desk wasn't designed to be flung wide. When she cracked it open, a stinging wave of cold night air rushed in. But the noise that draped her was as soft and heavy as fur.

At first all she saw was brightness, motion. The night sky had been swallowed by a white vortex. It was a circling, thrashing blizzard that caught her eye, and dragged it around and around until the solid ground underneath her heaved. Ma staggered and caught herself, gagging. *Moths,* she thought dizzily. The size and scale of them seemed wrong somehow, but what else could it be other than tens of thousands of moths called to die in the light?

Bowstrings twanged. Ma remembered the guards. They were on the roof ridges, silhouetted blackly against the circling mass, firing into it. The whiteness rained down.

Not moths. Birds. Birds that had once shimmered white as polished jade, and preened their curled and frilled and fanned feathers, were now carpeting the courtyard with their bloodied, fluttering, dying bodies. Madam Zhang's birds.

Strange things didn't always have significance. The birds could have escaped by accident. But, Ma thought with a falling heart, she knew this brand of strangeness. She had seen it so many times before: what seemed harmless and accidental, but bore the invisible mark of a mind—of intent, and desire.

What message was Zhu sending that was of such urgency

that she'd been forced to send it to Ma as she lay by the Great Khan's side?

Something must have happened that threatened to undo the plan, and it had happened too suddenly and catastrophically for Zhu to find any other solution.

A terrible foreboding built inside her. It felt like a ledge of ice pushing her out above frigid water. She thought, slowly, *An engineer, by the name of Jiao Yu.*

Jiao Yu, who had already told the Great Khan that Zhu Yuanzhang had a woman's body, and who was the only person in the palace who could recognize Zhu by sight.

As she stood naked at the window, her skin pimpling with cold and dread, Ma reached up and touched her hair, and felt gold beneath her fingers.

It seemed an eternity Ma had been sitting there, her back to the door of the Great Khan's chamber, waiting. She couldn't have read a word of the book in front of her if her life had depended on it. She was still naked under the coverlet she had wrapped herself in, and she couldn't stop her teeth chattering with cold and nerves. The Great Khan was asleep behind his drawn curtains, but she had no idea how much longer he would stay that way. Her heartbeats were shaking her apart. Had she guessed Zhu's message correctly? She dreaded being wrong, and dreaded even more that she wasn't. Each moment was a throb, a pulse, a prayer: *Please let him not come.*

The door behind her let in a person.

For just a moment, it could have been someone else. It could have been another official coming on another emergency, something Ma had no responsibility towards.

Jiao Yu said, "Consort. I have news for the Great Khan."

Ma had never heard Jiao speak Mongolian before. It sounded like he'd learned it from a book. But his tone was the same: cold, dismissive. In her mind, she saw him: mouth pursed with superiority above his wispy beard; the bright, weasel sparkle in his eye.

Ma had to force herself to speak. Her voice came out high, unnatural. "Esteemed Minister, the Great Khan is sleeping."

It was hopeless, but she found herself pleading silently with him. *Please, Jiao Yu. Don't do this. Leave.*

Jiao's incredulity felt like a physical pressure against her. "Consort, I don't think you understand. Would I come to the Great Khan's chambers if the matter wasn't urgent? Wake him." He added under his breath, in Han'er, "Who does this woman think she is?"

Somehow, Ma stood. Her body shuddered in revolt. It didn't want to be this person. It didn't want to feel this way; it didn't believe itself capable of containing the enormity and awfulness of these feelings for a single moment, let alone forever.

Even worse than the guilt was the shame of knowing that her pain was as much for herself as it was for Jiao. This had been her choice. She'd known that by killing for Zhu, she would lose a part of herself. She'd *known,* so what right did she have to self-pity?

But it hurt so much more than she'd imagined.

Somehow, she turned. She let him see her face. She said, crying, "I wish you could have believed in her, Jiao Yu."

Jiao's mind had always worked faster than anyone else's. Instead of wasting his last moments boggling, or trying to bolt, he opened his mouth to shout for the Great Khan. But the gold wire—wire that had once been a phoenix, on the end of a hairpin—had already tightened around his throat. Jiao's open mouth stayed open. All that came out was a faint creak. As Ma's head maid hauled on the looped ends of the wire with all her strength, the other maids rushed from the shadows to hold him.

Jiao's face purpled. The veins in his forehead were knotted tree roots. He was only a stringy scholar, so four women should have been enough to keep him still, but his approaching end gave him surprising new strength. He threw his head back, bloodying the head maid's nose, then swung himself one way and then the other like a buffalo trying to dislodge wolves. His mouth was open in a silent roar.

Ma gripped the coverlet around herself, shaking. How many times had she done this: watched a man die, and prayed for the end to come quickly? The only difference was that this time she wasn't praying for the man's sake. She felt mad with desperation for Jiao to give up. To *die.* Every extra moment was one that the Great Khan could wake; that the guards could wonder what was taking so long to wrap a consort for transport—

The women's slippered feet thumped faintly against the wooden floor as they were dragged back and forth. Jiao's eyes seemed to be coming out of his skull. The whites had burst all over into red. He heaved forwards, lost traction against the women's concerted effort and staggered violently back again, and the whole unbalanced mass of them landed with a crunch against the long maplewood sideboard. The walls shuddered.

"Great Khan! Is everything all right in there?"

The head maid set her teeth in a rictus of effort, and pulled. Jiao's open mouth opened further. It was wider than Ma had ever seen a person open their mouth, fissures springing open at the corners. Jiao's dark swollen tongue emerged from the void like a lake bed rising up under subterranean pressure.

Through her transfixing horror, Ma managed to call back, "One of my maids was too careless, and tripped. I'll punish her later."

The life went out of Jiao in jerky stages. The moment his knees buckled, the maids lowered him to the ground. Their nostrils were flared with silent effort. The tallest maid immediately shed her uniform and slippers as the others tore off Jiao's ministerial robe, scholar hat, undertrousers, and boots and handed them to her to put on. As soon as she was dressed, she slipped out the door with her head angled away from the guards. With the guards' own eyes lowered respectfully, hopefully all they would see would be a ministerial profile passing in the shadows.

They held their breath, then relaxed in unison as the guards murmured acknowledgment and the maid's footsteps continued down the corridor.

Quickly, Ma mouthed to the remaining maids, as she flung off the coverlet and lay down on the unrolled carpet. The maids dragged Jiao's body into place beside her. Then they flipped the end of the carpet over them, and rolled them up together.

Jiao's body was still warm. It shouldn't have felt that different from lying next to a living person. But all Ma could see in her mind's eye was his demonically dark tongue, protruding further and further from that widening mouth, and she felt like screaming.

The head maid tapped on the door to call in the eunuchs, and Ma heard her whisper a quick warning about the extra weight, before they hoisted the carpet with a suppressed grunt of effort and went out ahead of the procession of maids. Three maids, rather than four, but maids were even more beneath notice than the palace's furniture; none of the guards noticed one was missing. And then they were outside; they were crossing the palace, back towards Ma's residence.

This had been Ma's gift to Zhu. As she lay in the carpet, the corpse's flesh against her own, she knew that some essential part of herself had fallen down with Jiao into the darkness. Like the life she had taken from him, it was gone, and it would never be restored.

Zhu trotted behind Madam Zhang as she swept up to the top level of the Spring Hall. Her back stung. That morning all Madam Zhang's maids had been beaten as their collective punishment for whichever of them had been stupid enough to forget to latch the aviary door. Madam Zhang had already been in a foul mood due to the previous night's humiliation of being left waiting, and her fury upon finding out that her precious pigeons had escaped and been shot to death by the Great Khan's guards had been—extraordinary.

A beating had been a small price to pay. Since Zhu hadn't yet been dragged away by the Great Khan's guards—and she also hadn't heard any alarming rumors about Lady Shin's well-being—she assumed Ma had managed to at least partially resolve the Jiao situation without raising suspicions. But she was still worried. Had Ma permanently nullified Jiao as a threat, or only managed to bar his entry to the Great Khan? Was he still somewhere in the palace, poised to explode Zhu's plan at any moment? There was so much she didn't know, and she had no way of finding out.

It was cold at the top of the Spring Hall. Huge astrolabes had been set up at each corner of the exposed terrace, and a mechanical clock crowned the whole. From this third-story vantage point Zhu and Madam Zhang could see over the walls of both the Palace City and Imperial City, and glimpse the neatly sectioned outer city. On a dull day Dadu's outer wall was beige rather than gold. To the south, a banner of dust flew over the horizon.

"How near Zhu Yuanzhang comes!" Madam Zhang said, glaring at the dust. "My husband plans to overcome this last obstacle to his unfettered reign with the army *I* gave him, and he dares to put me on the shelf?"

Zhu saw in her mind's eye the familiar shape of her own army, Yuchun in her command tent. It was hard to tell, from a dust cloud, exactly how far away her army was from coming into contact with Dadu's defenders. Two or three days, she thought. Not more than four. Four more days, to keep everything on track despite Jiao. She had the unpleasant idea of her plan as a pile of stones balanced one atop another. The pile was currently wobbling—but if nothing happened to further destabilize it, it might hold together for long enough. But a single gust, or unexpected knock, and the entire thing would go down.

A small procession of women meandered into one of the courtyards below. Zhu's heart leapt in recognition. She wanted, desperately, to hold Ma; to ask her everything that had happened. But it would be enough to see her face. She feigned a casual tone, and said, "Look. There's Lady Shin."

"Indeed," Madam Zhang hissed. She swayed stiffly on her little feet for a moment, peering down with a narrow focus like an eagle on a rabbit. The true object of Madam Zhang's resentment might be out of reach, but here was this softer, juicier target that begged to release its blood. She sprang.

Zhu nearly had to run to keep up. The tininess of Madam Zhang's steps, and the way her feet stayed concealed beneath her billowing gown even as the wind caught it, made her seem like a celestial fairy descending from Heaven. Madam Zhang swooped into the courtyard and advanced on Ma, who startled and immediately dropped into a reverence with her eyes downcast.

"Lady Shin," Madam Zhang murmured. "I hear you've been satisfying the Great Khan very well lately."

Zhu only had eyes for Ma. She was still beautiful, still open in her vulnerability, but she seemed subtly changed with a new knowledge. A new sorrow. When Zhu saw how Ma's hair was pinned with flowers and a plain comb instead of the phoenix pin, she knew.

But if Ma had expended her one and only weapon upon Jiao . . . Zhu's relief at seeing Ma commingled with the feeling of having thrown a ladder over one treacherous crevasse on the path to the summit, only to realize another had opened ahead. Ma might be able to enter the Great Khan's chamber, and she could watch over him while he was vulnerably sleeping. But what use was either of those without a weapon?

Zhu's heart beat fast. There were still a few more days. A few more days, to get into Ma's hands what she needed, before Yuchun and her army met their opponents, and were destroyed.

Ma's eyes slid sideways to Zhu, full of grief, and Zhu sorrowed: not for Jiao, never, but for what she had made Ma do. For what she would make Ma do one more time, before it could all end.

"Why, Lady Shin," Madam Zhang purred with a malevolent satisfaction that had an edge of surprise, as if she hadn't expected such a present to be dropped into her lap, "did the Great Khan take away that magnificent hairpin of yours? Or perhaps you've grown so bold that you consider yourself above needing to wear it." Zhu's stomach lurched: of course there was no chance Madam Zhang had overlooked the missing pin. "I'd be careful, if I were you. This Great Khan doesn't take insult easily. You saw what happened to poor Bolud-Temur! A mere consort who dares make the Great Khan lose face by refusing his gift might find she's not as secure in his affections as she thought." Madam Zhang gave a cat's neat, white smile. "Men are fickle, after all."

Ma kept her composure, but Zhu saw the threat land. The Great Khan might have failed to notice a missing hair ornament, even one made of solid gold, but not when Madam Zhang made it her business to let him know. And if Ma's choices were either to admit having insulted the Great Khan, or confess to having lost something as valuable as the phoenix pin—

Zhu stared, stricken, at Ma. She didn't want to imagine what punishment awaited either of those transgressions. Ma gave her a ghost of a smile—which Zhu knew immediately was for her own reassurance, and therefore to be distrusted—even as Madam Zhang called impatiently, "Come, little cricket."

Zhu had no choice but to tear herself away, stealing one last backwards glance. Whatever happened now between Ma and the Great Khan, it would be between them alone. Zhu was powerless to intervene.

Though it was morning, and the eunuchs would come soon to remove Lady Shin and prepare him for his appointments, he let himself lie behind the bed-curtains for a few moments longer. Here was a world within the world, as private as a drop of water caught in the curl of a leaf. Beside him, Lady Shin's body made a moon curve towards the curtains, her head resting on the solid swell of her upper arm. She seemed unusually preoccupied. He could sense her thoughts churning.

"The Empress troubling you again?"

When she rolled over to face him, he was surprised by how apprehensive she looked. He frowned. "So that's it." He was annoyed at himself. Lady Shin's ordinary equanimity was such that it hadn't occurred to him that she might have been dreading his displeasure. "You were worrying about the pin thing? It's true, the Empress did request that I punish you for neglecting to wear it. She said a Great Khan shouldn't tolerate such an insult from a lowly consort. Apparently it constitutes the gravest threat to my reputation."

When she only stiffened further, he said with half-amused impatience, "Come now! You couldn't have thought I would have you beaten to death over a trifle. What further damage could I possibly do to my reputation? I don't care if you wear the pin or not. I told the Empress as much. Not that she was happy to hear it."

As he gathered her into his arms, he thought perhaps she *had* thought he would have her beaten: she looked positively nauseous. He tried to be reassuring. "If the Empress is so set on disturbing you, let's go up to the Summer Palace together. I'll make her stay in Khanbaliq for the season. Not that I think she'll spend the time reflecting on her behavior, but at least that will give us a few months of peace."

"You want to leave Khanbaliq?" He'd surprised her. "But what about Zhu Yuanzhang? Are you confident of defeating him so quickly, once he reaches the city?"

"Defeat him? That makes it sound like I intend to fight him." The mere idea filled him with contempt. "The least efficient way to a military victory is to have to win a battle for it. I'm perfectly happy to exchange the *glory* of battle for a solution that crushes the enemy without my forces ever needing to make contact." The slit of light between the bed-curtains intensified. His own dark anticipation of the forthcoming day's events seemed to strengthen in counterpoint. "The best way to make an army collapse is to cut off its head. Even the most well-organized army won't fight without the leader who holds the vision of what they're fighting for. Look at what happened to the Zhang army, when General Zhang was lost! It will be the same with Zhu Yuanzhang. That's why, the night before last, I sent a small force to infiltrate his position by stealth and seize him from his command tent. Just yesterday I received word of the team's success. They should be bringing him into the capital later today. Once his army learns of the warm welcome I gave him, I guarantee they'll cast their weapons down in a heartbeat."

"You captured Zhu Yuanzhang?" Lady Shin said in a strange tone. The room was cool, but there was a sudden gathering humidity between their bodies, as if she were on the verge of sweating. But then again, women did run hot at certain times of the month.

As he pushed down the coverlet to cool them, a thought occurred to him. "Remember that rumor—that Zhu Yuanzhang was a woman in disguise? There was nothing to it, after all. My team reported that he has all the parts you'd expect a man to have—with the exception of a hand. Although they did say it's a mystery he hasn't died of that particular wound yet, since even after all this time it hasn't healed well and was bleeding when they captured him." He shook his head in bemusement. "I have no idea why the Minister of Public Works said such a ridiculous thing in the first place. I tried to summon him yesterday to make an account of himself, but the eunuchs couldn't find him. They thought he might have left the city."

"Is it really necessary to execute Zhu Yuanzhang?" Lady Shin spoke so hoarsely that he wondered if her sweating was a sign of illness. "If you have him under your control, wouldn't it serve your purpose just as well to force him to make a public announcement of his surrender?"

It conjured a foreign scenario: that he *could* execute Zhu Yuanzhang, but might choose not to. He couldn't imagine it. "There's no mercy in me, Lady Shin. You know that."

A thicket of leafy plum branches had been placed in a tall blue-and-white vase just outside the bed-curtains. The angular leaves were the venous color of official robes. "Why can't there be?" Her sudden vehemence, still colored by that strange hoarseness, surprised him. "Why can't you choose to make yourself other than how you are, and have mercy? I don't know who they were, those people in your past who made you feel you had to be this way. They must have been important to you, even though they hurt you. But they're gone now. You're the Great Khan. Who in this world has the power to stop you from being how you want to be?"

She spread her small hand over the knobbled field of his sternum. He knew how to defend himself against force, but the softness of her touch penetrated him without resistance: it diffused his insufficient flesh and reached into the blackness inside, as if there was something there worth finding. "You can let go of the hurt, without letting go of your love."

The worst part, he thought as he stared at her with a tremolo of agony in his heart, was how she clearly *believed* what she was saying, even as she espoused the impossible. But there was as little point in wanting it to *be* different as there was in saying it. It was too late. He had purposefully stepped into the dark and let himself sink, and had wrenched the entire world into an orbit that held him at its center. There was no longer any possibility of change. He had already become.

As if she had read his mind, she insisted, "It's possible." How could softness be as strong as a seawall? "I know it is, because you choose it every time you're here with me. You don't hurt me. You aren't cruel to me."

But that had nothing to do with the future. Who he was when he was with her belonged to the past. It was a temporary reanimation of a person who'd had a name—a person who had once been capable of loving, and being loved. A shadow. A memory.

He said painfully, "None of this in here is real."

She tensed, and he had an abrupt sense of her withdrawal. It stung unreasonably. He realized he'd wanted her to deny it. Despite everything he knew about himself and the world, he had still yearned for her to insist that it was real; that what he felt was real. He'd hoped for the impossible, unaware he was even hoping until the moment he felt that hope crack like a seed between stones.

What a fool he was. He jerked himself from her and rose, sneering, "Don't think it's love because I call you every night. You're a convenient sleep aid, Lady Shin. That's it."

But his exhaustion made a lie of even that. He'd become so used to sleeping well that a single night's disturbed sleep now had the power to throw him into lingering disarray. As he thought about it, he felt a flash of unease. He couldn't tell if it was an afterimage from a fretful dream, or something overheard that he couldn't quite remember. Not last night, when he had learned of Zhu Yuanzhang's capture, but—

"That night with the birds. Did something else strange happen, while I was asleep? I thought I heard—" He dredged his memory, increasingly certain now that it *was* a memory and not a dream. "*—people.* And when I got up the next morning, you were gone. And then I found—"

His bare foot, encountering stickiness. When he'd peered at his sole to see what it was, the recognition had been as sharp as pain. "Blood."

She flinched as he looked back at her, and he had the sudden conviction, delivered from that dark place within him that was the worst, and thought the worst of everyone in turn, that she was hiding something. Her face, already unusually wan, had blanched to a color he'd never seen her be. He said, softly, "What happened, Lady Shin?"

A dark ocean pressure tunneled his vision, pressing so thickly into his ears that at first he couldn't make sense of what she said. She blurted it again, desperately, as if she was trying to force understanding into something that was as incapable of thought as a rock. "I'm pregnant."

The words hung between them: senseless, unmoored.

His lack of response made her panic. "That night with the birds. I tried to get back to sleep after being startled, but I felt a pain, and I realized I'd started bleeding. Then when I got up, I was overcome by dizziness—I fell. I was afraid something had gone wrong, that I might be having a— That was why I hurried to leave."

She went on, apologizing for having disturbed his rest, but he could only think, stupidly, that it was impossible. How could he create, when he had made himself into destruction? And yet—*this.* He felt a dismembering sense of the unchangeable world changing around him. He choked, "What of the—"

Child. His child. It wasn't possible, but somehow it was, because something had changed.

She was saying that bleeding wasn't unheard of in the early days; that it had stopped; that the physician had decreed everything to be progressing normally. He couldn't take it in. He needed to breathe, but found himself frozen in an anticipatory terror of what the next breath would feel like.

A knock startled them both. His head eunuch pronounced through the door, "May these unworthy ones enter to prepare the Great Khan for his appointments!"

The crowd of servants outside jumped in surprise as he flung the door open himself. "Your Majesty! We were about to—"

He strode past them, ignoring their pleas to be allowed to attend him. His bedchamber robe flapped unregally around his bare ankles. "Have Lady Shin's attendants collect her." He had no idea where he was going; he had no idea what he was feeling. "I have to—I have to go."

"He wouldn't hear a word against her," Madam Zhang fumed as Zhu painted on her eyebrows with a fine camel-hair brush. The caged birds twittered overhead.

Zhu felt a strange pang. She remembered Madam Zhang looking out over both their armies, with fire and hunger in her eyes. Zhu had been ambitious, but Madam Zhang equally so. Now Madam Zhang was the most powerful woman in the world, and yet she sat sidelined in her golden cage, battling over what status could be afforded her by a fickle man.

"He didn't even punish her?"

Madam Zhang twitched irritably. "He refused outright. What is she, a fox-spirit, to be able to enchant him past all rationality? She has the kind of body you mount like a broodmare, not someone to spend all your time with! I should call an exorcist."

Zhu had to control her relief about Ma avoiding punishment, lest her hand shake and mar the line she was drawing. As Madam Zhang continued her rant, her mind turned back to the problem of her approaching army. She still didn't have a weapon for Ma, or any way of getting one to her, and now there were perhaps only two days left before Yuchun reached Dadu and they would need to engineer the assassination. Perhaps Ma could beg the Great Khan for another hairpin, if he truly wasn't angry with her—but how would Zhu be able to meet Ma to tell her to do that?

When Zhu finished with the paint, Madam Zhang called over her jewelry box, then took out the most elaborate ceremonial headdress instead of her usual jade hairpins for the springtime.

"What's the occasion?" Zhu said, surprised, as she took it and started fixing it in place.

"I may no longer control my army," Madam Zhang said bitterly, "but at least I do still receive reports on their activities. The Great Khan didn't bother waiting for the armies to meet. He sent an infiltration force to capture Zhu Yuanzhang alive. They succeeded last night. The Great Khan has planned for his public execution this afternoon, as soon as he's brought back into the city."

In her shock Zhu stabbed in the headdress too hard. Madam Zhang exclaimed as it scratched her. She raised a hand to strike, then changed her mind and gave Zhu a magnanimous smile. "So clumsy, with your horrible mutilation! But I can forgive you the surprise. Finally, you'll see Zhu Yuanzhang receive his due."

Zhu was barely listening. Her mind whirled with horror, not only from the idea that Yuchun had been captured and was being brought to the capital for what would no doubt be the most spectacular execution the Great Khan could dream up. But if the Great Khan's team had captured Yuchun and not immediately realized that they had the wrong person—

She could see it in her mind's eye: Yuchun, realizing that his security had been breached and that the infiltrators intent upon his capture had mistaken him for Zhu Yuanzhang, slashing off his own right hand so the illusion could continue.

A wave of sadness stunned her. It mingled with her turbulent grief from Xu Da's death into a heaving slurry of pain. Unlike Zhu herself, who had been competent but never spectacular with a sword, Yuchun was the most talented fighter from a generation of young Nanren men. Zhu had sent him into training herself, and seen how he lived and breathed for the delight of using his body to its fullest potential. Now he had sacrificed his sword hand for her—and, in a few more hours, he would sacrifice himself wholly, and die in her place.

But—

Amidst her haze of pain, it occurred to Zhu that *Yuchun wasn't her.* The Great Khan had captured him on the assumption that the gruesome public execution of Zhu Yuanzhang would strike a fatal blow to the morale of the army closing in on Dadu. That they would crumble and run. But, Zhu thought slowly, that was the wrong assumption. Even if the Great Khan didn't know he didn't have the real Zhu, her *army* did. They knew their candidate for the throne was still alive.

If Zhu was willing to let Yuchun die in her place . . . her army wouldn't crumble. It would still continue towards Dadu in accordance with the plan, and Zhu herself would have her two days in which to find Ma a weapon. Two days to make sure she and Ma got it right, rather than rushing and perhaps failing in their assassination attempt.

Earlier in Zhu's life, she would have made her choice without hesitation. But now she did hesitate. She thought of Xu Da's agony, and Ma's gift to her of Jiao's death. She thought of Yuchun undergoing an execution in which the Great Khan kept him alive enough to scream for days on end. Would he still say then that it had been his willing choice—his gift to her, so she could win?

As she stood stricken behind Madam Zhang, a maid came

rushing to the circular window in the room partition that faced Madam Zhang's makeup table, where she temporarily replaced the view of the exquisitely trained waist-high indoors tree that the window had been designed to provide. "Empress! I just saw Lady Shin in the garden."

Madam Zhang flicked a bladed gaze through the window. "Is this supposed to interest me?"

But the maid, far from being cowed, was trembling with suppressed excitement at the importance of her news. "She was vomiting into the bushes."

Zhu startled again, her stricken feeling increasing, but this time Madam Zhang didn't notice: she stood so abruptly that the pearls hanging from her headdress clattered like hailstones.

She said, dreadful as a fired cannon, *"Take me to him."*

Madam Zhang hurried up the wooden stairs of the Palace of the Moon, the mirrored pagoda that spiked like a qilin's horn from the island in the middle of the Imperial City's lake. Zhu and the other maids squeezed their way up behind her. The temple's smell of incense and polished wood, in combination with the burn in Zhu's legs and lungs from the stairs, brought her novitiate years rushing back. Zhu had always disdained nostalgia, but she was suddenly subsumed by grief. Not for Wuhuang Monastery itself, but for the only other person who had known that vanished place. Now they were her memories alone, stored within her like the sutras inside the hollow gold Buddha on the temple's ground floor.

The Great Khan stood on the outside gallery of the pagoda's top level. His interest was directed towards the outer wall's main south gate, where the captured Zhu Yuanzhang would arrive. Five stories beneath, the lake had shed the last of its winter ice. The Imperial City's hunting grounds made a sea of white and pink flowering trees, a walled dream of lushness standing in stark comparison to Dadu's surrounding landscape and the army that filled the southern horizon. A few stray petals danced around the temple's lotus-bud finial that plunged upwards into the sky. Iron bells chimed from where they hung from the temple's five layers of skirted roofs, the melodious chorus joining the petals in their attempt on Heaven.

The Great Khan turned at Madam Zhang's arrival, seemingly unconcerned at how she had blown in like a thunderstorm. "Greetings, Empress wife."

The Great Khan was taller than Zhu had previously realized, now that she saw the two of them standing together. His impression of height was furthered by the black gown that seemed to swallow rather than enhance the gold dragons upon it, and the upsweep of his topknot within its gold collar. Another person in that same body, Zhu thought, could have made it seem masculine. But Wang Baoxiang clearly had no interest in shaping himself that way. His effeminacy was as deliberate as an argument.

"Is it true?" Madam Zhang said in high-pitched fury. "Is Lady Shin pregnant?"

The Great Khan raised his eyebrows, sardonic. "It does seem that way."

"This is how you would treat me, when I gave you everything! I gave you my army, my loyalty. *I gave you the throne.*"

"And I'm grateful for it. But why should you care about what happens with Lady Shin? You're the Empress. I'll never take that title from you. Isn't it everything you wanted?"

Madam Zhang had given him the world, and in return he had given Madam Zhang exactly what she'd asked for. His unconcern that she now found it empty seemed the deepest cruelty of all.

The Great Khan, clearly finished with the matter, said to his attendants, "We'll go to the Hall of Great Brilliance. I want to give Zhu Yuanzhang a personal audience before his execution. He should get to see the face of the one who beat him to the throne." Neither he nor his attendants gave so much as a glance at Madam Zhang as they left the gallery. Zhu heard him add to his head eunuch, "Ride ahead and tell Lady Shin to prepare herself to join me. I want her to be with me when I end it."

In that moment, Zhu knew what she could do. It felt like a brightness bursting inside her; it was a spark falling onto a bed of straw, setting her insides on fire with excitement. She had been spending all her time thinking about a weapon, when the opportunity had never been about a weapon in the first place. It was an opportunity that was about Zhu herself, who was as invisible to the Great Khan as a needle viewed end-on, and about Ma: so trusted and beloved by the Great Khan that he would want her by his side to share in his moment of victory.

Madam Zhang, on the gallery where the Great Khan left her, collapsed like a discarded puppet. She knelt, weeping in rage and despair. This was Zhu's chance to slip away, while Madam Zhang was consumed by emotion, and head back to the Palace City.

But she didn't. An unfamiliar feeling held her there with the weeping woman. Madam Zhang had wanted so fiercely. She had striven so hard, but she had never been able to see how she couldn't win while she remained in her gilded cage.

"Leave the carriage," Zhu instructed the other maids, her air of authority confusing them into acquiescence. "I'll bring her back when she's ready."

Zhu could feel Madam Zhang's weeping in her own body, the same way she'd felt Xu Da's pain. It was unpleasant, and she disliked it intensely, but she didn't try to chase it away. The wind brought a shower of new petals, and a ringing cascade of bells.

"Even had it been General Zhang who sat on that throne, he would have cast you aside too," Zhu said quietly. "Perhaps not as fast as this Great Khan did, but eventually. When he realized what's obvious. That all the fertility tea in the world won't create an heir in someone who's already too old to bear children."

Madam Zhang jerked to stare at Zhu, stricken.

"General Zhang had the Mandate," Zhu told her, "but I don't think he would have ever gained it of his own accord. He wasn't that ambitious. It only happened because you pushed him into it. The sad thing is: you never realized you could have claimed that Mandate yourself. You always found yourself a man to raise up, because you thought it had to belong to a man. You never believed it could be yours.

"When you chose to place yourself beneath a man, you ensured that this would be your fate, no matter which man it turned out to be in the end."

Out there on the plain to the south, Zhu's army waved their golden flags.

Madam Zhang said bloodlessly, "Who are you?"

"Do you truly not know me? We've met before. You offered to let me surrender to you, and I refused. I knew that to stand beneath you, a woman who stands beneath a man, is no victory at all."

Madam Zhang's mouth opened, then snapped shut. She couldn't bring herself to say it.

As Zhu stood over her fallen rival, she was suffused by the gloriousness of becoming her true self again. It was the pure rush of stepping back into her potential, and laying aside the misery of nothingness. "Yes. I am. Say my name. Say it before I take the throne, and you can never say it again."

"Impossible," Madam Zhang said, sounding as if she had strained something in order to say it. "Zhu Yuanzhang has the Mandate of Heaven."

"Why impossible? Because I'm not a man?" Zhu held out her hand and let the white light sparkle in her palm. "I claimed the Mandate, because I believed I could have it."

She let the light vanish and kept her hand out, offering it to Madam Zhang to help her up. "Let me return you the offer you once made me. Surrender, and join me as I rise to the throne."

But the look on Madam Zhang's face was wild as she recollected her rage. "Join you?" she spat. "Join someone who is neither man nor woman—someone even worse than a eunuch, because you deliberately refuse to take your allotted place under Heaven? A placeless person is no more than a beast! How could *you* ever be worthy of the throne?"

"I claim my place." Zhu gazed at where the glittering jewel roof of the Hall of Great Brilliance rose high above the walls of the Palace City. At the heart of the world, where she belonged. "And if the pattern of the world refuses to let that place exist, *I will change it."*

Madam Zhang laughed, a harsh and terrible sound. Zhu saw the fear in her, beneath the refusal and denial, and then it was gone as she launched herself at Zhu, hissing and scratching like a cat.

Madam Zhang's fingernails caught Zhu across the forehead, but even as they sank in Zhu was already twisting sideways, and Madam Zhang's furious momentum was too much for her tiny feet to divert. She stumbled past Zhu and was held for an instant, windmilling, at the railing, as if she might be able to muster a determination sufficient to overpower gravity itself.

She fell.

Zhu lunged to the railing and looked down. A burning sheet of blood had run down her forehead into her left eye, and she saw the world through a translucence of red. The shock of the sight sliced as deeply as grief. On the rocks beneath the lips of the five upcurled roofs, none of which protruded far enough to catch a falling woman, lay the broken body like a disjointed doll: its makeup unmarred; tiny shoes flung off by the impact of the fall; hair ornaments still glittering, beautiful, in the spring sunshine.

24

When Ma entered the Hall of Great Brilliance, the Great Khan came down from the gold-dragoned throne and took her hands as she made a reverence, saying, "Rise. I'm glad of your company, Lady Shin."

She'd known, from the way the guards had checked her for weapons before letting her enter, that she would find him alone. With the great doors closed, the hall was almost completely dark. Moonlike lanterns made solitary pools of light that didn't spread. The Great Khan's gaze flickered to the walls. In the gloom the beaten silver had taken on the deepness of pewter, but all Ma could see in it was their own distorted reflections. She could read the Great Khan well enough, though, to tell that he hated being in this hall. What did he see that she didn't? The thought made her shiver.

"Glad? I'd thought the Great Khan was angry with me. About the—"

She couldn't say the word. Her regret was too thick; it made her heart hurt. He should never have known about the child. Had it not been for Jiao, he never would have. It should have been a secret for her body to carry past this awful moment, into the future where it would have nothing to do with him.

"No. Not angry. But I confess, it caught me by surprise. The idea that I could be a—"

He gripped her hands as if she might vanish. His hands were his most feminine aspect, his fingers so graceful that Ma's eyes were always drawn to them with an almost tactile intensity. But now with her hands resting inside his, she was jarred by how much bigger they were than her own. She couldn't help remembering the buoyant pleasure that came from slipping her hand into Zhu's and feeling the private sameness that was the matching of their two small palms.

"I never knew the father of my blood," he said to their joined hands. With his face downturned, its Nanren shape was less apparent; the long angled sweep of his single-lidded eyes more pronounced. Ma had never seen him wear Mongol braids, but in that moment she could imagine it. "To all intents and purposes, the former Prince of Henan was my father. It was he who adopted me, raised me, had a father's expectations of me. He never forgot I wasn't his true son, but what man wouldn't hope for a child he raised to come to embody the qualities he values, and to bring pride to his old age? My brother had turned out so well, after all. I suppose my father thought he could do it again.

"For a long time, I tried to please him. But I was too fearful, cried too easily, and my natural interests ran towards the opposite of what he valued. And when I failed to give him what he wanted, he refused to believe I was trying. He thought that if I *had* tried, I would have succeeded, because Esen had. So my father rejected me."

His servants had shaved him so closely that there was no grain of beard visible on his jaw. His mandala earrings had fallen forwards, teardrop gleams of pearl and gold. Beautiful, but masculine. Ma had a memory of her own Semu father, long ago in this same city, wearing earrings with his general's armor. And yet, since all of Zhu's followers were Nanren, the only people Ma knew who wore earrings were women. Above his four lapped collars, the Great Khan's throat was as shadowed as an orchid.

He murmured, "I rejected him back. I rejected my brother for being what my father wanted, and so too everything they loved and valued. So the idea of becoming a father myself—I never thought about it. I'd refused every other way they wanted me to be, and I must have let go of that, too.

"But then—there was you."

He traced his thumb across the back of Ma's hand. Then, to Ma's heartbroken astonishment, he smiled. It didn't last: his upper lip caught on a crooked canine, which made him aware that he *was* smiling, so he stopped doing it. Ma had an overwhelming impression of self-consciousness, as if he'd been caught being silly. It was such a vulnerable, human reaction that it made her heart lurch with a wretched tenderness.

"I made myself into ruin, so I thought that was all I was good for. I thought that in having drowned the world in my own misery, I'd given up what I had always cherished: the ability to create. I couldn't write, I couldn't paint. But then you gave me this gift, Lady Shin. The gift of generation, the hope of bringing something into the world that isn't pain and despair. I can't change the past and everything I've done, I can't rewrite it, but I have the power to make a new future.

"That's why I wanted you here with me, for the end of it. This will be the start of our new beginning."

At that, Ma could no longer hold back her tears. She wasn't crying from happiness, as she knew he assumed, but because Zhu had always said the same thing. It was because of Zhu that Ma had learned how new beginnings were always heralded by one last terrible act. She was pathetically grateful that now that act was no longer up to her. Her heart broke to see him holding in a smile—at seeing his surprise at *having* to hold it in, because the existence of his own joy seemed impossible. But even if she and Zhu did decide to bring the child into the world, he would never father it. He would never get his chance to experience the new future he was imagining.

He said something in a language she didn't understand. At her puzzled look he flushed. "Was it such a bad pronunciation?"

Instead of repeating it, he turned her face towards him, and kissed her. It had a backwards quality: a first kiss, so gentle and closed-mouthed, when their bodies had already joined in other ways. And yet the intimacy of it shocked her. It was *him* in a way the simple intrusion of his body into hers hadn't been. She knew the character of this mouth: these thin lips that snarled, and compressed in bitter enjoyment of a cruelty inflicted or received, but that held too the potential for that lopsided, self-conscious smile with its one crooked tooth. She knew him here, as she knew that the warm press of his lips was saying something she didn't want to hear. His feelings were falling into that unbridgeable gap between them, the void he had no idea was there, before they could reach her on the other side. The kiss was warm, but it was dead. It was a kiss riven through the heart; a kiss without a future. It had none of the open-mouthed seeking hunger that Ma shared with Zhu. None of the feeling that in Zhu's small curious mouth and the glassy taste of her teeth Ma was always finding more of herself; that in each moment of seeking and finding they were joining deeper into connection, and fitting more closely, and thrilling more intensely in a mutuality that grew and grew.

He nuzzled the soft hair by her ear. Even as she curved towards him, even as the nearness of their faces created the bubble-intimacy of their togetherness, he was alone in there, as he'd always been alone, because Lady Shin didn't exist.

"Great Khan!"

His sallow cheeks were flushed when he pulled back. His eyes lingered on Ma even as he called to the guards outside, "You have Zhu Yuanzhang there?"

"Not yet, Great Khan. This is one of Lady Shin's maids. She says she came to deliver the anti-nausea medicine Lady Shin requested."

Zhu had always been going to come. It had the force of nature, of fate; it was the inevitable arrival of the future that Ma *wanted*. But at the same time she knew that same onrushing future would overcome everything else with its power. It would sweep away with its devastating brightness that one fragile spark that had just blossomed in the darkness.

"Lady Shin?" He was asking for her confirmation.

She couldn't speak for grief. She nodded, and felt the last slide of their hands together as they untangled, the brief press of his fingers against her own that was his promise to return.

The Great Khan resumed his throne and said, "Send her in."

The guards had made Zhu sip some of the medicine in front of them before they'd let her into the hall. They had taken her wooden hand. She'd known that she'd be facing the Great Khan with nothing but herself, as she now stepped inside and let her eyes adjust. It was an awful darkness inside, the darkness of the tomb or grave. In its lightlessness, the decorative sprays of spring leaves in their tall vases had already lost their vibrancy.

Although the hall's enormous dragon-carved wooden pillars obscured its emptiness, there was only a single person amongst them. Ma's wide Goryeo skirts were no longer the demure pastels of a low-ranked consort, but a queenly deep blue with crimson ribboning, as if the Great Khan had instructed her to dress appropriately to his triumph. But as Zhu passed her on the way to the throne, she saw that Ma's dress was the only celebratory thing about her. Her face was ashen. Her hands were buried in the rigid silk of her skirts, as if that grip were the only thing keeping her from falling. Zhu's heart clenched at the sight of her misery. Even if Ma had been spared the need to kill the Great Khan with her own hands, apparently the betrayal pained her almost as deeply. *Just one last thing, Yingzi,* Zhu thought to her. *One last thing, to end it.*

Zhu stood at the base of the steps leading up to the throne and regarded the Great Khan as he sat reading. As a maid, she was entirely beneath his notice. He would have paid more attention to a dog approaching him. It was only the glassy chime of their Mandates brushing each other that eventually drew his attention to her standing there in front of him. He frowned.

She could sense his rising punitive urge. Not only was she manifestly out of place, but she had dared intrude into his consciousness.

She said, "You were waiting for me."

That bald pronoun, *you,* with its sacrilegious implication of equals, landed between them like a gob of spit. He recoiled. "Has this scum gone mad, to address the Great Khan so? You're lucky we're fond of your mistress, or we would have you flayed! Give the medicine and go."

Zhu let the bowl drop. It bounced, splashing its contents to make a puddle that was only visible against the dark stone by its shine. It was a brighter shine than it should have had, because what it reflected wasn't just light, but a multiplicity of pale bodies. It seemed like a hole facing onto a bright sky in some other place. The bowl itself rolled in the direction Zhu had sent it, landing at the wall by the feet of one particular pale shape.

Ouyang's tattered white draperies were all the more awful

for Zhu's memory of the pride he had once taken in the magnificence of his armor, and his rigidly neat dress beneath it. He stood there with his head bowed, his hair tangled across his face. Zhu, remembering with a shudder the bloody malice and bared teeth of hungry ghosts, was glad she couldn't see it. His fist was still clenched around the hilt of his broken sword, as if he hadn't been able to release it even in death.

Pain radiated from the ghost in a soundless howl. This was the haunting, raging, grieving presence she had felt but not seen the first time she came into this hall. Now that awful presence beat against her with a tidal force that made her want to curl into herself in avoidance of its hunger. She had always had a connection to Ouyang, for their likeness. But now that likeness was gone, and it was a connection between herself and something dead—something monstrous. The pulpy horror of it pounded her in waves like nausea.

Zhu glanced back at the Great Khan in time to catch his realization of what she'd been looking at. *What she could see.*

He stared sharply, directly, at her. Taking in the emptiness of her sleeve, where a hand should have been; her boldness that didn't belong to any maid. Without a moment's disbelief, he understood who she must be. His hollow-cheeked face was controlled, but a flush of shock rushed into his cheeks and out again.

"Zhu Yuanzhang." He said her name with such exactitude that she had the idea he was writing crisp black characters in the air. As if he were writing out the fate she had enshrined in that name she had chosen for herself: that she was the tombstone of the Mongol Empire of the Great Yuan, of which he was the last element remaining. "So Jiao Yu did tell the truth about you. I had wondered."

The gold dragons on the throne writhed behind him, and opened their mouths to disgorge their clouds of golden water vapor. Their tangled bodies were so multitudinous that Zhu couldn't tell where any single one began and ended. She said, "I've come to claim what's mine."

"Have you." His fingers were white on his closed book. He called abruptly, "Guards! Come!"

"Great Khan!" came the faint reply from outside.

But they didn't come. The sharp thuds of fists and hilts on

the outside of those huge doors were transformed by the hall into booming echoes, as if they were in a black cave beneath the sea. "Great Khan! Unbar the door!"

Ma was still standing by the door she had barred. Zhu watched the Great Khan's confusion slowly bloom into self-hating realization. She hadn't realized there was any lightness in him until she saw its complete extinguishment. The dark rolled in.

"So Goryeo betrayed me," he said, after a long, terrible moment. "I confess: I didn't think they'd turn, even if you offered them independence. Their king is a weak character, and too many of his nobles find their lives perfectly comfortable under the patronage of the Great Yuan."

"Not all of Goryeo. Just one woman, who wanted to see you die."

"One—ah." She saw his self-hate increase until she thought it would overwhelm him, then with effort he regained control. "Lady Ki. I can't say she didn't have cause. So that was my mistake." His voice cracked with strain as he projected it across the hall to Ma. "It was a great performance! But greater still was my foolishness in believing it could have ever been real. Are you even from Goryeo?" As soon as he said it, pain crossed his face and he answered his own question. "Of course you aren't. When I spoke to you in that language, you had no idea what I said. Who are you?"

"Meet my wife, Ma Xiuying," Zhu said. "I don't blame you for becoming fond of her. She has the quality of drawing out the good in people. Did you feel it, when you were with her? That you were becoming your best possible self?"

She held out her left hand, and Ma came and took it. She was crying so much as she looked at the Great Khan that it seemed a miracle she could still breathe.

The Great Khan's own face was so agonized that Zhu could have believed he was dying. After a moment he rose from the throne. He was so pale it hardly seemed possible he had enough blood in him to stay upright, but an aura of viciousness rolled out from him in black waves. "Well, here we are. How do you plan to end me, Zhu Yuanzhang? You have no weapon. Do you expect me to dash myself against the floor so you can step over my body and take the throne?" His thin mouth twisted savagely. "I'm not generous enough to let you have it that easily."

For all his effeminacy, the Great Khan was taller and heavier than Zhu. He would be stronger. And he had two hands. In a brutal, unmediated body-to-body fight in which elbows smashed noses, arms were used to loop and strangle, and weight was used to crush, perhaps he would win.

The ghost stood motionless by the wall, silently gripping his broken sword, as Zhu approached. The radiating chill of his presence made her flesh contract around her bones, but when she came close enough to touch, she felt something worse. Though the ghost didn't move, she felt the sharp prickle of its attention. Zhu remembered the pirate women falling dead on the deck of her ship as the ghosts drained their life from them. And now she had caught the notice of this dreadful, hungry thing that was no longer *him,* but only the echo of his desire for revenge.

It was as precise a life-or-death moment as she'd ever experienced. She realized she was shaking with visceral fear. If it wanted to, this creature that had been Ouyang could kill her with a touch. She didn't know how much memory, if any, it retained of the acrimony and hatred with which they'd parted. "General," she said cautiously. "That one over there killed you. I know that nothing can make up for the rest of what happened to you. For what you did and lost. But for your own death, at least, will you let me have your revenge?"

She let her phantom hand flicker into being. That ghost hand, enrobed in white fire, had always felt like it burned. But now it burned with cold as she reached for the ghost's sword. And it was so cold. It was a cold that would drain her life force; it would stop her heart. Some terrified instinct told her that if she took too long, Ouyang would raise his head. He would look at her, and then with those sharp teeth he would devour her—

She drew back, suppressing a shuddering gasp, and the ghostly broken sword came with her.

Zhu remembered the pain and nothingness of the moment she had lost her hand, and how afterwards she had pulled herself out into brightness and the knowledge of herself. Ouyang's sword had been his revenge. It had killed the one he loved. But for Zhu, it was what had made her herself. She had held that blade within her. Her body knew it. And now, in the same way her Mandate traced the outline of her missing right hand, it traced Ouyang's sword, too. It ran along the broken edges and made them whole again, until Zhu was no longer holding a ghostly sword but one made from pure light.

"It's not real," the Great Khan said with sharp-edged fear, as if he was trying to unconvince himself of what he already knew: that it didn't have to be real, to hurt.

Zhu raised the sword. The light was her weapon, and her self, and it had the terrible brightness of the sun. To Ma she said, "Look away, Yingzi. Bear this one last thing for me. This last thing, that ends it."

The Great Khan didn't run. There was nowhere to run to. He could only shield his eyes with his arm as Zhu advanced on him. On the back of his upraised hand, and the unshielded parts of his face, the exposed skin reddened and blistered as Zhu brought the sword closer and closer. Light had no weight, but it had force, and now it pressed him to his knees as he cried out in pain. Behind Zhu, Ma was sobbing more wretchedly than she'd ever heard her cry before.

Zhu had taken a certain grim satisfaction in destroying Chen, and certainly in imagining what Ma had done to Jiao. But despite his manifest cruelty, the Great Khan wasn't like either of those men. He was, Zhu thought in an unpleasant moment of enlightenment, more like Zhu herself. Rather than being someone whom the world had hoisted to the top for his eminent worthiness, he had been scorned for what he was. The mere idea that he could have had ambition for the throne, let alone the capability to achieve it, had been considered laughable. He had put himself upon the throne as living revenge to those who would have denied it to him.

It was Ma who had told her: that those who had given Zhu their gifts had done so not so that she could be emperor, but so that she could be *herself* as emperor. Because they knew that Zhu understood what it was like to be nothing. Because they knew she would change the world, and leave behind the past that belonged to Chen and those other men who had always believed themselves worthy to be knelt to.

As Zhu brought the sword towards the Great Khan, she could

feel the awful pressure of the ghost's hunger for her to kill him. But—a ghost wasn't a person, with true desires. It was only an echo of pain and vengeance that wanted to see itself mirrored in the world it clung to, because that was all it knew. There was no life, no future, in a ghost. It belonged to the past as much as Chen did.

The Great Khan was in agony where he knelt beneath her sword. She hadn't even touched him with it, but she could see she was burning him alive. The ghost cried out soundlessly for its bloody vengeance.

She stopped.

It seemed like everything stopped. In that massive hall, with its pillars wider than the largest trees Zhu had ever seen, she had a sudden, aching sense of the tiny, unique humanity of each of them: the Great Khan gasping on his knees; Ma who was turned away and crying her heart out; and herself. But if they stayed like this forever, nothing would change; nothing could ever change.

She said into the vastness, "It has to be like this. I'm sorry."

The Great Khan flinched, bracing himself for the end. The back of his right hand that had been protecting his face was no longer just blistered, but an open red expanse. The sleeve of his black robe was smoking. The gilded paper thread of the dragons that had been embroidered there had been burned away, so that nothing remained but the shadow where they had been. But now Zhu turned from him and directed herself to the ghost. "I'm sorry, General. I know what you would have me do. But how can I make a new world if my first act within it is a continuation of the old? If this is to be a new beginning—I have to choose a new way to begin."

She let the sword and her right hand vanish. Her arm ended once again in that narrow pink stump. It was harmless and yet, she thought, her true self: the self she had chosen to be. She looked down at the Great Khan. "But for us to begin: there can't be two Mandates in the world. The one that must remain is mine. Give yours up."

But even as he knelt shuddering at her feet, it seemed like he might not do it. His chest heaved. There was torment on his face, but it wasn't solely from physical pain. He said with a hoarse desperation that was almost a plea, "I *can't*. I can't give it up. How can I, when it's what I am?"

Ma made a sound of anguish, then went forwards. She knelt in front of him and took his unburned hand between her own. It didn't seem like a romantic gesture, but a human one of comfort. Ma said to him in a low, aching voice that made Zhu feel as if she were eavesdropping, "What you felt was real, even if I wasn't."

As he stared at Ma, a tear ran across the pale skin where his raised arm had shielded his eyes, and over the triangle of blistered skin on his jaw. Zhu's own heart ached with understanding. She knew what it felt like, to face letting go. She remembered that moment of watching Xu Da's agony, while Chen told her to surrender. Her fate in one hand, and Xu Da in the other. Her fate was her self, but Xu Da was the beloved brother she had chosen for herself, and when the two had been put in balance it had felt like being torn apart.

Zhu had always been of the opinion that those who gave up their fates, like the original Zhu Chongba, simply hadn't been strong enough to carry them. She had always been strong enough. But perhaps when one's fate was one's means of survival and one's reason to continue—perhaps when one held it as tightly as she did, and the Great Khan did, and Ouyang had—giving up was the act that required the greater strength. As she watched the Great Khan struggle, she thought: it could be the hardest thing in the world.

Nothing was happening. And then, all at once: a shadow rose out of him, like cobwebs in the wind—a tatter that hung there for an instant, then dissolved into nothingness.

He gasped and fell forwards, and Ma caught him.

His fate had vanished. But in giving it up, Zhu thought, he hadn't made himself nothing. He had shed his name to become the Great Khan, and now the Great Khan was gone. In his place was this nameless, kneeling man who had the potential to be anyone. Anything.

"Go forth," she said to him, with a strange protective tenderness that seemed like reaching back to that self that had awoken from her duel with Ouyang to see her mutilated arm resting atop the covers. "Choose a new name for yourself, and live within it as you couldn't live before, as your true self. Go forth, and find a future in the brightness."

Then she went to the thing that had once been Ouyang. The twenty steps to reach him felt like walking headfirst into a gale of ice knives. The distorted connection between them was curdling her blood. She said to his unmoving form, "You also need to let go, General. Let go of the hurt and pain and revenge of this world and the people in it. Let it end here."

She let her right hand flicker back into being. As she reached for the ghost, he finally raised his head. For an instant she saw that hungry, nightmare face, but then the light touched him and made it once again that beautiful, pale, terrible face she had known. His eyes weren't black emptiness, but a human's, as if she had summoned *him* back—the true essence of him—by speaking to him. He looked at her with anguished longing as she told him, "I'll find his grave, and bury you together. You had no descendants, but I'll remember you. And my descendants, and their descendants, will remember you, and pray for you, at the monument I'll build to your names.

"Go into your next life. Live it, and bear its suffering. Do it again with the life after that, and the next, and with each one find it easier. Until one day, in a thousand years, the force of the universe will bring you and Esen-Temur back together to start afresh."

When she touched his pale cheek, it burned with such pure sensation that she couldn't tell whether it had been hot or cold. The terrible assonance of their connection resolved, turning back into that familiar resonance of their two strings that were alike amongst all the countless ones that made up the fabric of the universe. And then he vanished: blown away like a dandelion head in the wind, to be re-formed in some distant place, some distant future, to live again.

The room rang with absence. Zhu slowly became aware of the outside world again: a pounding and screaming upon the door.

She ascended the steps to the throne and stood there a moment, taking in the golden dragons that were the seat of the sun. Her triumph was muted by sorrow, for everything that had been given and lost for this moment. Those losses and sacrifices now formed the soil from which her new world would sprout. As the world grew, it would draw up the loving kindness of those sacrifices and knit it into the material of itself. With that as its foundation it could never be like the old world of violence and domination. It would be new. She thought with gratitude: *It will be itself.*

The man still on the floor, in the black robe of that old world, asked achingly, "What will you call it? Your new era."

Zhu sat. Her maid's uniform pulled awkwardly when she spread her legs apart like a man, like someone who sat atop the world. She rested one hand and one stump on her knees.

"Of the new dynasty founded by the Hongwu Emperor, the dynasty of radiant light that will shine unstopping for ten thousand years—"

The door broke down, and the guards tumbled in and halted in shock at the sight of her on the throne. As the light of her new dynasty spilled in, Zhu said, smiling, "Its name is Ming."

ACKNOWLEDGMENTS

Everyone knows that writing a second book is hard, and it turns out that writing a second book during a pandemic is an actual nightmare, so please consider the following thanks to be especially heartfelt.

Thanks to my editor at Tor, Will Hinton, for his unfailingly generous support during what was a very difficult time (for me, for him, for the entire world), and for his deceptively gentle questions that unlocked what this story was actually about. Also at Tor, particular thanks to Oliver Dougherty, Renata Sweeney, Libby Collins, and Devi Pillai. Thank you also to the many other people who labored mightily to bring this book into being, particularly those on the production, art and design, sales, marketing, publicity, contracts, and finance teams. Thanks to the copy editors and proofreaders, and to Rola Chang for another gorgeous cover illustration.

In the UK, all my thanks to Bella Pagan and Georgia Summers for so strongly championing the Radiant Emperor Duology both in-house and externally. I couldn't be more thrilled at how warmly these queer Chinese historicals have been received in the UK. Thank you to the entire Pan Macmillan team who worked so hard to make both books into the gorgeous physical (and digital) objects that they are. Thanks to Maria Rejt at Mantle, and to Stephen Haskins and Jamie-Lee Nardone at Black Crow PR.

Thank you to Natalie Naudus for narrating the audiobooks with verve and good humor (and for making the viral TikTok about *that* moment in book one), and the team at Macmillan Audio.

Thank you to Laura Rennert (Superstar agent of infinite patience! She who quails at nothing!) and the wonderful people at Andrea Brown Literary Agency, with particular thanks to Kara Reynolds and Kelli Kane.

Thank you to the publishers, editors, and translators of the foreign editions. Translation is such a skill and an art, and I'm grateful that readers of languages other than English are increasingly having access to a variety of queer stories.

To my there-from-the-beginning writing buddy Vanessa Len: look at us living the dream by sitting alone in our houses and crying! I'm so happy we managed to stay in lockstep throughout this process, to the point of our sequels coming out in the same month. Now onto book three, hopefully with less crying.

Bunker crew: I couldn't have done it without you. What a difference a community makes.

Thank you to the booksellers, librarians, book community members, awards committees and voters, queer and diverse literature advocates, and every reader who talked about and supported this series: it meant the world to me every time I saw love for my books full of terrible, murderous queers.

Thanks to the Sapphic Trifecta! It was a blast; I'm so glad we got to meet in person.

Finally, my deepest love and thanks to John and Erica for their patient support as I abandoned them to live in imperial China for years on end. If I had to be locked in a house for 267 days, I'm glad it was with the both of you.

I acknowledge the Wurundjeri people, who are the traditional custodians of the lands upon which I wrote this novel.

ABOUT THE AUTHOR

Harvard Wang

SHELLEY PARKER-CHAN is an Asian-Australian former international development adviser who worked on human rights, gender equality, and LGBTQ rights in Southeast Asia. Their debut historical fantasy novel, *She Who Became the Sun,* was a #1 *Sunday Times* best-seller and has been translated into twelve languages. Parker-Chan is a winner of the Astounding Award and the British Fantasy Awards for Best Fantasy Novel and Best Newcomer. They have also been a finalist for the Lambda, Locus, Aurealis, Ditmar, and British Book Awards. They live in Melbourne, Australia.

shelleyparkerchan.com